THE ARMOURER'S
PRENTICES

THE ARMOURER'S PRENTICES

Charlotte M. Yonge

WILDSIDE PRESS

THE ARMOURER'S PRENTICES

CHAPTER I.

The Verdurer's Lodge.

"Give me the poor allottery my father left me by testament, with that I
will go buy me fortunes."
"Get you with him, you old dog."

As You Like It.

The officials of the New Forest have ever since the days of the Conqueror
enjoyed some of the pleasantest dwellings that southern England can boast.

The home of the Birkenholt family was not one of the least delightful. It
stood at the foot of a rising ground, on which grew a grove of magnificent
beeches, their large silvery boles rising majestically like columns into a lofty
vaulting of branches, covered above with tender green foliage. Here and there
the shade beneath was broken by the gilding of a ray of sunshine on a lower
twig, or on a white trunk, but the floor of the vast arcades was almost entirely
of the russet brown of the fallen leaves, save where a fern or holly bush made a
spot of green. At the foot of the slope lay a stretch of pasture ground, some
parts covered by "lady-smocks, all silver white," with the course of the little
stream through the midst indicated by a perfect golden river of shining kingcups interspersed with ferns. Beyond lay tracts of brown heath and brilliant
gorse and broom, which stretched for miles and miles along the flats, while the
dry ground was covered with holly brake, and here and there woods of oak and
beech made a sea of verdure, purpling in the distance.

Cultivation was not attempted, but hardy little ponies, cows, goats,
sheep, and pigs were feeding, and picking their way about in the marshy mead
below, and a small garden of pot-herbs, inclosed by a strong fence of timber,
lay on the sunny side of a spacious rambling forest lodge, only one story high,
built of solid timber and roofed with shingle. It was not without strong pretensions to beauty, as well as to picturesqueness, for the posts of the door, the
architecture of the deep porch, the frames of the latticed windows, and the
verge boards were all richly carved in grotesque devices. Over the door was the
royal shield, between a pair of magnificent antlers, the spoils of a deer reported
to have been slain by King Edward the Fourth, as was denoted by the "glorious
sun of York" carved beneath the shield.

In the background among the trees were ranges of stables and kennels,
and on the grass-plat in front of the windows was a row of beehives. A tame
doe lay on the little green sward, not far from a large rough deer-hound, both
close friends who could be trusted at large. There was a mournful dispirited
look about the hound, evidently an aged animal, for the once black muzzle
was touched with grey, and there was a film over one of the keen beautiful eyes,
which opened eagerly as he pricked his ears and lifted his head at the rattle of

the door latch. Then, as two boys came out, he rose, and with a slowly waving tail, and a wistful appealing air, came and laid his head against one of the pair who had appeared in the pont. They were lads of fourteen and fifteen, clad in suits of new mourning, with the short belted doublet, puffed hose, small ruffs and little round caps of early Tudor times. They had dark eyes and hair, and honest open faces, the younger ruddy and sunburnt, the elder thinner and more intellectual—and they were so much the same size that the advantage of age was always supposed to be on the side of Stephen, though he was really the junior by nearly a year. Both were sad and grave, and the eyes and cheeks of Stephen showed traces of recent floods of tears, though there was more settled dejection on the countenance of his brother.

"Ay, Spring," said the lad, "'tis winter with thee now. A poor old rogue! Did the new housewife talk of a halter because he showed his teeth when her ill-nurtured brat wanted to ride on him? Nay, old Spring, thou shalt share thy master's fortunes, changed though they be. Oh, father! father! didst thou guess how it would be with thy boys!" And throwing himself on the grass, he hid his face against the dog and sobbed.

"Come, Stephen, Stephen; 'tis time to play the man! What are we to do out in the world if you weep and wail?"

"She might have let us stay for the month's mind," was heard from Stephen.

"Ay, and though we might be more glad to go, we might carry bitterer thoughts along with us. Better be done with it at once, say I."

"There would still be the Forest! And I saw the moorhen sitting yester eve! And the wild ducklings are out on the pool, and the woods are full of song. Oh! Ambrose! I never knew how hard it is to part—"

"Nay, now, Steve, where be all your plots for bravery? You always meant to seek your fortune—not bide here like an acorn for ever."

"I never thought to be thrust forth the very day of our poor father's burial, by a shrewish town-bred vixen, and a base narrow-souled—"

"Hist! hist!" said the more prudent Ambrose.

"Let him hear who will! He cannot do worse for us than he has done! All the Forest will cry shame on him for a mean-hearted skinflint to turn his brothers from their home, ere their father and his, be cold in his grave," cried Stephen, clenching the grass with his hands, in his passionate sense of wrong.

"That's womanish," said Ambrose.

"Who'll be the woman when the time comes for drawing cold steel?" cried Stephen, sitting up.

At that moment there came through the porch a man, a few years over thirty, likewise in mourning, with a paler, sharper countenance than the brothers, and an uncomfortable pleading expression of self-justification.

"How now, lads!" he said, "what means this? You have taken the matter too hastily. There was no thought that ye should part till you had some purpose in view. Nay, we should be fain for Ambrose to bide on here, so he would leave his portion for me to deal with, and teach little Will his primer and accidence. You are a quiet lad, Ambrose, and can rule your tongue better than Stephen."

"Thanks, brother John," said Ambrose, somewhat sarcastically, "but where Stephen goes I go."

"I would—I would have found Stephen a place among the prickers or rangers, if—" hesitated John. "In sooth, I would yet do it, if he would make it up with the housewife."

"My father looked higher for his son than a pricker's office," returned Ambrose.

"That do I wot," said John, "and therefore, 'tis for his own good that I would send him forth. His godfather, our uncle Birkenholt, he will assuredly provide for him, and set him forth—"

The door of the house was opened, and a shrewish voice cried, "Mr. Birkenholt—here, husband! You are wanted. Here's little Kate crying to have yonder smooth pouch to stroke, and I cannot reach it for her."

"Father set store by that otterskin pouch, for poor Prince Arthur slew the otter," cried Stephen. "Surely, John, you'll not let the babes make a toy of that?"

John made a helpless gesture, and at a renewed call, went indoors.

"You are right, Ambrose," said Stephen, "this is no place for us. Why should we tarry any longer to see everything moiled and set at nought? I have couched in the forest before, and 'tis summer time."

"Nay," said Ambrose, "we must make up our fardels and have our money in our pouches before we can depart. We must tarry the night, and call John to his reckoning, and so might we set forth early enough in the morning to lie at Winchester that night and take counsel with our uncle Birkenholt."

"I would not stop short at Winchester," said Stephen. "London for me, where uncle Randall will find us preferment!"

"And what wilt do for Spring!"

"Take him with me, of course!" exclaimed Stephen. "What! would I leave him to be kicked and pinched by Will, and hanged belike by Mistress Maud?"

"I doubt me whether the poor old hound will brook the journey."

"Then I'll carry him!"

Ambrose looked at the big dog as if he thought it would be a serious undertaking, but he had known and loved Spring as his brother's property ever since his memory began, and he scarcely felt that they could be separable for weal or woe.

The verdurers of the New Forest were of gentle blood, and their office was well-nigh hereditary. The Birkenholts had held it for many generations, and the reversion passed as a matter of course to the eldest son of the late holder, who had newly been laid in the burial-ground of Beaulieu Abbey. John Birkenholt, whose mother had been of knightly lineage, had resented his father's second marriage with the daughter of a yeoman on the verge of the Forest, suspected of a strain of gipsy blood, and had lived little at home, becoming a sort of agent at Southampton for business connected with the timber which was yearly cut in the Forest to supply material for the shipping. He had wedded the daughter of a person engaged in law business at Southampton, and had only been an occasional visitor at home, ever after the death of his stepmother. She had left these two boys, unwelcome appendages in his sight. They had obtained a certain amount of education at Beaulieu Abbey, where a school was kept, and where Ambrose daily studied, though for the last few months Stephen had assisted his father in his forest duties.

Death had come suddenly to break up the household in the early spring of 1515, and John Birkenholt had returned as if to a patrimony, bringing his wife and children with him. The funeral ceremonies had been conducted at Beaulieu Abbey on the extensive scale of the sixteenth century, the requiem, the feast, and the dole, all taking place there, leaving the Forest lodge in its ordinary quiet.

It had always been understood that on their father's death the two younger sons must make their own way in the world; but he had hoped to live until they were a little older, when he might himself have started them in life, or expressed his wishes respecting them to their elder brother. As it was, however, there was no commendation of them, nothing but a strip of parchment, drawn up by one of the monks of Beaulieu, leaving each of them twenty crowns, with a few small jewels and properties left by their own mother, while everything else went to their brother.

There might have been some jealousy excited by the estimation in which Stephen's efficiency—boy as he was—was evidently held by the plain-spoken underlings of the verdurer; and this added to Mistress Birkenholt's dislike to the presence of her husband's half-brothers, whom she regarded as interlopers without a right to exist. Matters were brought to a climax by old Spring's resentment at being roughly teased by her spoilt children. He had done nothing worse than growl and show his teeth, but the town-bred dame had taken alarm, and half in terror, half in spite, had insisted on his instant execution, since he was too old to be valuable. Stephen, who loved the dog only less than he loved his brother Ambrose, had come to high words with her; and the end of the altercation had been that she had declared that she would suffer no great lubbers of the half-blood to devour her children's inheritance, and teach them ill manners, and that go they must, and that instantly. John had muttered a little about "not so fast, dame," and "for very shame," but she had turned on him, and rated him with a violence that demonstrated who was ruler in the house, and took away all disposition to tarry long under the new dynasty.

The boys possessed two uncles, one on each side of the house. Their father's elder brother had been a man-at-arms, having preferred a stirring life to the Forest, and had fought in the last surges of the Wars of the Roses. Having become disabled and infirm, he had taken advantage of a corrody, or right of maintenance, as being of kin to a benefactor of Hyde Abbey at Winchester, to which Birkenholt some generations back had presented a few roods of land, in right of which, one descendant at a time might be maintained in the Abbey. Intelligence of his brother's death had been sent to Richard Birkenholt, but answer had been returned that he was too evil-disposed with the gout to attend the burial.

The other uncle, Harry Randall, had disappeared from the country under a cloud connected with the king's deer, leaving behind him the reputation of a careless, thriftless, jovial fellow, the best company in all the Forest, and capable of doing every one a work save his own.

The two brothers, who were about seven and six years old at the time of his flight, had a lively recollection of his charms as a playmate, and of their mother's grief for him, and refusal to believe any ill of her Hal. Rumours had come of his attainment to vague and unknown greatness at court, under the patronage of the Lord Archbishop of York, which the Verderer laughed to scorn, though his wife gave credit to them. Gifts bad come from time to time, passed through a succession of servants and officials of the king, such as a coral and silver rosary, a jewelled bodkin, an agate carved with Saint Catherine, an ivory pouncet box with a pierced gold coin as the lid; but no letter with them, as indeed Hal Randall had never been induced to learn to read or write. Master Birkenholt looked doubtfully at the tokens and hoped Hal had come honestly by them; but his wife had thoroughly imbued her sons with the belief that Uncle Hal was shining in his proper sphere, where he was better appreciated than at home. Thus their one plan was to go to London to find Uncle Hal, who was sure to put Stephen on the road to fortune, and enable Ambrose to become a great scholar, his favourite ambition.

His gifts would, as Ambrose observed, serve them as tokens, and with the purpose of claiming them, they re-entered the hall, a long low room, with a handsome open roof, and walls tapestried with dressed skins, interspersed with antlers, hung with weapons of the chase. At one end of the hall was a small polished barrel, always replenished with beer, at the other a hearth with a wood fire constantly burning, and there was a table running the whole length of the room; at one end of this was laid a cloth, with a few trenchers on it, and horn cups, surrounding a barley loaf and a cheese, this meagre irregular supper being considered as a sufficient supplement to the funeral baked meats which had abounded at Beaulieu. John Birkenholt sat at the table with a trencher and horn before him, uneasily using his knife to crumble, rather than cut, his bread. His wife, a thin, pale, shrewish-looking woman, was warming her child's feet at the fire, before putting him to bed, and an old woman sat spinning and nodding on a settle at a little distance.

"Brother," said Stephen, "we have thought on what you said. We will put our stuff together, and if you will count us out our portions, we will be afoot by sunrise tomorrow."

"Nay, nay, lad, I said not there was such haste; did I, mistress housewife?"—(she snorted); "only that thou art a well-grown lusty fellow, and 'tis time thou wentest forth. For thee, Ambrose, thou wottest I made thee a fair offer of bed and board."

"That is," called out the wife, "if thou wilt make a fair scholar of little

Will. 'Tis a mighty good offer. There are not many who would let their child be taught by a mere stripling like thee!"

"Nay," said Ambrose, who could not bring himself to thank her, "I go with Stephen, mistress; I would in end my scholarship ere I teach."

"As you please," said Mistress Maud, shrugging her shoulders, "only never say that a fair offer was not made to you."

"And," said Stephen, "so please you, brother John, hand us over our portions, and the jewels as bequeathed to us, and we will be gone."

"Portions, quotha?" returned John. "Boy, they be not due to you till you be come to years of discretion."

The brothers looked at one another, and Stephen said, "Nay, now, brother, I know not how that may be, but I do know that you cannot drive us from our father's house without maintenance, and detain what belongs to us."

And Ambrose muttered something about "my Lord of Beaulieu."

"Look you, now," said John, "did I ever speak of driving you from home without maintenance? Hath not Ambrose had his choice of staying here, and Stephen of waiting till some office be found for him? As for putting forty crowns into the hands of striplings like you, it were mere throwing it to the robbers."

"That being so," said Ambrose turning to Stephen, "we will to Beaulieu, and see what counsel my lord will give us."

"Yea, do, like the vipers ye are, and embroil us with my Lord of Beaulieu," cried Maud from the fire.

"See," said John, in his more caressing fashion, "it is not well to carry family tales to strangers, and—and—"

He was disconcerted by a laugh from the old nurse, "Ho! John Birkenholt, thou wast ever a lad of smooth tongue, but an thou, or madam here, think that thy brothers can be put forth from thy father's door without their due before the good man be cold in his grave, and the Forest not ring with it, thou art mightily out in thy reckoning!"

"Peace, thou old hag; what matter is't of thine?" began Mistress Maud, but again came the harsh laugh.

"Matter of mine! Why, whose matter should it be but mine, that have nursed all three of the lads, ay, and their father before them, besides four more that lie in the graveyard at Beaulieu? Rest their sweet souls! And I tell thee, Master John, an thou do not righteously by these thy brothers, thou mayst back to thy parchments at Southampton, for not a man or beast in the Forest will give thee good-day."

They all felt the old woman's authority. She was able and spirited in her homely way, and more mistress of the house than Mrs. Birkenholt herself; and such were the terms of domestic service, that there was no peril of losing her place. Even Maud knew that to turn her out was an impossibility, and that she must be accepted like the loneliness, damp, and other evils of Forest life. John had been under her dominion, and proceeded to persuade her. "Good now, Nurse Joan, what have I denied these rash striplings that my father would have granted them? Wouldst thou have them carry all their portion in their hands, to be cozened of it at the first alehouse, or robbed on the next heath?"

"I would have thee do a brother's honest part, John Birkenholt. A loving part I say not. Thou wert always like a very popple for hardness, and smoothness, ay, and slipperiness. Heigh ho! But what is right by the lads, thou *shalt* do."

John cowered under her eye as he had done at six years old, and faltered, "I only seek to do them right, nurse."

Nurse Joan uttered an emphatic grunt, but Mistress Maud broke in, "They are not to hang about here in idleness, eating my poor child's substance, and teaching him ill manners."

"We would not stay here if you paid us for it," returned Stephen.

"And whither would you go?" asked John.

"To Winchester first, to seek counsel with our uncle Birkenholt. Then to London, where uncle Randall will help us to our fortunes."

"Gipsy Hal! He is more like to help you to a halter," sneered John, *sotto voce*, and Joan herself observed, "Their uncle at Winchester will show them better than to run after that there go-by-chance."

However, as no one wished to keep the youths, and they were equally determined to go, an accommodation was come to at last. John was induced to give them three crowns apiece and to yield them up the five small trinkets specified, though not without some murmurs from his wife. It was no doubt safer to leave the rest of the money in his hands than to carry it with them, and he undertook that it should be forthcoming, if needed for any fit purpose, such as the purchase of an office, an apprentice's fee, or an outfit as a squire. It was a vague promise that cost him nothing just then, and thus could be readily made, and John's great desire was to get them away so that he could aver that they had gone by their own free will, without any hardship, for he had seen enough at his father's obsequies to show him that the love and sympathy of all the scanty dwellers in the Forest was with them.

Nurse Joan had fought their battles, but with the sore heart of one who was parting with her darlings never to see them again. She bade them doff their suits of mourning that she might make up their fardels, as they would travel in their Lincoln-green suits. To take these she repaired to the little rough shedlike chamber where the two brothers lay for the last time on their pallet bed, awake, and watching for her, with Spring at their feet. The poor old woman stood over them, as over the motherless nurslings whom she had tended, and she should probably never see more, but she was a woman of shrewd sense, and perceived that "with the new madam in the hall" it was better that they should be gone before worse ensued.

She advised leaving their valuables sealed up in the hands of my Lord Abbot, but they were averse to this—for they said their uncle Randall, who had not seen them since they were little children, would not know them without some pledge.

She shook her head. "The less you deal with Hal Randall the better," she said. "Come now, lads, be advised and go no farther than Winchester, where Master Ambrose may get all the book-learning he is ever craving for, and you, Master Stevie, may prentice yourself to some good trade."

"Prentice!" cried Stephen, scornfully.

"Ay, ay. As good blood as thine has been prenticed," returned Joan. "Better so than be a cutthroat sword-and-buckler fellow, ever slaying some one else or getting thyself slain—a terror to all peaceful folk. But thine uncle will see to that—a steady-minded lad always was he—was Master Dick."

Consoling herself with this hope, the old woman rolled up their new suits with some linen into two neat knapsacks; sighing over the thought that unaccustomed fingers would deal with the shirts she had spun, bleached, and sewn. But she had confidence in "Master Dick," and concluded that to send his nephews to him at Winchester gave a far better chance of their being cared for, than letting them be flouted into ill-doing by their grudging brother and his wife.

CHAPTER II.

The Grange of Silkstede.

"All Itchen's valley lay,
Saint Catherine's breezy side and the woodlands far away,
The huge Cathedral sleeping in venerable gloom,
The modest College tower, and the bedesmen's Norman home."

Lord Selborne.

Very early in the morning, even according to the habits of the time, were Stephen and Ambrose Birkenholt astir. They were full of ardour to enter on the new and unknown world beyond the Forest, and much as they loved it, any change that kept them still to their altered life would have been distasteful.

Nurse Joan, asking no questions, folded up their fardels on their backs, and packed the wallets for their day's journey with ample provision. She charged them to be good lads, to say their Pater, Credo, and Ave daily, and never omit Mass on a Sunday. They kissed her like their mother and promised heartily—and Stephen took his crossbow. They had had some hope of setting forth so early as to avoid all other *human* farewells, except that Ambrose wished to begin by going to Beaulieu to take leave of the Father who had been his kind master, and get his blessing and counsel. But Beaulieu was three miles out of their way, and Stephen had not the same desire, being less attached to his schoolmaster and more afraid of hindrances being thrown in their way.

Moreover, contrary to their expectation, their elder brother came forth, and declared his intention of setting them forth on their way, bestowing a great amount of good advice, to the same purport as that of nurse Joan, namely, that they should let their uncle Richard Birkenholt find them some employment at Winchester, where they, or at least Ambrose, might even obtain admission into the famous college of Saint Mary.

In fact, this excellent elder brother persuaded himself that it would be doing them an absolute wrong to keep such promising youths hidden in the Forest.

The purpose of his going thus far with them made itself evident. It was to see them past the turning to Beaulieu. No doubt he wished to tell the story in his own way, and that they should not present themselves there as orphans expelled from their father's house. It would sound much better that he had sent them to ask counsel of their uncle at Winchester, the fit person to take charge of them. And as he represented that to go to Beaulieu would lengthen their day's journey so much that they might hardly reach Winchester that night, while all Stephen's wishes were to go forward, Ambrose could only send his greetings. There was another debate over Spring, who had followed his master as usual. John uttered an exclamation of vexation at perceiving it, and bade Stephen drive the dog back. "Or give me the leash to drag him. He will never follow me."

"He goes with us," said Stephen.

"He! Thou'lt never have the folly! The old hound is half blind and past use. No man will take thee in with him after thee."

"Then they shall not take me in," said Stephen. "I'll not leave him to be hanged by thee."

"Who spoke of hanging him!"

"Thy wife will soon, if she hath not already."

"Thou wilt be for hanging him thyself ere thou have made a day's journey with him on the king's highway, which is not like these forest paths, I would have thee to know. Why, he limps already."

"Then I'll carry him," said Stephen, doggedly.

"What hast thou to say to that device, Ambrose?" asked John, appealing to the elder and wiser.

But Ambrose only answered "I'll help," and as John had no particular desire to retain the superannuated hound, and preferred on the whole to be spared sentencing him, no more was said on the subject as they went along, until all John's stock of good counsel had been lavished on his brothers' impatient ears. He bade them farewell, and turned back to the lodge, and they struck away along the woodland pathway which they had been told led to Winchester, though they had never been thither, nor seen any town save Southampton and Romsey at long intervals. On they went, sometimes through beech and oak woods of noble, almost primeval, trees, but more often across tracts of holly underwood, illuminated here and there with the snowy garlands of the wild cherry, and beneath with wide spaces covered with young green bracken, whose soft irregular masses on the undulating ground had somewhat the effect of the waves of the sea. These alternated with stretches of yellow gorse and brown heather, sheets of cotton-grass, and pools of white crowfoot, and all the vegetation of a mountain side, only that the mountain was not there.

The brothers looked with eyes untaught to care for beauty, but with a certain love of the home scenes, tempered by youth's impatience for something new. The nightingales sang, the thrushes flew out before them, the wild duck and moorhen glanced on the pools. Here and there they came on the furrows left by the snout of the wild swine, and in the open tracts rose the graceful heads of the deer, but of inhabitants or travellers they scarce saw any, save when they halted at the little hamlet of Minestead, where a small alehouse was kept by one Will Purkiss, who claimed descent from the charcoal-burner who had carried William Rufus's corpse to burial at Winchester—the one fact in history known to all New Foresters, though perhaps Ambrose and John were the only persons beyond the walls of Beaulieu who did not suppose the affair to have taken place in the last generation.

A draught of ale and a short rest were welcome as the heat of the day came on, making the old dog plod wearily on with his tongue out, so that Stephen began to consider whether he should indeed have to be his bearer—a serious matter, for the creature at full length measured nearly as much as he did. They met hardly any one, and they and Spring were alike too well known and trained, for difficulties to arise as to leading a dog through the Forest. Should they ever come to the term of the Forest? It was not easy to tell when they were really beyond it, for the ground was much of the same kind. Only the smooth, treeless hills, where they had always been told Winchester lay, seemed more defined, and they saw no more deer, but here and there were inclosures where wheat and barley were growing, and black timbered farmhouses began to show themselves at intervals. Herd boys, as rough and unkempt as their charges, could be seen looking after little tawny cows, black-faced sheep, or spotted pigs, with curs which barked fiercely at poor weary Spring, even as their masters were more disposed to throw stones than to answer questions.

By and by, on the further side of a green valley, could be seen buildings with an encircling wall of flint and mortar faced with ruddy brick, the dark red-tiled roofs rising among walnut-trees, and an orchard in full bloom spreading into a long green field.

"Winchester must be nigh. The sun is getting low," said Stephen.

"We will ask. The good folk will at least give us an answer," said Ambrose wearily.

As they reached the gate, a team of plough horses was passing in led by a peasant lad, while a lay brother, with his gown tucked up, rode sideways on one, whistling. An Augustinian monk, ruddy, burly, and sunburnt, stood in the farm-yard to receive an account of the day's work, and doffing his cap, Ambrose asked whether Winchester were near.

"Three mile or thereaway, my good lad," said the monk; "thou'lt see the towers an ye mount the hill. Whence art thou?" he added, looking at the two young strangers. "Scholars? The College elects not yet a while."

"We be from the Forest, so please your reverence, and are bound for Hyde Abbey, where our uncle, Master Richard Birkenholt, dwells."

"And oh, sir," added Stephen, "may we crave a drop of water for our dog?"

The monk smiled as he looked at Spring, who had flung himself down to take advantage of the halt, hanging out his tongue, and panting spasmodically. "A noble beast," he said, "of the Windsor breed, is't not?" Then laying his hand on the graceful head, "Poor old hound, thou art o'er travelled. He is aged for such a journey, if you came from the Forest since morn. Twelve years at the least, I should say, by his muzzle."

"Your reverence is right," said Stephen, "he is twelve years old. He is two years younger than I am, and my father gave him to me when he was a little whelp."

"So thou must needs take him to seek thy fortune with thee," said the good-natured Augustinian, not knowing how truly he spoke. "Come in, my lads, here's a drink for him. What said you was your uncle's name?" and as

Ambrose repeated it, "Birkenholt! Living on a corrody at Hyde! Ay! ay! My lads, I have a call to Winchester tomorrow, you'd best tarry the night here at Silkstede Grange, and fare forward with me."

The tired boys were heartily glad to accept the invitation, more especially as Spring, happy as he was with the trough of water before him, seemed almost too tired to stand over it, and after the first, tried to lap, lying down. Silkstede was not a regular convent, only a grange or farmhouse, presided over by one of the monks, with three or four lay brethren under him, and a little colony of hinds, in the surrounding cottages, to cultivate the farm, and tend a few cattle and numerous sheep, the special care of the Augustinians.

Father Shoveller, as the good-natured monk who had received the travellers was called, took them into the spacious but homely chamber which served as refectory, kitchen, and hall. He called to the lay brother who was busy over the open hearth to fry a few more rashers of bacon; and after they had washed away the dust of their Journey at the trough where Spring had slaked his thirst, they sat down with him to a hearty supper, which smacked more of the grange than of the monastery, spread on a large solid oak table, and washed down with good ale. The repast was shared by the lay brethren and farm servants, and also by two or three big sheepdogs, who had to be taught their manners towards Spring.

There was none of the formality that Ambrose was accustomed to at Beaulieu in the great refectory, where no one spoke, but one of the brethren read aloud some theological book from a stone pulpit in the wall. Here Brother Shoveller conversed without stint, chiefly with the brother who seemed to be a kind of bailiff, with whom he discussed the sheep that were to be taken into market the next day, and the prices to be given for them by either the college, the castle, or the butchers of Boucher Row. He however found time to talk to the two guests, and being sprung from a family in the immediate neighbourhood, he knew the verdurer's name, and ere he was a monk, had joined in the chase in the Forest.

There was a little oratory attached to the hall, where he and the lay brethren kept the hours, to a certain degree, putting two or three services into one, on a liberal interpretation of *laborare est orare*. Ambrose's responses made their host observe as they went out, "Thou hast thy Latin pat, my son, there's the making of a scholar in thee."

Then they took their first night's rest away from home, in a small guest-chamber, with a good bed, though bare in all other respects. Brother Shoveller likewise had a cell to himself but the lay brethren slept promiscuously among their sheepdogs on the floor of the refectory.

All were afoot in the early morning, and Stephen and Ambrose were awakened by the tumultuous bleatings of the flock of sheep that were being driven from their fold to meet their fate at Winchester market. They heard Brother Shoveller shouting his orders to the shepherds in tones a great deal more like those of a farmer than of a monk, and they made haste to dress themselves and join him as he was muttering a morning abbreviation of his obligatory devotions in the oratory, observing that they might be in time to hear mass at one of the city churches, but the sheep might delay them, and they had best break their fast ere starting.

It was Wednesday, a day usually kept as a moderate fast, so the breakfast was of oatmeal porridge, flavoured with honey, and washed down with mead, after which Brother Shoveller mounted his mule, a sleek creature, whose long ears had an air of great contentment, and rode off, accommodating his pace to that of his young companions up a stony cart-track which soon led them to the top of a chalk down, whence, as in a map, they could see Winchester, surrounded by its walls, lying in a hollow between the smooth green hills. At one end rose the castle, its fortifications covering its own hill, beneath, in the valley, the long, low massive Cathedral, the college buildings and tower with its pinnacles, and nearer at hand, among the trees, the Almshouse of Noble Poverty at Saint Cross, beneath the round hill of Saint Catherine. Churches and monastic buildings stood thickly in the town, and indeed, Brother Shoveller said, shaking his head, that there were well-nigh as many churches as folk to go to them; the place was decayed since the time he remembered when Prince Arthur was born there. Hyde Abbey he could not show them, from where they stood, as it lay further off by the river side, having been removed from the neighbourhood of the Minster, because the brethren of Saint Grimbald could not agree with those of Saint Swithun's belonging to the Minster, as indeed their buildings were so close together that it was hardly possible to pass between them, and their bells jangled in each other's ears.

Brother Shoveller did not seem to entertain a very high opinion of the monks of Saint Grimbald, and he asked the boys whether they were expected there. "No," they said; "tidings of their father's death had been sent by one of the woodmen, and the only answer that had been returned was that Master Richard Birkenholt was ill at ease, but would have masses said for his brother's soul."

"Hem?" said the Augustinian ominously; but at that moment they came up with the sheep, and his attention was wholly absorbed by them, as he joined the lay brothers in directing the shepherds who were driving them across the downs, steering them over the high ground towards the arched West Gate close to the royal castle. The street sloped rapidly down, and Brother Shoveller conducted his young companions between the overhanging houses, with stalls between serving as shops, till they reached the open space round the Market Cross, on the steps of which women sat with baskets of eggs, butter, and poultry, raised above the motley throng of cattle and sheep, with their dogs and drivers, the various cries of man and beast forming an incongruous accompaniment to the bells of the churches that surrounded the marketplace.

Citizens' wives in hood and wimple were there, shrilly bargaining for provision for their households, squires and grooms in quest of hay for their masters' stables, purveyors seeking food for the garrison, lay brethren and sisters for their convents, and withal, the usual margin of begging friars, wandering gleemen, jugglers and pedlars, though in no great numbers, as this was only a

Wednesday market-day, not a fair. Ambrose recognised one or two who made part of the crowd at Beaulieu only two days previously, when he had "seen through tears the juggler leap," and the jingling tune one of them was playing on a rebeck brought back associations of almost unbearable pain. Happily, Father Shoveller, having seen his sheep safely bestowed in a pen, bethought him of bidding the lay brother in attendance show the young gentlemen the way to Hyde Abbey, and turning up a street at right angles to the principal one, they were soon out of the throng.

It was a lonely place, with a decayed uninhabited appearance, and Brother Peter told them it had been the Jewry, whence good King Edward had banished all the unbelieving dogs of Jews, and where no one chose to dwell after them.

Soon they came in sight of a large extent of monastic buildings, partly of stone, but the more domestic offices of flint and brick or mortar. Large meadows stretched away to the banks of the Itchen, with cattle grazing in them, but in one was a set of figures to whom the lay brother pointed with a laugh of exulting censure.

"Long bows!" exclaimed Stephen. "Who be they?"

"Brethren of Saint Grimbald, sir. Such rule doth my Lord of Hyde keep, mitred abbot though he be. They say the good bishop hath called him to order, but what recks he of bishops? Good-day, Brother Bulpett, here be two young kinsmen of Master Birkenholt to visit him; and so *benedicite*, fair sirs. Saint Austin's grace be with you!"

Through a gate between two little red octagonal towers, Brother Bulpett led the two visitors, and called to another of the monks, "*Benedicite*, Father Segrim, here be two striplings wanting speech of old Birkenholt."

"Looking after dead men's shoes, I trow," muttered Father Segrim, with a sour look at the lads, as he led them through the outer court, where some fine horses were being groomed, and then across a second court surrounded with a beautiful cloister, with flower beds in front of it. Here, on a stone bench, in the sun, clad in a gown furred with rabbit skin, sat a decrepit old man, both his hands clasped over his staff. Into his deaf ears their guide shouted, "These boys say they are your kindred, Master Birkenholt."

"Anan?" said the old man, trembling with palsy. The lads knew him to be older than their father, but they were taken by surprise at such feebleness, and the monk did not aid them, only saying roughly, "There he is. Tell your errand."

"How fares it with you, uncle?" ventured Ambrose.

"Who be ye? I know none of you," muttered the old man, shaking his head still more.

"We are Ambrose and Stephen from the Forest," shouted Ambrose.

"Ah Steve! poor Stevie! The accursed boar has rent his goodly face so as I would never have known him. Poor Steve! Rest his soul!"

The old man began to weep, while his nephews recollected that they had heard that another uncle had been slain by the tusk of a wild boar in early manhood. Then to their surprise, his eyes fell on Spring, and calling the hound by name, he caressed the creature's head—"Spring, poor Spring! Stevie's faithful old dog. Hast lost thy master? Wilt follow me now?"

He was thinking of a Spring as well as of a Stevie of sixty years ago, and he babbled on of how many fawns were in the Queen's Bower this summer, and who had best shot at the butts at Lyndhurst, as if he were excited by the breath of his native Forest, but there was no making him understand that he was speaking with his nephews. The name of his brother John only set him repeating that John loved the greenwood, and would be content to take poor Stevie's place and dwell in the verdurer's lodge; but that he himself ought to be abroad, he had seen brave Lord Talbot's ships ready at Southampton, John might stay at home, but he would win fame and honour in Gascony.

And while he thus wandered, and the boys stood by perplexed and distressed, Brother Segrim came back, and said, "So, young sirs, have you seen enough of your doting kinsman? The sub-prior bids me say that we harbour no strange, idling, lubber lads nor strange dogs here. 'Tis enough for us to be saddled with dissolute old men-at-arms without all their idle kin making an excuse to come and pay their devoirs. These corrodies are a heavy charge and a weighty abuse, and if there be the visitation the king's majesty speaks of they will be one of the first matters to be amended."

Wherewith Stephen and Ambrose found themselves walked out of the cloister of Saint Grimbald, and the gates shut behind them.

CHAPTER III.

Kinsmen and Strangers.

"The reul of Saint Maure and of Saint Beneit
Because that it was old and some deale streit
This ilke monk let old things pace
He held ever of the new world the trace."

Chaucer.

"The churls!" exclaimed Stephen.

"Poor old man!" said Ambrose; "I hope they are good to him!"

"To think that thus ends all that once was gallant talk of fighting under Talbot's banner," sighed Stephen, thoughtful for a moment. "However, there's a good deal to come first."

"Yea, and what next?" said the elder brother.

"On to uncle Hal. I ever looked most to him. He will purvey me to a page's place in some noble household, and get thee a clerk's or scholar's place in my Lord of York's house. Mayhap there will be room for us both there, for my Lord of York hath a goodly following of armed men."

"Which way lies the road to London?"

"We must back into the town and ask, as well as fill our stomachs and our wallets," said Ambrose. "Talk of their rule! The entertaining of strangers is better understood at Silkstede than at Hyde."

"Tush! A grudged crust sticks in the gullet," returned Stephen. "Come on, Ambrose, I marked the sign of the White Hart by the marketplace. There will be a welcome there for foresters."

They returned on their steps past the dilapidated buildings of the old Jewry, and presently saw the market in full activity; but the sounds and sights of busy life where they were utter strangers, gave Ambrose a sense of loneliness and desertion, and his heart sank as the bolder Stephen threaded the way in the direction of a broad entry over which stood a slender-bodied hart with gold hoofs, horns, collar, and chain.

"How now, my sons?" said a full cheery voice, and to their joy, they found themselves pushed up against Father Shoveller.

"Returned already! Did you get scant welcome at Hyde? Here, come where we can get a free breath, and tell me."

They passed through the open gateway of the White Hart, into the court, but before listening to them, the monk exchanged greetings with the hostess, who stood at the door in a broad hat and velvet bodice, and demanded what cheer there was for noon-meat.

"A jack, reverend sir, eels and a grampus fresh sent up from Hampton; also fresh-killed mutton for such lay folk as are not curious of the Wednesday fast. They are laying the board even now."

"Lay platters for me and these two young gentlemen," said the Augustinian. "Ye be my guests, ye wot," he added, "since ye tarried not for meat at Hyde."

"Nor did they ask us," exclaimed Stephen; "lubbers and idlers were the best words they had for us."

"Ho! ho! That's the way with the brethren of Saint Grimbald! And your uncle?"

"Alas, sir, he doteth with age," said Ambrose. "He took Stephen for his own brother, dead under King Harry of Windsor."

"So! I had heard somewhat of his age and sickness. Who was it who thrust you out?"

"A lean brother with a thin red beard, and a shrewd, puckered visage."

"Ha! By that token 'twas Segrim the bursar. He wots how to drive a bargain. Saint Austin! but he deemed you came to look after your kinsman's corrody."

"He said the king spake of a visitation to abolish corrodies from religious houses," said Ambrose.

"He'll abolish the long bow from them first," said Father Shoveller. "Ay, and miniver from my Lord Abbot's hood. I'd admonish you, my good brethren of Saint Grimbald, to be in no hurry for a visitation which might scarce stop where you would fain have it. Well, my sons, are ye bound for the Forest again? An ye be, we'll wend back together, and ye can lie at Silkstede tonight."

"Alack, kind father, there's no more home for us in the Forest," said Ambrose.

"Methought ye had a brother?"

"Yea; but our brother hath a wife."

"Ho! ho! And the wife will none of you?"

"She would have kept Ambrose to teach her boy his primer," said Stephen; "but she would none of Spring nor of me."

"We hoped to receive counsel from our uncle at Hyde," added Ambrose.

"Have ye no purpose now?" inquired the Father, his jolly good-humoured face showing much concern.

"Yea," manfully returned Stephen. "'Twas what I ever hoped to do, to fare on and seek our fortune in London."

"Ha! To pick up gold and silver like Dick Whittington. Poor old Spring here will scarce do you the part of his cat," and the monk's hearty laugh angered Stephen into muttering, "We are no fools," but Father Shoveller only laughed the more, saying, "Fair and softly, my son, ye'll never pick up the gold if ye cannot brook a kindly quip. Have you friends or kindred in London?"

"Yea, that have we, sir," cried Stephen; "our mother's own brother, Master Randall, hath come to preferment there in my Lord Archbishop of York's household, and hath sent us tokens from time to time, which we will show you."

"Not while we be feasting," said Father Shoveller, hastily checking

Ambrose, who was feeling in his bosom. "See, the knaves be bringing their grampus across the court. Here, we'll clean our hands, and be ready for the meal;" and he showed them, under a projecting gallery in the inn yard a stone trough, through which flowed a stream of water, in which he proceeded to wash his hands and face, and to wipe them in a coarse towel suspended nigh at hand. Certainly after handling sheep freely there was need, though such ablutions were a refinement not indulged in by all the company who assembled round the well-spread board of the White Hart for the meal after the market. They were a motley company. By the host's side sat a knight on his way home from pilgrimage to Compostella, or perhaps a mission to Spain, with a couple of squires and other attendants, and converse of political import seemed to be passing between him and a shrewd-looking man in a lawyer's hood and gown, the recorder of Winchester, who preferred being a daily guest at the White Hart to keeping a table of his own. Country franklins and yeomen, merchants and men-at-arms, palmers and craftsmen, friars and monks, black, white, and grey, and with almost all, Father Shoveller had greeting or converse to exchange. He knew everybody, and had friendly talk with all, on canons or crops, on war or wool, on the prices of pigs or prisoners, on the news of the country side, or on the perilous innovations in learning at Oxford, which might, it was feared, even affect Saint Mary's College at Winchester.

He did not affect outlandish fishes himself, and dined upon pike, but observing the curiosity of his guests, he took good care to have them well supplied with grampus; also in due time with varieties of the pudding and cake kind which had never dawned on their forest—bred imagination, and with a due proportion of good ale-the same over which the knight might be heard rejoicing, and lauding far above the Spanish or French wines, on which he said he had been half starved.

Father Shoveller mused a good deal over his pike and its savoury stuffing. He was not by any means an ideal monk, but he was equally far from being a scandal. He was the shrewd man of business and manager of his fraternity, conducting the farming operations and making all the bargains, following his rule respectably according to the ordinary standard of his time, but not rising to any spirituality, and while duly observing the fast day, as to the quality of his food, eating with the appetite of a man who lived in the open fields.

But when their hunger was appeased, with many a fragment given to Spring, the young Birkenholts, wearied of the endless talk that was exchanged over the tankard, began to grow restless, and after exchanging signs across Father Shoveller's solid person, they simultaneously rose, and began to thank him and say they must pursue their journey.

"How now, not so fast, my sons," said the Father; "tarry a bit, I have more to say to thee. Prayers and provender, thou knowst—I'll come anon. So, sir, didst say yonder beggarly Flemings haggle at thy price for thy Southdown fleeces. Weight of dirt forsooth! Do not we wash the sheep in the Poolhole stream, the purest water in the shire?"

Manners withheld Ambrose from responding to Stephen's hot impatience, while the merchant in the sleek puce-coloured coat discussed the Flemish wool market with the monk for a good half-hour longer.

By this time the knight's horses were brought into the yard, and the merchant's men had made ready his palfrey, his pack-horse being already on the way; the host's son came round with the reckoning, and there was a general move. Stephen expected to escape, and hardly could brook the good-natured authority with which Father Shoveller put Ambrose aside, when he would have discharged their share of the reckoning, and took it upon himself. "Said I not ye were my guests?" quoth he. "We missed our morning mass, it will do us no harm to hear Nones in the Minster."

"Sir, we thank you, but we should be on our way," said Ambrose, incited by Stephen's impatient gestures.

"Tut, tut. Fair and softly, my son, or more haste may be worse speed. Methought ye had somewhat to show me."

Stephen's youthful independence might chafe, but the habit of submission to authorities made him obediently follow the monk out at the back entrance of the inn, behind which lay the Minster yard, the grand western front rising in front of them, and the buildings of Saint Swithun's Abbey extending far to their right. The hour was nearly noon, and the space was deserted, except for an old woman sitting at the great western doorway with a basket of rosaries made of nuts and of snail shells, and a workman or two employed on the bishop's new reredos.

"Now for thy tokens," said Father Shoveller. "See my young foresters, ye be new to the world. Take an old man's counsel, and never show, nor speak of such gear in an hostel. Mine host of the White Hart is an old gossip of mine, and indifferent honest, but who shall say who might be within earshot?"

Stephen had a mind to say that he did not see why the meddling monk should wish to see them at all, and Ambrose looked a little reluctant, but Father Shoveller said in his good-humoured way, "As you please, young sirs. 'Tis but an old man's wish to see whether he can do aught to help you, that you be not as lambs among wolves. Mayhap ye deem ye can walk into London town, and that the first man you meet can point you to your uncle—Randall call ye him?—as readily as I could show you my brother, Thomas Shoveller of Cranbury. But you are just as like to meet with some knave who might cozen you of all you have, or mayhap a beadle might take you up for vagabonds, and thrust you in the stocks, or ever you get to London town; so I would fain give you some commendation, an I knew to whom to make it, and ye be not too proud to take it."

"You are but too good to us, sir," said Ambrose, quite conquered, though Stephen only half believed in the difficulties. The Father took them within the west door of the Minster, and looking up and down the long arcade of the southern aisle to see that no one was watching, he inspected the tokens, and cross-examined them on their knowledge of their uncle.

His latest gift, the rosary, had come by the hand of Friar Hurst, a begging Minorite of Southampton, who had it from another of his order at

Winchester, who had received it from one of the king's archers at the Castle, with a message to Mistress Birkenholt that it came from her brother, Master Randall, who had good preferment in London, in the house of my Lord Archbishop of York, without whose counsel King Henry never stirred. As to the coming of the agate and the pouncet box, the minds of the boys were very hazy. They knew that the pouncet box had been conveyed through the attendants of the Abbot of Beaulieu, but they were only sure that from that time the belief had prevailed with their mother that her brother was prospering in the house of the all-powerful Wolsey. The good Augustinian, examining the tokens, thought they gave colour to that opinion. The rosary and agate might have been picked up in an ecclesiastical household, and the lid of the pouncet box was made of a Spanish coin, likely to have come through some of the attendants of Queen Katharine.

"It hath an appearance," he said. "I marvel whether there be still at the Castle this archer who hath had speech with Master Randall, for if ye know no more than ye do at present, 'tis seeking a needle in a bottle of hay. But see, here come the brethren that be to sing Nones—sinner that I am, to have said no Hours since the morn, being letted with lawful business."

Again the unwilling Stephen had to submit. There was no feeling for the incongruous in those days, and reverence took very different directions from those in which it now shows itself, so that nobody had any objection to Spring's pacing gravely with the others towards the Lady Chapel, where the Hours were sung, since the Choir was in the hands of workmen, and the sound of chipping stone could be heard from it, where Bishop Fox's elaborate lacework reredos was in course of erection. Passing the shrine of Saint Swithun, and the grand tomb of Cardinal Beaufort, where his life-coloured effigy filled the boys with wonder, they followed their leader's example, and knelt within the Lady Chapel, while the brief Latin service for the ninth hour was sung through by the canon, clerks, and boys. It really was the Sixth, but cumulative easygoing treatment of the Breviary had made this the usual time for it, as the name of noon still testifies. The boys' attention, it must be confessed, was chiefly expended on the wonderful miracles of the Blessed Virgin in fresco on the walls of the chapel, all tending to prove that here was hope for those who said their Ave in any extremity of fire or flood.

Nones ended, Father Shoveller, with many a halt for greeting or for gossip, took the lads up the hill towards the wide fortified space where the old Castle and royal Hall of Henry of Winchester looked down on the city, and after some friendly passages with the warder at the gate, Father Shoveller explained that he was in quest of some one recently come from court, of whom the striplings in his company could make inquiry concerning a kinsman in the household of my Lord Archbishop of York. The warder scratched his head, and bethinking himself that Eastcheap Jockey was the reverend father's man, summoned a horse-boy to call that worthy.

"Where was he?"

"Sitting over his pottle in the Hall," was the reply, and the monk, with a laugh savouring little of asceticism, said he would seek him there, and accordingly crossed the court to the noble Hall, with its lofty dark marble columns, and the Round Table of King Arthur suspended at the upper end. The governor of the Castle had risen from his meal long ago, but the garrison in the piping times of peace would make their ration of ale last as far into the afternoon as their commanders would suffer. And half a dozen men still sat there, one or two snoring, two playing at dice on a clear corner of the board, and another, a smart well-dressed fellow in a bright scarlet jerkin, laying down the law to a country bumpkin, who looked somewhat dazed. The first of these was, as it appeared, Eastcheap Jockey, and there was something both of the readiness and the impudence of the Londoner in his manner, when he turned to answer the question. He knew many in my Lord of York's house—as many as a man was like to know where there was a matter of two hundred folk between clerks and soldiers, he had often crushed a pottle with them. No; he had never heard of one called Randall, neither in hat nor cowl, but he knew more of them by face than by name, and more by by name than surname or christened name. He was certainly not the archer who had brought a token for Mistress Birkenholt, and his comrades all avouched equal ignorance on the subject. Nothing could be gained there, and while Father Shoveller rubbed his bald head in consideration, Stephen rose to take leave.

"Look you here, my fair son," said the monk. "Starting at this hour, though the days be long, you will not reach any safe halting place with daylight, whereas by lying a night in this good city, you might reach Alton tomorrow, and there is a home where the name of Brother Shoveller will win you free lodging and entertainment."

"And tonight, good Father?" inquired Ambrose.

"That will I see to, if ye will follow me."

Stephen was devoured with impatience during the farewells in the Castle, but Ambrose represented that the good man was giving them much of his time, and that it would be unseemly and ungrateful to break from him.

"What matter is it of his? And why should he make us lose a whole day?" grumbled Stephen.

"What special gain would a day be to us?" sighed Ambrose. "I am thankful that any should take heed for us."

"Ay, you love leading-strings," returned Stephen. "Where is he going now? All out of our way!"

Father Shoveller, however, as he went down the Castle hill, explained that the Warden of Saint Elizabeth's Hospital was his friend, and knowing him to have acquaintance among the clergy of Saint Paul's, it would be well to obtain a letter of commendation from him, which might serve them in good stead in case they were disappointed of finding their uncle at once.

"It would be better for Spring to have a little more rest," thought Stephen, thus mitigating his own longing to escape from the monks and friars, of whom Winchester seemed to be full.

They had a kindly welcome in the pretty little college of Saint Elizabeth of Hungary, lying in the meadows between William of Wykeham's College and the round hill of Saint Catherine. The Warden was a more scholarly and ecclesiastical-looking person than his friend, the good-natured Augustinian. After commending them to his care, and partaking of a drink of mead, the monk of Silkstede took leave of the youths, with a hearty blessing and advice to husband their few crowns, not to tell every one of their tokens, and to follow the counsel of the Warden of Saint Elizabeth's, assuring them that if they turned back to the Forest they should have a welcome at Silkstede. Moreover he patted Spring pitifully, and wished him and his master well through the journey.

Saint Elizabeth's College was a hundred years older than its neighbour Saint Mary's, as was evident to practised eyes by its arches and windows, but it had been so entirely eclipsed by Wykeham's foundation that the number of priests, students, and choir-boys it was intended to maintain, had dwindled away, so that it now contained merely the Warden, a superannuated priest, and a couple of big lads who acted as servants. There was an air of great quietude and coolness about the pointed arches of its tiny cloister on that summer's day, with the old monk dozing in his chair over the manuscript he thought he was reading, not far from the little table where the Warden was eagerly studying Erasmus's *Praise of Folly*. But the Birkenholts were of the age at which quiet means dulness, at least Stephen was, and the Warden had pity both on them and on himself; and hearing joyous shouts outside, he opened a little door in the cloister wall, and revealed a multitude of lads with their black gowns tucked up, "a playing at the ball"—these being the scholars of Saint Mary's. Beckoning to a pair of elder ones, who were walking up and down more quietly, he consigned the strangers to their care, sweetening the introduction by an invitation to supper, for which he would gain permission from their Warden.

One of the young Wykehamists was shy and churlish, and sheered off from the brothers, but the other catechised them on their views of becoming scholars in the college. He pointed out the cloister where the studies took place in all weathers, showed them the hall, the chapel, and the chambers, and expatiated on the chances of attaining to New College. Being moreover a scholarly fellow, he and Ambrose fell into a discussion over the passage of Virgil, copied out on a bit of paper, which he was learning by heart. Some other scholars having finished their game, and become aware of the presence of a strange dog and two strange boys, proceeded to mob Stephen and Spring, whereupon the shy boy stood forth and declared that the Warden of Saint Elizabeth's had brought them in for an hour's sport.

Of course, in such close quarters, the rival Warden was esteemed a natural enemy, and went by the name of "Old Bess," so that his recommendation went for worse than nothing, and a dash at Spring was made by the inhospitable young savages. Stephen stood to the defence in act to box, and the shy lad stood by him, calling for fair play and one at a time. Of course a fight ensued, Stephen and his champion on the one side, and two assailants on the other, till after a fall on either side, Ambrose's friend interfered with a voice as thundering as the manly crack would permit, peace was restored, Stephen found himself free of the meads, and Spring was caressed instead of being tormented.

Stephen was examined on his past present, and future, envied for his Forest home, and beguiled into magnificent accounts, not only of the deer that had fallen to his bow and the boars that had fallen to his father's spear, but of the honours to which his uncle in the Archbishop's household would prefer him—for he viewed it as an absolute certainty that his kinsman was captain among the men-at-arms, whom he endowed on the spot with scarlet coats faced with black velvet, and silver medals and chains.

Whereat one of the other boys was not behind in telling how his father was pursuivant to my Lord Duke of Norfolk, and never went abroad save with silver lions broidered on back and breast, and trumpets going before; and another dwelt on the splendours of the mayor and aldermen of Southampton with their chains and cups of gold. Stephen felt bound to surpass this with the last report that my Lord of York's men rode Flemish steeds in crimson velvet housings, passmented with gold and gems, and of course his uncle had the leading of them.

"Who be thine uncle?" demanded a thin, squeaky voice. "I have brothers likewise in my Lord of York's meiné."

"Mine uncle is Captain Harry Randall, of Shirley," quoth Stephen magnificently, scornfully surveying the small proportions of the speaker. "What is thy brother?"

"Head turnspit," said a rude voice, provoking a general shout of laughter; but the boy stood his ground, and said hotly: "He is page to the comptroller of my lord's household, and waits at the second table, and I know every one of the captains."

"He'll say next he knows every one of the Seven Worthies," cried another boy, for Stephen was becoming a popular character.

"And all the paladins to boot. Come on, little Rowley!" was the cry.

"I tell you my brother is page to the comptroller of the household, and my mother dwells beside the Gate House, and I know every man of them," insisted Rowley, waxing hot. "As for that Forest savage fellow's uncle being captain of the guard, 'tis more like that he is my lord's fool, Quipsome Hal!"

Whereat there was a cry, in which were blended exultation at the hit, and vituperation of the hitter. Stephen flew forward to avenge the insult, but a big bell was beginning to ring, a whole wave of black gowns rushed to obey it, sweeping little Rowley away with them; and Stephen found himself left alone with his brother and the two lads who had been invited to Saint Elizabeth's, and who now repaired thither with them.

The supper party in the refectory was a small one, and the rule of the foundation limited the meal to one dish and a pittance, but the dish was of savoury eels, and the Warden's good nature had added to it some cates and comfits in consideration of his youthful guests.

After some conversation with the elder Wykehamist, the Warden called

Ambrose and put him through an examination on his attainments, which proved so satis factory, that it ended in an invitation to the brothers to fill two of the empty scholarships of the college of the dear Saint Elizabeth. It was a good offer, and one that Ambrose would fain have accepted, but Stephen had no mind for the cloister or for learning.

The Warden had no doubt that he could be apprenticed in the city of Winchester, since the brother at home had in keeping a sum sufficient for the fee. Though the trade of "capping" had fallen off, there were still good substantial burgesses who would be willing to receive an active lad of good parentage, some being themselves of gentle blood. Stephen, however, would not brook the idea. "Out upon you, Ambrose!" said he, "to desire to bind your own brother to base mechanical arts."

"'Tis what Nurse Joan held to be best for us both," said Ambrose.

"Joan! Yea, like a woman, who deems a man safest when he is a tailor, or a perfumer. An you be minded to stay here with a black gown and a shaven crown, I shall on with Spring and come to preferment. Maybe thou'lt next hear of me when I have got some fat canonry for thee."

"Nay, I quit thee not," said Ambrose. "If thou fare forward, so do I. But I would thou couldst have brought thy mind to rest there."

"What! wouldst thou be content with this worn-out place, with more churches than houses, and more empty houses than full ones? No! let us on where there is something doing! Thou wilt see that my Lord of York will have room for the scholar as well as the man-at-arms."

So the kind offer was declined, but Ambrose was grieved to see that the Warden thought him foolish, and perhaps ungrateful.

Nevertheless the good man gave them a letter to the Reverend Master Alworthy, singing clerk at Saint Paul's Cathedral, telling Ambrose it might serve them in case they failed to find their uncle, or if my Lord of York's household should not be in town. He likewise gave them a recommendation which would procure them a night's lodging at the Grange, and after the morning's mass and meat, sped them on their way with his blessing, muttering to himself, "That elder one might have been the staff of mine age! Pity on him to be lost in the great and evil City! Yet 'tis a good lad to follow that fiery spark his brother. *Tanquam agnus inter lupes.* Alack!"

CHAPTER IV.

A Hero's Fall.

"These four came all afront and mainly made at me. I made no more
ado, but took their seven points on my target—thus—"

Shakespeare.

The journey to Alton was eventless. It was slow, for the day was a broiling
one, and the young foresters missed their oaks and beeches, as they toiled over
the chalk downs that rose and sank in endless succession; though they would
hardly have slackened their pace if it had not been for poor old Spring, who
was sorely distressed by the heat and the want of water on the downs. Every
now and then he lay down, panting distressfully, with his tongue hanging out,
and his young masters always waited for him, often themselves not sorry to
rest in the fragment of shade from a solitary thorn or juniper.

The track was plain enough, and there were hamlets at long intervals.
Flocks of sheep fed on the short grass, but there was no approaching the shepherds, as they and their dogs regarded Spring as an enemy, to be received with
clamour, stones, and teeth, in spite of the dejected looks which might have
acquitted him of evil intentions.

The travellers reached Alton in the cool of the evening, and were kindly
received by a monk, who had charge of a grange just outside the little town,
near one of the springs of the River Wey.

The next day's journey was a pleasanter one, for there was more of wood
and heather, and they had to skirt round the marshy borders of various bogs.
Spring was happier, being able to stop and lap whenever he would, and the
whole scene was less unfriendly to them. But they scarcely made speed enough,
for they were still among tall whins and stiff scrub of heather when the sun
began to get low, gorgeously lighting the tall plumes of golden broom, and
they had their doubts whether they might not be off the track; but in such
weather, there was nothing alarming in spending a night out of doors, if only
they had something for supper. Stephen took a bolt from the purse at his
girdle, and bent his crossbow, so as to be ready in case a rabbit sprang out, or a
duck flew up from the marshes.

A small thicket of trees was in sight, and they were making for it, when
sounds of angry voices were heard, and Spring, bristling up the mane on his
neck, and giving a few premonitory fierce growls like thunder, bounded forward as though he had been seven years younger. Stephen darted after him,
Ambrose rushed after Stephen, and breaking through the trees, they beheld the
dog at the throat of one of three men. As they came on the scene, the dog was
torn down and hurled aside, giving a howl of agony, which infuriated his
master. Letting fly his crossbow bolt full at the fellow's face, he dashed on,
reckless of odds, waving his knotted stick, and shouting with rage. Ambrose,

though more aware of the madness of such an assault, still hurried to his support, and was amazed as well as relieved to find the charge effectual. Without waiting to return a blow, the miscreants took to their heels, and Stephen, seeing nothing but his dog, dropped on his knees beside the quivering creature, from whose neck blood was fast pouring. One glance of the faithful wistful eyes, one feeble movement of the expressive tail, and Spring had made his last farewell! That was all Stephen was conscious of; but Ambrose could hear the cry, "Good sirs, good lads, set me free!" and was aware of a portly form bound to a tree. As he cut the rope with his knife, the rescued traveller hurried out thanks and demands—"Where are the rest of you?" and on the reply that there were no more, proceeded, "Then we must on, on at once, or the villains will return! They must have thought you had a band of hunters behind you. Two furlongs hence, and we shall be safe in the hostel at Dogmersfield. Come on, my boy," to Stephen, "the brave hound is quite dead, more's the pity. Thou canst do no more for him, and we shall soon be in his case if we dally here."

"I cannot cannot leave him thus," sobbed Stephen, who had the loving old head on his knees. "Ambrose! stay, we must bring him. There, his tail wagged! If the blood were staunched—"

"Stephen! Indeed he is stone dead! Were he our brother we could not do otherwise," reasoned Ambrose, forcibly dragging his brother to his feet. "Go on we must. Wouldst have us all slaughtered for his sake? Come! The rogues will be upon us anon. Spring saved this good man's life. Undo not his work. See Is yonder your horse, sir? This way, Stevie!"

The instinct of catching the horse roused Stephen, and it was soon accomplished, for the steed was a plump, docile, city-bred palfrey, with dapple-grey flanks like well-stuffed satin pincushions, by no means resembling the shaggy Forest ponies of the boys' experience, but quite astray in the heath, and ready to come at the master's whistle; and call of "Soh Soh!—now Poppet!" Stephen caught the bridle, and Ambrose helped the burgess into the saddle. "Now, good boys," he said, "each of you lay a hand on my pommel. We can make good speed ere the rascals find out our scant numbers."

"You would make better speed without us, sir," said Stephen, hankering to remain beside poor Spring.

"Eye think Giles Headley the man to leave two children, that have maybe saved my life as well as my purse, to bear the malice of the robbers?" demanded the burgess angrily. "That were like those fellows of mine who have shown their heels and left their master strapped to a tree! Thou! thou! what's thy name, that hast the most wit, bring thy brother, unless thou wouldst have him laid by the side of his dog."

Stephen was forced to comply, and run by Poppet's side, though his eyes were so full of tears that he could not see his way, even when the pace slackened, and in the twilight they found themselves among houses and gardens, and thus in safety, the lights of an inn shining not far off.

A figure came out in the road to meet them, crying, "Master! master! is it you? and without scathe? Oh, the saints be praised!"

"Ay, Tibble, 'tis I and no other, thanks to the saints and to these brave lads! What, man, I blame thee not, I know thou canst not strike; but where be the rest?"

"In the inn, sir. I strove to call up the hue and cry to come to the rescue, but the cowardly hinds were afraid of the thieves, and not one would come forth."

"I wish they may not be in league with them," said Master Headley. "See! I was delivered—ay, and in time to save my purse, by these twain and their good dog. Are ye from these parts, my fair lads?"

"We be journeying from the New Forest to London," said Ambrose. "The poor dog heard the tumult, and leapt to your aid, sir, and we made after him."

"'Twas the saints sent him!" was the fervent answer.

"And," (with a lifting of the cap), "I hereby vow to Saint Julian a hound of solid bronze a foot in length, with a collar of silver, to his shrine in Saint Faith's, in token of my deliverance in body and goods! To London are ye bound? Then will we journey on together!"

They were by this time near the porch of a large country hostel, from the doors and large bay window of which light streamed out. And as the casement was open, those without could both see and hear all that was passing within.

The table was laid for supper, and in the place of honour sat a youth of some seventeen or eighteen years, gaily dressed, with a little feather curling over his crimson cap, and thus discoursing:—

"Yea, my good host, two of the rogues bear my tokens, besides him whom I felled to the earth. He came on at me with his sword, but I had my point ready for him; and down he went before me like an ox. Then came on another, but him I dealt with by the back stroke as used in the tilt-yard at Clarendon."

"I trow we shall know him again, sir. Holy saints to think such rascals should haunt so nigh us," the hostess was exclaiming. "Pity for the poor goodman, Master Headley. A portly burgher was he, friendly of tongue and free of purse. I well remember him when he went forth on his way to Salisbury, little thinking, poor soul, what was before him. And is he truly sped?"

"I tell thee, good woman, I saw him go down before three of their pikes. What more could I do but drive my horse over the nearest rogue who was rifling him?"

"If he were still alive—which Our Lady grant!—the knaves will hold him to ransom," quoth the host, as he placed a tankard on the table.

"I am afraid he is past," said the youth, shaking his head. "But an if he be still in the rogues' hands and living, I will get me on to his house in Cheapside, and arrange with his mother to find the needful sum, as befits me, I being his heir and about to wed his daughter. However, I shall do all that in me lies to get the poor old seignior out of the hands of the rogues. Saints defend me!"

"The poor old seignior is much beholden to thee," said Master Headley, advancing amid a clamour of exclamations from three or four serving-men or grooms, one protesting that he thought his master was with him, another that his horse ran away with him, one showing an arm which was actually being bound up, and the youth declaring that he rode off to bring help.

"Well wast thou bringing it," Master Headley answered. "I might be still standing bound like an eagle displayed, against yonder tree, for aught you fellows reeked."

"Nay, sir, the odds—" began the youth.

"Odds! such odds as were put to rout—by what, deem you? These two striplings and one poor hound. Had but one of you had the heart of a sparrow, ye had not furnished a tale to be the laugh of the Barbican and Cheapside. Look well at them. How old be you, my brave lads?"

"I shall be sixteen come Lammas day, and Stephen fifteen at Martinmas day, sir," said Ambrose; "but verily we did nought. We could have done nought had not the thieves thought more were behind us."

"There are odds between going forward and backward," said Master Headley, dryly. "Ha! Art hurt? Thou bleedst," he exclaimed, laying his hand on Stephen's shoulder, and drawing him to the light.

"'Tis no blood of mine," said Stephen, as Ambrose likewise came to join in the examination. "It is my poor Spring's. He took the coward's blow. His was all the honour, and we have left him there on the heath!" And he covered his face with his hands.

"Come, come, my good child," said Master Headley; "we will back to the place by times tomorrow when rogues hide and honest men walk abroad. Thou shalt bury thine hound, as befits a good warrior, on the battle-field. I would fain mark his points for the effigy we will frame, honest Tibble, for Saint Julian. And mark ye, fellows, thou godson Giles, above all, who 'tis that boast of their valour, and who 'tis that be modest of speech. Yea, thanks, mine host. Let us to a chamber, and give us water to wash away soil of travel and of fray, and then to supper. Young masters, ye are my guests. Shame were it that Giles Headley let go farther them that have, under Heaven and Saint Julian, saved him in life, limb, and purse."

The inn was large, being the resort of many travellers from the south, often of nobles and knights riding to Parliament, and thus the brothers found themselves accommodated with a chamber, where they could prepare for the meal, while Ambrose tried to console his brother by representing that, after all, poor Spring had died gallantly, and with far less pain than if he had suffered a wasting old age, besides being honoured for ever by his effigy in Saint Faith's, wherever that might be, the idea which chiefly contributed to console his master.

The two boys appeared in the room of the inn looking so unlike the dusty, blood-stained pair who had entered, that Master Headley took a second glance to convince himself that they were the same, before beckoning them to seats on either side of him, saying that he must know more of them, and bidding the host load their trenchers well from the grand fabric of beef-pasty which had been set at the end of the board. The runaways, four or five in number, herded together lower down, with a few travellers of lower degree, all except the youth who had been boasting before their arrival, and who retained his seat at the board, thumping it with the handle of his knife to show his impatience for the commencement of supper; and not far off sat Tibble, the same who had hailed their arrival, a thin, slight, one-sided looking person, with a terrible red withered scar on one cheek, drawing the corner of his mouth awry. He, like Master Headley himself, and the rest of his party were clad in red, guarded with white, and wore the cross of Saint George on the white border of their flat crimson caps, being no doubt in the livery of their Company. The citizen himself, having in the meantime drawn his conclusions from the air and gestures of the brothers, and their mode of dealing with their food, asked the usual question in an affirmative tone, "Ye be of gentle blood, young sirs?"

To which they replied by giving their names, and explaining that they were journeying from the New Forest to find their uncle in the train of the Archbishop of York.

"Birkenholt," said Tibble, meditatively. "He beareth vert, a buck's head proper, on a chief argent, two arrows in saltire. Crest, a buck courant, pierced in the gorge by an arrow, all proper."

To which the brothers returned by displaying the handles of their knives, both of which bore the pierced and courant buck.

"Ay, ay," said the man. "'Twill be found in our books, sir. We painted the shield and new-crested the morion the first year of my prenticeship, when the Earl of Richmond, the late King Harry of blessed memory, had newly landed at Milford Haven."

"Verily," said Ambrose, "our uncle Richard Birkenholt fought at Bosworth under Sir Richard Pole's banner."

"A tall and stalwart esquire, methinks," said Master Headley. "Is he the kinsman you seek?"

"Not so, sir. We visited him at Winchester, and found him sorely old and with failing wits. We be on our way to our mother's brother, Master Harry Randall."

"Is he clerk or layman? My Lord of York entertaineth enow of both," said Master Headley.

"Lay assuredly, sir," returned Stephen; "I trust to him to find me some preferment as page or the like."

"Know'st thou the man, Tibble?" inquired the master.

"Not among the men-at-arms, sir," was the answer; "but there be a many of them whose right names we never hear. However, he will be easily found if my Lord of York be returned from Windsor with his train."

"Then will we go forward together, my young Masters Birkenholt. I am not going to part with my doughty champions!"—patting Stephen's shoulder. "Ye'd not think that these light-heeled knaves belonged to the brave craft of armourers."

"Certainly not," thought the lads, whose notion of armourers was derived from the brawny blacksmith of Lyndhurst, who sharpened their boar spears and shod their horses. They made some kind of assent, and Master Headley went on. "These be the times. This is what peace hath brought us to! I am called down to Salisbury to take charge of the goods, chattels, and estate of my kinsman, Robert Headley—Saints rest his soul!—and to bring home yonder spark, my godson, whose indentures have been made over to me. And I may not ride a mile after sunset without being set upon by a sort of robbers, who must have guessed over-well what a pack of cowards they had to deal with."

"Sir," cried the younger Giles, "I swear to you that I struck right and left. I did all that man could do, but these rogues of serving-men, they fled, and dragged me along with them, and I deemed you were of our company till we dismounted."

"Did you so? Methought anon you saw me go down with three pikes in my breast. Come, come, godson Giles, speech will not mend it! Thou art but a green, town-bred lad, a mother's darling, and mayst be a brave man yet, only don't dread to tell the honest truth that you were afeard, as many a better man might be."

The host chimed in with tales of the thieves and outlaws who then, and indeed for many later generations, infested Bagshot heath, and the wild moorland tracks around. He seemed to think that the travellers had had a hair's-breadth escape, and that a few seconds' more delay might have revealed the weakness of the rescuers and have been fatal to them.

However there was no danger so near the village in the morning, and, somewhat to Stephen's annoyance, the whole place turned out to inspect the spot, and behold the burial of poor Spring, who was found stretched on the heather, just as he had been left the night before. He was interred under the stunted oak where Master Headley had been tied. While the grave was dug with a spade borrowed at the inn, Ambrose undertook to cut out the dog's name on the bark, but he had hardly made the first incision when Tibble, the singed foreman, offered to do it for him, and made a much more sightly inscription than he could have done. Master Headley's sword was found honourably broken under the tree, and was reserved to form a base for his intended *ex voto*. He uttered the vow in due form like a funeral oration, when Stephen, with a swelling heart, had laid the companion of his life in the little grave, which was speedily covered in.

CHAPTER V.

The Dragon Court.

"A citizen
Of credit and renown
A trainband captain eke was he
Of famous London town."

Cowper.

In spite of his satisfaction at the honourable obsequies of his dog, Stephen Birkenholt would fain have been independent, and thought it provoking and strange that every one should want to direct his movements, and assume the charge of one so well able to take care of himself; but he could not escape as he had done before from the Warden of Saint Elizabeth, for Ambrose had readily accepted the proposal that they should travel in Master Headley's company, only objecting that they were on foot; on which the good citizen hired a couple of hackneys for them.

Besides the two Giles Headleys, the party consisted of Tibble, the scarred and withered foreman, two grooms, and two serving-men, all armed with the swords and bucklers of which they had made so little use. It appeared in process of time that the two namesakes, besides being godfather and godson, were cousins, and that Robert, the father of the younger one, had, after his apprenticeship in the paternal establishment at Salisbury, served for a couple of years in the London workshop of his kinsman to learn the latest improvements in weapons. This had laid the foundation of a friendship which had lasted through life, though the London cousin had been as prosperous as the country one had been the reverse. The provincial trade in arms declined with the close of the York and Lancaster wars. Men were not permitted to turn from one handicraft to another, and Robert Headley had neither aptitude nor resources. His wife was vain and thriftless, and he finally broke down under his difficulties, appointing by will his cousin to act as his executor, and to take charge of his only son, who had served out half his time as apprentice to himself. There had been delay until the peace with France had given the armourer some leisure for an expedition to Salisbury, a serious undertaking for a London burgess, who had little about him of the ancient northern weapon-smith, and had wanted to avail himself of the protection of the suite of the Bishop of Salisbury, returning from Parliament. He had spent some weeks in disposing of his cousin's stock in trade, which was far too antiquated for the London market; also of the premises, which were bought by an adjoining convent to extend its garden; and he had divided the proceeds between the widow and children. He had presided at the wedding of the last daughter, with whom the mother was to reside, and was on his way back to London with his godson, who had now become his apprentice.

Giles Headley the younger was a fine tall youth, but clumsy and untrained in the use of his limbs, and he rode a large, powerful brown horse, which brooked no companionship, lashing out with its shaggy hoofs at any of its kind that approached it, more especially at poor, plump, mottled Poppet. The men said he had insisted on retaining that, and no other, for his journey to London, contrary to all advice, and he was obliged to ride foremost, alone in the middle of the road; while Master Headley seemed to have an immense quantity of consultation to carry on with his foreman, Tibble, whose quiet-looking brown animal was evidently on the best of terms with Poppet. By day-light Tibble looked even more sallow, lean, and sickly, and Stephen could not help saying to the serving-man nearest to him, "Can such a weakling verily be an armourer?"

"Yea, sir. Wry-mouthed Tibble, as they call him, was a sturdy fellow till he got a fall against the mouth of a furnace, and lay ten months in Saint Bartholomew's Spital, scarce moving hand or foot. He cannot wield a hammer, but he has a cunning hand for gilding, and coloured devices, and is as good as Garter-king-at-arms himself for all bearings of knights and nobles."

"As we heard last night," said Stephen.

"Moreover in the spital he learnt to write and cast accompts like a very scrivener, and the master trusts him more than any, except maybe Kit Smallbones, the head smith."

"What will Smallbones think of the new prentice!" said one of the other men.

"Prentice! 'Tis plain enough what sort of prentice the youth is like to be who beareth the name of a master with one only daughter."

An emphatic grunt was the only answer, while Ambrose pondered on the good luck of some people, who had their futures cut out for them with no trouble on their own part.

This day's ride was through more inhabited parts, and was esteemed less perilous. They came in sight of the Thames at Lambeth, but Master Headley, remembering how ill his beloved Poppet had brooked the ferry, decided to keep to the south of the river by a causeway across Lambeth marsh, which was just passable in high and dry summers, and which conducted them to a raised road called Bankside, where they looked across to the towers of Westminster, and the Abbey in its beauty dawned on the imagination of Stephen and Ambrose. The royal standard floated over the palace, whence Master Headley perceived that the King was there, and augured that my Lord of York's meiné would not be far to seek. Then came broad green fields with young corn growing, or hay waving for the scythe, the tents and booths of May Fair, and the beautiful Market Cross in the midst of the village of Charing, while the Strand, immediately opposite, began to be fringed with great monasteries within their ample gardens, with here and there a nobleman's castellated house and terraced garden, with broad stone stairs leading to the Thames.

Barges and wherries plied up and down, the former often gaily canopied and propelled by livened oarsmen, all plying their arms in unison, so that the vessel looked like some brilliant many-limbed creature treading the water. Presently appeared the heavy walls inclosing the City itself, dominated by the tall openwork timber spire of Saint Paul's, with the four-square, four-turreted Tower acting, as it has been well said, as a padlock to a chain, and the river's breadth spanned by London bridge, a very street of houses built on the abutments. Now, Bankside had houses on each side of the road, and Wry-mouthed Tibble showed evident satisfaction when they turned to cross the bridge, where they had to ride in single file, not without some refractoriness on the part of young Headley's steed.

On they went, now along streets where each story of the tall houses projected over the last, so that the gables seemed ready to meet; now beside walls of convent gardens, now past churches, while the country lads felt bewildered with the numbers passing to and fro, and the air was full of bells.

Cap after cap was lifted in greeting to Master Headley by burgess, artisan, or apprentice, and many times did he draw Poppet's rein to exchange greetings and receive congratulations on his return. On reaching Saint Paul's Minster, he halted and bade the servants take home the horses, and tell the mistress, with his dutiful greetings, that he should be at home anon, and with guests.

"We must een return thanks for our safe journey and great deliverance," he said to his young companions, and thrusting his arm into that of a russet-vested citizen, who met him at the door, he walked into the cathedral, recounting his adventure.

The youths followed with some difficulty through the stream of loiterers in the nave, Giles the younger elbowing and pushing so that several of the crowd turned to look at him, and it was well that his kinsman soon astonished him by descending a stair into a crypt, with solid, short, clustered columns, and high-pitched vaulting, fitted up as a separate church, namely that of the parish of Saint Faith. The great cathedral, having absorbed the site of the original church, had given this crypt to the parishioners. Here all was quiet and solemn, in marked contrast to the hubbub in "Paul's Walk," above in the nave. Against the eastern pillar of one of the bays was a little altar, and the decorations included Saint Julian, the patron of travellers, with his saltire doubly crossed, and his stag beside him. Little ships, trees, and wonderful enamelled representations of perils by robbers, field and flood, hung thickly on Saint Julian's pillar, and on the wall and splay of the window beside it; and here, after crossing himself, Master Headley rapidly repeated a Paternoster, and ratified his vow of presenting a bronze image of the hound to whom he owed his rescue. One of the clergy came up to register the vow, and the good armourer proceeded to bespeak a mass of thanksgiving on the next morning, also ten for the soul of Master John Birkenholt, late Verdurer of the New Forest in Hampshire—a mode of showing his gratitude which the two sons highly appreciated.

Then, climbing up the steps again, and emerging from the cathedral by the west door, the boys beheld a scene for which their experiences of Romsey, and even of Winchester, had by no means prepared them. It was five o'clock on a summer evening, so that the whole place was full of stir. Old women sat with baskets of rosaries and little crosses, or images of saints, on the steps of the cathedral, while in the open space beyond, more than one horse was displaying his paces for the benefit; of some undecided purchaser, who had been chaffering for hours in Paul's Walk. Merchants in the costume of their countries, Lombard, Spanish, Dutch, or French, were walking away in pairs, attended by servants, from their Exchange, likewise in the nave. Women, some alone, some protected by serving-men or apprentices, were returning from their orisons, or, it might be, from their gossipings. Priests and friars, as usual, pervaded everything, and round the open space were galleried buildings with stalls beneath them, whence the holders were removing their wares for the night. The great octagonal structure of Paul's Cross stood in the centre, and just beneath the stone pulpit, where the sermons were wont to be preached, stood a man with a throng round him, declaiming a ballad at the top of his sing-song voice, and causing much loud laughter by some ribaldry about monks and friars.

Master Headley turned aside as quickly as he could, through Paternoster Row, which was full of stalls, where little black books, and larger sheets printed in black, letter, seemed the staple commodities, and thence the burgess, keeping a heedful eye on his young companions among all his greetings, entered the broader space of Cheapside, where numerous prentice lads seemed to be playing at different sports after the labours of the day.

Passing under an archway surmounted by a dragon with shining scales, Master Headley entered a paved courtyard, where the lads started at the figures of two knights in full armour, their lances in rest, and their horses with housings down to their hoofs, apparently about to charge any intruder. But at that moment there was a shriek of joy, and out from the scarlet and azure petticoats of the nearest steed, there darted a little girl, crying, "Father! father!" and in an instant she was lifted in Master Headley's arms, and was clinging round his neck, while he kissed and blessed her, and as he set her on her feet, he said, "Here, Dennet, greet thy cousin Giles Headley, and these two brave young gentlemen. Greet them like a courteous maiden, or they will think thee a little town mouse."

In truth the child had a pointed little visage, and bright brown eyes, somewhat like a mouse, but it was a very sweet face that she lifted obediently to be kissed not only by the kinsman, but by the two guests. Her father meantime was answering with nods to the respectful welcomes of the workmen, who thronged out below, and their wives looking down from the galleries above; while Poppet and the other horses were being rubbed down after their journey.

The ground-floor of the buildings surrounding the oblong court seemed to be entirely occupied by forges, workshops, warehouses and stables. Above, were open railed galleries, with outside stairs at intervals, giving access to the habitations of the workpeople on three sides. The fourth, opposite to the entrance, had a much handsomer, broad, stone stair, adorned on one side with a stone figure of the princess fleeing from the dragon, and on the other of Saint George piercing the monster's open mouth with his lance, the scaly convolutions of the two dragons forming the supports of the handrail on either side. Here stood, cap in hand, showing his thick curly hair, and with open front, displaying a huge hairy chest, a giant figure, whom his master greeted as Kit Smallbones, inquiring whether all had gone well during his absence.

"'Tis time you were back, sir, for there's a great tilting-match on hand for the Lady Mary's wedding. Here have been half the gentlemen in the Court after you, and my Lord of Buckingham sent twice for you since Sunday, and once for Tibble Steelman, and his squire swore that if you were not at his bidding before noon tomorrow, he would have his new suit of Master Hillyer of the Eagle."

"He shall see me when it suiteth me," said Mr. Headley coolly. "He wotteth well that Hillyer hath none who can burnish plate armour like Tibble here."

"Moreover the last iron we had from that knave Mepham is nought. It works short under the hammer."

"That shall be seen to, Kit. The rest of the budget tomorrow. I must on to my mother."

For at the doorway, at the head of the stairs, there stood the still trim and active figure of an old woman, with something of the mouse likeness seen in her grand-daughter, in the close cap, high hat, and cloth dress, that sumptuary opinion, if not law, prescribed for the burgher matron, a white apron, silver chain and bunch of keys at her girdle. Due and loving greetings passed between mother and son, after the longest and most perilous absence of Master Headley's life, and he then presented Giles, to whom the kindly dame offered hand and cheek, saying, "Welcome, my young kinsman, your good father was well known and liked here. May you tread in his steps!"

"Thanks, good mistress," returned Giles. "I am thought to have a pretty taste in the fancy part of the trade. My Lord of Montagu—"

Before he could get any farther, Mistress Headley was inquiring what was the rumour she had heard of robbers and dangers that had beset her son, and he was presenting the two young Birkenholts to her. "Brave boys! good boys," she said, holding out her hands and kissing each according to the custom of welcome, "you have saved my son for me, and this little one's father for her. Kiss them, Dennet, and thank them."

"It was the poor dog," said the child, in a clear little voice, drawing back with a certain quaint coquetting shyness; "I would rather kiss him."

"Would that thou couldst, little mistress," said Stephen. "My poor brave Spring!"

"Was he thine own? Tell me all about him," said Dennet, somewhat imperiously.

She stood between the two strangers looking eagerly in with sorrowfully interested eyes, while Stephen, out of his full heart, told of his faithful comradeship with his hound from the infancy of both. Her father meanwhile was exchanging serious converse with her grandmother, and Giles finding himself left in the background, began: "Come hither, pretty coz, and I will tell thee of my Lady of Salisbury's dainty little hounds."

"I care not for dainty little hounds," returned Dennet; "I want to hear of the poor faithful dog that flew at the wicked robber."

"A mighty stir about a mere chance." muttered Giles.

"I know what *you* did," said Dennet, turning her bright brown eyes full upon him. "You took to your heels."

Her look and little nod were so irresistibly comical that the two brothers could not help laughing; whereupon Giles Headley turned upon them in a passion.

"What mean ye by this insolence, you beggars' brats picked up on the heath?"

"Better born than thou, braggart and coward that thou art!" broke forth Stephen, while Master Headley exclaimed, "How now, lads? No brawling here!"

Three voices spoke at once.

"They were insolent."

"He reviled our birth."

"Father! they did but laugh when I told cousin Giles that he took to his heels, and he must needs call them beggars' brats picked up on the heath."

"Ha! ha! wench, thou art woman enough already to set them together by the ears," said her father, laughing. "See here, Giles Headley, none who bears my name shall insult a stranger on my hearth."

Stephen however had stepped forth holding out his small stock of coin, and saying, "Sir, receive for our charges, and let us go to the tavern we passed anon."

"How now, boy! Said I not ye were my guests?"

"Yea, sir, and thanks; but we can give no cause for being called beggars nor beggars' brats."

"What beggary is there in being guests, my young gentlemen?" said the master of the house. "If any one were picked up on the heath, it was I. We owned you for gentlemen of blood and coat armour, and thy brother there can tell thee that ye have no right to put an affront on me, your host, because a rude prentice from a country town hath not learnt to rule his tongue."

Giles scowled, but the armourer spoke with an authority that imposed on all, and Stephen submitted, while Ambrose spoke a few words of thanks, after which the two brothers were conducted by an external stair and gallery to a guest-chamber, in which to prepare for supper.

The room was small, but luxuriously filled beyond all ideas of the young foresters, for it was hung with tapestry, representing the history of Joseph; the bed was curtained, there was a carved chest for clothes, a table and a ewer and basin of bright brass with the armourer's mark upon it, a twist in which the letter H and the dragon's tongue and tail were ingeniously blended. The City was far in advance of the country in all the arts of life, and only the more magnificent castles and abbeys, which the boys had never seen, possessed the amount of comforts to be found in the dwellings of the superior class of Londoners. Stephen was inclined to look with contempt upon the effeminacy of a churl merchant.

"No churl," returned Ambrose, "if manners makyth man, as we saw at Winchester."

"Then what do they make of that cowardly clown, his cousin?"

Ambrose laughed, but said, "Prove we our gentle blood at least by not brawling with the fellow. Master Headley will soon teach him to know his place."

"That will matter nought to us. Tomorrow shall we be with our uncle Hal. I only wish his lord was not of the ghostly sort, but perhaps he may prefer me to some great knight's service. But oh! Ambrose, come and look. See! The fellow they call Smallbones is come out to the fountain in the middle of the court with a bucket in each hand. Look! Didst ever see such a giant? He is as big and brawny as Ascapart at the bar-gate at Southampton. See! he lifts that big pail full and brimming as though it were an egg shell. See his arm! 'Twere good to see him wield a hammer! I must look into his smithy before going forth tomorrow."

Stephen clenched his fist and examined his muscles ere donning his best mourning jerkin, and could scarce be persuaded to complete his toilet, so much was he entertained with the comings and goings in the court, a little world in itself, like a college quadrangle. The day's work was over, the forges out, and the smiths were lounging about at ease, one or two sitting on a bench under a large elm-tree beside the central well, enjoying each his tankard of ale. A few more were watching Poppet being combed down, and conversing with the newly-arrived grooms. One was carrying a little child in his arms, and a young man and maid sitting on the low wall round the well, seemed to be carrying on a courtship over the pitcher that stood waiting to be filled. Two lads were playing at skittles, children were running up and down the stairs and along the wooden galleries, and men and women went and came by the entrance gateway between the two effigies of knights in armour. Some were servants bringing helm or gauntlet for repair, or taking the like away. Some might be known by their flat caps to be apprentices, and two substantial burgesses walked in together, as if to greet Master Headley on his return. Immediately after, a man-cook appeared with white cap and apron, bearing aloft a covered dish surrounded by a steamy cloud, followed by other servants bearing other meats; a big bell began to sound, the younger men and apprentices gathered together and the brothers descended the stairs, and entered by the big door into the same large hall where they had been received. The spacious hearth was full of green boughs, with a beaupot of wild rose, honeysuckle, clove pinks and gilliflowers; the lower parts of the walls were hung with tapestry representing the adventures of Saint George; the mullioned windows had their upper squares filled with glass, bearing the shield of the City of London, that of the Armourers' Company, the rose and portcullis of the King, the pomegranate of Queen Catharine, and other like devices. Others, belonging to the Lancastrian kings, adorned the pendants from the handsome open roof and the front of a gallery for musicians which crossed one end of the hall in the taste of the times of Henry the Fifth and Whittington.

Far more interesting to the hungry travellers was it that the long table, running the whole breadth of the apartment, was decked with snowy linen, trenchers stood ready with horns or tankards beside them, and loaves of bread at intervals, while the dishes were being placed on the table. The master and his entire establishment took their meals together, except the married men, who lived in the quadrangle with their families. There was no division by the salt-cellar, as at the tables of the nobles and gentry, but the master, his family and guests, occupied the centre, with the hearth behind them, where the choicest of the viands were placed; next after them were the places of the journeymen according to seniority, then those of the apprentices, household servants, and stable-men, but the apprentices had to assist the serving-men in waiting on the master and his party before sitting down themselves. There was a dignity and regularity about the whole, which could not fail to impress Stephen and Ambrose with the weight and importance of a London burgher, warden of the Armourers' Company, and alderman of the Ward of Cheap. There were carved chairs for himself, his mother, and the guests, also a small Persian carpet extending from the hearth beyond their seats. This article filled the two for-esters with amazement. To put one's feet on what ought to be a coverlet! They would not have stepped on it, had they not been kindly summoned by old Mistress Headley to take their places among the company, which consisted, besides the family, of the two citizens who had entered, and of a priest who had likewise dropped in to welcome Master Headley's return, and had been invited to stay to supper. Young Giles, as a matter of course, placed himself amongst them, at which there were black looks and whispers among the apprentices, and even Mistress Headley wore an air of amazement.

"Mother," said the head of the family, speaking loud enough for all to hear, "you will permit our young kinsman to be placed as our guest this eve-ning. Tomorrow he will act as an apprentice, as we all have done in our time."

"I never did so at home!" cried Giles, in his loud, hasty voice.

"I trow not," dryly observed one of the guests.

Giles, however, went on muttering while the priest was pronouncing a Latin grace, and thereupon the same burgess observed, "never did I see it better proved that folk in the country give their sons no good breeding."

"Have patience with him, good Master Pepper," returned Mr. Headley. "He hath been an only son, greatly cockered by father, mother, and sisters, but ere long he will learn what is befitting."

Giles glared round, but he met nothing encouraging. Little Dennet sat with open mouth of astonishment, her grandmother looked shocked, the household which had been aggrieved by his presumption laughed at his rebuke, for there was not much delicacy in those days; but something generous in the gentle blood of Ambrose moved him to some amount of pity for the lad, who thus suddenly became conscious that the tie he had thought nominal at Salisbury, a mere preliminary to municipal rank, was here absolute subjection, and a bondage whence there was no escape. His was the only face that Giles met which had any friendliness in it, but no one spoke, for manners imposed silence upon youth at table, except when spoken to; and there was general hunger enough prevailing to make Mistress Headley's fat capon the most interesting contemplation for the present.

The elders conversed, for there was much for Master Headley to hear of civic affairs that had passed in his absence of two months, also of all the comings and goings, and it was ascertained that my Lord Archbishop of York was at his suburban abode, York House, now Whitehall.

It was a very late supper for the times, not beginning till seven o'clock, on account of the travellers; and as soon as it was finished, and the priest and burghers had taken their leave, Master Headley dismissed the household to their beds, although daylight was scarcely departed.

CHAPTER VI.

A Sunday in the City.

"The rod of Heaven has touched them all,
The word from Heaven is spoken
Rise, shine and sing, thou captive thrall,
Are not thy fetters broken!"

Keble.

On Sunday morning, when the young Birkenholts awoke, the whole air seemed full of bells from hundreds of Church and Minster steeples. The Dragon Court wore a holiday air, and there was no ring of hammers at the forges; but the men who stood about were in holiday attire: and the brothers assumed their best clothes.

Breakfast was not a meal much accounted of. It was reckoned effeminate to require more than two meals a day, though, just as in the verdurer's lodge at home, there was a barrel of ale on tap with drinking horns beside it in the hall, and on a small round table in the window a loaf of bread, to which city luxury added a cheese, and a jug containing sack, with some silver cups beside it, and a pitcher of fair water. Master Headley, with his mother and daughter, was taking a morsel of these refections, standing, and in out-door garments, when the brothers appeared at about seven o'clock in the morning.

"Ha! that's well," quoth he, greeting them. "No slugabeds, I see. Will ye come with us to hear mass at Saint Faith's?" They agreed, and Master Headley then told them that if they would tarry till the next day in searching out their uncle, they could have the company of Tibble Steelman, who had to see one of the captains of the guard about an alteration of his corslet, and thus would have every opportunity of facilitating their inquiries for their uncle.

The mass was an ornate one, though not more so than they were accustomed to at Beaulieu. Ambrose had his book of devotions, supplied by the good monks who had brought him up, and old Mrs. Headley carried something of the same kind; but these did not necessarily follow the ritual, and neither quiet nor attention was regarded as requisite in "hearing mass." Dennet, unchecked, was exchanging flowers from her Sunday posy with another little girl, and with hooded fingers carrying on in all innocence the satirical pantomime of Father Francis and Sister Catharine; and even Master Headley himself exchanged remarks with his friends, and returned greetings from burgesses and their wives while the celebrant priest's voice droned on, and the choir responded—the peals of the organ in the Minster above coming in at inappropriate moments, for there they were in a different part of High Mass using the Liturgy peculiar to Saint Paul's.

Thinking of last week at Beaulieu, Ambrose knelt meantime with his head buried in his hands, in an absorption of feeling that was not perhaps wholly devout, but which at any rate looked more like devotion than the demeanour of any one around. When the *Ite missa est* was pronounced, and all rose up, Stephen touched him and he rose, looking about, bewildered.

"So please you, young sir, I can show you another sort of thing by and by," said in his ear Tibble Steelman, who had come in late, and marked his attitude.

They went up from Saint Faith's in a flood of talk, with all manner of people welcoming Master Headley after his journey, and thence came back to dinner which was set out in the hall very soon after their return from church. Quite guests enough were there on this occasion to fill all the chairs, and Master Headley intimated to Giles that he must begin his duties at table as an apprentice, under the tuition of the senior, a tall young fellow of nineteen, by name Edmund Burgess. He looked greatly injured and discomfited, above all when he saw his two travelling companions seated at the table—though far lower than the night before; nor would he stir from where he was standing against the wall to do the slightest service, although Edmund admonished him sharply that unless he bestirred himself it would be the worse for him.

When the meal was over, and grace had been said, the boards were removed from their trestles, and the elders drew round the small table in the window with a flagon of sack and a plate of wastel bread in their midst to continue their discussion of weighty Town Council matters. Every one was free to make holiday, and Edmund Burgess good-naturedly invited the strangers to come to Mile End, where there was to be shooting at the butts, and a match at single-stick was to come off between Kit Smallbones and another giant, who was regarded as the champion of the brewer's craft.

Stephen was nothing loth, especially if he might take his own crossbow; but Ambrose never had much turn for these pastimes and was in no mood for them. The familiar associations of the mass had brought the grief of orphanhood, homelessness, and uncertainty upon him with the more force. His spirit yearned after his father, and his heart was sick for his forest home. Moreover, there was the duty incumbent on a good son of saying his prayers for the repose of his hither's soul. He hinted as much to Stephen, who, boylike, answered, "Oh, we'll see to that when we get into my Lord of York's house. Masses must be plenty there. And I must see Smallbones floor the brewer."

Ambrose could trust his brother under the care of Edmund Burgess, and resolved on a double amount of repetitions of the appointed intercessions for the departed.

He was watching the party of youths set off, all except Giles Headley, who sulkily refused the invitations, betook himself to a window and sat drumming on the glass, while Ambrose stood leaning on the dragon balustrade, with his eyes dreamily following the merry lads out at the gateway.

"You are not for such gear, sir," said a voice at his ear, and he saw the scathed face of Tibble Steelman beside him.

"Never greatly so, Tibble," answered Ambrose. "And *my* heart is too heavy for it now."

"Ay, ay, sir. So I thought when I saw you in Saint Faith's. I have known what it was to lose a good father in my time."

Ambrose held out his hand. It was the first really sympathetic word he had heard since he had left Nurse Joan.

"'Tis the week's mind of his burial," he said, half choked with tears. "Where shall I find a quiet church where I may say his *de profundis* in peace?"

"Mayhap," returned Tibble, "the chapel in the Pardon churchyard would serve your turn. 'Tis not greatly resorted to when mass time is over, when there's no funeral in hand, and I oft go there to read my book in quiet on a Sunday afternoon. And then, if 'tis your will, I will take you to what to my mind is the best healing for a sore heart."

"Nurse Joan was wont to say the best for that was a sight of the true Cross, as she once beheld it at Holy Rood church at Southampton," said Ambrose.

"And so it is, lad, so it is," said Tibble, with a strange light on his distorted features.

So they went forth together, while Giles again hugged himself in his doleful conceit, marvelling how a youth of birth and nurture could walk the streets on a Sunday with a scarecrow such as that!

The hour was still early, there was a whole summer afternoon before them; and Tibble, seeing how much his young companion was struck with the grand vista of church towers and spires, gave him their names as they stood, though coupling them with short dry comments on the way in which their priests too often perverted them.

The Cheap was then still in great part an open space, where boys were playing, and a tumbler was attracting many spectators; while the ballad-singer of yesterday had again a large audience, who laughed loudly at every coarse jest broken upon mass-priests and friars.

Ambrose was horrified at the stave that met his ears, and asked how such profanity could be allowed. Tibble shrugged his shoulders, and cited the old saying, "The nearer the church,"—adding, "Truth hath a voice, and will out."

"But surely this is not the truth?"

"'Tis mighty like it, sir, though it might be spoken in a more seemly fashion."

"What's this?" demanded Ambrose. "'Tis a noble house."

"That's the Bishop's palace, sir—a man that hath much to answer for."

"Liveth he so ill a life then?"

"Not so. He is no scandalous liver, but he would fain stifle all the voices that call for better things. Ay, you look back at yon ballad-monger! Great folk despise the like of him, never guessing at the power there may be in such ribald stuff; while they would fain silence that which might turn men from their evil ways while yet there is time."

Tibble muttered this to himself, unheeded by Ambrose, and then presently crossing the churchyard, where a grave was being filled up, with numerous idle children around it, he conducted the youth into a curious little chapel, empty now, but with the Host enthroned above the altar, and the trestles on which the bier had rested still standing in the narrow nave.

It was intensely still and cool, a fit place indeed for Ambrose's filial devotions, while Tibble settled himself on the step, took out a little black book, and became absorbed. Ambrose's Latin scholarship enabled him to comprehend the language of the round of devotions he was rehearsing for the benefit of his father's soul; but there was much repetition in them, and he had been so trained as to believe their correct recital was much more important than attention to their spirit, and thus, while his hands held his rosary, his eyes were fixed upon the walls where was depicted the Dance of Death. In terrible repetition, the artist had aimed at depicting every rank or class in life as alike the prey of the grisly phantom. Triple-crowned pope, scarlet-hatted cardinal, mitred prelate, priests, monks, and friars of every degree; emperors, kings, princes, nobles, knights, squires, yeomen, every sort of trade, soldiers of all kinds, beggars, even thieves and murderers, and, in like manner, ladies of every degree, from the queen and the abbess, down to the starving beggar, were each represented as grappled with, and carried off by the crowned skeleton. There was no truckling to greatness. The bishop and abbot writhed and struggled in the grasp of Death, while the miser clutched at his gold, and if there were some nuns, and some poor ploughmen who willingly clasped his bony fingers and obeyed his summons joyfully, there were countesses and prioresses who tried to beat him off, or implored him to wait. The infant smiled in his arms, but the middle-aged fought against his scythe.

The contemplation had a most depressing effect on the boy, whose heart was still sore for his father. After the sudden shock of such a loss, the monotonous repetition of the snatching away of all alike, in the midst of their characteristic worldly employments, and the anguish and hopeless resistance of most of them, struck him to the heart. He moved between each bead to a fresh group; staring at it with fixed gaze, while his lips moved in the unconscious hope of something consoling; till at last, hearing some uncontrollable sobs, Tibble Steelman rose and found him crouching rather than kneeling before the figure of an emaciated hermit, who was greeting the summons of the King of Terrors, with crucifix pressed to his breast, rapt countenance and outstretched arms, seeing only the Angel who hovered above. After some minutes of bitter weeping, which choked his utterance, Ambrose, feeling a friendly hand on his shoulder, exclaimed in a voice broken by sobs, "Oh, tell me, where may I go to become an anchorite! There's no other safety! I'll give all my portion, and spend all my time in prayer for my father and the other poor souls in purgatory."

Two centuries earlier, nay, even one, Ambrose would have been encouraged to follow out his purpose. As it was, Tibble gave a little dry cough and said, "Come along with me, sir, and I'll show you another sort of way."

"I want no entertainment!" said Ambrose, "I should feel only as if he," pointing to the phantom, "were at hand, clutching me with his deadly claw," and he looked over his shoulder with a shudder.

There was a box by the door to receive alms for masses on behalf of the souls in purgatory, and here he halted and felt for the pouch at his girdle, to pour in all the contents; but Steelman said, "Hold, sir, are you free to dispose of your brother's share, you who are purse-bearer for both?"

"I would fain hold my brother to the only path of safety."

Again Tibble gave his dry cough, but added, "He is not in the path of safety who bestows that which is not his own but is held in trust. I were foully to blame if I let this grim portrayal so work on you as to lead you to beggar not only yourself, but your brother, with no consent of his."

For Tibble was no impulsive Italian, but a sober-minded Englishman of sturdy good sense, and Ambrose was reasonable enough to listen and only drop in a few groats which he knew to be his own.

At the same moment, a church bell was heard, the tone of which Steelman evidently distinguished from all the others, and he led the way out of the Pardon churchyard, over the space in front of Saint Paul's. Many persons were taking the same route; citizens in gowns and gold or silver chains, their wives in tall pointed hats; craftsmen, black-gowned scholarly men with fur caps, but there was a much more scanty proportion of priests, monks or friars, than was usual in any popular assemblage. Many of the better class of women carried folding stools, or had them carried by their servants, as if they expected to sit and wait.

"Is there a procession toward? or a relic to be displayed?" asked Ambrose, trying to recollect whose feast-day it might be.

Tibble screwed up his mouth in an extraordinary smile as he said, "Relic quotha? yea, the soothest relic there be of the Lord and Master of us all."

"Methought the true Cross was always displayed on the High Altar," said Ambrose, as all turned to a side aisle of the noble nave.

"Rather say hidden," muttered Tibble. "Thou shalt have it displayed, young sir, but neither in wood nor gilded shrine. See, here he comes who setteth it forth."

From the choir came, attended by half a dozen clergy, a small, pale man, in the ordinary dress of a priest, with a square cap on his head. He looked spare, sickly, and wrinkled, but the furrows traced lines of sweetness, his mouth was wonderfully gentle, and there was a keen brightness about his clear grey eye. Every one rose and made obeisance as he passed along to the stone stair leading to a pulpit projecting from one of the columns.

Ambrose saw what was coming, though he had only twice before heard preaching. The children of the ante-reformation were not called upon to hear sermons; and the few exhortations given in Lent to the monks of Beaulieu were so exclusively for the religious that seculars were not invited to them. So that Ambrose had only once heard a weary and heavy discourse there plentifully garnished with Latin; and once he had stood among the throng at a wake at Millbrook, and heard a begging friar recommend the purchase of briefs of indulgence and the daily repetition of the Ave Maria by a series of extraordinary miracles for the rescue of desperate sinners, related so jocosely as to keep the crowd in a roar of laughter. He had laughed with the rest, but he could not imagine his guide, with the stern, grave eyebrows, writhen features and earnest, ironical tone, covering—as even he could detect—the deepest feeling, enjoying such broad sallies as tickled the slow merriment of village clowns and forest deer-stealers.

All stood for a moment while the Paternoster was repeated. Then the owners of stools sat down on them, some leant on adjacent pillars, others curled themselves on the floor, but most remained on their feet as unwilling to miss a word, and of these were Tibble Steelman and his companion.

Omnis qui facit peccattum, servus est peccati, followed by the rendering in English, "Whosoever doeth sin is sin's bond thrall." The words answered well to the ghastly delineations that seemed stamped on Ambrose's brain and which followed him about into the nave, so that he felt himself in the grasp of the cruel fiend, and almost expected to feel the skeleton claw of Death about to hand him over to torment. He expected the consolation of hearing that a daily "Hail Mary," persevered in through the foulest life, would obtain that beams should be arrested in their fall, ships fail to sink, cords to hang, till such confession had been made as should insure ultimate salvation, after such a proportion of the flames of purgatory as masses and prayers might not mitigate.

But his attention was soon caught. Sinfulness stood before him not as the liability to penalty for transgressing an arbitrary rule, but as a taint to the entire being, mastering the will, perverting the senses, forging fetters out of habit, so as to be a loathsome horror paralysing and enchaining the whole being and making it into the likeness of him who brought sin and death into the world. The horror seemed to grow on Ambrose, as his boyish faults and errors rushed on his mind, and he felt pervaded by the contagion of the pestilence, abhorrent even to himself. But behold, what was he hearing now? "The bond thrall abideth not in the house for ever, but the Son abideth ever. *Si ergo Filius liberavit, verè liberi eritis*." "If the Son should make you free, then are ye free indeed." And for the first time was the true liberty of the redeemed soul comprehensibly proclaimed to the young spirit that had begun to yearn for something beyond the outside. Light began to shine through the outward ordinances; the Church; the world, life, and death, were revealed as something absolutely new; a redeeming, cleansing, sanctifying power was made known, and seemed to inspire him with a new life, joy, and hope. He was no longer feeling himself necessarily crushed by the fetters of death, or only delivered from absolute peril by a mechanism that had lost its heart, but he could enter into the glorious liberty of the sons of God, in process of being saved, not *in* sin but *from* sin.

It was an era in his life, and Tibble heard him sobbing, but with very different sobs from those in the Pardon chapel. When it was over, and the blessing given, Ambrose looked up from the hands which had covered his face with a new radiance in his eyes, and drew a long breath. Tibble saw that he was like one in another world, and gently led him away.

"Who is he? What is he? Is he an angel from Heaven?" demanded the boy, a little wildly, as they neared the southern door.

"If an angel be a messenger of God, I trow he is one," said Tibble. "But men call him Dr. Colet. He is Dean of Saint Paul's Minster, and dwelleth in the house you see below there."

"And are such words as these to be heard every Sunday?"

"On most Sundays doth he preach here in the nave to all sorts of folk."

"I must—I must hear it again!" exclaimed Ambrose.

"Ay, ay," said Tibble, regarding him with a well-pleased face. "You are one with whom it works."

"Every Sunday!" repeated Ambrose. "Why do not all—your master and all these," pointing to the holiday crowds going to and fro—"why do they not all come to listen?"

"Master doth come by times," said Tibble, in the tone of irony that was hard to understand. "He owneth the dean as a rare preacher."

Ambrose did not try to understand. He exclaimed again, panting as if his thoughts were too strong for his words—

"Lo you, that preacher-dean call ye him?—putteth a soul into what hath hitherto been to me but a dead and empty framework."

Tibble held out his hand almost unconsciously, and Ambrose pressed it. Man and boy, alike they had felt the electric current of that truth, which, suppressed and ignored among mans inventions, was coming as a new revelation to many, and was already beginning to convulse the Church and the world.

Ambrose's mind was made up on one point. Whatever he did, and wherever he went, he felt the doctrine he had just heard as needful to him as vital air, and he must be within reach of it. This, and not the hermit's cell, was what his instinct craved. He had always been a studious, scholarly boy, supposed to be marked out for a clerical life, because a book was more to him than a bow, and he had been easily trained in good habits and practices of devotion; but all in a childish manner, without going beyond simple receptiveness, until the experiences of the last week had made a man of him, or more truly, the Pardon chapel and Dean Colet's sermon had made him a new being, with the realities of the inner life opened before him.

His present feeling was relief from the hideous load he had felt while dwelling on the Dance of Death, and therewith general goodwill to all men, which found its first issue in compassion for Giles Headley, whom he found on his return seated on the steps—moody and miserable.

"Would that you had been with us," said Ambrose, sitting down beside him on the step. "Never have I heard such words as today."

"I would not be seen in the street with that scarecrow," murmured Giles. "If my mother could have guessed that he was to be set over me, I had never come here."

"Surely you knew that he was foreman."

"Yea, but not that I should be under him—I whom old Giles vowed should be as his own son—I that am to wed yon little brown moppet, and be master here! So, forsooth," he said, "now he treats me like any common low-bred prentice."

"Nay," said Ambrose, "an if you were his son, he would still make you serve. It's the way with all craftsmen—yea and with gentlemen's sons also. They must be pages and squires ere they can be knights."

"It never was the way at home. I was only bound prentice to my father for the name of the thing, that I might have the freedom of the city, and become head of our house."

"But how could you be a wise master without learning the craft?"

"What are journeymen for?" demanded the lad. "Had I known how Giles Headley meant to serve me, he might have gone whistle for a husband for his wench. I would have ridden in my Lady of Salisbury's train."

"You might have had rougher usage there than here," said Ambrose. "Master Headley lays nothing on you but what he has himself proved. I would I could see you make the best of so happy a home."

"Ay, that's all very well for you, who are certain of a great man's house."

"Would that I were certified that my brother would be as well off as you, if you did but know it," said Ambrose. "Ha! here come the dishes! 'Tis supper-time come on us unawares, and Stephen not returned from Mile End!"

Punctuality was not, however, exacted on these summer Sunday evenings, when practice with the bow and other athletic sports were enjoined by Government, and, moreover, the youths were with so trustworthy a member of the household as Kit Smallbones.

Sundry City magnates had come to supper with Master Headley, and whether it were the effect of Ambrose's counsel, or of the example of a hand-some lad who had come with his father, one of the worshipful guild of Merchant Taylors, Giles did vouchsafe to bestir himself in waiting, and in consideration of the effort it must have cost him, old Mrs. Headley and her son did not take notice of his blunders, but only Dennet fell into a violent fit of laughter, when he presented the stately alderman with a nutmeg under the impression that it was an overgrown peppercorn. She suppressed her mirth as well as she could, poor little thing, for it was a great offence in good manners, but she was detected, and, only child as she was, the consequence was the being banished from the table and sent to bed.

But when, after supper was over, Ambrose went out to see if there were any signs of the return of Stephen and the rest, he found the little maiden curled up in the gallery with her kitten in her arms.

"Nay!" she said, in a spoilt-child tone, "I'm not going to bed before my time for laughing at that great oaf! Nurse Alice says he is to wed me, but I won't have him! I like the pretty boy who had the good dog and saved father, and I like you, Master Ambrose. Sit down by me and tell me the story over again, and we shall see Kit Smallbones come home. I know he'll have beaten the brewer's fellow."

Before Ambrose had decided whether thus far to abet rebellion, she jumped up and cried: "Oh, I see Kit! He's got my ribbon! He has won the match!"

And down she rushed, quite oblivious of her disgrace, and Ambrose presently saw her uplifted in Kit Smallbones' brawny arms to utter her congratulations.

Stephen was equally excited. His head was full of Kit Smallbones' exploits, and of the marvels of the sports he had witnessed and joined in with fair success. He had thought Londoners poor effeminate creatures, but he found that these youths preparing for the trained bands understood all sorts of martial exercises far better than any of his forest acquaintance, save perhaps the hitting of a mark. He was half wild with a boy's enthusiasm for Kit Smallbones and Edmund Burgess, and when, after eating the supper that had been reserved for the late comers, he and his brother repaired to their own chamber, his tongue ran on in description of the feats he had witnessed and his hopes of emulating them, since he understood that Archbishop as was my Lord of York, there was a tilt-yard at York House. Ambrose, equally full of his new feelings, essayed to make his brother a sharer in them, but Stephen entirely failed to understand more than that his book-worm brother had heard something that delighted him in his own line of scholarship, from which Stephen had happily escaped a year ago!

CHAPTER VII.

York House.

"Then hath he servants five or six score,
Some behind and some before
A marvellous great company
Of which are lords and gentlemen,
With many grooms and yeomen
And also knaves among them."

Contemporary Poem on Wolsey.

Early were hammers ringing on anvils in the Dragon Court, and all was activity. Master Headley was giving his orders to Kit Smallbones before setting forth to take the Duke of Buckingham's commands; Giles Headley, very much disgusted, was being invested with a leathern apron, and entrusted to Edmund Burgess to learn those primary arts of furbishing which, but for his mother's vanity and his father's weakness, he would have practised four years sooner. Tibble Steelman was superintending the arrangement of half a dozen corslets, which were to be carried by three stout porters, under his guidance, to what is now Whitehall, then the residence of the Archbishop of York, the king's prime adviser, Thomas Wolsey.

"Look you, Tib," said the kind-hearted armourer, "if those lads find not their kinsman, or find him not what they look for, bring them back hither, I cannot have them cast adrift. They are good and brave youths, and I owe a life to them."

Tibble nodded entire assent, but when the boys appeared in their mourning suits, with their bundles on their backs, they were sent back again to put on their forest green, Master Headley explaining that it was reckoned ill-omened, if not insulting, to appear before any great personage in black, unless to enhance some petition directly addressed to himself. He also bade them leave their fardels behind, as, if they tarried at York House, these could be easily sent after them.

They obeyed—even Stephen doing so with more alacrity than he had hitherto shown to Master Headley's behests; for now that the time for departure had come, he was really sorry to leave the armourer's household. Edmund Burgess had been very good-natured to the raw country lad, and Kit Smallbones was, in his eyes, an Ascapart in strength, and a Bevis in prowess and kindliness. Mistress Headley too had been kind to the orphan lads, and these two days had given a feeling of being at home at the Dragon. When Giles wished them a moody farewell, and wished he were going with them, Stephen returned, "Ah! you don't know when you are well off."

Little Dennet came running down after them with two pinks in her hands. "Here's a sop-in-wine for a token for each of you young gentlemen," she cried, "for you came to help father, and I would you were going to stay and wed me instead of Giles."

"What, both of us, little maid?" said Ambrose, laughing, as he stooped to receive the kiss her rosy lips tendered to him.

"Not but what she would have royal example," muttered Tibble aside.

Dennet put her head on one side, as considering. "Nay, not both; but you are gentle and courteous, and he is brave and gallant—and Giles there is moody and glum, and can do nought."

"Ah! you will see what a gallant fellow Giles can be when thou hast cured him of his home-sickness by being good to him," said Ambrose, sorry for the youth in the universal laughter at the child's plain speaking.

And thus the lads left the Dragon, amid friendly farewells. Ambrose looked up at the tall spire of Saint Paul's with a strong determination that he would never put himself out of reach of such words as he had there drunk in, and which were indeed spirit and life to him.

Tibble took them down to the Saint Paul's stairs on the river, where at his whistle a wherry was instantly brought to transport them to York stairs, only one of the smiths going any further in charge of the corslets. Very lovely was their voyage in the brilliant summer morning, as the glittering water reflected in broken ripples church spire, convent garden, and stately house. Here rows of elm-trees made a cool walk by the river side, there strawberry beds sloped down the Strand, and now and then the hooded figures of nuns might be seen gathering the fruit. There, rose the round church of the Temple, and the beautiful gardens surrounding the buildings, half monastic, half military, and already inhabited by lawyers. From a barge at the Temple stairs a legal personage descended, with a square beard, and open, benevolent, shrewd face, before whom Tibble removed his cap with eagerness, saying to Ambrose, "Yonder is Master More, a close friend of the dean's, a good and wise man, and forward in every good work."

Thus did they arrive at York House. Workmen were busy on some portions of it, but it was inhabited by the great Archbishop, the king's chief adviser. The approach of the boat seemed to be instantly notified, as it drew near the stone steps giving entrance to the gardens, with an avenue of trees leading up to the principal entrance.

Four or five yeomen ran down the steps, calling out to Tibble that their corslets had tarried a long time, and that Sir Thomas Drury had been storming for him to get his tilting armour into order.

Tibble followed the man who had undertaken to conduct him through a path that led to the offices of the great house, bidding the boys keep with him, and asking for their uncle Master Harry Randall.

The yeoman shook his head. He knew no such person in the household, and did not think there ever had been such. Sir Thomas Drury was found in the stable court, trying the paces of the horse he intended to use in the approaching joust. "Ha! old Wrymouth," he cried, "welcome at last! I must have my new device damasked on my shield. Come hither, and I'll show it thee."

Private rooms were seldom enjoyed, even by knights and gentlemen, in such a household, and Sir Thomas could only conduct Tibble to the armoury, where numerous suits of armour hung on blocks, presenting the semblance of armed men. The knight a good-looking personage, expatiated much on the device he wished to dedicate to his lady-love, a pierced heart with a forget-me-not in the midst and it was not until the directions were finished that Tibble ventured to mention the inquiry for Randall.

"I wot of no such fellow," returned Sir Thomas, "you had best go to the comptroller, who keeps all the names."

Tibble had to go to this functionary at any rate, to obtain an order for payment for the corslets he had brought home. Ambrose and Stephen followed him across an enormous hall, where three long tables were being laid for dinner.

The comptroller of the household, an esquire of good birth, with a stiff little ruff round his neck, sat in a sort of office inclosed by panels at the end of the hall. He made an entry of Tibble's account in a big book, and sent a message to the cofferer to bring the amount. Then Tibble again put his question on behalf of the two young foresters, and the comptroller shook his head. He did not know the name. "Was the gentleman," (he chose that word as he looked at the boys), "layman or clerk?"

"Layman, certainly," said Ambrose, somewhat dismayed to find how little, on interrogation, he really knew.

"Was he a yeoman of the guard, or in attendance on one of my lord's nobles in waiting?"

"We thought he had been a yeoman," said Ambrose.

"See," said the comptroller, stimulated by a fee administered by Tibble, "'tis just dinner-time, and I must go to attend on my Lord Archbishop; but do you, Tibble, sit down with these striplings to dinner, and then I will cast my eye over the books, and see if I can find any such name. What, hast not time? None ever quits my lord's without breaking his fast."

Tibble had no doubt that his master would be willing that he should give up his time for this purpose, so he accepted the invitation. The tables were by this time nearly covered, but all stood waiting, for there flowed in from the great doorway of the hall a gorgeous train—first, a man bearing the double archiepiscopal cross of York, fashioned in silver, and thick with gems—then, with lofty mitre enriched with pearls and jewels, and with flowing violet lace-covered robes came the sturdy square-faced ruddy prelate, who was then the chief influence in England, and after him two glittering ranks of priests in square caps and richly embroidered copes, all in accordant colours. They were returning, as a yeoman told Tibble, from some great ecclesiastical ceremony, and dinner would be served instantly.

"That for which Ralf Bowyer lives!" said a voice close by. "He would fain that the dial's hands were Marie bones, the face blancmange, wherein the figures should be grapes of Corinth!"

Stephen looked round and saw a man close beside him in what he knew at once to be the garb of a jester. A tall scarlet velvet cap, with three peaks, bound with gold braid, and each surmounted with a little gilded bell, crowned his head, a small crimson ridge to indicate the cock's comb running along the front. His jerkin and hose were of motley, the left arm and right leg being blue, their opposites, orange tawny, while the nether socks and shoes were in like manner black and scarlet counterchanged. And yet, somehow, whether from the way of wearing it, or from the effect of the gold embroidery meandering over all, the effect was not distressing, but more like that of a gorgeous bird. The figure was tall, lithe, and active, the brown ruddy face had none of the blank stare of vacant idiocy, but was full of twinkling merriment, the black eyes laughed gaily, and perhaps only so clear-sighted and shrewd an observer as Tibble would have detected a weakness of purpose about the mouth.

There was a roar of laughter at the gibe, as indeed there was at whatever was uttered by the man whose profession was to make mirth.

"Thou likest thy food well enough thyself, quipsome one," muttered Ralf.

"Hast found one who doth not, Ralf? Then should he have a free gift of my bauble," responded the jester, shaking on high that badge, surmounted with the golden head of an ass, and jingling with bells. "How now, friend Wrymouth? 'Tis long since thou wert here! This house hath well-nigh been forced to its ghostly weapons for lack of thy substantial ones. Where hast thou been?"

"At Salisbury, good Merryman."

"Have the Wilts men raked the moon yet out of the pond? Did they lend thee their rake, Tib, that thou hast raked up a couple of green Forest palmerworms, or be they the sons of the man in the moon, raked out and all astray?"

"Mayhap, for we met them with dog and bush," said Tibble, "and they dropped as from the moon to save my poor master from the robbers on Bagshot heath! Come now, mine honest fellow, aid me to rake, as thou sayest, this same household. They are come up from the Forest, to seek out their uncle, one Randall, who they have heard to be in this meiné. Knowest thou such a fellow?"

"To seek a spider in a stubble-field! Truly he needs my bauble who sent them on such an errand," said the jester, rather slowly, as if to take time for consideration. "What's your name, my Forest flies?"

"Birkenholt sir," answered Ambrose, "but our uncle is Harry Randall."

"Here's fools enow to take away mine office," was the reply. "Here's a couple of lads would leave the greenwood and the free oaks and beeches, for this stinking, plague-smitten London."

"We'd not have quitted it could we have tarried at home," began Ambrose; but at that moment there was a sudden commotion, a trampling of horses was heard outside, a loud imperious voice demanded, "Is my Lord Archbishop within?" a whisper ran round, "the King," and there entered the hall with hasty steps, a figure never to be forgotten, clad in a bunting dress of green velvet embroidered with gold, with a golden hunting horn slung round his neck.

Henry the Eighth was then in the splendid prime of his youth, in his twenty-seventh year, and in the eyes, not only of his own subjects, but of all others, the very type of a true king of men. Tall, and as yet of perfect form for strength, agility, and grace; his features were of the beautiful straight Plantagenet type, and his complexion of purely fair rosiness, his large well-opened blue eyes full at once of frankness and keenness, and the short golden beard that fringed his square chin giving the manly air that otherwise might have seemed wanting to the feminine tinting of his regular lineaments. All caps were instantly doffed save the little bonnet with one drooping feather that covered his short, curled, yellow hair; and the Earl of Derby, who was at the head of Wolsey's retainers, made haste, bowing to the ground, to assure him that my Lord Archbishop was but doffing his robes, and would be with his Grace instantly. Would his Grace vouchsafe to come on to the privy chamber where the dinner was spread?

At the same moment Quipsome Hal sprang forward, exclaiming, "How now, brother and namesake? Wherefore this coil? Hath cloth of gold wearied yet of cloth of frieze? Is she willing to own her right to this?" as he held out his bauble.

"Holla, old Blister! art thou there?" said the King, good-humouredly. "What! knowest not that we are to have such a wedding as will be a sight for sore eyes!"

"Sore! that's well said, friend Hal. Thou art making progress in mine art! Sore be the eyes wherein thou wouldst throw dust."

Again the King laughed, for every one knew that his sister Mary had secretly been married to the Duke of Suffolk for the last two months, and that this public marriage and the tournament that was to follow were only for the sake of appearances. He laid his hand good-naturedly on the jester's shoulder as he walked up the hall towards the Archbishop's private apartments, but the voices of both were loud pitched, and bits of the further conversation could be picked up. "Weddings are rife in your family," said the jester, "none of you get weary of fitting on the noose. What, thou thyself, Hal? Ay, thou hast not caught the contagion yet! Now ye gods forefend! If thou hast the chance, thou'lt have it strong."

Therewith the Archbishop, in his purple robes, appeared in the archway at the other end of the hall, the King joined him, and still followed by the jester, they both vanished. It was presently made known that the King was about to dine there, and that all were to sit down to eat. The King dined alone with the Archbishop as his host; the two noblemen who had formed his suite joined the first table in the higher hall; the knights that of the steward of the household, who was of knightly degree, and with whom the superior clergy of the household ate; and the grooms found their places among the vast array of yeomen and serving-men of all kinds with whom Tibble and his two young companions had to eat. A week ago, Stephen would have contemned the idea of being classed with serving-men and grooms, but by this time he was quite bewildered, and anxious enough to be thankful to keep near a familiar face on any terms, and to feel as if Tibble were an old friend, though he had only known him for five days.

Why the King had come had not transpired, but there was a whisper that despatches from Scotland were concerned in it. The meal was a lengthy one, but at last the King's horses were ordered, and presently Henry came forth, with his arm familiarly linked in that of the Archbishop, whose horse had likewise been made ready that he might accompany the King back to Westminster. The jester was close at hand, and as a parting shaft he observed, while the King mounted his horse, "Friend Hal! give my brotherly commendations to our Madge, and tell her that one who weds Anguish cannot choose but cry out."

Wherewith, affecting to expect a stroke from the King's whip, he doubled himself up, performed the contortion now called turning a coachwheel, then, recovering himself, put his hands on his hips and danced wildly on the steps; while Henry, shaking his whip at him, laughed at the only too obvious pun, for Anguish was the English version of Angus, the title of Queen Margaret's second husband, and it was her complaints that had brought him to his counsellor.

The jester then, much to the annoyance of the two boys, thought proper to follow them to the office of the comptroller, and as that dignitary read out from his books the name of every Henry, and of all the varieties of Ralf and Randolf among the hundred and eighty persons composing the household, he kept on making comments. "Harry Hempseed, clerk to the kitchen; ay, Hempseed will serve his turn one of these days. Walter Randall, groom of the chamber; ah, ha! my lads, if you want a generous uncle who will look after you well, there is your man! He'll give you the shakings of the napery for largesse, and when he is in an open-handed mood, will let you lie on the rushes that have served the hall. Harry of Lambeth, yeoman of the stable. He will make you free of all the taverns in Eastchepe."

And so on, accompanying each remark with a pantomime mimicry of the air and gesture of the individual. He showed in a second the contortions of Harry Weston in drawing the bow, and in another the grimaces of Henry Hope, the choir man, in producing bass notes, or the swelling majesty of Randall Porcher, the cross-bearer, till it really seemed as if he had shown off the humours of at least a third of the enormous household. Stephen had laughed at first, but as failure after failure occurred, the antics began to weary even him, and seem unkind and ridiculous as hope ebbed away, and the appalling idea began to grow on him of being cast loose on London without a friend or protector. Ambrose felt almost despairing as he heard in vain the last name. He would almost have been willing to own Hal the scullion, and his hopes rose when he heard of Hodge Randolph, the falconer, but alas, that same Hodge came from Yorkshire.

"And mine uncle was from the New Forest in Hampshire," he said.

"Maybe he went by the name of Shirley," added Stephen, "'tis where his home was."

But the comptroller, unwilling to begin a fresh search, replied at once that the only Shirley in the household was a noble esquire of the Warwickshire family.

"You must e'en come back with me, young masters," said Tibble, "and see what my master can do for you."

"Stay a bit," said the fool. "Harry of Shirley! Harry of Shirley! Methinks I could help you to the man, if so be as you will deem him worth the finding," he added, suddenly turning upside down, and looking at them standing on the palms of his hands, with an indescribable leer of drollery, which in a moment dashed all the hopes with which they had turned to him. "Should you know this nunks of yours?" he added.

"I think I should," said Ambrose. "I remember best how he used to carry me on his shoulder to cull mistletoe for Christmas."

"Ah, ha! A proper fellow of his inches now, with yellow hair?"

"Nay," said Ambrose, "I mind that his hair was black, and his eyes as black as sloes—or as thine own, Master Jester."

The jester tumbled over into a more extraordinary attitude than before, while Stephen said—

"John was wont to twit us with being akin to Gipsy Hal."

"I mean a man sad and grave as the monks of Beaulieu," said the jester.

"He!" they both cried. "No, indeed! He was foremost in all sports." "Ah!" cried Stephen, "mind you not, Ambrose, his teaching us leap-frog, and aye leaping over one of us himself, with the other in his arms."

"Ah! sadly changed, sadly changed," said the jester, standing upright, with a most mournful countenance. "Maybe you'd not thank me if I showed him to you, young sirs, that is, if he be the man."

"Nay! is he in need, or distress?" cried the brothers.

"Poor Hal!" returned the fool, shaking his head with mournfulness in his voice.

"Oh, take us to him, good—good jester," cried Ambrose. "We are young and strong. We will work for him."

"What, a couple of lads like you, that have come to London seeking for him to befriend you—deserving well cap for that matter. Will ye be guided to him, my broken and soured—no more gamesome, but a sickly old runagate?"

"Of course," cried Ambrose. "He is our mother's brother. We must care for him."

"Master Headley will give us work, mayhap," said Stephen, turning to Tibble. "I could clean the furnaces."

"Ah, ha! I see fools' caps must hang thick as beech masts in the Forest," cried the fool, but his voice was husky, and he turned suddenly round with his back to them, then cut three or four extraordinary capers, after which he observed—

"Well, young gentlemen, I will see the man I mean, and if he be the same, and be willing to own you for his nephews, he will meet you in the Temple Gardens at six of the clock this evening, close to the rose-bush with the flowers in my livery—motley red and white."

"But how shall we know him?"

"D'ye think a pair of green caterpillars like you can't be marked—unless indeed the gardener crushes you for blighting his roses." Wherewith the jester quitted the scene, walking on his hands, with his legs in the air.

"Is he to be trusted?" asked Tibble of the comptroller.

"Assuredly," was the answer; "none hath better wit than Quipsome Hal, when he chooseth to be in earnest. In very deed, as I have heard Sir Thomas More say, it needeth a wise man to be fool to my Lord of York."

CHAPTER VIII.

Quipsome Hal.

"The sweet and bitter fool
Will presently appear,
The one in motley here
The other found out there."

Shakespeare.

There lay the quiet Temple Gardens, on the Thames bank, cut out in formal walks, with flowers growing in the beds of the homely kinds beloved by the English. Musk roses, honeysuckle and virgin's bower, climbed on the old grey walls; sops-in-wine, bluebottles, bachelor's buttons, stars of Bethlehem and the like, filled the borders; May thorns were in full sweet blossom; and near one another were the two rose-bushes, one damask and one white provence, whence Somerset and Warwick were said to have plucked their fatal badges; while on the opposite side of a broad grass-plot was another bush, looked on as a great curiosity of the best omen, where the roses were streaked with alternate red and white, in honour, as it were, of the union of York and Lancaster.

By this rose-tree stood the two young Birkenholts. Edmund Burgess having, by his master's desire, shown them the way, and passed them in by a word and sign from his master, then retired unseen to a distance to mark what became of them, they having promised also to return and report of themselves to Master Headley.

They stood together earnestly watching for the coming of the uncle, feeling quite uncertain whether to expect a frail old broken man, or to find themselves absolutely deluded, and made game of by the jester.

The gardens were nearly empty, for most people were sitting over their supper-tables after the business of the day was over, and only one or two figures in black gowns paced up and down in conversation.

"Come away, Ambrose," said Stephen at last. "He only meant to make fools of us! Come, before he comes to gibe us for having heeded a moment. Come, I say—here's this man coming to ask us what we are doing here."

For a tall, well-made, well personage in the black or sad colour of a legal official, looking like a prosperous householder, or superior artisan, was approaching them, some attendant, as the boys concluded belonging to the Temple. They expected to be turned out, and Ambrose in an apologetic tone, began, "Sir, we were bidden to meet a—a kinsman here."

"And even so am I," was the answer, in a grave, quiet tone, "or rather to meet twain."

Ambrose looked up into a pair of dark eyes, and exclaimed, "Stevie, Stevie, 'tis he. 'Tis uncle Hal."

"Ay, 'tis all you're like to have for him," answered Harry Randall, enfolding each in his embrace. "Lad, how like thou art to my poor sister! And is she indeed gone—and your honest father too—and none left at home but that hunks, little John? How and when died she?"

"Two years agone come Lammastide," answered Stephen. "There was a deadly creeping fever and ague through the Forest. We two sickened, and Ambrose was so like to die that Diggory went to the abbey for the priest to housel and anneal him, but by the time Father Simon came he was sound asleep, and soon was whole again. But before we were on our legs, our blessed mother took the disease, and she passed away ere many days were over. Then, though poor father took not that sickness, he never was the same man again, and only twelve days after last Pasch-tide he was taken with a fit and never spake again."

Stephen was weeping by this time, and his uncle had a hand on his shoulder, and with tears in his eyes, threw in ejaculations of pity and affection. Ambrose finished the narrative with a broken voice indeed, but as one who had more self-command than his brother, perhaps than his uncle, whose exclamations became bitter and angry as he heard of the treatment the boys had experienced from their half-brother, who, as he said, he had always known as a currish mean-spirited churl, but scarce such as this.

"Nor do I think he would have been, save for his wife, Maud Pratt of Hampton," said Ambrose. "Nay, truly also, he deemed that we were only within a day's journey of council from our uncle Richard at Hyde."

"Richard Birkenholt was a sturdy old comrade! Methinks he would give Master Jack a piece of his mind."

"Alack, good uncle, we found him in his dotage, and the bursar of Hyde made quick work with us, for fear, good Father Shoveller said, that we were come to look after his corrody."

"Shoveller—what, a Shoveller of Cranbury? How fell ye in with him?"

Ambrose told the adventures of their journey, and Randall exclaimed, "By my bau—I mean by my faith—if ye have ill-luck in uncles, ye have had good luck in friends."

"No ill-luck in thee, good, kind uncle," said Stephen, catching at his hand with the sense of comfort that kindred blood gives.

"How wottest thou that, child? Did not I—I mean did not Merryman tell you, that mayhap ye would not be willing to own your uncle?"

"We deemed he was but jesting," said Stephen.

For a sudden twinkle in the black eyes, an involuntary twist of the muscles of the face, were a sudden revelation to him. He clutched hold of Ambrose with a sudden grasp; Ambrose too looked and recoiled for a moment, while the colour spread over his face.

"Yes, lads. Can you brook the thought!—Harry Randall is the poor fool!"

Stephen, whose composure had already broken down, burst into tears again, perhaps mostly at the downfall of all his own expectations and glorifications of the kinsman about whom he had boasted. Ambrose only exclaimed,

"O uncle, you must have been hard pressed." For indeed the grave, almost melancholy man, who stood before them, regarding them wistfully, had little in common with the lithe tumbler full of absurdities whom they had left at York House.

"Even so, my good lad. Thou art right in that," said he gravely. "Harder than I trust will ever be the lot of you two, my sweet Moll's sons. She never guessed that I was come to this."

"O no," said Stephen. "She always thought thou—thou hadst some high preferment in—"

"And so I have," said Randall with something of his ordinary humour. "There's no man dares to speak such plain truth to my lord—or for that matter to King Harry himself, save his own Jack-a-Lee—and he, being a fool of nature's own making, cannot use his chances, poor rogue! And so the poor lads came up to London hoping to find a gallant captain who could bring them to high preferment, and found nought but—Tom Fool! I could find it in my heart to weep for them! And so thou mindest clutching the mistletoe on nunk Hal's shoulder. I warrant it groweth still on the crooked May bush? And is old Bobbin alive?"

They answered his questions, but still as if under a great shock, and presently he said, as they paced up and down the garden walks, "Ay, I have been sore bestead, and I'll tell you how it came about, boys, and mayhap ye will pardon the poor fool, who would not own you sooner, lest ye should come in for mockery ye have not learnt to brook." There was a sadness and pleading in his tone that touched Ambrose, and he drew nearer to his uncle, who laid a hand on his shoulder, and presently the other on that of Stephen, who shrank a little at first, but submitted. "Lads, I need not tell you why I left fair Shirley and the good greenwood. I was a worse fool then than ever I have been since I wore the cap and bells, and if all had been brought home to me, it might have brought your father and mother into trouble—my sweet Moll who had done her best for me. I deemed, as you do now, that the way to fortune was open, but I found no path before me, and I had tightened my belt many a time, and was not much more than a bag of bones, when, by chance, I fell in with a company of tumblers and gleemen. I sang them the old hunting-song, and they said I did it tunably, and, whereas they saw I could already dance a hornpipe and turn a somersault passably well, the leader of the troop, old Nat Fire-eater, took me on, and methinks he did not repent—nor I neither—save when I sprained my foot and had time to lie by and think. We had plenty to fill our bellies and put on our backs; we had welcome wherever we went, and the groats and pennies rained into our caps. I was Clown and Jack Pudding and whatever served their turn, and the very name of Quipsome Hal drew crowds. Yea, 'twas a merry life! Ay, I feel thee wince and shrink, my lad; and so should I have shuddered when I was of thine age, and hoped to come to better things."

"Methinks 'twere better than this present," said Stephen rather gruffly.

"I had my reasons, boy," said Randall, speaking as if he were pleading his cause with their father and mother rather than with two such young lads.

"There was in our company an old man-at-arms who played the lute and the rebeck, and sang ballads so long as hand and voice served him, and with him went his grandchild, a fair and honest little maiden, whom he kept so jealously apart that 'twas long ere I knew of her following the company. He had been a franklin on my Lord of Warwick's lands, and had once been burnt out by Queen Margaret's men, and just as things looked up again with him, King Edward's folk ruined all again, and slew his two sons. When great folk play the fool, small folk pay the scot, as I din into his Grace's ears whenever I may. A minion of the Duke of Clarence got the steading, and poor old Martin Fulford was turned out to shift as best he might. One son he had left, and with him he went to the Low Countries, where they would have done well had they not been bitten by faith in the fellow Perkin Warbeck. You've heard of him?"

"Yea," said Ambrose; "the same who was taken out of sanctuary at Beaulieu, and borne off to London. Father said he was marvellous like in the face to all the kings he had ever seen hunting in the Forest."

"I know not; but to the day of his death old Martin swore that he was a son of King Edward's, and they came home again with the men the Duchess of Burgundy gave Perkin—came bag and baggage, for young Fulford had wedded a fair Flemish wife, poor soul! He left her with his father nigh to Taunton ere the battle, and he was never heard of more, but as he was one of the few men who knew how to fight, belike he was slain. Thus old Martin was left with the Flemish wife and her little one on his hands, for whose sake he did what went against him sorely, joined himself to this troop of jugglers and players, so as to live by the minstrelsy he had learnt in better days, while his daughter-in-law mended and made for the company and kept them in smart and shining trim. By the time I fell in with them his voice was well-nigh gone, and his hand sorely shaking, but Fire-eating Nat, the master of our troop, was not an ill-natured fellow, and the glee-women's feet were well used to his rebeck. More-over, the Fire-eater had an eye to little Perronel, though her mother had never let him train her—scarce let him set an eye on her; and when Mistress Fulford died, poor soul, of ague, caught when we showed off before the merry Prior of Worcester, her last words were that Perronel should never be a glee-maiden. Well, to make an end of my tale, we had one day a mighty show at Windsor, when the King and Court were at the castle, and it was whispered to me at the end that my Lord Archbishop's household needed a jester, and that Quipsome Hal had been thought to make excellent fooling. I gave thanks at first, but said I would rather be a free man, not bound to be a greater fool than Dame Nature made me all the hours of the day. But when I got back to the Garter, what should I find but that poor old Martin had been stricken with the dead palsy while he was playing his rebeck, and would never twang a note more; and there was pretty Perronel weeping over him, and Nat Fire-eater pledging his word to give the old man bed, board, and all that he could need, if so be that Perronel should be trained to be one of his glee-maidens, to dance and tumble and sing. And there was the poor old franklin shaking his head more than the palsy made it shake already, and trying to frame his lips to say, 'rather they both should die.'"

"Oh, uncle, I wot now what thou didst!" cried Stephen.

"Yea, lad, there was nought else to be done. I asked Master Fulford to give me Perronel, plighting my word that never should she sing or dance for any one's pleasure save her own and mine, and letting him know that I came of a worthy family. We were wedded out of hand by the priest that had been sent for to housel him, and in our true names. The Fire-eater was fiery enough, and swore that, wedded or not, I was bound to him, that he would have both of us, and would not drag about a helpless old man unless he might have the wench to do his bidding. I verily believe that, but for my being on the watch and speaking a word to two or three stout yeomen of the king's guard that chanced to be crushing a pot of sack at the Garter, he would have played some villainous trick on us. They gave a hint to my Lord of York's steward and he came down and declared that the Archbishop required Quipsome Hal, and would-of his grace-send a purse of nobles to the Fire-eater, wherewith he was to be off on the spot without more ado, or he might find it the worse for him, and they, together with mine host's good wife, took care that the rogue did not carry away Perronel with him, as he was like to have done. To end my story, here am I, getting showers of gold coins one day and nought but kicks and gibes the next, while my good woman keeps \zavprn=house=hau/s\ house nigh here on the banks of the Thames with Gaffer Martin. Her Flemish thrift has set her to the washing and clear—starching of the lawyers' ruffs, whereby she makes enough to supply the defects of my scanty days, or when I have to follow my lord's grace out of her reach, sweet soul. There's my tale, nevoys. And now, have ye a hand for Quipsome Hal?"

"O uncle! Father would have honoured thee!" cried Stephen.

"Why didst thou not bring her down to the Forest?" said Ambrose.

"I conned over the thought," said Randall, "but there was no way of living. I wist not whether the Ranger might not stir up old tales, and moreover old Martin is ill to move. We brought him down by boat from Windsor, and he has never quitted the house since, nor his bed for the last two years. You'll come and see the housewife? She hath a supper laying out for you, and on the way we'll speak of what ye are to do, my poor lads."

"I'd forgotten that," said Stephen.

"So had not I," returned his uncle; "I fear me I cannot aid you to preferment as you expected. None know Quipsome Hal by any name but that of Harry Merryman, and it were not well that ye should come in there as akin to the poor fool."

"No," said Stephen, emphatically.

"Your father left you twenty crowns apiece?"

"Ay, but John hath all save four of them."

"For that there's remedy. What saidst thou of the Cheapside armourer? His fellow, the Wrymouth, seemed to have a care of you. Ye made in to the rescue with poor old Spring."

"Even so," replied Ambrose, "and if Stevie would brook the thought, I trow that Master Headley would be quite willing to have him bound as his apprentice."

"Well said, my good lad!" cried Hal. "What sayest thou, Stevie?"

"I had liefer be a man-at-arms."

"That thou couldst only be after being sorely knocked about as horse-boy and as groom. I tried that once, but found it meant kicks, and oaths, and vile company—such as I would not have for thy mother's son, Steve. Headley is a well-reported, God-fearing man, and will do well by thee. And thou wilt learn the use of arms as well as handle them."

"I like Master Headley and Kit Smallbones well enough," said Stephen, rather gloomily, "and if a gentleman must be a prentice, weapons are not so bad a craft for him."

"Whittington was a gentleman," said Ambrose.

"I am sick of Whittington," muttered Stephen.

"Nor is he the only one," said Randall, "there's Middleton and Pole-ay, and many another who have risen from the flat cap to the open helm, if not to the coronet. Nay, these London companies have rules against taking any prentice not of gentle blood. Come in to supper with my good woman, and then I'll go with thee and hold converse with good Master Headley, and if Master John doth not send the fee freely, why then I know of them who shall make him disgorge it. But mark," he added, as he led the way out of the gardens, "not a breath of Quipsome Hal. Down here they know me as a clerk of my lord's chamber, sad and sober, and high in his trust and therein they are not far out."

In truth, though Harry Randall had been a wild and frolicsome youth in his Hampshire home, the effect of being a professional buffoon had actually made it a relaxation of effort to him to be grave, quiet, and slow in movement; and this was perhaps a more effectual disguise than the dark garments, and the false brown hair, beard, and moustache, with which he concealed the shorn and shaven condition required of the domestic jester. Having been a player, he was well able to adapt himself to his part, and yet Ambrose had considerable doubts whether Tibble had not suspected his identity from the first, more especially as both the lads had inherited the same dark eyes from their mother, and Ambrose for the first time perceived a considerable resemblance between him and Stephen, not only in feature but in unconscious gesture.

Ambrose was considering whether he had better give his uncle a hint, lest concealment should excite suspicion; when, niched as it were against an abutment of the wall of the Temple courts, close to some steps going down to the Thames, they came upon a tiny house, at whose open door stood a young woman in the snowiest of caps and aprons over a short black gown, beneath which were a trim pair of blue hosen and stout shoes; a suspicion of yellow hair was allowed to appear framing the honest, fresh, Flemish face, which beamed a good-humoured welcome.

"Here they be! here be the poor lads, Pernel mine." She held out her hand, and offered a round comfortable cheek to each, saying, "Welcome to

London, young gentlemen."

Good Mistress Perronel did not look, exactly the stuff to make a glee-maiden of, nor even the beauty for whom to sacrifice everything, even liberty and respect. She was substantial in form, and broad in face and mouth, without much nose, and with large almost colourless eyes. But there was a wonderful look of heartiness and friendliness about her person and her house; the boys had never in their lives seen anything so amazingly and spotlessly clean and shining. In a corner stood an erection like a dark oaken cupboard or wardrobe, but in the middle was an opening about a yard square through which could be seen the night-capped face of a white-headed white-bearded old man, propped against snowy pillows. To him Randall went at once, saying, "So, gaffer, how goes it? You see I have brought company, my poor sister's sons—rest her soul!"

Gaffer Martin mumbled something to them incomprehensible, but which the jester comprehended, for he called them up and named them to him, and Martin put out a bony hand, and gave them a greeting. Though his speech and limbs had failed him, his intelligence was evidently still intact, and there was a tenderly-cared-for look about him, rendering his condition far less pitiable than that of Richard Birkenholt, who was so palpably treated as an incumbrance.

The table was already covered with a cloth, and Perronel quickly placed on it a yellow bowl of excellent beef broth, savoury with vegetables and pot-herbs, and with meat and dumplings floating in it. A lesser bowl was provided for each of the company, with horn spoons, and a loaf of good wheaten bread, and a tankard of excellent ale. Randall declared that his Perronel made far daintier dishes than my Lord Archbishop's cook, who went every day in silk and velvet.

He explained to her his views on the armourer, to which she agreed with all her might, the old gentleman in bed adding something which the boys began to understand, that there was no worthier nor more honourable condition than that of an English burgess, specially in the good town of London, where the kings knew better than to be ever at enmity with their good towns.

"Will the armourer take both of you?" asked Mistress Randall.

"Nay, it was only for Stephen we devised it," said Ambrose.

"And what wilt thou do?"

"I wish to be a scholar," said Ambrose.

"A lean trade," quoth the jester; "a monk now or a friar may be a right jolly fellow, but I never yet saw a man who throve upon books!"

"I had rather study than thrive," said Ambrose rather dreamily.

"He wotteth not what he saith," cried Stephen.

"Oh ho! so thou art of that sort!" rejoined his uncle. "I know them! A crabbed black and white page is meat and drink to them! There's that Dutch fellow, with a long Latin name, thin and weazen as never was Dutchman before; they say he has read all the books in the world, and can talk in all the tongues, and yet when he and Sir Thomas More and the Dean of Saint Paul's get together at my lord's table one would think they were bidding for my bauble. Such excellent fooling do they make, that my lord sits holding his sides."

"The Dean of Saint Paul's!" said Ambrose, experiencing a shock.

"Ay! He's another of your lean scholars, and yet he was born a wealthy man, son to a Lord Mayor, who, they say, reared him alone out of a round score of children."

"Alack! poor souls," sighed Mistress Randall under her breath, for, as Ambrose afterwards learnt, her two babes had scarce seen the light. Her husband, while giving her a look of affection, went on—"Not that he can keep his wealth. He has bestowed the most of it on Stepney church, and on the school he hath founded for poor children, nigh to Saint Paul's."

"Could I get admittance to that school?" exclaimed Ambrose.

"Thou art a big fellow for a school," said his uncle, looking him over. "However, faint heart never won fair lady."

"I have a letter from the Warden of Saint Elizabeth's to one of the clerks of Saint Paul's," added Ambrose. "Alworthy is his name."

"That's well. We'll prove that same," said his uncle. "Meantime, if ye have eaten your fill, we must be on our way to thine armourer, nevoy Stephen, or I shall be called for."

And after a private colloquy between the husband and wife, Ambrose was by both of them desired to make the little house his home until he could find admittance into Saint Paul's School, or some other. He demurred somewhat from a mixture of feelings, in which there was a certain amount of Stephen's longing for freedom of action, and likewise a doubt whether he should not thus be a great inconvenience in the tiny household—a burden he was resolved not to be. But his uncle now took a more serious tone.

"Look thou, Ambrose, thou art my sister's son, and fool though I be, thou art bound in duty to me, and I to have charge of thee, nor will I—for the sake of thy father and mother—have thee lying I know not where, among gulls, and cutpurses, and beguilers of youth here in this city of London. So, till better befalls thee, and I wot of it, thou must be here no later than curfew, or I will know the reason why."

"And I hope the young gentleman will find it no sore grievance," said Perronel, so good-humouredly that Ambrose could only protest that he had feared to be troublesome to her, and promise to bring his bundle the next day.

CHAPTER IX.

Arms Spiritual and Temporal.

"For him was leifer to have at his bedde's hedde
Twenty books clothed in blacke or redde
Of Aristotle and his philosophie
Than robes riche or fiddle or psalterie."

Chaucer.

Master Headley was found spending the summer evening in the bay window of the hall. Tibble sat on a three-legged stool by him, writing in a crabbed hand, in a big ledger, and Kit Smallbones towered above both, holding in his hand a bundle of tally-sticks. By the help of these, and of that accuracy of memory which writing has destroyed, he was unfolding, down to the very last farthing, the entire account of payments and receipts during his master's absence, the debtor and creditor account being preserved as perfectly as if he had always had a pen in his huge fingers, and studied book-keeping by double or single entry.

On the return of the two boys with such an apparently respectable member of society as the handsome well-dressed personage who accompanied them, little Dennet, who had been set to sew her sampler on a stool by her grandmother, under penalty of being sent off to bed if she disturbed her father, sprang up with a little cry of gladness, and running up to Ambrose, entreated for the tales of his good greenwood Forest, and the pucks and pixies, and the girl who daily shared her breakfast with a snake and said, "Eat your own side, Speckleback." Somehow, on Sunday night she had gathered that Ambrose had a store of such tales, and she dragged him off to the gallery, there to revel in them, while his brother remained with her father.

Though Master Stephen had begun by being high and mighty about mechanical crafts, and thought it a great condescension to consent to be bound apprentice, yet when once again in the Dragon court, it looked so friendly and felt so much like a home that he found himself very anxious that Master Headley should not say that he could take no more apprentices at present, and that he should be satisfied with the terms uncle Hal would propose. And oh! suppose Tibble should recognise Quipsome Hal!

However, Tibble was at this moment entirely engrossed by the accounts, and his master left him and his big companion to unravel them, while he himself held speech with his guest at some distance—sending for a cup of sack, wherewith to enliven the conversation.

He showed himself quite satisfied with what Randall chose to tell of himself as a well known "housekeeper" close to the Temple, his wife a "lavender" there, while he himself was attached to the suite of the Archbishop of York. Here alone was there any approach to shuffling, for Master Headley was left to suppose that Randall attended Wolsey in his capacity of king's counsellor, and therefore, having a house of his own, had not been found in the roll of the domestic retainers and servants. He did not think of inquiring further, the more so as Randall was perfectly candid as to his own inferiority of birth to the Birkenholt family, and the circumstances under which he had left the Forest.

Master Headley professed to be quite willing to accept Stephen as an apprentice, with or without a fee; but he agreed with Randall that it would be much better not to expose him to having it cast in his teeth that he was accepted out of charity; and Randall undertook to get a letter so written and conveyed to John Birkenholt that he should not dare to withhold the needful sum, in earnest of which Master Headley would accept the two crowns that Stephen had in hand, as soon as the indentures could be drawn out by one of the many scriveners who lived about Saint Paul's.

This settled, Randall could stay no longer, but he called both nephews into the court with him. "Ye can write a letter?" he said.

"Ay, sure, both of us; but Ambrose is the best scribe," said Stephen.

"One of you had best write then. Let that cur John know that I have my Lord of York's ear, and there will be no fear but he will give it. I'll find a safe hand among the clerks, when the judges ride to hold the assize. Mayhap Ambrose might also write to the Father at Beaulieu. The thing had best be bruited."

"I wished to do so," said Ambrose. "It irked me to have taken no leave of the good Fathers."

Randall then took his leave, having little more than time to return to York House, where the Archbishop might perchance come home wearied and chafed from the King, and the jester might be missed if not there to put him in good humour.

The curfew sounded, and though attention to its notes was not compulsory by law, it was regarded as the break-up of the evening and the note of recall in all well-ordered establishments. The apprentices and journeymen came into the court, among them Giles Headley, who had been taken out by one of the men to be provided with a working dress, much to his disgust; the grandmother summoned little Dennet and carried her off to bed. Stephen and Ambrose bade good-night, but Master Headley and his two confidential men remained somewhat longer to wind up their accounts. Doors were not, as a rule, locked within the court, for though it contained from forty to fifty persons, they were all regarded as a single family, and it was enough to fasten the heavily bolted, iron-studded folding doors of the great gateway leading into Cheapside, the key being brought to the master like that of a castle, seven minutes, measured by the glass, after the last note of the curfew in the belfry outside Saint Paul's.

The summer twilight, however, lasted long after this time of grace, and when Tibble had completed his accountant's work, and Smallbones' deep voiced "Good-night, comrade," had resounded over the court, he beheld a figure rise up from the steps of the gallery, and Ambrose's voice said: "May I speak to thee, Tibble? I need thy counsel."

"Come hither, sir," said the foreman, muttering to himself, "Methought 'twas working in him! The leaven! the leaven!"

Tibble led the way up one of the side stairs into the open gallery, where he presently opened a door, admitting to a small, though high chamber, the walls of bare brick, and containing a low bed, a small table, a three-legged stool, a big chest, and two cupboards, also a cross over the head of the bed. A private room was a luxury neither possessed nor desired by most persons of any degree, and only enjoyed by Tibble in consideration of his great value to his master, his peculiar tastes, and the injuries he had received. In point of fact, his fall had been owing to a hasty blow, given in a passion by the master himself when a young man. Dismay and repentance had made Giles Headley a cooler and more self-controlled man ever since, and even if Tibble had not been a superior workman, he might still have been free to do almost anything he chose. Tibble gave his visitor the stool, and himself sat down on the chest, saying: "So you have found your uncle, sir."

"Ay," said Ambrose, pausing in some expectation that Tibble would mention some suspicion of his identity; but if the foreman had his ideas on the subject he did not disclose them, and waited for more communications.

"Tibble!" said Ambrose, with a long gasp, "I must find means to hear more of him thou tookedst me to on Sunday."

"None ever truly tasted of that well without longing to come back to it," quoth Tibble. "But hath not thy kinsman done aught for thee?"

"Nay," said Ambrose, "save to offer me a lodging with his wife, a good and kindly lavender at the Temple."

Tibble nodded.

"So far am I free," said Ambrose, "and I am glad of it. I have a letter here to one of the canons, one Master Alworthy, but ere I seek him I would know somewhat from thee, Tibble. What like is he?"

"I cannot tell, sir," said Tibble. "The canons are rich and many, and a poor smith like me wots little of their fashions."

"Is it true," again asked Ambrose, "that the Dean—he who spake those words yesterday—hath a school here for young boys?"

"Ay. And a good and mild school it be, bringing them up in the name and nurture of the Holy Child Jesus, to whom it is dedicated."

"Then they are taught this same doctrine?"

"I trow they be. They say the Dean loves them like the children of his old age, and declares that they shall be made in love with holy lore by gentleness rather than severity."

"Is it likely that this same Alworthy could obtain me entrance there?"

"Alack, sir, I fear me thou art too old. I see none but little lads among them. Didst thou come to London with that intent?"

"Nay, for I only wist today that there was such a school. I came with I scarce know what purpose, save to see Stephen safely bestowed, and then to find some way of learning myself. Moreover, a change seems to have come on me, as though I had hitherto been walking in a dream."

Tibble nodded, and Ambrose, sitting there in the dark, was moved to pour forth all his heart, the experience of many an ardent soul in those spirit searching days. Growing up happily under the care of the simple monks of Beaulieu he had never looked beyond their somewhat mechanical routine, accepted everything implicitly, and gone on acquiring knowledge with the receptive spirit but dormant thought of studious boyhood as yet unawakened, thinking that the studious clerical life to which every one destined him would only be a continuation of the same, as indeed it had been to his master, Father Simon. Not that Ambrose expressed this, beyond saying, "They are good and holy men, and I thought all were like them, and fear that was all!"

Then came death, for the first time nearly touching and affecting the youth, and making his soul yearn after further depths, which he might yet have found in the peace of the good old men, and the holy rites and doctrine that they preserved; but before there was time for these things to find their way into the wounds of his spirit, his expulsion from home had sent him forth to see another side of monkish and clerkly life.

Father Shoveller, kindly as he was, was a mere yeoman with nothing spiritual about him; the monks of Hyde were, the younger, gay comrades, only trying how loosely they could sit to their vows; the elder, churlish and avaricious; even the Warden of Elizabeth College was little more than a student. And in London, fresh phases had revealed themselves; the pomp, state, splendour and luxury of Archbishop Wolsey's house had been a shock to the lad's ideal of a bishop drawn from the saintly biographies he had studied at Beaulieu; and he had but to keep his ears open to hear endless scandals about the mass-priests, as they were called, since they were at this time very unpopular in London, and in many cases deservedly so. Everything that the boy had hitherto thought the way of holiness and salvation seemed invaded by evil and danger, and under the bondage of death, whose terrible dance continued to haunt him.

"I saw it, I saw it," he said, "all over those halls at York House. I seemed to behold the grisly shape standing behind one and another, as they ate and laughed; and when the Archbishop and his priests and the King came in it seemed only to make the pageant complete! Only now and then could I recall those blessed words, 'Ye are free indeed.' Did he say from the bondage of death?"

"Yea," said Tibble, "into the glorious freedom of God's children."

"Thou knowst it. Thou knowst it, Tibble. It seems to me that life is no life, but living death, without that freedom! And I *must* hear of it, and know whether it is mine, yea, and Stephen's, and all whom I love. O Tibble, I would beg my bread rather than not have that freedom ever before mine eyes."

"Hold it fast! hold it fast, dear sir," said Tibble, holding out his hands with tears in his eyes, and his face working in a manner that happily Ambrose could not see.

"But how—how? The barefoot friar said that for an *Ave* a day, our Blessed Lady will drag us back from purgatory. I saw her on the wall of her chapel at Winchester saving a robber knight from the sea, yea and a thief from the gallows; but that is not being free."

"Fond inventions of pardon-mongers," muttered Tibble.

"And is one not free when the priest hath assoilsied him?" added Ambrose.

"If, and if—" said Tibble. "But none shall make me trow that shrift in words, without heart—sorrow for sin, and the Latin heard with no thought of Him that bore the guilt, can set the sinner free. 'Tis none other that the Dean sets forth, ay, and the book that I have here. I thank my God," he stood up and took off his cap reverently, "that He hath opened the eyes of another!"

His tone was such that Ambrose could have believed him some devout almost inspired hermit rather than the acute skilful artisan he appeared at other times; and in fact, Tibble Steelman, like many another craftsman of those days, led a double life, the outer one that of the ordinary workman, the inner one devoted to those lights that were shining unveiled and new to in any; and especially here in the heart of the City, partly from the influence of Dean Colet's sermons and catechisings at Saint Paul's, but also from remnants of Lollardism, which had never been entirely quenched. The ordinary clergy looked at it with horror, but the intelligent and thoughtful of the burgher and craftsman classes studied it with a passionate fervour which might have sooner broken out and in more perilous forms save for the guidance it received in the truly Catholic and open-spirited public teachings of Colet, in which he persisted in spite of the opposition of his brother clergy.

Not that as yet the inquirers had in the slightest degree broken with the system of the Church, or with her old traditions. They were only beginning to see the light that had been veiled from them, and to endeavour to clear the fountain from the mire that had fouled it; and there was as yet no reason to believe that the aspersions continually made against the mass-priests and the friars were more than the chronic grumblings of Englishmen, who had found the same faults in them for the last two hundred years.

"And what wouldst thou do, young sir?" presently inquired Tibble.

"That I came to ask thee, good Tibble. I would work to the best of my power in any craft so I may hear those words and gain the key to all I have hitherto learnt, unheeding as one in a dream. My purpose had been to be a scholar and a clerk, but I must see mine own way, and know whither I am being carried, ere I can go farther."

Tibble writhed and wriggled himself about in consideration. "I would I wist how to take thee to the Dean himself," he said, "but I am but a poor man, and his doctrine is 'new wine in old bottles' to the master, though he be a right good man after his lights. See now, Master Ambrose, me seemeth that thou hadst best take thy letter first to this same priest. It may be that he can prefer thee to some post about the minster. Canst sing?"

"I could once, but my voice is nought at this present. If I could but be a servitor at Saint Paul's School!"

"It might be that the will which hath led thee so far hath that post in store for thee, so bear the letter to Master Alworthy. And if he fail thee, wouldst thou think scorn of aiding a friend of mine who worketh a printing-press in Warwick Inner Ward? Thou wilt find him at his place in Paternoster Row, hard by Saint Paul's. He needeth one who is clerk enough to read the Latin, and the craft being a new one 'tis fenced by none of those prentice laws that would bar the way to thee elsewhere, at thy years."

"I should dwell among books!"

"Yea, and holy books, that bear on the one matter dear to the true heart. Thou might serve Lucas Hansen at the sign of the Winged Staff till thou hast settled thine heart, and then it may be the way would be opened to study at Oxford or at Cambridge, so that thou couldst expound the faith to others."

"Good Tibble, kind Tibble, I knew thou couldst aid me! Wilt thou speak to this Master Hansen for me?"

Tibble, however, held that it was more seemly that Ambrose should first try his fate with Master Alworthy, but in case of this not succeeding, he promised to write a billet that would secure attention from Lucas Hansen.

"I warn thee, however, that he is Low Dutch," he added, "though he speaketh English well." He would gladly have gone with the youth, and at any other time might have been sent by his master, but the whole energies of the Dragon would be taken up for the next week by preparations for the tilting-match at court, and Tibble could not be spared for another working hour.

Ambrose, as he rose to bid his friend good-night, could not help saying that he marvelled that one such as he could turn his mind to such vanities as the tilt-yard required.

"Nay," said Tibble, "'twas the craft I was bred to—yea, and I have a good master; and the Apostle Paul himself—as I've heard a preacher say—bade men continue in the state wherein they were, and not be curious to chop and change. Who knoweth whether in God's sight, all our wars and policies be no more than the games of the tilt-yard. Moreover, Paul himself made these very weapons read as good a sermon as the Dean himself. Didst never hear of the shield of faith, and helmet of salvation, and breastplate of righteousness? So, if thou comest to Master Hansen, and provest worthy of his trust, thou wilt hear more, ay, and maybe read too thyself, and send forth the good seed to others," he murmured to himself, as he guided his visitor across the moonlit court up the stairs to the chamber where Stephen lay fast asleep.

CHAPTER X.

Two Vocations.

"The smith, a mighty man is he
With large and sinewy hands;
And the muscles of his brawny arms
Are strong as iron bands."

Longfellow.

Stephen's first thought in the morning was whether the *ex voto* effigy of poor Spring was put in hand, while Ambrose thought of Tibble's promised commendation to the printer. They both, however, found their affairs must needs wait. Orders for weapons for the tilting-match had come in so thickly the day before that every hand must be employed on executing them, and the Dragon court was ringing again with the clang of hammers and screech of grind-stones.

Stephen, though not yet formally bound, was to enter on his apprentice life at once; and Ambrose was assured by Master Headley that it was of no use to repair to any of the dignified clergy of Saint Paul's before mid-day, and that he had better employ the time in writing to his elder brother respecting the fee. Materials were supplied to him, and he used them so as to do credit to the monks of Beaulieu, in spite of little Dennet spending every spare moment in watching his pen as if he were performing some cabalistic operation.

He was a long time about it. There were two letters to write, and the wording of them needed to be very careful, besides that the old court hand took more time to frame than the Italian current hand, and even thus, when dinner-time came, at ten o'clock, the household was astonished to find that he had finished all that regarded Stephen, though he had left the letters open, until his own venture should have been made.

Stephen flung himself down beside his brother hot and panting, shaking his shoulder-blades and declaring that his arms felt ready to drop out. He had been turning a grindstone ever since six o'clock. The two new apprentices had been set on to sharpening the weapon points as all that they were capable of, and had been bidden by Smallbones to turn and hold alternately, but "that oaf Giles Headley," said Stephen, "never ground but one lance, and made me go on turning, threatening to lay the butt about mine ears if I slacked."

"The lazy lubber!" cried Ambrose. "But did none see thee, or couldst not call out for redress?"

"Thou art half a wench thyself, Ambrose, to think I'd complain. Besides, he stood on his rights as a master, and he is a big fellow."

"That's true," said Ambrose, "and he might make it the worse for thee."

"I would I were as big as he," sighed Stephen, "I would soon show him which was the better man."

Perhaps the grinding match had not been as unobserved as Stephen fancied, for on returning to work, Smallbones, who presided over all the rougher parts of the business, claimed them both. He set Stephen to stand by him, sort out and hand him all the rivets needed for a suit of proof armour that hung on a frame, while he required Giles to straighten bars of iron heated to a white heat. Ere long Giles called out for Stephen to change places, to which Smallbones coolly replied, "Turnabout is the rule here, master."

"Even so," replied Giles, "and I have been at work like this long enough, ay, and too long!"

"Thy turn was a matter of three hours this morning," replied Kit—not coolly, for nobody was cool in his den, but with a brevity which provoked a laugh.

"I shall see what my cousin the master saith!" cried Giles, in great wrath.

"Ay, that thou wilt," returned Kit, "if thou dost loiter over thy business, and hast not those bars ready when called for."

"He never meant me to be put on work like this, with a hammer that breaks mine arm."

"What! crying out for that!" said Edmund Burgess, who had just come in to ask for a pair of tongs. "What wouldst say to the big hammer that none can wield save Kit himself?"

Giles felt there was no redress, and panted on, feeling as if he were melting away, and with a dumb, wild rage in his heart, that could get no outlet, for Smallbones was at least as much bigger than he as he was than Stephen. Tibble was meanwhile busy over the gilding and enamelling of Buckingham's magnificent plate armour in Italian fashion, but he had found time to thrust into Ambrose's hand an exceedingly small and curiously folded billet for Lucas Hansen, the printer, in case of need. "He would be found at the sign of the Winged Staff in Paternoster Row," said Tibble, "or if not there himself, there would be his servant who would direct Ambrose to the place where the Dutch printer lived and worked." No one was at leisure to show the lad the way, and he set out with a strange feeling of solitude, as his path began decisively to be away from that of his brother.

He did not find much difficulty in discovering the quadrangle on the south side of the minster where the minor canons lived near the deanery; and the porter, a stout lay brother, pointed out to him the doorway belonging to Master Alworthy. He knocked, and a young man with a tonsured head but a bloated face opened it. Ambrose explained that he had brought a letter from the Warden of Saint Elizabeth's College at Winchester.

"Give it here," said the young man.

"I would give it to his reverence himself," said Ambrose.

"His reverence is taking his after-dinner nap and may not be disturbed," said the man.

"Then I will wait," said Ambrose.

The door was shut in his face, but it was the shady side of the court, and he sat down on a bench and waited. After full an hour the door was opened, and the canon, a good-natured looking man, in a square cap, and gown and cassock of the finest cloth, came slowly out. He had evidently heard nothing of the message, and was taken by surprise when Ambrose, doffing his cap and bowing low, gave him the greeting of the Warden of Saint Elizabeth's and the letter.

"Hum! Ha! My good friend—Fielder—I remember him. He was always a scholar. So he hath sent thee here with his commendations. What should I do with all the idle country lads that come up to choke London and feed the plague? Yet stay—that lurdane Bolt is getting intolerably lazy and insolent, and methinks he robs me! What canst do, thou stripling?"

"I can read Latin, sir, and know the Greek alphabeta."

"Tush! I want no scholar more than enough to serve my mass. Canst sing?"

"Not now; but I hope to do so again."

"When I rid me of Bolt there—and there's an office under the sacristan that he might fill as well as another knave—the fellow might do for me well enow as a body servant," said Mr. Alworthy, speaking to himself. "He would brush my gowns and make my bed, and I might perchance trust him with my marketings, and by and by there might be some office for him when he grew saucy and idle. I'll prove him on mine old comrade's word."

"Sir," said Ambrose, respectfully, "what I seek for is occasion for study. I had hoped you could speak to the Dean, Dr. John Colet, for some post at his school."

"Boy," said Alworthy, "I thought thee no such fool! Why crack thy brains with study when I can show thee a surer path to ease and preferment? But I see thou art too proud to do an old man a service. Thou writst thyself gentleman, forsooth, and high blood will not stoop."

"Not so, sir," returned Ambrose, "I would work in any way so I could study the humanities, and hear the Dean preach. Cannot you commend me to his school?"

"Ha!" exclaimed the canon, "this is your sort, is it? I'll have nought to do with it! Preaching, preaching! Every idle child's head is agog on preaching nowadays! A plague on it! Why can't Master Dean leave it to the black friars, whose vocation 'tis, and not cumber us with his sermons for ever, and set every lazy lad thinking he must needs run after them? No, no, my good boy, take my advice. Thou shalt have two good bellyfuls a day, all my cast gowns, and a pair of shoes by the year, with a groat a month if thou wilt keep mine house, bring in my meals, and the like, and by and by, so thou art a good lad, and runst not after these new-fangled preachments which lead but to heresy, and set folk racking their brains about sin and such trash, we'll get thee shorn and into minor orders, and who knows what good preferment thou mayst not win in due time!"

"Sir, I am beholden to you, but my mind is set on study."

"What kin art thou to a fool?" cried the minor canon, so startling Ambrose that he had almost answered, and turning to another ecclesiastic whose siesta seemed to have ended about the same time, "Look at this varlet, Brother Cloudesley! Would you believe it? He comes to me with a letter from mine old friend, in consideration of which I offer him that saucy lubber Bolt's place, a gown of mine own a year, meat and preferment, and, lo you, he tells me all he wants is to study Greek, forsooth, and hear the Dean's sermons!"

The other canon shook his head in dismay at such arrant folly. "Young stripling, be warned," he said. "Know what is good for thee. Greek is the tongue of heresy."

"How may that be, reverend sir," said Ambrose, "when the holy Apostles and the Fathers spake and wrote in the Greek?"

"Waste not thy time on him, brother," said Mr. Alworthy. "He will find out his error when his pride and his Greek forsooth have brought him to fire and faggot."

"Ay! ay!" added Cloudesley. "The Dean with his Dutch friend and his sermons, and his new grammar and accidence, is sowing heretics as thick as groundsel."

Wherewith the two canons of the old school waddled away, arm in arm, and Bolt put out his head, leered at Ambrose, and bade him shog off, and not come sneaking after other folk's shoes.

Sooth to say, Ambrose was relieved by his rejection. If he were not to obtain admission in any capacity to Saint Paul's School, he felt more drawn to Tibble's friend the printer; for the self-seeking luxurious habits into which so many of the beneficed clergy had fallen were repulsive to him, and his whole soul thirsted after that new revelation, as it were, which Colet's sermon had made to him. Yet the word heresy was terrible and confusing, and a doubt came over him whether he might not be forsaking the right path, and be lured aside by false lights.

He would think it out before he committed himself. Where should he do so in peace? He thought of the great Minster, but the nave was full of a surging multitude, and there was a loud hum of voices proceeding from it, which took from him all inclination to find his way to the quieter and inner portions of the sanctuary.

Then he recollected the little Pardon Church, where he had seen the *Dance of Death* on the walls; and crossing the burial-ground he entered, and, as he expected, found it empty, since the hours for masses for the dead were now past. He knelt down on a step, repeated the sext office, in warning for which the bells were chiming all round, covering his face with his hands, and thinking himself back to Beaulieu; then, seating himself on a step, leaning against the wall, he tried to think out whether to give himself up to the leadings of the new light that had broken on him, or whether to wrench himself from it. Was this, which seemed to him truth and deliverance, verily the heresy respecting which rumours had come to horrify the country convents? If he had only heard of it from Tibble Wrymouth, he would have doubted, in spite of its power over him, but he had heard it from a man, wise, good, and high in place, like Dean Colet. Yet to his further perplexity, his uncle had spoken of

Colet as jesting at Wolsey's table. What course should he take? Could he bear to turn away from that which drew his soul so powerfully, and return to the bounds which seem to him to be grown so narrow, but which he was told were safe? Now that Stephen was settled, it was open to him to return to Saint Elizabeth's College, but the young soul within him revolted against the repetition of what had become to him unsatisfying, unless illumined by the brightness he seemed to have glimpsed at.

But Ambrose had gone through much unwonted fatigue of late, and while thus musing he fell asleep, with his head against the wall. He was half wakened by the sound of voices, and presently became aware that two persons were examining the walls, and comparing the paintings with some others, which one of them had evidently seen. If he had known it, it was with the *Dance of Death* on the bridge of Lucerne.

"I question," said a voice that Ambrose had heard before, "whether these terrors be wholesome for men's souls."

"For priests' pouches, they be," said the other, with something of a foreign accent.

"Alack, when shall we see the day when the hope of paradise and dread of purgatory shall be no longer made the tools of priestly gain; and hatred of sin taught to these poor folk, instead of servile dread of punishment."

"Have a care, my Colet," answered the yellow bearded foreigner; "thou art already in ill odour with those same men in authority; and though a Dean's stall be fenced from the episcopal crook, yet there is a rod at Rome which can reach even thither."

"I tell thee, dear Erasmus, thou art too timid; I were well content to leave house and goods, yea, to go to prison or to death, could I but bring home to one soul, for which Christ died, the truth and hope in every one of those prayers and creeds that our poor folk are taught to patter as a senseless charm."

"These are strange times," returned Erasmus. "Methinks yonder phantom, be he skeleton or angel, will have snatched both of us away ere we behold the full issue either of thy preachings, or my Greek Testament, or of our More's Utopian images. Dost thou not feel as though we were like children who have set some mighty engine in motion, like the great water-wheels in my native home, which, whirled by the flowing streams of time and opinion, may break up the whole foundations, and destroy the oneness of the edifice?"

"It may be so," returned Colet. "What read we? 'The net brake' even in the Master's sight, while still afloat on the sea. It was only on the shore that the hundred and fifty-three, all good and sound, were drawn to His feet."

"And," returned Erasmus, "I see wherefore thou hast made thy children at Saint Paul's one hundred and fifty and three."

The two friends were passing out. Their latter speeches had scarce been understood by Ambrose, even if he heard them, so full was he of conflicting feelings, now ready to cast himself before their feet, and entreat the Dean to help him to guidance, now withheld by bashfulness, unwillingness to interrupt, and ingenuous shame at appearing like an eavesdropper towards such dignified and venerable personages. Had he obeyed his first impulse, mayhap his career had been made safer and easier for him, but it was while shyness chained his limbs and tongue that the Dean and Erasmus quitted the chapel, and the opportunity of accosting them had slipped away.

Their half comprehended words had however decided him in the part he should take, making him sure that Colet was not controverting the formularies of the Church, but drawing out those meanings which in repetition by rote were well-nigh forgotten. It was as if his course were made clear to him.

He was determined to take the means which most readily presented themselves of hearing Colet; and leaving the chapel, he bent his steps to the Row which his book-loving eye had already marked. Flanking the great Cathedral on the north, was the row of small open stalls devoted to the sale of books, or "objects of devotion," all so arranged that the open portion might be cleared, and the stock-in-trade locked up if not carried away. Each stall had its own sign, most of them sacred, such as the Lamb and Flag, the Scallop Shell, or some patron saint, but classical emblems were oddly intermixed, such as Minerva's aegis, Pegasus, and the Lyre of Apollo. The sellers, some middle-aged men, some lads, stretched out their arms with their wares to attract the passengers in the street, and did not fail to beset Ambrose. The more lively looked at his Lincoln-green and shouted verses of ballads at him, fluttering broad sheets with verses on the lamentable fate of Jane Shore, or Fair Rosamond, the same woodcut doing duty for both ladies, without mercy to their beauty. The scholastic judged by his face and step that he was a student, and they flourished at him black-bound copies of Virgilius Maro, and of Tully's Offices, while others, hoping that he was an incipient clerk, offered breviaries, missals or portuaries, with the Use of Saint Paul's, or of Sarum, or mayhap Saint Austin's Confessions. He made his way along, with his eye diligently heedful of the signs, and at last recognised the Winged Staff or caduceus of Hermes, over a stall where a couple of boys in blue caps and gowns and yellow stockings were making a purchase of a small, grave-looking, elderly but bright cheeked man, whose yellow hair and beard were getting intermingled with grey. They were evidently those Saint Paul's School boys whom Ambrose envied so much, and as they finished their bargaining and ran away together, Ambrose advanced with a salutation, asked if he did not see Master Lucas Hansen, and gave him the note with the commendations of Tibble Steelman the armourer.

He was answered with a ready nod and "yea, yea," as the old man opened the billet and cast his eyes over it; then scanning Ambrose from head to foot, said with some amazement, "But you are of gentle blood, young sir."

"I am," said Ambrose; "but gentle blood needs at times to work for bread, and Tibble let me hope that I might find both livelihood for the body and for the soul with you, sir."

"Is it so?" asked the printer, his face lighting up. "Art thou willing to labour and toil, and give up hope of fee and honour, if so thou mayst win the truth?"

Ambrose folded his hands with a gesture of earnestness, and Lucas

Hansen said, "Bless thee, my son! Methinks I can aid thee in thy quest, so thou canst lay aside," and here his voice grew sharper and more peremptory, "all thy gentleman's airs and follies, and serve—ay, serve and obey."

"I trust so," returned Ambrose; "my brother is even now becoming prentice to Master Giles Headley, and we hope to live as honest men by the work of our hands and brains."

"I forgot that you English herren are not so puffed up with pride and scorn like our Dutch nobles," returned the printer. "Canst live sparingly, and lie hard, and see that thou keepst the house clean, not like these English swine?"

"I hope so," said Ambrose, smiling; "but I have an uncle and aunt, and they would have me lie every night at their house beside the Temple gardens."

"What is thine uncle?"

"He hath a post in the meiné of my Lord Archbishop of York," said Ambrose, blushing and hesitating a little. "He cometh to and fro to his wife, who dwells with her old father, doing fine lavender's work for the lawyer folk therein."

It was somewhat galling that this should be the most respectable occupation that could be put forward, but Lucas Hansen was evidently reassured by it. He next asked whether Ambrose could read Latin, putting a book into his hand as he did so; Ambrose read and construed readily, explaining that he had been trained at Beaulieu.

"That is well!" said the printer; "and hast thou any Greek?"

"Only the alphabeta," said Ambrose, "I made that out from a book at Beaulieu, but Father Simon knew no more, and there was nought to study from."

"Even so," replied Hansen, "but little as thou knowst 'tis as much as I can hope for from any who will aid me in my craft. 'Tis I that, as thou hast seen, furnish for the use of the children at the Dean's school of Saint Paul's. The best and foremost scholars of them are grounded in their Greek, that being the tongue wherein the Holy Gospels were first writ. Hitherto I have had to get me books for their use from Holland, whither they are brought from Basle, but I have had sent me from Hamburg a fount of type of the Greek character, whereby I hope to print at home, the accidence, and mayhap the *Dialogues* of Plato, and it might even be the sacred Gospel itself, which the great Doctor, Master Erasmus, is even now collating from the best authorities in the universities."

Ambrose's eyes kindled with unmistakable delight. "You have the accidence!" he exclaimed. "Then could I study the tongue even while working for you! Sir, I would do my best! It is the very opportunity I seek."

"Fair and softly," said the printer with something of a smile. "Thou art new to cheapening and bargaining, my fair lad. Thou hast spoken not one word of the wage."

"I recked not of that," said Ambrose. "'Tis true, I may not burthen mine uncle and aunt, but verily, sir, I would live on the humblest fare that will keep body and soul together so that I may have such an opportunity."

"How knowst thou what the opportunity may be?" returned Lucas, drily. "Thou art but a babe! Some one should have a care of thee. If I set thee to stand here all day and cry what d'ye lack? or to carry bales of books 'twixt this and Warwick Inner Ward, thou wouldst have no ground to complain."

"Nay, sir," returned Ambrose, "I wot that Tibble Steelman would never send me to one who would not truly give me what I need."

"Tibble Steelman is verily one of the few who are both called and chosen," replied Lucas, "and I think thou art the same so far as green youth may be judged, since thou art one who will follow the word into the desert, and never ask for the loaves and fishes. Nevertheless, I will take none advantage of thy youth and zeal, but thou shalt first behold what thou shalt have to do for me, and then if it still likes thee, I will see thy kindred. Hast no father?"

Ambrose explained, and at that moment Master Hansen's boy made his appearance, returning from an errand; the stall was left in his charge, while the master took Ambrose with him into the precincts of what had once been the splendid and hospitable mansion of the great king-maker, Warwick, but was now broken up into endless little tenements with their courts and streets, though the baronial ornaments and the arrangement still showed what the place had been.

Entering beneath a wide archway, still bearing the sign of the Bear and Ragged Staff, Lucas led the way into what must have been one of the courts of offices, for it was surrounded with buildings and sheds of different heights and sizes, and had on one side a deep trough of stone, fed by a series of water-taps, intended for the use of the stables. The doors of one of these buildings was unlocked by Master Hansen, and Ambrose found himself in what had once perhaps been part of a stable, but had been partitioned off from the rest. There were two stalls, one serving the Dutchman for his living room, the other for his workshop. In one corner stood a white earthenware stove—so new a spectacle to the young forester that he supposed it to be the printing-press. A table, shiny with rubbing, a wooden chair, a couple of stools, a few vessels, mirrors for brightness, some chests and corner cupboards, a bed shutting up like a box and likewise highly polished, completed the furniture, all arranged with the marvellous orderliness and neatness of the nation. A curtain shut off the opening to the other stall, where stood a machine with a huge screw, turned by leverage. Boxes of type and piles of paper surrounded it, and Ambrose stood and looked at it with a sort of awe-struck wonder and respect as the great fount of wisdom. Hansen showed him what his work would be, in setting up type, and by and by correcting after the first proof. The machine could only print four pages at a time, and for this operation the whole strength of the establishment was required. Moreover, Master Hansen bound, as well as printed his books. Ambrose was by no means daunted. As long as he might read as well as print, and while he had Sundays at Saint Paul's to look to, he asked no more—except indeed that his gentle blood stirred at the notion of acting salesman in the book-stall, and Master Hansen assured him with a smile that

Will Wherry, the other boy, would do that better than either of them, and that he would be entirely employed here.

The methodical master insisted however on making terms with the boy's relations; and with some misgivings on Ambrose's part, the two—since business hours were almost over—walked together to the Temple and to the little house, where Perronel was ironing under her window.

Ambrose need not have doubted. The Dutch blood on either side was stirred; and the good housewife commanded the little printer's respect as he looked round on a kitchen as tidy as if it in his own country. And the bargain was struck that Ambrose Birkenholt should serve Master Hansen for his meals and two pence a week, while he was to sleep at the little house of Mistress Randall, who would keep his clothes and linen in order.

And thus it was that both Ambrose and Stephen Birkenholt had found their vocations for the present, and both were fervent in them. Master Headley pshawed a little when he heard that Ambrose had engaged himself to a printer and a foreigner; and when he was told it was to a friend of Tibble's, only shook his head, saying that Tib's only fault was dabbling in matters of divinity, as if a plain man could not be saved without them! However, he respected the lad for having known his own mind and not hung about in idleness, and he had no opinion of clerks, whether monks or priests. Indeed, the low esteem in which the clergy as a class were held in London was one of the very evil signs of the times. Ambrose was invited to dine and sup at the Dragon court every Sunday and holiday, and he was glad to accept, since the hospitality was so free, and he thus was able to see his brother and Tibble; besides that, it prevented him from burthening Mistress Randall, whom he really liked, though he could not see her husband, either in bis motley or his plain garments, without a shudder of repulsion.

Ambrose found that setting up type had not much more to do with the study of new books than Stephen's turning the grindstone had with fighting in the lists; and the mistakes he made in spelling from right to left, and in confounding the letters, made him despair, and prepare for any amount of just indignation from his master; but he found on the contrary that Master Hansen had never had a pupil who made so few blunders on the first trial, and augured well of him from such a beginning. Paper was too costly, and pressure too difficult, for many proofs to be struck off, but Hansen could read and correct his type as it stood, and assured Ambrose that practice would soon give him the same power; and the correction was thus completed, when Will Wherry, a big, stout fellow, came in to dinner—the stall being left during that time, as nobody came for books during the dinner-hour, and Hansen, having an understanding with his next neighbour, by which they took turns to keep guard against thieves.

The master and the two lads dined together on the contents of a cauldron, where pease and pork had been simmering together on the stove all the morning. Their strength was then united to work the press and strike off a sheet, which the master scanned, finding only one error in it. It was a portion of Lilly's *Grammar*, and Ambrose regarded it with mingled pride and delight, though he longed to go further into those deeper revelations for the sake of which he had come here.

Master Hansen then left the youths to strike off a couple of hundred sheets, after which they were to wash the types and re-arrange the letters in the compartments in order, whilst he returned to the stall. The customers requiring his personal attention were generally late ones. When all this was accomplished, and the pot put on again in preparation for supper, the lads might use the short time that remained as they would, and Hansen himself showed Ambrose a shelf of books concealed by a blue curtain, whence he might read.

Will Wherry showed unconcealed amazement that this should be the taste of his companion. He himself hated the whole business, and would never have adopted it, but that he had too many brothers for all to take to the water on the Thames, and their mother was too poor to apprentice them, and needed the small weekly pay the Dutchman gave him. He seemed a good-natured, dull fellow, whom no doubt Hansen had hired for the sake of the strong arms, developed by generations of oarsmen upon the river. What he specially disliked was that his master was a foreigner. The whole court swarmed with foreigners, he said, with the utmost disgust, as if they were noxious insects. They made provisions dear, and undersold honest men, and he wondered the Lord Mayor did not see to it and drive them out. He did not so much object to the Dutch, but the Spaniards—no words could express his horror of them.

By and by, Ambrose going out to fetch some water from the conduit, found standing by it a figure entirely new to him. It was a young girl of some twelve or fourteen years old, in the round white cap worn by all of her age and sex; but from beneath it hung down two thick plaits of the darkest hair he had ever seen, and though the dress was of the ordinary dark serge with a coloured apron, it was put on with an air that made it look like some strange and beautiful costume on the slender, lithe, little form. The vermilion apron was further trimmed with a narrow border of white, edged again with deep blue, and it chimed in with the bright coral earrings and necklace. As Ambrose came forward the creature tried to throw a crimson handkerchief over her head, and ran into the shelter of another door, but not before Ambrose had seen a pair of large dark eyes so like those of a terrified fawn that they seemed to carry him back to the Forest. Going back amazed, he asked his companion who the girl he had seen could have been.

Will stared. "I trow you mean the old blackamoor sword-cutler's wench. He is one of those pestilent strangers. An 'Ebrew Jew who worships Mahound and is too bad for the Spanish folk themselves."

This rather startled Ambrose, though he knew enough to see that the accusations could not both be true, but he forgot it in the delight, when Will pronounced the work done, of drawing back the curtain and feasting his eyes upon the black backs of the books, and the black-letter brochures that lay by them. There were scarcely thirty, yet he gloated on them as on an inexhaustible store, while Will, whistling wonder at his taste, opined that since some one was there to look after the stove, and the iron pot on it, he might go out and have a turn at ball with Hob and Martin.

Ambrose was glad to be left to go over his coming feast. There was Latin, English, and, alas! baffling Dutch. High or Low it was all the same to him. What excited his curiosity most was the *Enchiridion Militis Christiani* of Erasmus—in Latin of course, and that he could easily read—but almost equally exciting was a Greek and Latin vocabulary; or again, a very thin book in which he recognised the New Testament in the Vulgate. He had heard chapters of it read from the graceful stone pulpit overhanging the refectory at Beaulieu, and, of course, the Gospels and Epistles at mass, but they had been read with little expression and no attention; and that Sunday's discourse had filled him with eagerness to look farther; but the mere reading the titles of the books was pleasure enough for the day, and his master was at home before he had fixed his mind on anything. Perhaps this was as well, for Lucas advised him what to begin with, and how to divide his studies so as to gain a knowledge of the Greek, his great ambition, and also to read the Scripture.

The master was almost as much delighted as the scholar, and it was not till the curfew was beginning to sound that Ambrose could tear himself away. It was still daylight, and the door of the next dwelling was open. There, sitting on the ground cross-legged, in an attitude such as Ambrose had never seen, was a magnificent old man, with a huge long white beard, wearing, indeed, the usual dress of a Londoner of the lower class, but the gown flowed round him in a grand and patriarchal manner, corresponding with his noble, somewhat aquiline features; and behind him Ambrose thought he caught a glimpse of the shy fawn he had seen in the morning.

CHAPTER XI.
Ay Di Me Grenada.

"In sooth it was a thing to weep
If then as now the level plain
Beneath was spreading like the deep,
The broad unruffled main.
If like a watch-tower of the sun
Above, the Alpuxarras rose,
Streaked, when the dying day was done,
With evening's roseate snows."

Archbishop Trench.

When Mary Tudor, released by death from her first dreary marriage, contracted for her brother's pleasure, had appeased his wrath at her second marriage made to please herself, Henry the Eighth was only too glad to mark his
assent by all manner of festivities; and English chroniclers, instead of record-
ing battles and politics, had only to write of pageantries and tournaments
during the merry May of the year 1515—a May, be it remembered, which,
thanks to the old style, was at least ten days nearer to Midsummer than our
present month.

How the two queens and all their court had gone a-maying on Shooter's
Hill, ladies and horses poetically disguised and labelled with sweet summer
titles, was only a nine days' wonder when the Birkenholts had come to
London, but the approaching tournament at Westminster on the Whitsun holiday was the great excitement to the whole population, for, with all its faults,
the Court of bluff King Hal was thoroughly genial, and every one, gentle and
simple, might participate in his pleasures.

Seats were reserved at the lists for the city dignitaries and their families,
and though old Mistress Headley professed that she ought to have done with
such vanities, she could not forbear from going to see that her son was not too
much encumbered with the care of little Dennet, and that the child herself ran
into no mischief. Master Headley himself grumbled and sighed but he put
himself into his scarlet gown, holding that his presence was a befitting attention to the king, glad to gratify his little daughter, and not without a desire to
see how his workmanship—good English ware—held out against "mail and
plate of Milan steel," the fine armour brought home from France by the new
Duke of Suffolk. Giles donned his best in the expectation of sitting in the
places of honour as one of the family, and was greatly disgusted when Kit
Smallbones observed, "What's all that bravery for? The tilting-match quotha?
Ha! ha! my young springald, if thou see it at all, thou must be content to gaze
as thou canst from the armourers' tent, if Tibble there chooses to be cumbered
with a useless lubber like thee."

"I always sat with my mother when there were matches at Clarendon," muttered Giles, who had learnt at least that it was of no use to complain of Smallbones' plain speaking.

"If folks cocker malapert lads at Sarum we know better here," was the answer.

"I shall ask the master, my kinsman," returned the youth.

But he got little by his move. Master Headley told him, not unkindly, for he had some pity for the spoilt lad, that not the Lord Mayor himself would take his own son with him while yet an apprentice. Tibble Steelman would indeed go to one of the attendants' tents at the further end of the lists, where repairs to armour and weapons might be needed, and would take an assistant or two, but who they might be must depend on his own choice, and if Giles had any desire to go, he had better don his working dress.

In fact, Tibble meant to take Edmund Burgess and one workman for use, and one of the new apprentices for pleasure, letting them change in the middle of the day. The swagger of Giles actually forfeited for him the first turn, which—though he was no favourite with the men—would have been granted to his elder years and his relationship to the master; but on his overbearing demand to enter the boat which was to carry down a little anvil and charcoal furnace, with a few tools, rivets, nails, and horse-shoes, Tibble coolly returned that he needed no such gay birds; but if Giles chose to be ready in his leathern coat when Stephen Birkenholt came home at mid-day, mayhap he might change with him.

Stephen went joyously in the plainest of attire, though Tibble in fur cap, grimy jerkin, and leathern apron was no elegant steersman; and Edmund, who was at the age of youthful foppery, shrugged his shoulders a little, and disguised the garments of the smithy with his best flat cap and newest mantle.

They kept in the wake of the handsome barge which Master Headley shared with his friend and brother alderman, Master Hope the draper, whose young wife, in a beautiful black velvet hood and shining blue satin kirtle, was evidently petting Dennet to her heart's content, though the little damsel never lost an opportunity of nodding to her friends in the plainer barge in the rear.

The Tudor tilting-matches cost no lives, and seldom broke bones. They were chiefly opportunities for the display of brilliant enamelled and gilt armour, at the very acme of cumbrous magnificence; and of equally gorgeous embroidery spread out over the vast expanse provided by elephantine Flemish horses. Even if the weapons had not been purposely blunted, and if the champions had really desired to slay one another, they would have found the task very difficult, as in effect they did in the actual game of war. But the spectacle was a splendid one, and all the apparatus was ready in the armourers' tent, marked by Saint George and the Dragon. Tibble ensconced himself in the innermost corner with a "tractate," borrowed from his friend Lucas, and sent the apprentices to gaze their fill at the rapidly filling circles of seats. They saw King Harry, resplendent in gilded armour—"from their own anvil, true English steel," said Edmund, proudly—hand to her seat his sister the bride, one of the most beautiful women then in existence, with a lovely and delicate bloom on her fair face and exquisite Plantagenet features. No more royally handsome creatures could the world have offered than that brother and sister, and the English world appreciated them and made the lists ring with applause at the fair lady who had disdained foreign princes to wed her true love, an honest Englishman.

He—the cloth of frieze—in blue Milanese armour, made to look as classical as possible, and with clasps and medals engraven from antique gems—handed in Queen Katharine, whose dark but glowing Spanish complexion made a striking contrast to the dazzling fairness of her young sister-in-law. Near them sat a stout burly figure in episcopal purple, and at his feet there was a form which nearly took away all Stephen's pleasure for the time. For it was in motley, and he could hear the bells jingle, while the hot blood rose in his cheeks in the dread lest Burgess should detect the connection, or recognise in the jester the grave personage who had come to negotiate with Mr. Headley for his indentures, or worse still, that the fool should see and claim him.

However, Quipsome Hal seemed to be exchanging drolleries with the young dowager of France, who, sooth to say, giggled in a very unqueenly manner at jokes which made the grave Spanish-born queen draw up her stately head, and converse with a lady on her other hand—an equally stately lady, somewhat older, with the straight Plantagenet features, and by her side a handsome boy, who, though only eight or nine years old, was tonsured, and had a little scholar's gown. "That," said Edmund, "is my Lady Countess of Salisbury, of whom Giles Headley prates so much."

A tournament, which was merely a game between gorgeously equipped princes and nobles, afforded little scope for adventure worthy of record, though it gave great diversion to the spectators. Stephen gazed like one fascinated at the gay panoply of horse and man, with the huge plumes on the heads of both, as they rushed against one another, and he shared with Edmund the triumph when the lance from their armoury held good, the vexation if it were shivered. All would have been \bvprn=perfect=pu|/fikt\ perfect but for the sight of his uncle, playing off his drolleries in a manner that gave him a sense of personal degradation.

To escape from the sight almost consoled him when, in the pause after the first courses had been run, Tibble told him and Burgess to return, and send Headley and another workman with a fresh bundle of lances for the afternoon's tilting. Stephen further hoped to find his brother at the Dragon court, as it was one of those holidays that set every one free, and separation began to make the brothers value their meetings.

But Ambrose was not at the Dragon court, and when Stephen went in quest of him to the Temple, Perronel had not seen him since the early morning, but she said he seemed so much bitten with the little old man's scholarship that she had small doubt that he would be found poring over a book in Warwick Inner Ward.

Thither therefore did Stephen repair. The place was nearly deserted, for the inhabitants were mostly either artisans or that far too numerous race who lived on the doles of convents, on the alms of churchgoers, and the largesses scattered among the people on public occasions, and these were for the most part pursuing their vocation both of gazing and looking out for gain among the spectators outside the lists. The door that Stephen had been shown as that of Ambrose's master was, however, partly open, and close beside it sat in the sun a figure that amazed him. On a small mat or rug, with a black and yellow handkerchief over her head, and little scarlet legs crossed under a blue dress, all lighted up by the gay May sun, there slept the little dark, glowing maiden, with her head bent as it leant against the wall, her rosy lips half open, her long black plaits on her shoulders.

Stepping up to the half open door, whence he heard a voice reading, his astonishment was increased. At the table were his brother and his master, Ambrose with a black book in hand, Lucas Hansen with some papers, and on the ground was seated a venerable, white-bearded old man, something between Stephen's notions of an apostle and of a magician, though the latter idea predominated at sight of a long parchment scroll covered with characters such as belonged to no alphabet that he had ever dreamt of. What were they doing to his brother? He was absolutely in an enchanter's den. Was it a pixie at the door, guarding it? "Ambrose!" he cried aloud.

Everybody started. Ambrose sprang to his feet, exclaiming, "Stephen!" The pixie gave a little scream and jumped up, flying to the old man, who quietly rolled up his scroll.

Lucas rose up as Ambrose spoke.

"Thy brother?" said he.

"Yea—come in search of me," said Ambrose.

"Thou hadst best go forth with him," said Lucas.

"It is not well that youth should study over long," said the old man. "Thou hast aided us well, but do thou now unbend the bow. Peace be with thee, my son."

Ambrose complied, but scarcely willingly, and the instant they had made a few steps from the door, Stephen exclaimed in dismay, "Who—what was it? Have they bewitched thee, Ambrose?"

Ambrose laughed merrily. "Not so. It is holy lore that those good men are reading."

"Nay now, Ambrose. Stand still—if thou canst, poor fellow," he muttered, and then made the sign of the cross three times over his brother, who stood smiling, and said, "Art satisfied Stevie? Or wilt have me rehearse my *Credo*?" Which he did, Stephen listening critically, and drawing a long breath as he recognised each word, pronounced without a shudder at the critical points. "Thou art safe so far," said Stephen. "But sure he is a wizard. I even beheld his familiar spirit—in a fair shape doubtless—like a pixie! Be not deceived, brother. Sorcery reads backwards—and I saw him so read from that scroll of his. Laughest thou! Nay! what shall I do to free thee? Enter here!"

Stephen dragged his brother, still laughing, into the porch of the nearest church, and deluged him with holy water with such good will, that Ambrose, putting up his hands to shield his eyes, exclaimed, "Come now, have done with this folly, Stephen—though it makes me laugh to think of thy scared looks, and poor little Aldonza being taken for a familiar spirit." And Ambrose laughed as he had not laughed for weeks.

"But what is it, then?"

"The old man is of thy calling, or something like it, Stephen, being that he maketh and tempereth sword-blades after the prime Damascene or Toledo fashion, and the familiar spirit is his little daughter."

Stephen did not however look mollified. "Sword-blades! None have a right to make them save our craft. This is one of the rascaille Spaniards who have poured into the city under favour of the queen to spoil and ruin the lawful trade. Though could you but have seen, Ambrose, how our tough English ashwood in King Harry's band—from our own armoury too—made all go down before it, you would never uphold strangers and their false wares that can only get the better by sorcery."

"How thou dost harp upon sorcery!" exclaimed Ambrose. "I must tell thee the good old man's story as 'twas told to me, and then wilt thou own that he is as good a Christian as ourselves—ay, or better—and hath little cause to love the Spaniards."

"Come on, then," said Stephen. "Methought if we, went towards Westminster we might yet get where we could see the lists. Such a rare show, Ambrose, to see the King in English armour, ay, and Master Headley's, every inch of it, glittering in the sun, so that one could scarce brook the dazzling, on his horse like a rock shattering all that came against him! I warrant you the lances cracked and shivered like faggots under old Purkis's bill-hook. And that you should liefer pore over crabbed monkish stuff with yonder old men! My life on it, there must be some spell!"

"No more than of old, when I was ever for book and thou for bow," said Ambrose; "but I'll make thee rueful for old Michael yet. Hast heard tell of the Moors in Spain?"

"Moors—blackamoors who worship Mahound and Termagant. I saw a blackamoor last week behind his master, a merchant of Genoa, in Paul's Walk. He looked like the devils in the Miracle Play at Christ Church, with blubber lips and wool for hair. I marvelled that he did not writhe and flee when he came within the Minster, but Ned Burgess said he was a christened man."

"Moors be not all black, neither be they all worshippers of Mahound," replied Ambrose.

However, as Ambrose's information, though a few degrees more correct and intelligent than his brother's, was not complete, it will be better not to give the history of Lucas's strange visitors in his words.

They belonged to the race of Saracen Arabs who had brought the arts of life to such perfection in Southern Spain, but who had received the general appellation of Moors from those Africans who were continually reinforcing them, and, bringing a certain Puritan strictness of Mohammedanism with them, had done much towards destroying the highest cultivation among them before the Spanish kingdoms became united, and finally triumphed over them. During the long interval of two centuries, while Castille was by Italian occupied by internal wars, and Aragon conquests, there had been little aggression on the Moorish borderland, and a good deal of friendly intercourse both in the way of traffic and of courtesy, nor had the bitter persecution and distrust of new converts then set in, which followed the entire conquest of Granada. Thus, when Ronda was one of the first Moorish cities to surrender, a great merchant of the unrivalled sword-blades whose secret had been brought from Damascus, had, with all his family, been accepted gladly when he declared himself ready to submit and receive baptism. Miguel Abenali was one of the sons, and though his conversion had at first been mere compliance with his father's will and the family interests, he had become sufficiently convinced of Christian truth not to take part with his own people in the final struggle. Still, however, the inbred abhorrence of idolatry had influenced his manner of worship, and when, after half a lifetime, Granada had fallen, and the Inquisition had begun to take cognisance of new Christians from among the Moors as well as the Jews, there were not lacking spies to report the absence of all sacred images or symbols from the house of the wealthy merchant, and that neither he nor any of his family had been seen kneeling before the shrine of Nuestra Señora. The sons of Abenali did indeed feel strongly the power of the national reaction, and revolted from the religion which they saw cruelly enforced on their conquered countrymen. The Moor had been viewed as a gallant enemy, the Morisco was only a being to be distrusted and persecuted; and the efforts of the good Bishop of Granada, who had caused the Psalms, Gospels, and large portions of the Breviary to be translated into Arabic, were frustrated by the zeal of those who imagined that heresy lurked in the vernacular, and perhaps that objections to popular practices might be strengthened.

By order of Cardinal Ximenes, these Arabic versions were taken away and burnt; but Miguel Abenali had secured his own copy, and it was what he there learnt that withheld him from flying to his countrymen and resuming their faith when he found that the Christianity he had professed for forty years was no longer a protection to him. Having known the true Christ in the Gospel, he could not turn back to Mohammed, even though Christians persecuted in the Name they so little understood.

The crisis came in 1507, when Ximenes, apparently impelled by the dread that simulated conformity should corrupt the Church, quickened the persecution of the doubtful "Nuevos Cristianos," and the Abenali family, who had made themselves loved and respected, received warning that they had been denounced, and that their only hope lay in flight.

The two sons, high-spirited young men, on whom religion had far less hold than national feeling, fled to the Alpuxarra Mountains, and renouncing the faith of the persecutors, joined their countrymen in their gallant and desperate warfare. Their mother, who had long been dead, had never been more than an outward Christian; but the second wife of Abenali shared his belief and devotion with the intelligence and force of character sometimes found among the Moorish ladies of Spain. She and her little ones fled with him in disguise to Cadiz, with the precious Arabic Scriptures rolled round their waists, and took shelter with an English merchant, who had had dealings in sword-blades with Señor Miguel, and had been entertained by him in his beautiful Saracenic house at Ronda with Eastern hospitality. This he requited by giving them the opportunity of sailing for England in a vessel laden with Xeres sack; but the misery of the voyage across the Bay of Biscay in a ship lit for nothing but wine, was excessive, and creatures reared in the lovely climate and refined luxury of the land of the palm and orange, exhausted too already by the toils of the mountain journey, were incapable of enduring it, and Abenali's brave wife and one of her children were left beneath the waves of the Atlantic. With the one little girl left to him, he arrived in London, and the recommendation of his Cadiz friend obtained for him work from a dealer in foreign weapons, who was not unwilling to procure them nearer home. Happily for him, Moorish masters, however rich, were always required to be proficients in their own trade; and thus Miguel, or Michael as he was known in England, was able to maintain himself and his child by the fabrication of blades that no one could distinguish from those of Damascus. Their perfection was a work of infinite skill, labour, and industry, but they were so costly, that their price, and an occasional job of inlaying gold in other metal, sufficed to maintain the old man and his little daughter. The armourers themselves were sometimes forced to have recourse to him, though unwillingly, for he was looked on with distrust and dislike as an interloper of foreign birth, belonging to no guild. A Biscayan or Castillian of the oldest Christian blood incurred exactly the same obloquy from the mass of London craftsmen and apprentices, and Lucas himself had small measure of favour, though Dutchmen were less alien to the English mind than Spaniards, and his trade did not lead to so much rivalry and competition.

As much of this as Ambrose knew or understood he told to Stephen, who listened in a good deal of bewilderment, understanding very little, but with a strong instinct that his brother's love of learning was leading him into dangerous company. And what were they doing on this fine May holiday, when every one ought to be out enjoying themselves?

"Well, if thou wilt know," said Ambrose, pushed hard, "there is one Master William Tindal, who hath been doing part of the blessed Evangel into English, and for better certainty of its correctness, Master Michael was comparing it with his Arabic version, while I overlooked the Latin."

"O Ambrose, thou wilt surely run into trouble. Know you not how nurse Joan used to tell us of the burning of the Lollard books?"

"Nay, nay, Stevie, this is no heresy. 'Tis such work as the great scholar, Master Erasmus, is busied on—ay, and he is loved and honoured by both the Archbishops and the King's grace. Ask Tibble Steelman what he thinks thereof."

"Tibble Steelman would think nought of a beggarly stranger calling himself a sword-cutler, and practising the craft without prenticeship or license," said Stephen, swelling with indignation. "Come on, Ambrose, and sweep the cobwebs from thy brain. If we cannot get into our own tent again, we can mingle with the outskirts, and learn how the day is going, and how our lances and breastplates have stood where the knaves at the Eagle have gone like reeds and egg-shells—just as I threw George Bates, the prentice at the Eagle yesterday, in a wrestling match at the butts with the trick old Diggory taught me."

CHAPTER XII.

A King in a Quagmire.

"For my pastance
Hunt, sing, and dance,
My heart is set
All godly sport
To my comfort.
Who shall me let?"
The King's Balade,

attributed to Henry the Eighth.

Life was a rough, hearty thing in the early sixteenth century, strangely divided between thought and folly, hardship and splendour, misery and merriment, toil and sport.

The youths in the armourer's household had experienced little of this as yet in their country life, but in London they could not but soon begin to taste both sides of the matter. Master Headley himself was a good deal taken up with city affairs, and left the details of his business to Tibble Steelman and Kit Smallbones, though he might always appear on the scene, and he had a wonderful knowledge of what was going on.

The breaking-in and training of the two new country lads was entirely left to them and to Edmund Burgess. Giles soon found that complaints were of no avail, and only made matters harder for him, and that Tibble Steelman and Kit Smallbones had no notion of favouring their master's cousin.

Poor fellow, he was very miserable in those first weeks. The actual toil, to which he was an absolute novice, though nominally three years an apprentice, made his hands raw, and his joints full of aches, while his groans met with nothing but laughter; and he recognised with great displeasure, that more was laid on him than on Stephen Birkenholt. This was partly in consideration of Stephen's youth, partly of his ready zeal and cheerfulness. His hands might be sore too, but he was rather proud of it than otherwise, and his hero worship of Kit Smallbones made him run on errands, tug at the bellows staff, or fetch whatever was called for with a bright alacrity that won the foremens' hearts, and it was noted that he who was really a gentleman, had none of the airs that Giles Headley showed.

Giles began by some amount of bullying, by way of slaking his wrath at the preference shown for one whom he continued to style a beggarly brat picked up on the heath; but Stephen was good-humoured, and accustomed to give and take, and they both found their level, as well in the Dragon court as among the world outside, where the London prentices were a strong and redoubtable body, with rude, not to say cruel, rites of initiation among themselves, plenty of rivalries and enmities between house and house, guild and guild, but a united, not to say ferocious, *esprit de corps* against every one else. Fisticuffs and wrestlings were the amenities that passed between them, though always with a love of fair play so long as no cowardice, or what was looked on as such, was shown, for there was no mercy for the weak or weakly. Such had better betake themselves at once to the cloister, or life was made intolerable by constant jeers, blows, baiting and huntings, often, it must be owned, absolutely brutal.

Stephen and Giles had however passed through this ordeal. The letter to John Birkenholt had been despatched by a trusty clerk riding with the Judges of Assize, whom Mistress Perronel knew might be safely trusted, and who actually brought back a letter which might have emanated from the most affectionate of brothers, giving his authority for the binding Stephen apprentice to the worshipful Master Giles Headley, and sending the remainder of the boy's portion.

Stephen was thereupon regularly bound apprentice to Master Headley. It was a solemn affair, which took place in the Armourer's Hall in Coleman Street, before sundry witnesses. Harry Randall, in his soberest garb and demeanour, acted as guardian to his nephew, and presented him, clad in the regulation prentice garb—"flat round cap, close-cut hair, narrow falling bands, coarse side coat, close hose, cloth stockings," coat with the badge of the Armourers' Company, and Master Headley's own dragon's tail on the sleeve, to which was added a blue cloak marked in like manner. The instructions to apprentices were rehearsed, beginning, "Ye shall constantly and devoutly on your knees every day serve God, morning and evening,"—pledging him to "avoid evil company, to make speedy return when sent on his master's business, to be fair, gentle and lowly in speech and carriage with all men," and the like.

Mutual promises were interchanged between him and his master, Stephen on his knees; the indentures were signed, for Quipsome Hal could with much ado produce an autograph signature, though his penmanship went no further, and the occasion was celebrated by a great dinner of the whole craft at the Armourers' Hall, to which the principal craftsmen who had been apprentices, such as Tibble Steelman and Kit Smallbones, were invited, sitting at a lower table, while the masters had the higher one on the days, and a third was reserved for the apprentices after they should have waited on their masters—in fact it was an imitation of the orders of chivalry, knights, squires, and pages, and the gradation of rank was as strictly observed as by the nobility. Giles, considering the feast to be entirely in his honour, though the transfer of his indentures had been made at Salisbury, endeavoured to come out in some of his bravery, but was admonished that such presumption might be punished, the first time, at his master's discretion, the second time, by a whipping at the Hall of his Company, and the third time by six months being added to the term of his apprenticeship.

Master Randall was entertained in the place of honour, where he comported himself with great gravity, though he could not resist alarming Stephen with an occasional wink or gesture as the boy approached in the course of the duties of waiting at the upper board—a splendid sight with cups and flagons of gold and silver, with venison and capons and all that a City banquet could command before the invention of the turtle.

There was drinking of toasts, and among the foremost was that of Wolsey, who had freshly received his nomination of cardinal, and whose hat was on its way from Rome—and here the jester could not help betraying his knowledge of the domestic policy of the household, and telling the company how it had become known that the scarlet hat was actually on the way, but in a "varlet's budget—a mere Italian common knave, no better than myself," quoth Quip-some Hal, whereat his nephew trembled standing behind his chair, forgetting that the decorous solid man in the sad-coloured gown and well-crimped ruff, neatest of Perronel's performances, was no such base comparison for any varlet. Hal went on to describe, however, how my Lord of York had instantly sent to stay the messenger on his landing at Dover, and equip him with all manner of costly silks by way of apparel, and with attendants, such as might do justice to his freight, "that so," he said, "men may not rate it but as a scarlet cock's comb, since all men be but fools, and the sole question is, who among them hath wit enough to live by his folly." Therewith he gave a wink that so disconcerted Stephen as nearly to cause an upset of the bowl of perfumed water that he was bringing for the washing of hands.

Master Headley, however, suspected nothing, and invited the grave Master Randall to attend the domestic festival on the presentation of poor Spring's effigy at the shrine of Saint Julian. This was to take place early in the morning of the 14th of September, Holy Cross Day, the last holiday in the year that had any of the glory of summer about it, and on which the apprentices claimed a prescriptive right to go out nutting in Saint John's Wood, and to carry home their spoil to the lasses of their acquaintance.

Tibble Steelman had completed the figure in bronze, with a silver collar and chain, not quite without protest that the sum had better have been bestowed in alms. But from his master's point of view this would have been giving to a pack of lying beggars and thieves what was due to the holy saint; no one save Tibble, who could do and say what he chose, could have ventured on a word of remonstrance on such a subject; and as the full tide of iconoclasm, consequent on the discovery of the original wording of the second commandment, had not yet set in, Tibble had no more conscientious scruple against making the figure, than in moulding a little straight-tailed lion for Lord Harry Percy's helmet.

So the party in early morning heard their mass, and then, repairing to Saint Julian's pillar, while the rising sun came peeping through the low eastern window of the vaulted Church of Saint Faith, Master Headley on his knees gave thanks for his preservation, and then put forward his little daughter, holding on her joined hands the figure of poor Spring, couchant, and beautifully modelled in bronze with all Tibble's best skill.

Hal Randall and Ambrose had both come up from the little home where

Perronel presided, for the hour was too early for the jester's absence to be remarked in the luxurious household of the Cardinal elect, and he even came to break his fast afterwards at the Dragon court, and held such interesting discourse with old Dame Headley on the farthingales and coifs of Queen Katharine and her ladies, that she pronounced him a man wondrous wise and understanding, and declared Stephen happy in the possession of such a kinsman.

"And whither away now, youngsters?" he said, as he rose from table.

"To Saint John's Wood! The good greenwood, uncle," said Ambrose.

"Thou too, Ambrose?" said Stephen joyfully. "For once away from thine ink and thy books!"

"Ay," said Ambrose, "mine heart warms to the woodlands once more. Uncle, would that thou couldst come."

"Would that I could, boy! We three would show these lads of Cockayne what three foresters know of wood-craft! But it may not be. Were I once there, the old blood might stir again and I might bring you into trouble, and ye have not two faces under one hood as I have! So fare ye well, I wish you many a bagful of nuts!"

The four months of city life, albeit the City was little bigger than our moderate sized country towns, and far from being an unbroken mass of houses, had yet made the two young foresters delighted to enjoy a day of thorough country in one another's society. Little Dennet longed to go with them, but the prentice world was far too rude for little maidens to be trusted in it, and her father held out hopes of going one of these days to High Park as he called it, while Edmund and Stephen promised her all their nuts, and as many blackberries as could be held in their flat caps.

"Giles has promised me none," said Dennet, with a pouting lip, "nor Ambrose."

"Why sure, little mistress, thou'lt have enough to crack thy teeth on!" said Edmund Burgess.

"They *ought* to bring theirs to me," returned the little heiress of the Dragon court with an air of offended dignity that might have suited the heiress of the kingdom.

Giles, who looked on Dennet as a kind of needful appendage to the Dragon, a piece of property of his own, about whom he need take no trouble, merely laughed and said, "Want must be thy master then." But Ambrose treated her petulance in another fashion. "Look here, pretty mistress," said he, "there dwells by ne a poor little maid nigh about thine age, who never goeth further out than to Saint Paul's minster, nor plucketh flower, nor hath sweet cake, nor manchet bread, nor sugar-stick, nay, and scarce ever saw English hazel-nut nor blackberry. 'Tis for her that I want to gather them."

"Is she thy master's daughter?" demanded Dennet, who could admit the claims of another princess.

"Nay, my master hath no children, but she dwelleth near him."

"I will send her some, and likewise of mine own comfits and cakes," said

Mistress Dennet. "Only thou must bring all to me first."

Ambrose laughed and said, "It's a bargain then, little mistress?"

"I keep my word," returned Dennet marching away, while Ambrose obeyed a summons from good-natured Mistress Headley to have his wallet filled with bread and cheese like those of her own prentices.

Off went the lads under the guidance of Edmund Burgess, meeting parties of their own kind at every turn, soon leaving behind them the City bounds, as they passed under New Gate, and by and by skirting the fields of the great Carthusian monastery, or Charter House, with the burial-ground given by Sir Walter Manny at the time of the Black Death. Beyond came marshy ground through which they had to pick their way carefully, over stepping-stones—this being no other than what is now the Regent's Park, not yet in any degree drained by the New River, but all quaking ground, overgrown with rough grass and marsh-plants, through which Stephen and Ambrose bounded by the help of stout poles with feet and eyes well used to bogs, and knowing where to look for a safe footing, while many a flat-capped London lad floundered about and sank over his yellow ankles or left his shoes behind him, while lapwings shrieked pee-wheet, and almost flapped him with their broad wings, and moorhens dived in the dark pools, and wild ducks rose in long families.

Stephen was able to turn the laugh against his chief adversary and rival, George Bates of the Eagle, who proposed seeking for the lapwing's nest in hopes of a dainty dish of plovers' eggs; being too great a cockney to remember that in September the contents of the eggs were probably flying over the heather, as well able to shift for themselves as their parents.

Above all things the London prentices were pugnacious, but as every one joined in the laugh against George, and he was, besides, stuck fast on a quaking tussock of grass, afraid to proceed or advance, he could not have his revenge. And when the slough was passed, and the slight rise leading to the copse of Saint John's Wood was attained, behold, it was found to be in possession of the lower sort of lads, the black guard as they were called. They were of course quite as ready to fight with the prentices as the prentices were with them, and a battle royal took place, all along the front of the hazel bushes—in which Stephen of the Dragon and George of the Eagle fought side by side. Sticks and fists were the weapons, and there were no very severe casualties before the prentices, being the larger number as well as the stouter and better fed, had routed their adversaries, and driven them off towards Harrow.

There was crackling of boughs and filling of bags, and cracking of nuts, and wild cries in pursuit of startled hare or rabbit, and though Ambrose and Stephen indignantly repelled the idea of Saint John's Wood being named in the same day with their native forest, it is doubtful whether they had ever enjoyed themselves more; until just as they were about to turn homeward, whether moved by his hostility to Stephen, or by envy at the capful of juicy blackberries, carefully covered with green leaves, George Bates, rushing up from behind, shouted out, "Here's a skulker! Here's one of the black guard! Off to thy fellows, varlet!" at the same time dealing a dexterous blow under the cap, which sent the blackberries up into Ambrose's face. "Ha! ha!" shouted the ill-conditioned fellow. "So much for a knave that serves rascally strangers! Here! hand over that bag of nuts!"

Ambrose was no fighter, but in defence of the bag that was to purchase a treat for little Aldonza, he clenched his fists, and bade George Bates come and take them if he would. The quiet scholarly boy was, however, no match for the young armourer, and made but poor reply to the buffets of his adversary, who had hold of the bag, and was nearly choking him with the string round his neck.

However, Stephen had already missed his brother, and turning round, shouted out that the villain Bates was mauling him, and rushed back, falling on Ambrose's assailant with a sudden well-directed pommelling that made him hastily turn about, with cries of "Two against one!"

"Not at all," said Stephen. "Stand by, Ambrose; I'll give the coward his deserts."

In fact, though the boys were nearly of a size, George somewhat the biggest, Stephen's country activity, and perhaps the higher spirit of his gentle blood, generally gave him the advantage, and on this occasion he soon reduced Bates to roar for mercy.

"Thou must purchase it!" said Stephen. "Thy bag of nuts, in return for the berries thou hast wasted!"

Peaceable Ambrose would have remonstrated, but Stephen was implacable. He cut the string, and captured the bag, then with a parting kick bade Bates go after his comrades, for his Eagle was nought but a thieving kite.

Bates made off pretty quickly, but the two brothers tarried a little to see how much damage the blackberries had suffered, and to repair the losses as they descended into the bog by gathering some choice dewberries.

"I marvel these fine fellows 'scaped our company," said Stephen presently.

"Are we in the right track, thinkst thou? Here is a pool I marked not before," said Ambrose anxiously.

"Nay, we can't be far astray while we see Saint Paul's spire and the Tower full before us," said Stephen. "Plainer marks than we had at home."

"That may be. Only where is the safe footing?" said Ambrose. "I wish we had not lost sight of the others!"

"Pish! what good are a pack of City lubbers!" returned Stephen. "Don't we know a quagmire when we see one, better than they do?"

"Hark, they are shouting for us."

"Not they! That's a falconer's call. There's another whistle! See, there's the hawk. She's going down the wind, as I'm alive," and Stephen began to bound wildly along, making all the sounds and calls by which falcons were recalled, and holding up as a lure a lapwing which he had knocked down. Ambrose, by no means so confident in bog-trotting as his brother, stood still to await him, hearing the calls and shouts of the falconer coming nearer, and presently seeing a figure, flying by the help of a pole over the pools and dykes that here made some attempt at draining the waste. Suddenly, in mid career over one of these broad ditches, there was a collapse, and a lusty shout for help as the form disappeared. Ambrose instantly perceived what had happened, the leaping pole had broken to the downfall of its owner. Forgetting all his doubts as to bogholes and morasses, he grasped his own pole, and sprang from tussock to tussock, till he had reached the bank of the ditch or water-course in which the unfortunate sportsman was floundering. He was a large, powerful man, but this was of no avail, for the slough afforded no foothold. The further side was a steep bank built up of sods, the nearer sloped down gradually, and though it was not apparently very deep, the efforts of the victim to struggle out had done nothing but churn up a mass of black muddy water in which he sank deeper every moment, and it was already nearly to his shoulders when with a cry of joy, half choked however, by the mud, he cried, "Ha! my good lad! Are there any more of ye?"

"Not nigh, I fear," said Ambrose, beholding with some dismay the breadth of the shoulders which were all that appeared above the turbid water.

"Soh! Lie down, boy, behind that bunch of osier. Hold out thy pole. Let me see thine hands. Thou art but a straw, but, our Lady be my speed! Now hangs England on a pair of wrists!"

There was a great struggle, an absolute effort for life, and but for the osier stump Ambrose would certainly have been dragged into the water, when the man had worked along the pole, and grasping his hands, pulled himself upwards. Happily the sides of the dyke became harder higher up, and did not instantly yield to the pressure of his knees, and by the time Ambrose's hands and shoulders felt nearly wrenched from their sockets, the stem of the osier had been attained, and in another minute, the rescued man, bareheaded, plastered with mud, and streaming with water, sat by him on the bank, panting, gasping, and trying to gather breath and clear his throat from the mud he had swallowed.

"Thanks, good lad, well done," he articulated. "Those fellows! where are they?" And feeling in his bosom, he brought out a gold whistle suspended by a chain. "Blow it," he said, taking off the chain, "my mouth is too full of slime."

Ambrose blew a loud shrill call, but it seemed to reach no one but Stephen, whom he presently saw dashing towards them.

"Here is my brother coming, sir," he said, as he gave his endeavours to help the stranger to free himself from the mud that clung to him, and which was in some places thick enough to be scraped off with a knife. He kept up a continual interchange of exclamations at his plight, whistles and shouts for his people, and imprecations on their tardiness, until Stephen was near enough to show that the hawk had been recovered, and then he joyfully called out, "Ha! hast thou got her? Why, flat-caps as ye are, ye put all my fellows to shame! How now, thou errant bird, dost know thy master, or take him for a mud wall? Kite that thou art, to have led me such a dance! And what's your name, my brave lads? Ye must have been bred to wood-craft."

Ambrose explained both their parentage and their present occupation, but was apparently heeded but little. "Wot ye how to get out of this quagmire?" was the question.

"I never was here before, sir," said Stephen; "but yonder lies the Tower, and if we keep along by this dyke, it must lead us out somewhere."

"Well said, boy, I must be moving, or the mud will dry on me, and I shall stand here as though I were turned to stone by the Gorgon's head! So have with thee! Go on first, master hawk-tamer. What will bear thee will bear me!"

There was an imperative tone about him that surprised the brothers, and Ambrose looking at him from head to foot, felt sure that it was some great man at the least, whom it had been his hap to rescue. Indeed, he began to have further suspicions when they came to a pool of clearer water, beyond which was firmer ground, and the stranger with an exclamation of joy, borrowed Stephen's cap, and, scooping up the water with it, washed his face and head, disclosing the golden hair and beard, fair complexion, and handsome square face he had seen more than once before.

He whispered to Stephen, "'Tis the King!"

"Ha! ha!" laughed Henry, "hast found him out, lads? Well, it may not be the worse for ye. Pity thou shouldst not be in the Forest still, my young falconer, but we know our good city of London too well to break thy indentures. And thou—"

He was turning to Ambrose when further shouts were heard. The King hallooed, and bade the boys do so, and in a few moments more they were surrounded by the rest of the hawking party, full of dismay at the king's condition, and deprecating his anger for having lost him.

"Yea," said Henry; "an it had not been for this good lad, ye would never have heard more of the majesty of England! Swallowed in a quagmire had made a new end for a king, and ye would have to brook the little Scot."

The gentlemen who had come up were profuse in lamentations. A horse was brought up for the king's use, and he prepared to mount, being in haste to get into dry clothes. He turned round, however, to the boys, and said, "I'll not forget you, my lads. Keep that!" he added, as Ambrose, on his knee, would have given him back the whistle, "'tis a token that maybe will serve thee, for I shall know it again. And thou, my black-eyed lad—My purse, Howard!"

He handed the purse to Stephen—a velvet bag richly wrought with gold, and containing ten gold angels, besides smaller money—bidding them divide, like good brothers as he saw they were, and then galloped off with his train.

Twilight was coming on, but following in the direction of the riders, the boys were soon on the Islington road. The New Gate was shut by the time they reached it, and their explanation that they were belated after a nutting expedition would not have served them, had not Stephen produced the sum of twopence which softened the surliness of the guard.

It was already dark, and though curfew had not yet sounded, preparations were making for lighting the watch-fires in the open spaces and throwing chains across the streets, but the little door in the Dragon court was open, and Ambrose went in with his brother to deliver up his nuts to Dennet and claim her promise of sending a share to Aldonza.

They found their uncle in his sober array sitting by Master Headley, who was rating Edmund and Giles for having lost sight of them, the latter excusing himself by grumbling out that he could not be marking all Stephen's brawls with George Bates.

When the two wanderers appeared, relief took the form of anger, and there were sharp demands why they had loitered. Their story was listened to with many exclamations: Dennet jumped for joy, her grandmother advised that the angels should be consigned to her own safe keeping, and when Master Headley heard of Henry's scruples about the indentures, he declared that it was a rare wise king who knew that an honest craft was better than court favour.

"Yet mayhap he might do something for thee, friend Ambrose," added the armourer. "Commend thee to some post in his chapel royal, or put thee into some college, since such is thy turn. How sayst thou, Master Randall, shall he send in this same token, and make his petition?"

"If a foo— if a plain man may be heard where the wise hath spoken," said Randall, "he had best abstain. Kings love not to be minded of mishaps, and our Hal's humour is not to be reckoned on! Lay up the toy in case of need, but an thou claim overmuch he may mind thee in a fashion not to thy taste."

"Sure our King is of a more generous mould!" exclaimed Mrs. Headley.

"He is like other men, good mistress, just as you know how to have him, and he is scarce like to be willing to be minded of the taste of mire, or of floundering like a hog in a salt marsh. Ha! ha!" and Quipsome Hal went off into such a laugh as might have betrayed his identity to any one more accustomed to the grimaces of his professional character, but which only infected the others with the same contagious merriment. "Come thou home now," he said to Ambrose; "my good woman hath been in a mortal fright about thee, and would have me come out to seek after thee. Such are the women folk, Master Headley. Let them have but a lad to look after, and they'll bleat after him like an old ewe that has lost her lamb."

Ambrose only stayed for Dennet to divide the spoil, and though the blackberries had all been lost or crushed, the little maiden kept her promise generously, and filled the bag not only with nuts but with three red-cheeked apples, and a handful of comfits, for the poor little maid who never tasted fruit or sweets.

CHAPTER XIII.

A London Holiday.

"Up then spoke the apprentices tall
Living in London, one and all."

Old Ballad.

Another of the many holidays of the Londoners was enjoyed on the occasion of the installation of Thomas Wolsey as Cardinal of Saint Cecilia, and Papal Legate.

A whole assembly of prelates and "lusty gallant gentlemen" rode out to Blackheath to meet the Roman envoy, who, robed in full splendour, with Saint Peter's keys embroidered on back and breast and on the housings of his mule, appeared at the head of a gallant train in the papal liveries, two of whom carried the gilded pillars, the insignia of office, and two more, a scarlet and gold-covered box or casket containing the Cardinal's hat. Probably no such reception of the dignity was ever prepared elsewhere, and all was calculated to give magnificent ideas of the office of Cardinal and of the power of the Pope to those who had not been let into the secret that the messenger had been met at Dover; and thus magnificently fitted out to satisfy the requirements of the butcher's son of Ipswich, and of one of the most ostentatious of courts.

Old Gaffer Martin Fulford had muttered in his bed that such pomp had not been the way in the time of the true old royal blood, and that display had come in with the upstart slips of the Red Rose—as he still chose to style the Tudors; and he maundered away about the beauty and affability of Edward the Fourth till nobody could understand him, and Perronel only threw in her "ay, grandad," or "yea, gaffer," when she thought it was expected of her.

Ambrose had an unfailing appetite for the sermons of Dean Colet, who was to preach on this occasion in Westminster Abbey, and his uncle had given him counsel how to obtain standing ground there, entering before the procession. He was alone, his friends Tibble and Lucas both had that part of the Lollard temper which loathed the pride and wealth of the great political clergy, and in spite of their admiration for the Dean they could not quite forgive his taking part in the pomp of such a raree-show.

But Ambrose's devotion to the Dean, to say nothing of youthful curiosity, outweighed all those scruples, and as he listened, he was carried along by the curious sermon in which the preacher likened the orders of the hierarchy below to that of the nine orders of the Angels, making the rank of Cardinal correspond to that of the Seraphim, aglow with love. Of that holy flame, the scarlet robes were the type to the spiritualised mind of Colet, while others saw in them only the relic of the imperial purple of old Rome; and some beheld them as the token that Wolsey was one step nearer the supreme height that he coveted so earnestly. But the great and successful man found himself personally addressed, bidden not to be puffed up with his own greatness, and stringently reminded of the highest example of humility, shown that he that exalteth himself shall be abased, and he that humbleth himself be exalted. The preacher concluded with a strong personal exhortation to do righteousness and justice alike to rich and poor, joined with truth and mercy, setting God always before him.

The sermon ended, Wolsey knelt at the altar, and Archbishop Wareham, who, like his immediate predecessors, held legatine authority, performed the act of investiture, placing the scarlet hat with its many loops and tassels on his brother primate's head, after which a magnificent *Te Deum* rang through the beautiful church, and the procession of prelates, peers, and ecclesiastics of all ranks in their richest array formed to escort the new Cardinal to banquet at his palace with the King and Queen.

Ambrose, stationed by a column, let the throng rush, tumble, and jostle one another to behold the show, till the Abbey was nearly empty, while he tried to work out the perplexing question whether all this pomp and splendour were truly for the glory of God, or whether it were a delusion for the temptation of men's souls. It was a debate on which his old and his new guides seemed to him at issue, and he was drawn in both directions—now by the beauty, order, and deep symbolism of the Catholic ritual, now by the spirituality and earnestness of the men among whom he lived. At one moment the worldly pomp, the mechanical and irreverent worship, and the gross and vicious habits of many of the clergy repelled him; at another the reverence and conservatism of his nature held him fast.

Presently he felt a hand on his shoulder, and started, "Lost in a stud, as we say at home, boy," said the jester, resplendent in a bran new motley suit. "Wilt come in to the banquet? 'Tis open house, and I can find thee a seat without disclosing the kinship that sits so sore on thy brother. Where is he?"

"I have not seen him this day."

"That did I," returned Randall, "as I rode by on mine ass. He was ruffling it so lustily that I could not but give him a wink, the which my gentleman could by no means stomach! Poor lad! Yet there be times, Ambrose, when I feel in sooth that mine office is the only honourable one, since who besides can speak truth? I love my lord; he is a kind, open-handed master, and there's none I would so willingly serve, whether by jest or earnest, but what is he but that which I oft call him in joke—the greater fool than I, selling peace and ease, truth and hope, this life and the next, for yonder scarlet hat, which is after all of no more worth than this jingling head-gear of mine."

"Deafening the spiritual ears far more, it may be," said Ambrose, "since *humiles exaltaverint.*"

It was no small shock that there, in the midst of the nave, the answer was a bound, like a ball, almost as high as the capital of the column by which they stood. "There's exaltation!" said Randall in a low voice, and Ambrose perceived that some strangers were in sight. "Come, seek thy brother out, boy, and bring him to the banquet. I'll speak a word to Peter Porter, and he'll let you in.

There'll be plenty of fooling all the afternoon, before my namesake King Hal, who can afford to be an honester man in his fooling than any about him, and whose laugh at a hearty jest is goodly to hear."

Ambrose thanked him and undertook the quest. They parted at the great west door of the Abbey, where, by way of vindicating his own character for buffoonery, Randall exclaimed, "Where be mine ass?" and not seeing the animal, immediately declared, "There he is!" and at the same time sprang upon the back and shoulders of a gaping and astonished clown who was gazing at the rear of the procession.

The crowd applauded with shouts of coarse laughter, but a man, who seemed to belong to the victim, broke in with an angry oath, and "How now, sir?"

"I cry you mercy," quoth the jester; "'twas mine own ass I sought, and if I have fallen on thine, I will but ride him to York House and then restore him. So ho! good jackass," crossing his ankles on the poor fellow's chest so that he could not be shaken off.

The comrade lifted a cudgel, but there was a general cry of "My Lord Cardinal's jester, lay not a finger on him!"

But Harry Randall was not one to brook immunity on the score of his master's greatness. In another second he was on his feet, had wrested the staff from the hands of his astounded beast of burden, flourished it round his head after the most approved manner of Shirley champions at Lyndhurst fair, and called to his adversary to "come on."

It did not take many rounds before Hal's dexterity had floored his adversary, and the shouts of "Well struck, merry fool!" "Well played, Quipsome Hal!" were rising high when the Abbot of Westminster's yeomen were seen making way through the throng, which fell back in terror on either side as they came to seize on the brawlers in their sacred precincts.

But here again my Lord Cardinal's fool was a privileged person, and no one laid a hand on him, though his blood being up, he would, spite of his gay attire, have enjoyed a fight on equal terms. His quadruped donkey was brought up to him amid general applause, but when he looked round for Ambrose, the boy had disappeared.

The better and finer the nature that displayed itself in Randall, the more painful was the sight of his buffooneries to his nephew, and at the first leap, Ambrose had hurried away in confusion. He sought his brother here, there, everywhere, and at last came to the conclusion that Stephen must have gone home to dinner. He walked quickly across the fields separating Westminster from the City of London, hoping to reach Cheapside before the lads of the Dragon should have gone out again; but just as he was near Saint Paul's, coming round Amen Corner, he heard the sounds of a fray. "Have at the country lubbers! Away with the moonrakers! Flat-caps, come on!" "Hey! lads of the Eagle! Down with the Dragons! Adders! Snakes–s–s s–s–s!"

There was a kicking, struggling mass of blue backs and yellow legs before him, from out of which came "Yah! Down with the Eagles! Cowards! Kites!

Cockneys!" There were plenty of boys, men, women with children in their arms hallooing on, "Well done, Eagle!" "Go it, Dragon!"

The word Dragon filled the quiet Ambrose with hot impulse to defend his brother. All his gentle, scholarly habits gave way before that cry, and a shout that he took to be Stephen's voice in the midst of the *mêlée*.

He was fairly carried out of himself, and doubling his fists, fell on the back of the nearest boys, intending to break through to his brother, and he found an unexpected ally. Will Wherry's voice called out, "Have with you, comrade!"—and a pair of hands and arms considerably stouter and more used to fighting than his own, began to pommel right and left with such good will that they soon broke through to the aid of their friends; and not before it was time, for Stephen, Giles, and Edmund, with their backs against the wall, were defending themselves with all their might against tremendous odds; and just as the new allies reached them, a sharp stone struck Giles in the eye, and levelled him with the ground, his head striking against the wall. Whether it were from alarm at his fall, or at the unexpected attack in the rear, or probably from both causes, the assailants dispersed in all directions without waiting to perceive how slender the succouring force really was.

Edmund and Stephen were raising up the unlucky Giles, who lay quite insensible, with blood pouring from his eye. Ambrose tried to wipe it away, and there were anxious doubts whether the eye itself were safe. They were some way from home, and Giles was the biggest and heaviest of them all.

"Would that Kit Smallbones were here!" said Stephen, preparing to take the feet, while Edmund took the shoulders.

"Look here," said Will Wherry, pulling Ambrose's sleeve, "our yard is much nearer, and the old Moor, Master Michael, is safe to know what to do for him. That sort of cattle always are leeches. He wiled the pain from my thumb when 'twas crushed in our printing-press. Mayhap if he put some salve to him, he might get home on his own feet."

Edmund listened. "There's reason in that," he said. "Dost know this leech, Ambrose?"

"I know him well. He is a good old man, and wondrous wise. Nay, no black arts; but he saith his folk had great skill in herbs and the like, and though he be no physician by trade, he hath much of their lore."

"Have with thee, then," returned Edmund, "the rather that Giles is no small weight, and the guard might come on us ere we reached the Dragon."

"Or those cowardly rogues of the Eagle might set on us again," added Stephen; and as they went on their way to Warwick Inner Ward, he explained that the cause of the encounter had been that Giles had thought fit to prank himself in his father's silver chain, and thus George Bates, always owing the Dragon a grudge, and rendered specially malicious since the encounter on Holy Rood Day, had raised the cry against him, and caused all the flat-caps around to make a rush at the gaud as lawful prey.

"'Tis clean against prentice statutes to wear one, is it not?" asked Ambrose.

"Ay," returned Stephen; "yet none of us but would stand up for our own comrade against those meddling fellows of the Eagle."

"But," added Edmund, "we must beware the guard, for if they looked into the cause of the fray, our master might he called on to give Giles a whipping in the Company's hall, this being a second offence of going abroad in these vanities."

Ambrose went on before to prepare Miguel Abenali, and entreat his good offices, explaining that the youth's master, who was also his kinsman, would be sure to give handsome payment for any good offices to him. He scarcely got out half the words; the grand old Arab waved his hand and said, "When the wounded is laid before the tent of Ben Ali, where is the question of recompense? Peace be with thee, my son! Bring him hither. Aldonza, lay the carpet yonder, and the cushions beneath the window, where I may have light to look to his hurt."

Therewith he murmured a few words in an unknown tongue, which, as Ambrose understood, were an invocation to the God of Abraham to bless his endeavours to heal the stranger youth, but which happily were spoken before the arrival of the others, who would certainly have believed them an incantation.

The carpet though worn threadbare, was a beautiful old Moorish rug, once glowing with brilliancy, and still rich in colouring, and the cushion was of thick damask faded to a strange pale green. All in that double-stalled partition, once belonging to the great earl's war-horses, was scrupulously clean, for the Christian Moor had retained some of the peculiar virtues born of Mohammedanism and of high civilisation. The apprentice lads tramped in much as if they had been entering a wizard's cave, though Stephen had taken care to assure Edmund of his application of the test of holy water.

Following the old man's directions, Edmund and Stephen deposited their burden on the rug. Aldonza brought some warm water, and Abenali washed and examined the wound, Aldonza standing by and handing him whatever he needed, now and then assisting with her slender brown hands in a manner astonishing to the youths, who stood by anxious and helpless, while their companion began to show signs of returning life.

Abenali pronounced that the stone had missed the eyeball, but the cut and bruise were such as to require constant bathing, and the blow on the head was the more serious matter, for when the patient tried to raise himself he instantly became sick and giddy, so that it would be wise to leave him where he was. This was much against the will of Edmund Burgess, who shared all the prejudices of the English prentice against the foreigner—perhaps a wizard and rival in trade; but there was no help for it, and he could only insist that Stephen should mount guard over the bed until he had reported to his master, and returned with his orders. Therewith he departed, with such elaborate thanks and courtesies to the host, as betrayed a little alarm in the tall apprentice, who feared not quarter-staff, nor wrestler, and had even dauntlessly confronted the masters of his guild!

Stephen, sooth to say, was not very much at ease; everything around had such a strange un-English aspect, and he imploringly muttered, "Bide with me, Am!" to which his brother willingly assented, being quite as comfortable in Master Michael's abode as by his aunt's own hearth.

Giles meanwhile lay quiet and then, as his senses became less confused, and he could open one eye, he looked dreamily about him, and presently began to demand where he was, and what had befallen him, grasping at the hand of Ambrose as if to hold fast by something familiar; but he still seemed too much dazed to enter into the explanation, and presently murmured something about thirst. Aldonza came softly up with a cup of something cool. He looked very hard at her, and when Ambrose would have taken it from her hand to give it to him, he said, "Nay! *Site!*"

And *site*, with a sweet smile in her soft, dark, shady eyes, and on her full lips, held the cup to his lips far more daintily and dexterously than either of his boy companions could have done; then when he moaned and said his head and eye pained him, the white-bearded elder came and bathed his brow with the soft sponge. It seemed all to pass before him like a dream, and it was not much otherwise with his unhurt companions, especially Stephen, who followed with wonder the movements made by the slippered feet of father and daughter upon the mats which covered the stone flooring of the old stable. The mats were only of English rushes and flags, and had been woven by Abenali and the child; but loose rashes strewing the floor were accounted a luxury in the Forest, and even at the Dragon court the upper end of the hall alone had any covering. Then the water was heated, and all such other operations carried on over a curious round vessel placed over charcoal; the window and the door had dark heavy curtains; and a matted partition cut off the further stall, no doubt to serve as Aldonza's chamber. Stephen looked about for something to assure him that the place belonged to no wizard enchanter, and was glad to detect a large white cross on the wall, with a holy-water stoup beneath it, but of images there were none.

It seemed to him a long time before Master Headley's ruddy face, full of anxiety, appeared at the door.

Blows were, of course, no uncommon matter; perhaps so long as no permanent injury was inflicted, the master-armourer had no objection to anything that might knock the folly out of his troublesome young inmate; but Edmund had made him uneasy for the youth's eye, and still more so about the quarters he was in, and he had brought a mattress and a couple of men to carry the patient home, as well as Steelman, his prime minister, to advise him.

He had left all these outside, however, and advanced, civilly and condescendingly thanking the sword-cutler, in perfect ignorance that the man who stood before him had been born to a home that was an absolute palace compared with the Dragon court. The two men were a curious contrast. There stood the Englishman with his sturdy form inclining, with age, to corpulence, his broad honest face telling of many a civic banquet, and his short stubbly brown grizzled beard; his whole air giving a sense of worshipful authority and weight; and opposite to him the sparely made, dark, thin, aquiline-faced, white-bearded Moor, a far smaller man in stature, yet with a patriarchal dignity, refinement, and grace in port and countenance, belonging as it were to another sphere.

Speaking English perfectly, though with a foreign accent, Abenali informed Master Headley that his young kinsman would by Heaven's blessing soon recover without injury to the eye, though perhaps a scar might remain.

Mr. Headley thanked him heartily for his care, and said that he had brought men to carry the youth home, if he could not walk; and then he went up to the couch with a hearty "How now, Giles? So thou hast had hard measure to knock the foolery out of thee, my poor lad. But come, we'll have thee home, and my mother will see to thee."

"I cannot walk," said Giles, heavily, hardly raising his eyes, and when he was told that two of the men waited to bear him home, he only entreated to be let alone. Somewhat sharply, Mr. Headley ordered him to sit up and make ready, but when he tried to do so, he sank back with a return of sickness and dizziness.

Abenali thereupon intreated that he might be left to his care for that night, and stepping out into the court so as to be unheard by the patient, explained that the brain had had a shock, and that perfect quiet for some hours to come was the only way to avert a serious illness, possibly dangerous. Master Headley did not like the alternative at all, and was a good deal perplexed. He beckoned to Tibble Steelman, who had all this time been talking to Lucas Hansen, and now came up prepared with his testimony that this Michael was a good man and true, a godly one to boot, who had been wealthy in his own land and was a rare artificer in his own craft.

"Though he hath no license to practise it here," threw in Master Headley, *sotto voce*; but he accepted the assurance that Michael was a good Christian, and, with his daughter, regularly went to mass; and since better might not be, he reluctantly consented to leave Giles under his treatment, on Lucas reiterating the assurance that he need have no fears of magic or foul play of any sort. He then took the purse that hung at his girdle, and declared that Master Michael, (the title of courtesy was wrung from him by the stately appearance of the old man), must be at no charges for his cousin.

But Abenali with a grace that removed all air of offence from his manner, returned thanks for the intention, but declared that it never was the custom of the sons of Ali to receive reward for the hospitality they exercised to the stranger within their gates. And so it was that Master Headley, a good deal puzzled, had to leave his apprentice under the roof of the old sword-cutler for the night at least.

"'Tis passing strange," said he, as he walked back; "I know not what my mother will say, but I wish all may be right. I feel—I feel as if I had left the lad Giles with Abraham under the oak tree, as we saw him in the miracle play!"

This description did not satisfy Mrs. Headley, indeed she feared that her son was likewise bewitched; and when, the next morning, Stephen, who had been sent to inquire for the patient, reported him better, but still unable to be moved, since he could not lift his head without sickness, she became very anxious. Giles was transformed in her estimate from a cross-grained slip to poor Robin Headley's boy, the only son of a widow, and nothing would content her but to make her son conduct her to Warwick Inner Ward to inspect matters, and carry thither a precious relic warranted proof against all sorcery.

It was with great trepidation that the good old dame ventured, but the result was that she was fairly subdued by Abenali's patriarchal dignity. She had never seen any manners to equal his, not *even* when King Edward the Fourth had come to her father's house at the Barbican, chucked her under the chin, and called her a dainty duck!

It was Aldonza, however, who specially touched her feelings. Such a sweet little wench, with the air of being bred in a kingly or knightly court, to be living there close to the very dregs of the city was a scandal and a danger—speaking so prettily too, and knowing how to treat her elders. She would be a good example for Dennet, who, sooth to say, was getting too old for spoilt-child sauciness to be always pleasing, while as to Giles, he could not be in better quarters. Mrs. Headley, well used to the dressing of the burns and bruises incurred in the weapon-smiths' business, could not but confess that his eye had been dealt with as skilfully as she could have done it herself.

CHAPTER XIV.

The Knight of the Badger.

"I am a gentleman of a company."

Shakespeare.

Giles Headley's accident must have amounted to concussion of the brain, for though he was able to return to the Dragon in a couple of days, and the cut over his eye was healing fast, he was weak and shaken, and did not for several weeks recover his usual health.

The noise and heat of the smithy were distressing to him, and there was no choice but to let him lie on settles, sun himself on the steps, and attempt no work.

It had tamed him a good deal. Smallbones said the letting out of malapert blood was wholesome, and others thought him still under a spell; but he seemed to have parted with much of his arrogance, either because he had not spirits for self-assertion, or because something of the grand eastern courtesy of Abenali had impressed him. For intercourse with the Morisco had by no means ceased. Giles went, as long as the injury required it, to have the hurt dressed, and loitered in the Inner Ward a long time every day, often securing some small dainty for Aldonza—an apple, a honey cake, a bit of marchpane, a dried plum, or a comfit. One day he took her a couple of oranges. To his surprise, as he entered, Abenali looked up with a strange light in his eyes, and exclaimed, "My son! thy scent is to my nostrils as the court of my fathouse!" Then, as he beheld the orange, he clasped his hands, took it in them, and held it to his breast, pouring out a chant in an unknown tongue, while the tears flowed down his cheeks.

"Father, father!" Aldonza cried, terrified, while Giles marvelled whether the orange worked on him like a spell. But he perceived their amazement, and spoke again in English, "I thank thee, my son! Thou hast borne me back for a moment to the fountain in my father's house, where ye grow, ye trees of the unfading leaf, the spotless blossom, and golden fruit! Ah Ronda! Ronda! Land of the sunshine, the deep blue sky, and snow-topped hills! Land where are the graves of my father and mother! How pines and sickens the heart of the exile for thee! O happy they who died beneath the sword or flame, for they knew not the lonely home-longing of the exile. Ah! ye golden fruits! One fragrant breath of thee is as a waft of the joys of my youth! Are ye foretastes of the fruits of Paradise, the true home to which I may yet come, though I may never, never see the towers and hills of Ronda more?"

Giles knew not what to make of this outburst. He kept it to himself as too strange to be told. The heads of the family were willing that he should carry these trifles to the young child of the man who would accept no reward for his hospitality. Indeed, Master Headley spent much consideration on how to recompense the care bestowed on his kinsman.

Giles suggested that Master Michael had just finished the most beautiful sword blade he had ever seen, and had not yet got a purchaser for it; it was far superior to the sword Tibble had just completed for my Lord of Surrey. Thereat the whole court broke into an outcry; that any workman should be supposed to turn out any kind of work surpassing Steelman's was rank heresy, and Master Headley bluntly told Giles that he knew not what he was talking of! He might perhaps purchase the blade by way of courtesy and return of kindness, but—good English workmanship for him!

However, Giles was allowed to go and ask the price of the blade, and bring it to be looked at. When he returned to the court he found, in front of the building where finished suits were kept for display, a tall, thin, wiry, elderly man, deeply bronzed, and with a scar on his brow. Master Headley and Tibble were both in attendance, Tib measuring the stranger, and Stephen, who was standing at a respectful distance, gave Giles the information that this was the famous Captain of Free-lances, Sir John Fulford, who had fought in all the wars in Italy, and was going to fight in them again, but wanted a suit of "our harness."

The information was hardly needed, for Sir John, in a voice loud enough to lead his men to the battle-field, and with all manner of strong asseverations in all sorts of languages, was explaining the dints and blows that had befallen the mail he had had from Master Headley eighteen years ago, when he was but a squire; how his helmet had endured tough blows, and saved his head at Novara, but had been crushed like an egg shell by a stone from the walls at Barletta, which had nearly been his own destruction: and how that which he at present wore (beautifully chased and in a classical form) was taken from a dead Italian Count on the field of Ravenna, but always sat amiss on him; and how he had broken his good sword upon one of the rascally Swiss only a couple of months ago at Marignano. Having likewise disabled his right arm, and being well off through the payment of some ransoms, he had come home partly to look after his family, and partly to provide himself with a full suit of English harness, his present suit being a patchwork of relics of numerous battle-fields. Only one thing he desired, a true Spanish sword, not only Toledo or Bilboa in name, but nature. He had seen execution done by the weapons of the soldiers of the Great Captain, and been witness to the endurance of their metal, and this made him demand whether Master Headley could provide him with the like.

Giles took the moment for stepping forward and putting Abenali's work into the master's hand. The Condottiere was in raptures. He pronounced it as perfect a weapon as Gouzalo de Cordova himself could possess; showed off its temper and his own dexterity by piercing and cutting up an old cuirass, and invited the bystanders to let him put it to further proof by letting him slice through an apple placed on the open palm of the hand.

Giles's friendship could not carry him so far as to make the venture; Kit Smallbones observed that he had a wife and children, and could not afford to risk his good right hand on a wandering soldier's bravado; Edmund was heard saying, "Nay, nay, Steve, don't be such a fool," but Stephen was declaring he would not have the fellow say that English lads hunt back from what rogues of France and Italy would dare.

"No danger for him who winceth not," said the knight.

Master Headley, a very peaceful citizen in his composition in spite of his trade, was much inclined to forbid Stephen from the experiment, but he refrained, ashamed and unwilling to daunt a high spirit; and half the household, eager for the excitement, rushed to the kitchen in quest of apples, and brought out all the women to behold, and add a clamour of remonstrance.

Sir John, however, insisted that they should all be ordered back again. "Not that the noise and clamour of women folk makes any odds to me," said the grim old warrior, "I've seen too many towns taken for that, but it might make the lad queasy, and cost him a thumb or so."

Of course this renewed the dismay and excitement, and both Tibble and his master entreated Stephen to give up the undertaking if he felt the least misgiving as to his own steadiness, arguing that they should not think him any more a craven than they did Kit Smallbones or Edmund Burgess. But Stephen's mind was made up, his spirit was high, and he was resolved to go through with it.

He held out his open hand, a rosy-checked apple was carefully laid on it. The sword flashed through the air—divided in half the apple which remained on Stephen's palm. There was a sharp shriek from a window, drowned in the acclamations of the whole court, while the Captain patted Stephen on the shoulder, exclaiming, "Well done, my lad. There's the making of a tall fellow in thee! If ever thou art weary of making weapons and wouldst use them instead, seek out John Fulford, of the Badger troop, and thou shalt have a welcome. Our name is the Badger, because there's no troop like us for digging out mines beneath the walls."

A few months ago such an invitation would have been bliss to Stephen. Now he was bound in all honour and duty to his master, and could only thank the knight of the Badger, and cast a regretful eye at him, as he drank a cup of wine, and flung a bag of gold and silver, supplemented by a heavy chain, to Master Headley, who prudently declined working for Free Companions, unless he were paid beforehand; and, at the knight's request, took charge of a sufficient amount to pay his fare back again to the Continent. Then mounting a tall, lean, bony horse, the knight said he should call for his armour on returning from Somerset, and rode off, while Stephen found himself exalted as a hero in the eyes of his companions for an act common enough at feats of arms among modern cavalry, but quite new to the London flat-caps. The only sufferer was little Dennet, who had burst into an agony of crying at the sight, needed that Stephen should spread out both hands before her, and show her the divided apple, before she would believe that his thumb was in its right place, and at night screamed out in her sleep that the ill-favoured man was cutting off Stephen's hands.

The sword was left behind by Sir John in order that it might be fitted with a scabbard and belt worthy of it; and on examination, Master Headley and Tibble both confessed that they could produce nothing equal to it in workmanship, though Kit looked with contempt at the slight weapon of deep blue steel, with lines meandering on it like a watered silk, and the upper part inlaid with gold wire in exquisite arabesque patterns. He called it a mere toy, and muttered something about sorcery, and men who had been in foreign parts not thinking honest weight of English steel good enough for them.

Master Headley would not trust one of the boys with the good silver coins that had been paid as the price of the sword—French crowns and Milanese ducats, with a few Venetian gold bezants—but he bade them go as guards to Tibble, for it was always a perilous thing to carry a sum of money through the London streets. Tibble was not an unwilling messenger. He knew Master Michael to be somewhat of his own way of thinking, and he was a naturally large-minded man who could appreciate skill higher than his own without jealousy. Indeed, he and his master held a private consultation on the mode of establishing a connection with Michael and profiting by his ability.

To have lodged him at the Dragon court and made him part of the establishment might have seemed the most obvious way, but the dogged English hatred and contempt of foreigners would have rendered this impossible, even if Abenali himself would have consented to give up his comparative seclusion and live in a crowd and turmoil.

But he was thankful to receive and execute orders from Master Headley, since so certain a connection would secure Aldonza from privation such as the child had sometimes had to endure in the winter; when, though the abstemious Eastern nature needed little food, there was great suffering from cold and lack of fuel. And Tibble moreover asked questions and begged for instructions in some of the secrets of the art. It was an effort to such a prime artificer as Steelman to ask instruction from any man, especially a foreigner, but Tibble had a nature of no common order, and set perfection far above class prejudice; and moreover, he felt Abenali to be one of those men who had their inner eyes devotedly fixed on the truth, though little knowing where the quest would lead them.

On his side Abenali underwent a struggle. "Woe is me!" he said. "Wottest thou, my son, that the secrets of the sword of light and swiftness are the heritage that Abdallah Ben Ali brought from Damascus in the hundred and fifty-third year of the flight of him whom once I termed the prophet; nor have they departed from our house, but have been handed on from father to son. And shall they be used in the wars of the stranger and the Christian?"

"I feared it might be thus," said Tibble.

"And yet," went on the old man, as if not hearing him, "wherefore should I guard the secret any longer? My sons? Where are they? They brooked not the scorn and hatred of the Castillian which poisoned to them the new faith. They cast in their lot with their own people, and that their bones may lie bleaching on the mountains is the best lot that can have befallen the children of my youth and hope. The house of Miguel Abenali is desolate and childless, save for the little maiden who sits by my hearth in the land of my exile! Why should I guard it longer for him who may wed her, and whom I may never behold? The will of Heaven be done! Young man, if I bestow this knowledge on thee, wilt thou swear to be as a father to my daughter, and to care for her as thine own?"

It was a good while since Tibble had been called a young man, and as he listened to the flowing Eastern periods in their foreign enunciation, he was for a moment afraid that the price of the secret was that he should become the old Moor's son-in-law! His seared and scarred youth had precluded marriage, and he entertained the low opinion of women frequent in men of superior intellect among the uneducated. Besides, the possibilities of giving umbrage to Church authorities were dawning on him, and he was not willing to form any domestic ties, so that in every way such a proposition would have been unwelcome to him. But he had no objection to pledge himself to fatherly guardianship of the pretty child in case of a need that might never arise. So he gave the promise, and became a pupil of Abenali, visiting Warwick Inner Ward with his master's consent whenever he could be snared, while the workmanship at the Dragon began to profit thereby.

The jealousy of the Eagle was proportionately increased. Alderman Itillyeo, the head of the Eagle, was friendly enough to Mr. Headley, but it was undeniable that they were the rival armourers of London, dividing the favours of the Court equally between them, and the bitterness of the emulation increased the lower it went in the establishment. The prentices especially could hardly meet without gibes and sneers, if nothing worse, and Stephen's exploit had a peculiar flavour because it was averred that no one at the Eagle would have done the like.

But it was not till the Sunday that Ambrose chanced to hear of the feat, at which he turned quite pale, but he was prouder of it than any one else, and although he rejoiced that he had not seen it performed, he did not fail to boast of it at home, though Perronel began by declaring that she did not care for the mad pranks of roistering prentices; but presently she paused, as she stirred her grandfather's evening posset, and said, "What saidst thou was the strange soldier's name?"

"Fulford—Sir John Fulford," said Ambrose. "What? I thought not of it, is not that Gaffer's name?"

"Fulford, yea! Mayhap—" and Perronel sat down and gave an odd sort of laugh of agitation—"mayhap 'tis mine own father."

"Shouldst thou know him, good aunt?" cried Ambrose, much excited.

"Scarce," she said. "I was not seven years old when he went to the wars—if so be he lived through the battle—and he recked little of me, being but a maid. I feared him greatly and so did my mother. 'Twas happier with only Gaffer! Where saidst thou he was gone?"

Ambrose could not tell, but he undertook to bring Stephen to answer all queries on the subject. His replies that the Captain was gone in quest of his family to Somersetshire settled the matter, since there had been old Martin Fulford's abode, and there John Fulford had parted with his wife and father. They did not, however, tell the old man of the possibility of his son's being at home, he had little memory, and was easily thrown into a state of agitation; besides, it was a doubtful matter how the Condottiere would feel as to the present fortunes of the family. Stephen was to look out for his return in quest of his suit of armour, inform him of his father's being alive, and show him the way to the little house by the Temple Gardens; but Perronel gave the strictest injunctions that her husband's profession should not be explained. It would be quite enough to say that he was of the Lord Cardinal's household.

Stephen watched, but the armour was finished and Christmas passed by before anything was seen of the Captain. At last, however, he did descend on the Dragon court, looking so dilapidated that Mr. Headley rejoiced in the having received payment beforehand. He was louder voiced and fuller of strange oaths than ever, and in the utmost haste, for he had heard tidings that, "there was to be a lusty game between the Emperor and the Italians, and he must have his share."

Stephen made his way up to speak to him, and was received with, "Ha, my gallant lad! Art weary of hammer and anvil? Wouldst be a brave Badger, slip thine indentures, and hear helm and lance ring in good earnest?"

"Not so, sir," said Stephen, "but I have been bidden to ask if thou hast found thy father?"

"What's that to thee, stripling? When thou hast cut thy wisdom teeth, thou'lt know old fathers be not so easy found. 'Twas a wild goose chase, and I wot not what moved me to run after it. I met jolly comrades enough, bumpkins that could drink with an honest soldier when they saw him, but not one that ever heard the name of Fulford."

"Sir," said Stephen, "I know an old man named Fulford. His granddaughter is my uncle's wife, and they dwell by the Temple."

The intelligence seemed more startling and less gratifying than Stephen had expected. Sir John demanded whether they were poor, and declared that he had better have heard of them when his purse was fuller. He had supposed that his wife had given him up and found a fresh mate, and when he heard of her death, he made an exclamation which might be pity, but had in it something of relief. He showed more interest about his old father; but as to his daughter, if she had been a lad now, a' might have been a stout comrade by this time, ready to do the Badger credit. Yea, his poor Kate was a good lass, but she was only a Flemish woman and hadn't the sense to rear aught but a whining little wench, who was of no good except to turn fools' heads, and she was wedded and past all that by this time.

Stephen explained that she was wedded to one of the Lord Cardinal's meine.

"Ho!" said the Condottiere, pausing, "be that the butcher's boy that is pouring out his gold to buy scarlet hats, if not the three crowns. 'Tis no bad household wherein to have a footing. Saidst thou I should find my wench and the old Gaffer there?"

Stephen had to explain, somewhat to the disappointment of the Captain, who had, as it appeared, in the company of three or four more adventurous spirits like himself, taken a passage in a vessel lying off Gravesend, and had only turned aside to take up his new armour and his deposit of passage-money. He demurred a little, he had little time to spare, and though, of course, he could take boat at the Temple Stairs, and drop down the river, he observed that it would have been a very different thing to go home to the old man when he first came back with a pouch full of ransoms and plunder, whereas now he had barely enough to carry him to the place of meeting with his Badgers. And there was the wench too—he had fairly forgotten her name. Women were like she wolves for greed when they had a brood of whelps.

Stephen satisfied him that there was no danger on that score, and heard him muttering, that it was no harm to secure a safe harbour in case a man hadn't the luck to be knocked on the head ere he grew too old to trail a pike. And he would fain see the old man.

So permission was asked for Stephen to show the way to Master Randall's, and granted somewhat reluctantly, Master Headley saying, "I'll have thee back within an hour, Stephen Birkenholt, and look thou dost not let thy brain be set afire with this fellow's windy talk of battles and sieges, and deeds only fit for pagans and wolves."

"Ay!" said Tibble, perhaps with a memory of the old fable, "better be the trusty mastiff than the wolf."

And like the wolf twitting the mastiff with his chain, the soldier was no sooner outside the door of the Dragon court before he began to express his wonder how a lad of mettle could put up with a flat cap, a blue gown, and the being at the beck and call of a greasy burgher, when a bold, handsome young knave like him might have the world before him and his stout pike.

Stephen was flattered, but scarcely tempted. The hard selfishness and want of affection of the Condottiere shocked him, while he looked about, hoping some of his acquaintance would see him in company with this tall figure clanking in shining armour, and with a knightly helmet and gilt spurs. The armour, new and brilliant, concealed the worn and shabby leathern dress beneath, and gave the tall, spare figure a greater breadth, diminishing the look of a hungry wolf which Sir John Fulford's aspect suggested. However, as he passed some of the wealthier stalls, where the apprentices, seeing the martial figure, shouted, "What d'ye lack, sir knight?" and offered silk and velvet robes and mantles, gay sword knots, or even rich chains, under all the clamour, Stephen heard him swearing by Saint George what a place this would be for a sack, if his Badgers were behind him.

"If that poor craven of a Warbeck had had a spark of valour in him," quoth he, as he passed a stall gay with bright tankards and flagons, "we would have rattled some of that shining gear about the lazy citizens' ears! He, jolly King Edward's son! I'll never give faith to it! To turn his back when there was such a booty to be had for the plundering."

"He might not have found it so easy. Our trainbands are sturdy enough," said Stephen, whose *esprit de corps* was this time on the Londoners' side, but the knight of the Badger snapped his fingers, and said, "So much for your burgher trainbands! All they be good for with their show of fight is to give honest landsknechts a good reason to fall on to the plunder, if so be one is hampered by a squeamish prince. But grammercy to Saint George, there be not many of that sort after they be once fleshed!"

Perhaps a year ago, when fresh from the Forest, Stephen might have been more captivated by the notion of adventure and conquest. Now that he had his place in the community and looked on a civic position with wholesome ambition, Fulford's longings for havoc in these peaceful streets made his blood run cold. He was glad when they reached their destination, and he saw Perronel with bare arms, taking in some linen cuffs and bands from a line across to the opposite wall. He could only call out, "Good naunt, here he be!"

Perronel turned round, the colour rising in her cheeks, with an obeisance, but trembling a good deal. "How now, wench? Thou art grown a buxom dame. Thou makst an old man of me," said the soldier with a laugh. "Where's my father? I have not the turning of a cup to stay, for I'm come home poor as a cat in a plundered town, and am off to the wars again; but hearing that the old man was nigh at hand, I came this way to see him, and let thee know thou art a knight's daughter. Thou art indifferent comely, girl, what's thy name? but not the peer of thy mother when I wooed her as one of the bonny lasses of Bruges."

He gave a kind of embrace, while she gave a kind of gasp of "Welcome, sir," and glanced somewhat reproachfully at Stephen for not having given her more warning. The cause of her dismay was plain as the Captain, giving her no time to precede him, strode into the little chamber, where Hal Randall, without his false beard or hair, and in his parti-coloured hose, was seated by the cupboardlike bed, assisting old Martin Fulford to take his mid-day meal.

"Be this thine husband, girl? Ha! ha! He's more like a jolly friar come in to make thee merry when the good man is out!" exclaimed the visitor, laughing loudly at his own rude jest; but heeding little either Hal's appearance or his reply, as he caught the old man's bewildered eyes, and heard his efforts to utter his name.

For eighteen years had altered John Fulford less than either his father or his daughter, and old Martin recognised him instantly, and held out the only arm he could use, while the knight, softened, touched, and really feeling more natural affection than Stephen had given him credit for, dropped on his knee, breaking into indistinct mutterings with rough but hearty greetings, regretting that he had not found his father sooner, when his pouch was full, lamenting the change in him, declaring that he must hurry away now, but promising to come back with sacks of Italian ducats to provide for the old man.

Those who could interpret the imperfect utterance, now further choked by tears and agitation, knew that there was a medley of broken rejoicings, blessings, and weepings, in the midst of which the soldier, glad perhaps to end a scene where he became increasingly awkward and embarrassed, started up, hastily kissed the old man on each of his withered cheeks, gave another kiss to his daughter, threw her two Venetian ducats, bidding her spend them for the old man, and he would bring a pouchful more next time, and striding to the door, bade Stephen call a boat to take him down to Gravesend.

Randall, who had in the meantime donned his sober black gown in the inner chamber, together with a dark hood, accompanied his newly found father-in-law down the river, and Stephen would fain have gone too, but for the injunction to return within the hour.

Perronel had hurried back to her grandfather's side to endeavour to compose him after the shock of gladness. But it had been too much for his enfeebled powers. Another stroke came on before the day was over, and in two or three days more old Martin Fulford was laid to rest, and his son's ducats were expended on masses for his soul's welfare.

CHAPTER XV.

Heave Half a Brick at him.

"For strangers then did so increase,
By reason of King Henry's queen,
And privileged in many a place
To dwell, as was in London seen.
Poor tradesmen had small dealing then
And who but strangers bore the bell,
Which was a grief to Englishmen
To see them here in London dwell."

"Ill May Day,"
by Churchill, a Contemporary Poet.

Time passed on, and Edmund Burgess, who had been sent from York to learn the perfection of his craft, completed his term and returned to his home, much regretted in the Dragon court, where his good humour and good sense had generally kept the peace, both within and without.

Giles Headley was now the eldest prentice. He was in every way greatly improved, thoroughly accepting his position, and showing himself quite ready both to learn and to work; but he had not the will or the power of avoiding disputes with outsiders, or turning them aside with a merry jest; and rivalries and quarrels with the armoury at the Eagle began to increase. The Dragon, no doubt, turned out finer workmanship, and this the Eagle alleged was wholly owing to nefarious traffic with the old Spanish or Moorish sorcerer in Warwick Inner Ward, a thing unworthy of honest Englishmen.

This made Giles furious, and the cry never failed to end in a fight, in which Stephen supported the cause of the one house, and George Bates and his comrades of the other.

It was the same with even the archery at Mile End, where the butts were erected, and the youth contended with the long bow, which was still considered as the safeguard of England. King Henry often looked in on these matches, and did honour to the winners. One match there was in especial, on Mothering Sunday, when the champions of each guild shot against one another at such a range that it needed a keen eye to see the popinjay—a stuffed bird at which they shot.

Stephen was one of these, his forest lore having always given him an advantage over many of the others. He even was one of the last three who were to finish the sport by shooting against one another. One was a butcher named Barlow. The other was a Walloon, the best shot among six hundred foreigners of various nations, all of whom, though with little encouragement, joined in the national sport on these pleasant spring afternoons. The first contest threw out the Walloon, at which there were cries of ecstasy; now the trial was between

Barlow and Stephen, and in this final effort, the distance of the pole to which the popinjay was fastened was so much increased that strength of arm told as much as accuracy of aim, and Stephen's seventeen years' old muscles could not, after so long a strain, cope with those of Ralph Barlow, a butcher of full thirty years old. His wrist and arm began to shake with weariness, and only one of his three last arrows went straight to the mark, while Barlow was as steady as ever, and never once failed. Stephen was bitterly disappointed, his eyes filled with tears, and he flung himself down on the turf, feeling as if the shouts of "A Barlow! a Barlow!" which were led by the jovial voice of King Harry himself, were all exulting over him.

Barlow was led up to the king, who hailed him "King of Shoreditch," a title borne by the champion archer ever after, so long as bowmanship in earnest lasted. A tankard which the king filled with silver pieces was his prize, but Henry did not forget Number 2. "Where's the other fellow?" he said. "He was but a stripling, and to my mind, his feat was a greater marvel than that of a stalwart fellow like Barlow."

Half a dozen of the spectators, among them the cardinal's hurried in search of Stephen, who was roused from his fit of weariness and disappointment by a shake of the shoulder as his uncle jingled his bells in his ears, and exclaimed, "How now, here I own a cousin!" Stephen sat up and stared with angry, astonished eyes, but only met a laugh. "Ay, ay, 'tis but striplings and fools that have tears to spend for such as this! Up, boy! D'ye hear? The other Hal is asking for thee."

And Stephen, hastily brushing away his tears, and holding his flat cap in his hand, was marshalled across the mead, hot, shy, and indignant, as the jester mopped and mowed, and cut all sorts of antics before him, turning round to observe in an encouraging voice, "Pluck up a heart, man! One would think Hal was going to cut off thine head!" And then, on arriving where the king sat on his horse, "Here he is, Hal, such as he is come humbly to crave thy gracious pardon for hitting the mark no better! He'll mend his ways, good my lord, if your grace will pardon him this time."

"Ay, marry, and that will I," said the king. "The springald bids fair to be King of Shoreditch by the time the other fellow abdicates. How old art thou, my lad?"

"Seventeen, an it please your grace," said Stephen, in the gruff voice of his age.

"And thy name?"

"Stephen Birkenholt, my liege," and he wondered whether he would be recognised; but Henry only said—

"Methinks I've seen those sloe-black eyes before. Or is it only that the lad is thy very marrow, quipsome one?"

"The which," returned the jester, gravely, while Stephen tingled all over with dismay, "may account for the tears the lad was wasting at not having the thews of the fellow double his age! But I envy him not! Not I! He'll never have wit for mine office, but will come in second there likewise."

"I dare be sworn he will," said the king. "Here, take this, my good lad, and prank thee in it when thou art out of thy time, and goest a-hunting in Epping!"

It was a handsome belt with a broad silver clasp, engraven with the Tudor rose and portcullis; and Stephen bowed low and made his acknowledgments as best he might.

He was hailed with rapturous acclamations by his own contemporaries, who held that he had saved the credit of the English prentice world, and insisted on carrying him enthroned on their shoulders back to Cheapside, in emulation of the journeymen and all the butcher kind, who were thus bearing home the King of Shoreditch.

Shouts, halloos, whistles, every jubilant noise that youth and boyhood could invent, were the triumphant music of Stephen on his surging and uneasy throne, as he was shifted from one bearer to another when each in turn grew tired of his weight. Just, however, as they were nearing their own neighbourhood, a counter cry broke out, "Witchcraft! His arrows are bewitched by the old Spanish sorcerer! Down with Dragons and Wizards!" And a handful of mud came full in the face of the enthroned lad, aimed no doubt by George Bates. There was a yell and rush of rage, but the enemy was in numbers too small to attempt resistance, and dashed off before their pursuers, only pausing at safe corners to shout Parthian darts of "Wizards!" "Magic!" "Sorcerers!" "Heretics!"

There was nothing to be done but to collect again, and escort Stephen, who had wiped the mud off his face, to the Dragon court, where Dennet danced on the steps for joy, and Master Headley, not a little gratified, promised Stephen a supper for a dozen of his particular friends at Armourers' Hall on the ensuing Easter Sunday.

Of course Stephen went in search of his brother, all the more eagerly because he was conscious that they had of late drifted apart a good deal. Ambrose was more and more absorbed by the studies to which Lucas Hansen led him, and took less and less interest in his brother's pursuits. He did indeed come to the Sunday's dinner according to the regular custom, but the moment it was permissible to leave the board he was away with Tibble Steelman to meet friends of Lucas, and pursue studies, as if, Stephen thought, he had not enough of books as it was. When Dean Colet preached or catechised in Saint Paul's in the afternoon they both attended and listened, but that good man was in failing health, and his wise discourses were less frequent.

Where they were at other times, Stephen did not know, and hardly cared, except that he had a general dislike to, and jealousy of, anything that took his brother's sympathy away from him. Moreover Ambrose's face was thinner and paler, he had a strange absorbed look, and often even when they were together seemed hardly to attend to what his brother was saying.

"I will make him come," said Stephen to himself, as he went with swinging gait towards Warwick Inner Ward, where, sure enough, he found Ambrose sitting at the door, frowning over some black-letter which looked most uninviting in the eyes of the apprentice, and he fell upon his brother with half angry, half merry reproofs for wasting the fine spring afternoon over such studies.

Ambrose looked up with a dreamy smile and greeted his brother; but all the time Stephen was narrating the history of the match, (and he *did* tell the fate of each individual arrow of his own or Barlow's), his eyes were wandering back to the crabbed page in his hand, and when Stephen impatiently wound up his history with the invitation to supper on Easter Sunday, the reply was, "Nay, brother, thanks, but that I cannot do."

"Cannot!" exclaimed Stephen.

"Nay, there are other matters in hand that go deeper."

"Yea, I know whatever concerns musty books goes deeper with thee than thy brother," replied Stephen, turning away much mortified.

Ambrose's warm nature was awakened. He held his brother by the arm and declared himself anything but indifferent to him, but he owned that he did not love noise and revelry, above all on Sunday.

"Thou art addling thy brains with preachings!" said Stephen. "Pray Heaven they make not a heretic of thee. But thou mightest for once have come to mine own feast."

Ambrose, much perplexed and grieved at thus vexing his brother, declared that he would have done so with all his heart, but that this very Easter Sunday there was coming a friend of Master Hansen's from Holland: who was to tell them much of the teaching in Germany, which was so enlightening men's eyes.

"Yea, truly, making heretics of them, Mistress Headley saith," returned Stephen. "O Ambrose, if thou wilt run after these books and parchments, canst not do it in right fashion, among holy monks, as of old?"

"Holy monks!" repeated Ambrose. "Holy monks! Where be they?"

Stephen stared at him.

"Hear uncle Hal talk of monks whom he sees at my Lord Cardinal's table! What holiness is there among them? Men, that have vowed to renounce all worldly and carnal things flaunt like peacocks and revel like swine—my Lord Cardinal with his silver pillars foremost of them! He poor and mortified! 'Tis verily as our uncle saith, he plays the least false and shameful part there!"

"Ambrose, Ambrose, thou wilt be distraught, poring over these matters that were never meant for lads like us! Do but come and drive them out for once with mirth and good fellowship."

"I tell thee, Stephen, what thou callest mirth and good fellowship do but drive the pain in deeper. Sin and guilt be everywhere. I seem to see the devils putting foul words on the tongue and ill deeds in the hands of myself and all around me, that they may accuse us before God. No, Stephen, I cannot, cannot come. I must go where I can hear of a better way."

"Nay," said Stephen, "what better way can there be than to be shriven—clean shriven—and then housled, as I was ere Lent, and trust to be again on next Low Sunday morn? That's enough for a plain lad." He crossed himself reverently, "Mine own Lord pardoneth and cometh to me."

But the two minds, one simple and practical, the other sensitive and speculative, did not move in the same atmosphere, and could not understand one another. Ambrose was in the condition of excitement and bewilderment produced by the first stirrings of the Reformation upon enthusiastic minds. He had studied the Vulgate, made out something of the Greek Testament, read all fragments of the Fathers that came in his way, and also all the controversial "tractates," Latin or Dutch, that he could meet with, and attended many a secret conference between Lucas and his friends, when men, coming from Holland or Germany, communicated accounts of the lectures and sermons of Dr. Martin Luther, which already were becoming widely known.

He was wretched under the continual tossings of his mind. Was the entire existing system a vast delusion, blinding the eyes and destroying the souls of those who trusted to it; and was the only safety in the one point of faith that Luther pressed on all, and ought all that he had hitherto revered to crumble down to let that alone be upheld? Whatever he had once loved and honoured at times seemed to him a lie, while at others real affection and veneration, and dread of sacrilege, made him shudder at himself and his own doubts! It was his one thought, and he passionately sought after all those secret conferences which did but feed the flame that consumed him.

The elder men who were with him were not thus agitated. Lucas's convictions had not long been fixed. He did not court observation nor do anything unnecessarily to bring persecution on himself, but he quietly and secretly acted as an agent in dispersing the Lollard books and those of Erasmus, and lived in the conviction that there would one day be a great crash, believing himself to be doing his part by undermining the structure, and working on undoubtingly. Abenali was not aggressive. In fact, though he was reckoned among Lucas's party, because of his abstinence from all cult of saints or images, and the persecution he had suffered, he did not join in their general opinions, and held aloof from their meetings. And Tibble Steelman, as has been before said, lived two lives, and that as foreman at the Dragon court, being habitual to him, and requiring much thought and exertion, the speculations of the reformers were to him more like an intellectual relaxation than the business of life. He took them as a modern artisan would in this day read his newspaper, and attend his club meeting.

Ambrose, however, had the enthusiastic practicalness of youth. On that which he fully believed, he must act, and what did he fully believe?

Boy as he was—scarcely yet eighteen—the toils and sports that delighted his brother seemed to him like toys amusing infants on the verge of an abyss, and he spent his leisure either in searching in the Vulgate for something to give him absolute direction, or in going in search of preachers, for, with the stirring of men's minds, sermons were becoming more frequent.

There was much talk just now of the preaching of one Doctor Beale, to whom all the tradesmen, Journeymen, and apprentices were resorting, even those who were of no special religious tendencies. Ambrose went on Easter

Tuesday to hear him preach at Saint Mary's Spitall. The place was crowded with artificers, and Beale began by telling them that he had "a pitiful bill," meaning a letter, brought to him declaring how aliens and strangers were coming in to inhabit the City and suburbs, to eat the bread from poor fatherless children, and take the living from all artificers and the intercourse from merchants, whereby poverty was so much increased that each bewaileth the misery of others. Presently coming to his text, "*Caelum caeli Domini, terram autem dedit filiis hominis,*" (the Heaven of Heavens is the Lord's, the earth hath He given to the children of men), the doctor inculcated that England was given to Englishmen, and that as birds would defend their nests, so ought Englishmen to defend themselves, *and to hurt and grieve aliens for the common weal!* The corollary a good deal resembled that of "hate thine enemy" which was foisted by "them of the old time" upon "thou shalt love thy neighbour." And the doctor went on upon the text, "*Pugna pro patriâ,*" to demonstrate that fighting for one's country meant rising upon and expelling all the strangers who dwelt and traded within it. Many of these foreigners were from the Hanse towns which had special commercial privileges, there were also numerous Venetians and Genoese, French and Spaniards, the last of whom were, above all, the objects of dislike. Their imports of silks, cloth of gold, stamped leather, wine and oil, and their superior skill in many handicrafts, had put English wares out of fashion; and their exports of wool, tin, and lead excited equal jealousy, which Dr. Beale, instigated as was well known by a broker named John Lincoln, was thus stirring up into fierce passion. His sermon was talked of all over London; blacker looks than ever were directed at the aliens, stones and dirt were thrown at them, and even Ambrose, as he walked along the street, was reviled as the Dutchkin's knave. The insults became each day more daring and outrageous. George Bates and a skinner's apprentice named Studley were caught in the act of tripping up a portly old Flanderkin and forthwith sent to Newgate, and there were other arrests, which did but inflame the smouldering rage of the mob. Some of the wealthier foreigners, taking warning by the signs of danger, left the City, for there could be no doubt that the whole of London and the suburbs were in a combustible condition of discontent, needing only a spark to set it alight.

It was just about this time that a disreputable clerk—a lewd priest, as Hall calls him—a hanger-on of the house of Howard, was guilty of an insult to a citizen's wife as she was quietly walking home through the Cheap. Her husband and brother, who were nearer at hand than he guessed, avenged the outrage with such good wills that this disgrace to the priesthood was left dead on the ground. When such things happened, and discourses like Beale's were heard, it was not surprising that Ambrose's faith in the clergy as guides received severe shocks.

CHAPTER XVI.

May Eve.

"The rich, the poor, the old, the young,
Beyond the seas though born and bred,
By prentices they suffered wrong,
When armèd thus they gather'd head."

Ill May Day.

May Eve had come, and little Dennet Headley was full of plans for going out early with her young play-fellows to the meadow to gather May dew in the early morning, but her grandmother, who was in bed under a heavy attack of rheumatism, did not like the reports brought to her, and deferred her consent to the expedition.

In the afternoon there were tidings that the Lord Mayor, Sir Thomas Rest, had been sent for to my Lord Cardinal, who just at this time, during the building at York House, was lodging in his house close to Temple Bar. Some hours later a message came to Master Alderman Headley to meet the Lord Mayor and the rest of the Council at the Guildhall. He shook himself into his scarlet gown, and went off, puffing and blowing, and bidding Giles and Stephen take heed that they kept close, and ran into no mischief.

But they agreed, and Kit Smallbones with them, that there could be no harm in going into the open space of Cheapside and playing out a match with bucklers between Giles and Wat Ball, a draper's prentice who had challenged him. The bucklers were huge shields, and the weapons were wooden swords. It was an exciting sport, and brought out all the youths of Cheapside in the summer evening, bawling out encouragement, and laying wagers on either side. The curfew rang, but there were special privileges on May Eve, and the game went on louder than ever.

There was far too much noise for any one to hear the town crier, who went along jingling his bell, and shouting, "O yes! O yes! O yes! By order of the Lord Mayor and Council, no householder shall allow any one of his household to be abroad beyond his gate between the hours of nine o'clock at night and seven in the morning," or if any of the outermost heard it, as did Ambrose who was on his way home to his night quarters, they were too much excited not to turn a deaf ear to it.

Suddenly, however, just as Giles was preparing for a master-stroke, he was seized roughly by the shoulder and bidden to give over. He looked round. It was an alderman, not his master, but Sir John Mundy, an unpopular, harsh man.

"Wherefore?" demanded Giles.

"Thou shalt know," said the alderman, seizing his arm to drag him to the Counter prison, but Giles resisted. Wat Ball struck at Sir John's arm with his wooden sword, and as the alderman shouted for the watch and city-guard, the lads on their side raised their cry, "Prentices and Clubs! Flat-caps and Clubs!" Master Headley, struggling along, met his colleague, with his gown torn into shreds from his back, among a host of wildly yelling lads, and panting, "Help, help, brother Headley!" With great difficulty the two aldermen reached the door of the Dragon, whence Smallbones sallied out to rescue them, and dragged them in.

"The boys!—the boys!" was Master Headley's first cry, but he might as well have tried to detach two particular waves from a surging ocean as his own especial boys from the multitude on that wild evening. There was no moon, and the twilight still prevailed, but it was dark enough to make the confusion greater, as the cries swelled and numbers flowed into the open space of Cheapside. In the words of Hall, the chronicler, "Out came serving-men, and watermen, and courtiers, and by eleven of the clock there were six or seven hundreds in Cheap. And out of Pawle's Churchyard came three hundred which wist not of the others." For the most part all was involved in the semi-darkness of the summer night, but here and there light came from an upper window on some boyish face, perhaps full of mischief, perhaps somewhat bewildered and appalled. Here and there were torches, which cast a red glare round them, but whose smoke blurred everything, and seemed to render the darkness deeper.

Perhaps if the tumult had only been of the apprentices, provoked by Alderman Mundy's interference, they would soon have dispersed, but the throng was pervaded by men with much deeper design, and a cry arose—no one knew from whence—that they would break into Newgate and set free Studley and Bates.

By this time the torrent of young manhood was quite irresistible by any force that had yet been opposed to it. The Mayor and Sheriffs stood at the Guildhall, and read the royal proclamation by the light of a wax candle, held in the trembling hand of one of the clerks; but no one heard or heeded them, and the uproar was increased as the doors of Newgate fell, and all the felons rushed out to join the rioters.

At the same time another shout rose, "Down with the aliens!" and there was a general rush towards Saint Martin's gate, in which direction many lived. There was, however, a pause here, for Sir Thomas More, Recorder of London, stood in the way before Saint Martin's gate, and with his full sweet voice began calling out and entreating the lads to go home, before any heads were broken more than could be mended again. He was always a favourite, and his good humour seemed to be making some impression, when, either from the deter-mination of the more evil-disposed, or because the inhabitants of Saint Martin's Lane were beginning to pour down hot water, stones, and brickbats on the dense mass of heads below them, a fresh access of fury seized upon the mob. Yells of, "Down with the strangers!" echoed through the narrow streets, drowning Sir Thomas's voice. A lawyer who stood with him was knocked down and much hurt, the doors were battered down, and the household stuff thrown from the windows. Here, Ambrose, who had hitherto been pushed helplessly about, and knocked hither and thither, was driven up against Giles, and, to avoid falling and being trampled down, clutched hold of him breathless and panting.

"Thou here!" exclaimed Giles. "Who would have thought of sober Ambrose in the midst of the fray? See here, Stevie!"

"Poor old Ambrose!" cried Stephen, "keep close to us! We'll see no harm comes to thee. 'Tis hot work, eh?"

"Oh, Stephen! could I but get out of the throng to warn my master and Master Michael!"

Those words seemed to strike Giles Headley. He might have cared little for the fate of the old printer, but as he heard the screams of the women in the houses around, he exclaimed, "Ay! there's the old man and the little maid! We will have her to the Dragon!"

"Or to mine aunt's," said Ambrose.

"Have with thee then," said Giles: "Take his other arm, Steve;" and locking their arms together the three fought and forced their way from among the plunderers in Saint Martin's with no worse mishap than a shower of hot water, which did not hurt them much through their stout woollen coats. They came at last to a place where they could breathe, and stood still a moment to recover from the struggle, and vituperate the hot water.

Then they heard fresh howls and yells in front as well as behind.

"They are at it everywhere," exclaimed Stephen. "I hear them somewhere out by Cornhill."

"Ay, where the Frenchmen live that calender worsted," returned Giles. "Come on; who knows how it is with the old man and little maid?"

"There's a sort in our court that are ready for aught," said Ambrose.

On they hurried in the darkness, which was now at the very deepest of the night; now and then a torch was borne across the street, and most of the houses had lights in the upper windows, for few Londoners slept on that strange night. The stained glass of the windows of the Churches beamed in bright colours from the Altar lights seen through them, but the lads made slower progress than they wished, for the streets were never easy to walk in the dark, and twice they came on mobs assailing houses, from the windows of one of which, French shoes and boots were being hailed down. Things were moderately quiet around Saint Paul's, but as they came into Warwick Lane they heard fresh shouts and wild cries, and at the archway leading to the inner yard they could see that there was a huge bonfire in the midst of the court—of what composed they could not see for the howling figures that exulted round it.

"George Bates, the villain!" cried Stephen, as his enemy in exulting ferocious delight was revealed for a moment throwing a book on the fire, and shouting, "Hurrah! there's for the old sorcerer, there's for the heretics!"

That instant Giles was flying on Bates, and Stephen, with equal, if not greater fury, at one of his comrades; but Ambrose dashed through the outskirts of the wildly screaming and shouting fellows, many of whom were the miscreant population of the mews, to the black yawning doorway of his master. He saw only a fellow staggering out with the screw of the press to feed the flame, and hurried on in the din to call, "Master, art thou there?"

There was no answer, and he moved on to the next door, calling again softly, while all the spoilers seemed absorbed in the fire and the combat. "Master Michael! 'Tis I, Ambrose!"

"Here, my son," cautiously answered a voice he knew for Lucas Hansen's.

"Oh, master! master!" was his low, heart-stricken cry, as by the leaping light of a flame he saw the pale face of the old printer, who drew him in.

"Yea! 'tis ruin, my son," said Lucas. "And would that that were the worst."

The light flashed and flickered through the broken window so that Ambrose saw that the hangings had been torn down and everything wrecked, and a low sound as of stifled weeping directed his eyes to a corner where Aldonza sat with her father's head on her lap. "Lives he? Is he greatly hurt?" asked Ambrose, awe-stricken.

"The life is yet in him, but I fear me greatly it is passing fast," said Lucas, in a low voice. "One of those lads smote him on the back with a club, and struck him down at the poor maid's feet, nor hath he moved since. It was that one young Headley is fighting with," he added.

"Bates! ah! Would that we had come sooner! What! more of this work—"

For just then a tremendous outcry broke forth, and there was a rush and panic among those who had been leaping round the fire just before. "The guard!—the King's men!" was the sound they presently distinguished. They could hear rough abusive voices, shrieks and trampling of feet. A few seconds more and all was still, only the fire remained, and in the stillness the suppressed sobs and moans of Aldonza were heard.

"A light! Fetch a light from the fire!" said Lucas.

Ambrose ran out. The flame was lessening, but he could see the dark bindings, and the blackened pages of the books he loved so well. A corner of a page of Saint Augustine's Confessions was turned towards him and lay on a singed fragment of Aldonza's embroidered curtain, while a little red flame was licking the spiral folds of the screw, trying, as it were, to gather energy to do more than blacken it. Ambrose could have wept over it at any other moment, but now he could only catch up a brand—it was the leg of his master's carved chair—and run back with it. Lucas ventured to light a lamp, and they could then see the old man's face pale, but calm and still, with his long white beard flowing over his breast. There was no blood, no look of pain, only a set look about the eyes; and Aldonza cried, "Oh, father, thou art better! Speak to me! Let Master Lucas lift thee up!"

"Nay, my child. I cannot move hand or foot. Let me lie thus till the Angel of Death come for me. He is very near." He spoke in short sentences. "Water—nay—no pain," he added then, and Ambrose ran for some water in the first battered fragment of a tin pot he could find. They bathed his face and he gathered strength after a time to say, "A priest!—oh for a priest to shrive and housel me."

"I will find one," said Ambrose, speeding out into the court over fragments of the beautiful work for which Abenali was hated, and over the torn, half burnt leaves of the beloved store of Lucas. The fire had died down, but morning twilight was beginning to dawn, and all was perfectly still after the recent tumult though for a moment or two Ambrose heard some distant cries.

Where should he go? Priests indeed were plentiful, but both his friends were in bad odour with the ordinary ones. Lucas had avoided both the Lenten shrift and Easter Communion, and what Miguel might have done, Ambrose was uncertain. Some young priests had actually been among the foremost in sacking the dwellings of the unfortunate foreigners, and Ambrose was quite uncertain whether he might not fall on one of that stamp—or on one who might vex the old man's soul—perhaps deny him the Sacraments altogether. As he saw the pale lighted windows of Saint Paul's, it struck him to see whether any one were within. The light might be only from some of the tapers burning perpetually, but the pale light in the north-east, the morning chill, and the clock striking three, reminded him that it must be the hour of Prime, and he said to himself, "Sure, if a priest be worshipping at this hour, he will be a good and merciful man. I can but try."

The door of the transept yielded to his hand. He came forward, lighted through the darkness by the gleam of the candles, which cast a huge and awful shadow from the crucifix of the rood-screen upon the pavement. Before it knelt a black figure in prayer. Ambrose advanced in some awe and doubt how to break in on these devotions, but the priest had heard his step, rose and said, "What is it, my son? Dost thou seek sanctuary after these sad doings?"

"Nay, reverend sir," said Ambrose. "'Tis a priest for a dying man I seek;" and in reply to the instant question, where it was, he explained in haste who the sufferer was, and how he had received a fatal blow, and was begging for the Sacraments. "And oh, sir!" he added, "he is a holy and God-fearing man, if ever one lived, and hath been cruelly and foully entreated by jealous and wicked folk, who hated him for his skill and industry."

"Alack for the unhappy lads; and alack for those who egged them on," said the priest. "Truly they knew not what they did. I will come with thee, my good youth. Thou hast not been one of them?"

"No, truly sir, save that I was carried along and could not break from the throng. I work for Lucas Hansen, the Dutch printer, whom they have likewise plundered in their savage rage."

"'Tis well. Thou canst then bear this," said the priest, taking a thick wax candle. Then reverently advancing to the Altar, whence he took the pyx, or gold case in which the Host was reserved, he lighted the candle, which he gave, together with his stole, to the youth to bear before him.

Then, when the light fell full on his features, Ambrose with a strange thrill of joy and trust perceived that it was no other than Dean Colet, who had here been praying against the fury of the people. He was very thankful, feeling intuitively that there was no fear but that Abenali would be understood, and for his own part, the very contact with the man whom he revered seemed to calm and soothe him, though on that solemn errand no word could be spoken. Ambrose went on slowly before, his dark head uncovered, the priestly stole hanging over his arm, his hands holding aloft the tall candle of virgin wax, while the Dean followed closely with feeble steps, looking frail and worn, but with a grave, sweet solemnity on his face. It was a perfectly still morning, and as they slowly paced along, the flame burnt steadily with little flickering, while the pure, delicately-coloured sky overhead was becoming every moment lighter, and only the larger stars were visible. The houses were absolutely still, and the only person they met, a lad creeping homewards after the fray, fell on his knees bareheaded as he perceived their errand. Once or twice again sounds came up from the city beneath, like shrieks or wailing breaking strangely on that fair peaceful May morn; but still that pair went on till Ambrose had guided the Dean to the yard, where, except that the daylight was revealing more and more of the wreck around, all was as he had left it. Aldonza, poor child, with her black hair hanging loose like a veil, for she had been startled from her bed, still sat on the ground making her lap a pillow for the white-bearded head, nobler and more venerable than ever. On it lay, in the absolute immobility produced by the paralysing blow, the fine features already in the solemn grandeur of death, and only the movement of the lips under the white flowing beard and of the dark eyes showing life.

Dean Colet said afterwards that he felt as if he had been called to the death-bed of Israel, or of Barzillai the Gileadite, especially when the old man, in the Oriental phraseology he had never entirely lost, said, "I thank Thee, my God, and the God of my fathers, that Thou hast granted me that which I had prayed for."

The Dutch printer was already slightly known to the Dean, having sold him many books. A few words were exchanged with him, but it was plain that the dying man could not be moved, and that his confession must be made on the lap of the young girl. Colet knelt over him so as to be able to hear, while Lucas and Ambrose withdrew, but were soon called back for the remainder of the service for the dying. The old man's face showed perfect peace. All worldly thought and care seemed to have been crushed out of him by the blow, and he did not even appear to think of the unprotected state of his daughter, although he blessed her with solemn fervour immediately after receiving the Viaticum—then lay murmuring to himself sentences which Ambrose, who had learnt much from him, knew to be from his Arabic breviary about palm-branches, and the twelve manner of fruits of the Tree of Life.

It was a strange scene—the grand, calm, patriarchal old man, so peaceful on his dark-haired daughter's lap in the midst of the shattered home in the old feudal stable. All were silent a while in awe, but the Dean was the first to move and speak, calling Lucas forward to ask sundry questions of him.

"Is there no good woman," he asked, "who could be with this poor child and take her home, when her father shall have passed away?"

"Mine uncle's wife, sir," said Ambrose, a little doubtfully. "I trow she would come—since I can certify her that your reverence holds him for a holy man."

"I had thy word for it," said the Dean. "Ah! reply not, my son, I see well how it may be with you here. But tell those who will take the word of John Colet that never did I mark the passing away of one who had borne more for the true holy Catholic faith, nor held it more to his soul's comfort."

For the Dean, a man of vivid intelligence, knew enough of the Moresco persecutions to be able to gather from the words of Lucas and Ambrose, and the confession of the old man himself, a far more correct estimate of Abenali's sufferings, and constancy to the truth, than any of the more homebred wits could have divined. He knew, too, that his own orthodoxy was so called in question by the narrower and more unspiritual section of the clergy that only the appreciative friendship of the King and the Cardinal kept him securely in his position.

Ambrose sped away, knowing that Perronel would be quite satisfied. He was sure of her ready compassion and good-will, but she had so often bewailed his running after learning and possibly heretical doctrine, that he had doubted whether she would readily respond to a summons, on his own authority alone, to one looked on with so much suspicion as Master Michael. Colet intimated his intention of remaining a little longer to pray with the dying man, and further wrote a few words on his tablets, telling Ambrose to leave them with one of the porters at his house as he went past Saint Paul's.

It was broad daylight now, a lovely May morning, such as generally called forth the maidens, small and great, to the meadows to rub their fresh cheeks with the silvery dew, and to bring home kingcups, cuckoo flowers, blue bottles, and cowslips for the Maypoles that were to be decked. But all was silent now, not a house was open, the rising sun made the eastern windows of the churches a blaze of light, and from the west door of Saint Paul's the city beneath seemed sleeping, only a wreath or two of smoke rising. Ambrose found the porter looking out for his master in much perturbation. He groaned as he looked at the tablets, and heard where the Dean was, and said that came of being a saint on earth. It would be the death of him ere long! What would old Mistress Colet, his mother, say? He would have detained the youth with his inquiries, but Ambrose said he had to speed down to the Temple on an errand from the Dean, and hurried away. All Ludgate Hill was now quiet, every house closed, but here and there lay torn shreds of garments, or household vessels.

As he reached Fleet Street, however, there was a sound of horses' feet, and a body of men-at-arms with helmets glancing in the sun were seen. There was a cry, "There's one! That's one of the lewd younglings! At him!"

And Ambrose to his horror and surprise saw two horsemen begin to gallop towards him, as if to ride him down. Happily he was close to a narrow archway leading to an alley down which no war-horse could possibly make its way, and dashing into it and round a corner, he eluded his pursuers, and reached the bank of the river, whence, being by this time experienced in the byways of London, he could easily reach Perronel's house.

She was standing at her door looking out anxiously, and as she saw him she threw up her hands in thanksgiving to our Lady that here he was at last, and then turned to scold him. "O lad, lad, what a night thou hast given me! I trusted at least that thou hadst wit to keep out of a fray and to let the poor aliens alone, thou that art always running after yonder old Spaniard. Hey! what now? Did they fall on him! Fie! Shame on them!—a harmless old man like that."

"Yea, good aunt, and what is more, they have slain him, I fear me, outright."

Amidst many a "good lack" and exclamation of pity and indignation from Perronel, Ambrose told his tale of that strange night, and entreated her to come with him to do what was possible for Abenali and his daughter. She hesitated a little; her kind heart was touched, but she hardly liked to leave her house, in case her husband should come in, as he generally contrived to do in the early morning, now that the Cardinal's household was lodged so near her. Sheltered as she was by the buildings of the Temple, she had heard little or nothing of the noise of the riot, though she had been alarmed at her nephew's absence, and an officious neighbour had run in to tell her first that the prentice lads were up and sacking the houses of the strangers, and next that the Tower was firing on them, and the Lord Mayor's guard and the gentlemen of the Inns of Court were up in arms to put them down. She said several times, "Poor soul!" and, "Yea, it were a shame to leave her to the old Dutchkin," but with true Flemish deliberation she continued her household arrangements, and insisted that the bowl of broth, which she set on the table, should be partaken of by herself and Ambrose before she would stir a step. "Not eat! Now out on thee, lad! what good dost thou think thou or I can do if we come in faint and famished, where there's neither bite nor sup to be had? As for me, not a foot will I budge, till I have seen thee empty that bowl. So to it, my lad! Thou hast been afoot all night, and lookst so grimed and ill-favoured a varlet that no man would think thou camest from an honest wife's house. Wash thee at the pail! Get thee into thy chamber and put on clean garments, or I'll not walk the street with thee! 'Tis not safe—thou wilt be put in ward for one of the rioters."

Everybody who entered that little house obeyed Mistress Randall, and Ambrose submitted, knowing it vain to resist, and remembering the pursuit he had recently escaped; yet the very refreshment of food and cleanliness revealed to him how stiff and weary were his limbs, though he was in no mood for rest. His uncle appeared at the door just as he had hoped Perronel was ready.

"Ah! there's one of you whole and safe!" he exclaimed. "Where is the other?"

"Stephen?" exclaimed Ambrose. "I saw him last in Warwick Inner Ward." And in a few words he explained. Hal Randall shook his head. "May all be well," he exclaimed, and then he told how Sir Thomas Parr had come at midnight and roused the Cardinal's household with tidings that all the rabble of London were up, plundering and murdering all who came in their way, and that he had then ridden on to Richmond to the King with the news. The Cardinal had put his house into a state of defence, not knowing against whom the riot might be directed—and the jester had not been awakened till too late to get out to send after his wife, besides which, by that time, intelligence had come in that the attack was directed entirely on the French and Spanish merchants and artificers in distant parts of the city and suburbs, and was only conducted by lads with no better weapons than sticks, so that the Temple and its precincts were in no danger at all.

The mob had dispersed of its own accord by about three or four o'clock, but by that hour the Mayor had got together a force, the Gentlemen of the Inns of Court and the Yeomen of the Tower were up in arms, and the Earl of Shrewsbury had come in with a troop of horse. They had met the rioters, and had driven them in herds like sheep to the different prisons, after which Lord Shrewsbury had come to report to the Cardinal that all was quiet, and the jester having gathered as much intelligence as he could, had contrived to slip into the garments that concealed his motley, and to reach home. He gave ready consent to Perronel's going to the aid of the sufferers in Warwick Inner Ward, especially at the summons of the Dean of Saint Paul's, and even to her bringing home the little wench. Indeed, he would escort her thither himself, for he was very anxious about Stephen, and Ambrose was so dismayed by the account he gave as to reproach himself extremely for having parted company with his brother, and never having so much as thought of him as in peril, while absorbed in care for Abenali. So the three set out together, when no doubt the sober, solid appearance which Randall's double suit of apparel and black gown gave him, together with his wife's matronly and respectable look, were no small protection to Ambrose, for men-at-arms were prowling about the streets, looking hungry to pick up straggling victims; and one actually stopped Randall to interrogate him as to who the youth was, and what was his errand.

Before Saint Paul's they parted, the husband and wife going towards Warwick Inner Ward, whither Ambrose, fleeter of foot, would follow, so soon as he had ascertained at the Dragon court whether Stephen was at home.

Alas! at the gate he was hailed with the inquiry whether he had seen his brother or Giles. The whole yard was disorganised, no work going on. The lads had not been seen all night, and the master himself had in the midst of his displeasure and anxiety been summoned to the Guildhall. The last that was known was Giles's rescue, and the assault on Alderman Mundy. Smallbones and Steelman had both gone in different directions to search for the two apprentices, and Dennet, who had flown down unheeded and unchecked at the first hope of news, pulled Ambrose by the sleeve, and exclaimed, "Oh! Ambrose, Ambrose! they can never hurt them! They can never do any harm to *our* lads, can they?"

Ambrose hoped for the same security, but in his dismay, could only hurry after his uncle and aunt.

He found the former at the door of the old stable—whence issued wild screams and cries. Several priests and attendants were there now, and the kind Dean with Lucas was trying to induce Aldonza to relax the grasp with which she embraced the body, whence a few moments before the brave and constant spirit had departed. Her black hair hanging over like a veil, she held the inanimate head to her bosom, sobbing and shrieking with the violence of her Eastern nature. The priest who had been sent for to take care of the corpse, and bear it to the mortuary of the Minster, wanted to move her by force; but the Dean insisted on one more gentle experiment, and beckoned to the kindly woman, whom he saw advancing with eyes full of tears. Perronel knelt down by her, persevered when the poor girl stretched out her hand to beat her off, crying, "Off! go! Leave me my father! O father, father, joy of my life! my one only hope and stay, leave me not! Wake! wake, speak to thy child, O my father!"

Though the child had never seen or heard of Eastern wailings over the dead, yet hereditary nature prompted her to the lamentations that scandalised the priests and even Lucas, who broke in with, "Fie, maid, thou mournest as one who hath no hope." But Dr. Colet still signed to them to have patience, and Perronel somehow contrived to draw the girl's head on her breast and give her a motherly kiss, such as the poor child had never felt since she, when almost a babe, had been lifted from her dying mother's side in the dark stifling hold of the vessel in the Bay of Biscay. And in sheer surprise and sense of being soothed she ceased her cries, listened to the tender whispers and persuasions about holy men who would care for her father, and his wishes that she should be a good maid—till at last she yielded, let her hands be loosed, allowed Perronel to lift the venerable head from her knee, and close the eyes—then to gather her in her arms, and lead her to the door, taking her, under Ambrose's guidance, into Lucas's abode, which was as utterly and mournfully dismantled as their own, but where Perronel, accustomed in her wandering days to all sorts of contrivances, managed to bind up the streaming hair, and, by the help of her own cloak, to bring the poor girl into a state in which she could be led through the streets.

The Dean meantime had bidden Lucas to take shelter at his own house, and the old Dutchman had given a sort of doubtful acceptance.

Ambrose, meanwhile, half distracted about his brother, craved counsel of the jester where to seek him.

CHAPTER XVII.

Ill May Day.

"With two and two together tied,
Through Temple Bar and Strand they go,
To Westminster, there to be tried,
Ropes about their necks also."

Ill May Day.

And where was Stephen? Crouching, wretched with hunger, cold, weariness, blows, and what was far worse, sense of humiliation and disgrace, and tenor for the future, in a corner of the yard of Newgate—whither the whole set of lads, surprised in Warwick Inner Court by the law students of the Inns of Court, had been driven like so many cattle, at the sword's point, with no attention or perception that he and Giles had been struggling against the spoilers.

Yet this fact made them all the more forlorn. The others, some forty in number, their companions in misfortune, included most of the Barbican prentices, who were of the Eagle faction, special enemies alike to Abenali and to the Dragon, and these held aloof from Headley and Birkenholt, nay, reviled them for the attack which they declared had caused the general capture.

The two lads of the Dragon had, in no measured terms, denounced the cruelty to the poor old inoffensive man, and were denounced in their turn as friends of the sorcerer. But all were too much exhausted by the night's work to have spirit for more than a snarling encounter of words, and the only effect was that Giles and Stephen were left isolated in their misery outside the shelter of the handsome arched gateway under which the others congregated.

Newgate had been rebuilt by Whittington out of pity to poor prisoners and captives. It must have been unspeakably dreadful before, for the foulness of the narrow paved court, shut in by strong walls, was something terrible. Tired, spent, and aching all over, and with boyish callousness to dirt, still Giles and Stephen hesitated to sit down, and when at last they could stand no longer, they rested, leaning against one another. Stephen tried to keep up hope by declaring that his master would soon get them released, and Giles alternated between despair, and declarations that he would have justice on those who so treated his father's son. They dropped asleep—first one and then the other—from sheer exhaustion, waking from time to time to realise that it was no dream, and to feel all the colder and more cramped.

By and by there were voices at the gate. Friends were there asking after their own Will, or John, or Thomas, as the case might be. The jailer opened a little wicket-window in the heavy door, and, no doubt for a consideration, passed in food to certain lads whom he called out, but it did not always reach its destination. It was often torn away as by hungry wolves. For though the felons had been let out, when the doors were opened; the new prisoners were not by any means all apprentices. There were watermen, husbandmen, beggars, thieves, among them, attracted by the scent of plunder; and even some of the elder lads had no scruple in snatching the morsel from the younger ones.

Poor little Jasper Hope, a mischievous little curly-headed idle fellow, only thirteen, just apprenticed to his brother the draper, and rushing about with the other youths in the pride of his flat cap, was one of the sufferers. A servant had been at the door, promising that his brother would speedily have him released, and handing in bread and meat, of which he was instantly robbed by George Bates and three or four more big fellows, and sent away reeling and sobbing, under a heavy blow, with all the mischief and play knocked out of him. Stephen and Giles called "Shame!" but were unheeded, and they could only draw the little fellow up to them, and assure him that his brother would soon come for him.

The next call at the gate was Headley and Birkenholt—

"Master Headley's prentices—Be they here?"

And at their answer, not only the window, but the door in the gate was opened, and stooping low to enter, Kit Smallbones came in, and not empty-handed.

"Ay, ay, youngsters," said he, "I knew how it would be, by what I saw elsewhere, so I came with a fee to open locks. How came ye to get into such plight as this? And poor little Hope too! A fine pass when they put babes in jail."

"I'm prenticed!" said Jasper, though in a very weak little voice.

"Have you had bite or sup?" asked Kit.

And on their reply, telling how those who had had supplies from home had been treated, Smallbones observed, "Let them try it," and stood, at all his breadth, guarding the two youths and little Jasper, as they ate, Stephen at first with difficulty, in the dampness and foulness of the place, but then ravenously. Smallbones lectured them on their folly all the time, and made them give an account of the night. He said their master was at the Guildhall taking counsel with the Lord Mayor, and there were reports that it would go hard with the rioters, for murder and plunder had been done in many places, and he especially looked at. Giles with pity, and asked how he came to embroil himself with Master Mundy? Still his good-natured face cheered them, and he promised further supplies. He also relieved Stephen's mind about his brother, telling of his inquiry at the Dragon in the morning. All that day the condition of such of the prisoners as had well-to-do friends was improving. Fathers, brothers, masters, and servants, came in quest of them, bringing food and bedding, and by exorbitant fees to the jailers obtained for them shelter in the gloomy cells. Mothers could not come, for a proclamation had gone out that none were to babble, and men were to keep their wives at home. And though there were more material comforts, prospects were very gloomy. Ambrose came when Kit Smallbones returned with what Mrs. Headley had sent the captives. He looked sad and dazed, and clung to his brother, but said very little, except that they ought to be locked up together, and he really would have been left in Newgate, if Kit had not laid a great hand on his shoulder and almost forced him away.

Master Headley himself arrived with Master Hope in the afternoon. Jasper sprang to his brother, crying, "Simon! Simon! you are come to take me out of this dismal, evil place?" But Master Hope—a tall, handsome, grave young man, who had often been much disturbed by his little brother's pranks—could only shake his head with tears in his eyes, and, sitting down on the roll of bedding, take him on his knee and try to console him with the hope of liberty in a few days.

He had tried to obtain the boy's release on the plea of his extreme youth, but the authorities were hotly exasperated, and would hear of no mercy. The whole of the rioters were to be tried three days hence, and there was no doubt that some would be made an example of; the only question was, how many?

Master Headley closely interrogated his own two lads, and was evidently sorely anxious about his namesake, who, he feared, might be recognised by Alderman Mundy and brought forward as a ringleader of the disturbance; nor did he feel at all secure that the plea that he had no enmity to the foreigners, but had actually tried to defend Lucas and Abenali, would be attended to for a moment, though Lucas Hansen had promised to bear witness of it. Giles looked perfectly stunned at the time, unable to take in the idea, but at night Stephen was wakened on the pallet that they shared with little Jasper, by hearing him weeping and sobbing for his mother at Salisbury.

Time lagged on till the 4th of May. Some of the poor boys whiled away their time with dreary games in the yard, sometimes wrestling, but more often gambling with the dice, that one or two happened to possess, for the dinners that were provided for the wealthier, sometimes even betting on what the sentences would be, and who would be hanged, or who escape.

Poor lads, they did not, for the most part, realise their real danger, but Stephen was more and more beset with home-sick longing for the glades and thickets of his native forest, and would keep little Jasper and even Giles for an hour together telling of the woodland adventures of those happy times, shutting his eyes to the grim stone walls, and trying to think himself among the beeches, hollies, cherries, and hawthorns, shining in the May sun! Giles and he were close friends now, and with little Jasper, said their Paters and Ayes together, that they might be delivered from their trouble. At last, on the 4th, the whole of the prisoners were summoned roughly into the court, where harsh-looking men-at-arms proceeded to bind them together in pairs to be marched through the streets to the Guildhall. Giles and Stephen would naturally have been put together, but poor little Jasper cried out so lamentably, when he was about to be bound to a stranger, that Stephen stepped forward in his stead, begging that the boy might go with Giles. The soldier made a contemptuous sound, but consented, and Stephen found that his companion in misfortune, whose left elbow was tied to his right, was George Bates.

The two lads looked at each other in a strange, rueful manner, and Stephen said, "Shake hands, comrade. If we are to die, let us bear no ill-will."

George gave a cold, limp, trembling hand. He looked wretched, subdued, tearful, and nearly starved, for he had no kinsfolk at hand, and his master was too angry with him, and too much afraid of compromising himself to have sent him any supplies. Stephen tried to unbutton his own pouch, but not succeeding with his left hand, bade George try with his right. "There's a cake of bread there," he said. "Eat that, and thou'lt be able better to stand up like a man, come what will."

George devoured it eagerly. "Ah!" he said, in a stronger voice, "Stephen Birkenholt, thou art an honest fellow. I did thee wrong. If ever we get out of this plight—"

Here they were ordered to march, and in a long and doleful procession they set forth. The streets were lined with men-at-arms, for all the affections and sympathies of the people were with the unfortunate boys, and a rescue was apprehended.

In point of fact, the Lord Mayor and aldermen were afraid of the King's supposing them to have organised the assault on their rivals, and each was therefore desirous to show severity to any one's apprentices save his own; while the nobility were afraid of contumacy on the part of the citizens, and were resolved to crush down every rioter among them, so that they had filled the city with their armed retainers. Fathers and mothers, masters and dames, sisters and fellow prentices, found their doors closely guarded, and could only look with tearful, anxious eyes, at the processions of poor youths, many of them mere children, who were driven from each of the jails to the Guildhall. There when all collected the entire number amounted to two hundred and seventy-eight though a certain proportion of these were grown men, priests, wherrymen and beggars, who had joined the rabble in search of plunder.

It did not look well for them that the Duke of Norfolk and his son, the Earl of Surrey, were joined in the commission with the Lord Mayor. The upper end of the great hall was filled with aldermen in their robes and chains, with the sheriffs of London and the whole imposing array, and the Lord Mayor with the Duke sat enthroned above them in truly awful dignity. The Duke was a hard and pitiless man, and bore the City a bitter grudge for the death of his retainer, the priest killed in Cheapside, and in spite of all his poetical fame, it may be feared that the Earl of Surrey was not of much more merciful mood, while their men-at-arms spoke savagely of hanging, slaughtering, or setting the City on fire.

The arraignment was very long, as there were so large a number of names to be read, and, to the horror of all, it was not for a mere riot, but for high treason. The King, it was declared, being in amity with all Christian princes, it was high treason to break the truce and league by attacking their subjects resident in England. The terrible punishment of the traitor would thus be the doom of all concerned, and in the temper of the Howards and their retainers, there was little hope of mercy, nor, in times like those, was there even much prospect that, out of such large numbers, some might escape.

A few were more especially cited, fourteen in number, among them George Bates, Walter Ball, and Giles Headley, who had certainly given cause for the beginning of the affray. There was no attempt to defend George Bates, who seemed to be stunned and bewildered beyond the power of speaking or even of understanding, but as Giles cast his eyes round in wild, terrified appeal, Master Headley rose up in his alderman's gown, and prayed leave to be heard in his defence, as he had witnesses to bring in his favour.

"Is he thy son, good Armourer Headley?" demanded the Duke of Norfolk, who held the work of the Dragon court in high esteem.

"Nay, my Lord Duke, but he is in the place of one, my near kinsman and godson, and so soon as his time be up, bound to wed my only child! I pray you to hear his cause, ere cutting off the heir of an old and honourable house."

Norfolk and his sons murmured something about the Headley skill in armour, and the Lord Mayor was willing enough for mercy, but Sir John Mundy here rose: "My Lord Duke, this is the very young man who was first to lay hands on me! Yea, my lords and sirs, ye have already heard how their rude sport, contrary to proclamation, was the cause of the tumult. When I would have bidden them go home, the one brawler asks me insolently, 'Wherefore?' the other smote me with his sword, whereupon the whole rascaille set on me, and as Master Alderman Headley can testify, I scarce reached his house alive. I ask should favour overcome justice, and a ringleader, who hath assaulted the person of an alderman, find favour above others?"

"I ask not for favour," returned Headley, "only that witnesses be heard on his behalf, ere he be condemned."

Headley, as a favourite with the Duke, prevailed to have permission to call his witnesses; Christopher Smallbones, who had actually rescued Alderman Mundy from the mob, and helped him into the Dragon court, could testify that the proclamation had been entirely unheard in the din of the youths looking on at the game. And this was followed up by Lucas Hansen declaring that so far from having attacked or plundered him and the others in Warwick Inner Ward, the two, Giles Headley and Stephen Birkenholt, had come to their defence, and fallen on those who were burning their goods.

On this a discussion followed between the authorities seated at the upper end of the hall. The poor anxious watchers below could only guess by the gestures what was being agitated as to their fate, and Stephen was feeling it sorely hard that Giles should be pleaded for as the master's kinsman, and he left to so cruel a fate, no one saying a word for him but unheeded Lucas. Finally, without giving of judgment, the whole of the miserable prisoners, who had been standing without food for hours, were marched back, still tied, to their several prisons, while their guards pointed out the gibbets where they were to suffer the next day.

Master Headley was not quite so regardless of his younger apprentice as Stephen imagined. There was a sort of little council held in his hall when he returned—sad, dispirited, almost hopeless—to find Hal Randall anxiously awaiting him. The alderman said he durst not plead for Stephen, lest he should lose both by asking too much, and his young kinsman had the first right, besides being in the most peril as having been singled out by name; whereas

Stephen might escape with the multitude if there were any mercy. He added that the Duke of Norfolk was certainly inclined to save one who knew the secret of Spanish sword-blades; but that he was fiercely resolved to be revenged for the murder of his lewd priest in Cheapside, and that Sir John Mundy was equally determined that Giles should not escape.

"What am I to say to his mother? Have I brought him from her for this?" mourned Master Headley. "Ay, and Master Randall, I grieve as much for thy nephew, who to my mind hath done nought amiss. A brave lad! A good lad, who hath saved mine own life. Would that I could do aught for him! It is a shame!"

"Father," said Dennet, who had crept to the back of his chair, "the King would save him! Mind you the golden whistle that the grandame keepeth?"

"The maid hath hit it!" exclaimed Randall. "Master alderman! Let me but have the little wench and the whistle tomorrow morn, and it is done. How sayest thou, pretty mistress? Wilt thou go with me and ask thy cousin's life, and poor Stephen's, of the King?"

"With all my heart, sir," said Dennet, coming to him with outstretched hands. "Oh! sir, canst thou save them? I have been vowing all I could think of to our Lady and the saints, and now they are going to grant it!"

"Tarry a little," said the alderman. "I must know more of this. Where wouldst thou take my child? How obtain access to the King's Grace?"

"Worshipful sir, trust me," said Randall. "Thou know'st I am sworn servant to my Lord Cardinal, and that his folk are as free of the Court as the King's own servants. If thine own folk will take us up the river to Richmond, and there wait for us while I lead the maid to the King, I can well-nigh swear to thee that she will prevail."

The alderman looked greatly distressed. Ambrose threw himself on his knees before him, and in an agony entreated him to consent, assuring him that Master Randall could do what he promised. The alderman was much perplexed. He knew that his mother, who was confined to her bed by rheumatism, would be shocked at the idea. He longed to accompany his daughter himself, but for him to be absent from the sitting of the court might be fatal to Giles, and he could not bear to lose any chance for the poor youths.

Meantime an interrogative glance and a nod had passed between Tibble and Randall, and when the alderman looked towards the former, always his prime minister, the answer was, "Sir, me seemeth that it were well to do as Master Randall counselleth. I will go with Mistress Dennet, if such be your will. The lives of two such youths as our prentices may not lightly be thrown away, while by God's providence there is any means of striving to save them."

Consent then was given, and it was further arranged that Dennet and her escort should be ready at the early hour of half-past four, so as to elude the guards who were placed in the streets; and also because King Henry in the summer went very early to mass, and then to some out-of-door sport. Randall said he would have taken his own good woman to have the care of the little mistress, but that the poor little orphan Spanish wench had wept herself so sick, that she could not be left to a stranger.

Master Headley himself brought the child by back streets to the river, and thence down to the Temple stairs, accompanied by Tibble Steelman, and a maidservant on whose presence her grandmother had insisted. Dennet had hardly slept all night for excitement and perturbation, and she looked very white, small, and insignificant for her thirteen years, when Randall and Ambrose met her, and placed her carefully in the barge which was to take them to Richmond. It was somewhat fresh in the very early morning, and no one was surprised that Master Randall wore a large dark cloak as they rowed up the river. There was very little speech between the passengers; Dennet sat between Ambrose and Tibble. They kept their heads bowed. Ambrose's brow was on one hand, his elbow on his knee, but he spared the other to hold Dennet. He had been longing for the old assurance he would once have had, that to vow himself to a life of hard service in a convent would be the way to win his brother's life; but he had ceased to be able to feel that such bargains were the right course, or that a convent necessarily afforded sure way of service, and he never felt more insecure of the way and means to prayer than in this hour of anguished supplication.

When they came beyond the City, within sight of the trees of Sheen, as Richmond was still often called, Randall insisted that Dennet should eat some of the bread and meat that Tibble had brought in a wallet for her. "She must look her best," he said aside to the foreman. "I would that she were either more a babe or better favoured! Our Hal hath a tender heart for a babe and an eye for a buxom lass."

He bade the maid trim up the child's cap and make the best of her array, and presently reached some stairs leading up to the park. There he let Ambrose lift her out of the boat. The maid would fain have followed, but he prevented this, and when she spoke of her mistress having bidden her follow wherever the child went, Tibble interfered, telling her that his master's orders were that Master Randall should do with her as he thought meet. Tibble himself followed until they reached a thicket entirely concealing them from the river. Halting here, Randall, with his nephew's help, divested himself of his long gown and cloak, his beard and wig, produced cockscomb and bauble from his pouch, and stood before the astonished eyes of Dennet as the jester!

She recoiled upon Tibble with a little cry, "Oh, why should he make sport of us? Why disguise himself?"

"Listen, pretty mistress," said Randall. "'Tis no disguise, Tibble there can tell you, or my nephew. My disguise lies there," pointing to his sober raiment. "Thus only can I bring thee to the King's presence! Didst think it was jest? Nay, verily, I am as bound to try to save my sweet Stevie's life, my sister's own gallant son, as thou canst be to plead for thy betrothed." Dennet winced.

"Ay, Mistress Dennet," said Tibble, "thou mayst trust him, spite of his garb, and 'tis the sole hope. He could only thus bring thee in. Go thou on, and the lad and I will fall to our prayers."

Dennet's bosom heaved, but she looked up in the jester's dark eyes, saw the tears in them, made an effort, put her hand in his, and said, "I will go with him."

Hal led her away, and they saw Tibble and Ambrose both fall on their knees behind the hawthorn bush, to speed them with their prayers, while all the joyous birds singing their carols around seemed to protest against the cruel captivity and dreadful doom of the young gladsome spirits pent up in the City prisons.

One full gush of a thrush's song in especial made Dennet's eyes overflow, which the jester perceived and said, "Nay, sweet maid, no tears. Kings brook not to be approached with blubbered faces. I marvel not that it seems hard to thee to go along with such as I, but let me be what I will outside, mine heart is heavy enough, and thou wilt learn sooner or later, that fools are not the only folk who needs must smile when they have a load within."

And then, as much to distract her thoughts and prevent tears as to reassure her, he told her what he had before told his nephews of the inducements that had made him Wolsey's jester, and impressed on her the forms of address.

"Thou'lt hear me make free with him, but that's part of mine office, like the kitten I've seen tickling the mane of the lion in the Tower. Thou must say, 'An it please your Grace,' and thou needst not speak of his rolling in the mire, thou wottest, or it may anger him."

The girl showed that her confidence became warmer by keeping nearer to his side, and presently she said, "I must beg for Stephen first, for 'tis his whistle."

"Blessings on thee, fair wench, for that, yet seest thou, 'tis the other springald who is in the greater peril, and he is closer to thy father and to thee."

"He fled, when Stephen made in to the rescue of my father," said Dennet.

"The saints grant we may so work with the King that he may spare them both," ejaculated Randall.

By this time the strange pair were reaching the precincts of the great dwelling-house, where about the wide-open door loitered gentlemen, grooms, lacqueys, and attendants of all kinds. Randall reconnoitred.

"An we go up among all these," he said, "they might make their sport of us both, so that we might lose time. Let us see whether the little garden postern be open."

Henry the Eighth had no fears of his people, and kept his dwellings more accessible than were the castles of many a subject. The door in the wall proved to be open, and with an exclamation of joy, Randall pointed out two figures, one in a white silken doublet and hose, with a short crimson cloak over his shoulder, the other in scarlet and purple robes, pacing the walk under the wall—Henry's way of holding a cabinet council with his prime minister on a summer's morning.

"Come on, mistress, put a brave face on it!" the jester encouraged the girl, as he led her forward, while the king, catching sight of them, exclaimed, "Ha! there's old Patch. What doth he there?"

But the Cardinal, impatient of interruption, spoke imperiously, "What dost thou here, Merriman? Away, this is no time for thy fooleries and frolics."

But the King, with some pleasure in teasing, and some of the enjoyment of a schoolboy at a break in his tasks, called out, "Nay, come hither, quipsome one! What new puppet hast brought hither to play off on us?"

"Yea, brother Hal," said the jester, "I have brought one to let thee know how Tom of Norfolk and his crew are playing the fool in the Guildhall, and to ask who will be the fool to let them wreak their spite on the best blood in London, and leave a sore that will take many a day to heal."

"How is this, my Lord Cardinal?" said Henry; "I bade them make an example of a few worthless hinds, such as might teach the lusty burghers to hold their lads in bounds and prove to our neighbours that their churlishness was by no consent of ours."

"I trow," returned the Cardinal, "that one of these same hinds is a boon companion of the fool's—*hinc illae lachrymae*, and a speech that would have befitted a wise man's mouth."

"There is work that may well make even a fool grave, friend Thomas," replied the jester.

"Nay, but what hath this little wench to say?" asked the King, looking down on the child from under his plumed cap with a face set in golden hair, the fairest and sweetest, as it seemed to her, that she had ever seen, as he smiled upon her. "Methinks she is too small to be thy love. Speak out, little one. I love little maids, I have one of mine own. Hast thou a brother among these misguided lads?"

"Not so, an please your Grace," said Dennet, who fortunately was not in the least shy, and was still too young for a maiden's shamefastness. "He is to be my betrothed. I would say, one of them is, but the other—he saved my father's life once."

The latter words were lost in the laughter of the King and Cardinal at the unblushing avowal of the small, prim-faced maiden.

"Oh ho! So 'tis a case of true love, whereto a King's face must needs show grace. Who art thou, fair suppliant, and who may this swain of thine be?"

"I am Dennet Headley, so please your Grace; my father is Giles Headley the armourer, Alderman of Cheap Ward," said Dennet, doing her part bravely, though puzzled by the King's tone of banter; "and see here, your Grace!"

"Ha! the hawk's whistle that Archduke Philip gave me! What of that? I gave it—ay, I gave it to a youth that came to mine aid, and reclaimed a falcon for me! Is't he, child?"

"Oh, sir, 'tis he who came in second at the butts, next to Barlow, 'tis Stephen Birkenholt! And he did nought! They bore no ill-will to strangers! No, they were falling on the wicked fellows who had robbed and slain good old Master Michael, who taught our folk to make the only real true Damascus blades welded in England. But the lawyers of the Inns of Court fell on them all alike, and have driven them off to Newgate, and poor little Jasper Hope too. And Alderman Mundy bears ill-will to Giles. And the cruel Duke of Norfolk and his men swear they'll have vengeance on the Cheap, and there'll be hanging and quartering this very morn. Oh! your Grace, your Grace, save our lads! for Stephen saved my father."

"Thy tongue wags fast, little one," said the King, good-naturedly, "with thy Stephen and thy Giles. Is this same Stephen, the knight of the whistle and the bow, thy betrothed, and Giles thy brother?"

"Nay, your Grace," said Dennet, hanging her head, "Giles Headley is my betrothed—that is, when his time is served, he will be—father sets great store by him, for he is the only one of our name to keep up the armoury, and he has a mother, Sir, a mother at Salisbury. But oh, Sir, Sir! Stephen is so good and brave a lad! He made in to save father from the robbers, and he draws the best bow in Cheapside, and he can grave steel as well as Tibble himself, and this is the whistle your Grace wots of."

Henry listened with an amused smile that grew broader as Dennet's voice all unconsciously became infinitely more animated and earnest, when she began to plead Stephen's cause.

"Well, well, sweetheart," he said, "I trow thou must have the twain of them, though," he added to the Cardinal, who smiled broadly, "it might perchance be more for the maid's peace than she wots of now, were we to leave this same knight of the whistle to be strung up at once, ere she have found her heart; but in sooth that I cannot do, owing well-nigh a life to him and his brother. Moreover, we may not have old Headley's skill in weapons lost!"

Dennet held her hands close clasped while these words were spoken apart. She felt as if her hope, half granted, were being snatched from her, as another actor appeared on the scene, a gentleman in a lawyer's gown, and square cap, which he doffed as he advanced and put his knee to the ground before the King, who greeted him with, "Save you, good Sir Thomas, a fair morning to you."

"They told me your Grace was in Council with my Lord Cardinal," said Sir Thomas More; "but seeing that there was likewise this merry company, I durst venture to thrust in, since my business is urgent."

Dennet here forgot court manners enough to cry out, "O your Grace! your Grace, be pleased for pity's sake to let me have the pardon for them first, or they'll be hanged and dead. I saw the gallows in Cheapside, and when they are dead, what good will your Grace's mercy do them?"

"I see," said Sir Thomas. "This little maid's errand jumps with mine own, which was to tell your Grace that unless there be speedy commands to the Howards to hold their hands, there will be wailing like that of Egypt in the City. The poor boys, who were but shouting and brawling after the nature of mettled youth—the most with nought of malice—are penned up like sheep for the slaughter—ay, and worse than sheep, for we quarter not our mutton alive, whereas these poor younglings—babes of thirteen, some of them—be indicted for high treason! Will the parents, shut in from coming to them by my Lord of Norfolks men, ever forget their agonies, I ask your Grace?"

Henry's face grew red with passion. "If Norfolk thinks to act the King, and turn the city into a shambles,"—with a mighty oath—"he shall abye it.

Here, Lord Cardinal—more, let the free pardon be drawn up for the two lads. And we will ourselves write to the Lord Mayor and to Norfolk that though they may work their will on the movers of the riot—that pestilent Lincoln and his sort—not a prentice lad shall be touched till our pleasure be known. There now, child, thou hast won the lives of thy lads, as thou callest them. Wilt thou rue the day, I marvel? Why cannot some of their mothers pluck up spirit and beg them off as thou hast done?"

"Yea," said Wolsey. "That were the right course. If the Queen were moved to pray your Grace to pity the striplings, then could the Spaniards make no plaint of too much clemency being shown."

They were all this time getting nearer the palace, and being now at a door opening into the hall, Henry turned round. "There, pretty maid, spread the tidings among thy gossips, that they have a tender-hearted Queen, and a gracious King. The Lord Cardinal will presently give thee the pardon for both thy lads, and by and by thou wilt know whether thou thankest me for it!" Then putting his hand under her chin, he turned up her face to him, kissed her on each cheek, and touched his feathered cap to the others, saying, "See that my bidding be done," and disappeared.

"It must be prompt, if it be to save any marked for death this morn," More in a low voice observed to the Cardinal. "Lord Edmund Howard is keen as a bloodhound on his vengeance."

Wolsey was far from being a cruel man, and besides, there was a natural antagonism between him and the old nobility, and he liked and valued his fool, to whom he turned, saying, "And what stake hast thou in this, sirrah? Is't all pure charity?"

"I'm scarce such a fool as that, Cousin Red Hat," replied Randall, rallying his powers. "I leave that to Mr. More here, whom we all know to be a good fool spoilt. But I'll make a clean breast of it. This same Stephen is my sister's son, an orphan lad of good birth and breeding—whom, my lord, I would die to save."

"Thou shalt have the pardon instantly, Merriman," said the Cardinal, and beckoning to one of the attendants who clustered round the door, he gave orders that a clerk should instantly, and very briefly, make out the form. Sir Thomas More, hearing the name of Headley, added that for him indeed the need of haste was great, since he was one of the fourteen sentenced to die that morning.

Quipsome Hal was interrogated as to how he had come, and the Cardinal and Sir Thomas agreed that the river would be as speedy a way of returning as by land; but they decided that a King's pursuivant should accompany him, otherwise there would be no chance of forcing his way in time through the streets, guarded by the Howard retainers.

As rapidly as was in the nature of a high officer's clerk to produce a dozen lines, the precious document was indicted, and it was carried at last to Dennet, bearing Henry's signature and seal. She held it to her bosom, while, accompanied by the pursuivant, who—happily for them—was interested in one of the unfortunate fourteen, and therefore did not wait to stand on his dignity, they hurried across to the place where they had left the barge—Tibble and Ambrose joining them on the way. Stephen was safe. Of his life there could be no doubt, and Ambrose almost repented of feeling his heart so light while Giles's fate hung upon their speed.

The oars were plied with hearty good-will, but the barge was somewhat heavy, and by and by coming to a landing-place where two watermen had a much smaller and lighter boat, the pursuivant advised that he should go forward with the more necessary persons, leaving the others to follow. After a few words, the light weights of Tibble and Dennet prevailed in their favour, and they shot forward in the little boat.

They passed the Temple—on to the stairs nearest Cheapside—up the street. There was an awful stillness, only broken by heavy knells sounding at intervals from the churches. The back streets were thronged by a trembling, weeping people, who all eagerly made way for the pursuivant, as he called, "Make way, good people—a pardon!"

They saw the broader space of Cheapside. Horsemen in armour guarded it, but they too opened a passage for the pursuivant. There was to be seen above the people's heads a scaffold. A fire burnt on it—the gallows and noosed rope hung above.

A figure was mounting the ladder. A boy! Oh, Heavens! would it be too late? Who was it? They were still too far off to see. They might only be cruelly holding out hope to one of the doomed.

The pursuivant shouted aloud—"In the King's name, Hold!" He lifted Dennet on his shoulder, and bade her wave her parchment. An overpowering roar arose. "A pardon! a pardon! God save the King!"

Every hand seemed to be forwarding the pursuivant and the child, and it was Giles Headley, who, loosed from the hold of the executioner, stared wildly about him, like one distraught.

CHAPTER XVIII.

Pardon.

*"'What if,' quoth she, 'by Spanish blood
Have London's stately streets been wet,
Yet will I seek this country's good
And pardon for these young men get.'"*

Churchill.

The night and morning had been terrible to the poor boys, who only had begun to understand what awaited them. The fourteen selected had little hope, and indeed a priest came in early morning to hear the confessions of Giles Headley and George Bates, the only two who were in Newgate.

George Bates was of the stolid, heavy disposition that seems armed by outward indifference, or mayhap pride. He knew that his case was hopeless, and he would not thaw even to the priest. But Giles had been quite unmanned, and when he found that for the doleful procession to the Guildhall he was to be coupled with George Bates, instead of either of his room-fellows, he flung himself on Stephen's neck, sobbing out messages for his mother, and entreaties that, if Stephen survived, he would be good to Aldonza. "For you will wed Dennet, and—"

There the jailers roughly ordered him to hold his peace, and dragged him off to be pinioned to his fellow-sufferer. Stephen was not called till some minutes later, and had not seen him since. He himself was of course overshadowed by the awful gloom of apprehension for himself, and pity for his comrades, and he was grieved at not having seen or heard of his brother or master, but he had a very present care in Jasper, who was sickening in the prison atmosphere, and when fastened to his arm, seemed hardly able to walk. Leashed as they were, Stephen could only help him by holding the free hand, and when they came to the hall, supporting him as much as possible, as they stood in the miserable throng during the conclusion of the formalities, which ended by the horrible sentence of the traitor being pronounced on the whole two hundred and seventy-eight. Poor little Jasper woke for an interval from the sense of present discomfort to hear it. He seemed to stiffen all over with the shock of horror, and then hung a dead weight on Stephen's arm. It would have dragged him down, but there was no room to fall, and the wretchedness of the lad against whom he staggered found vent in a surly imprecation, which was lost among the cries and the entreaties of some of the others. The London magistracy were some of them in tears, but the indictment for high treason removed the poor lads from their jurisdiction to that of the Earl Marshal, and thus they could do nothing to save the fourteen foremost victims. The others were again driven out of the hall to return to their prisons; the nearest pair of lads doing their best to help Stephen drag his burthen along in the halt outside, to arrange the sad processions, one of the guards, of milder mood, cut the cord that bound the lifeless weight to Stephen, and permitted the child to be laid on the stones of the court, his collar unbuttoned, and water to be brought. Jasper was just reviving when the word came to march, but still he could not stand, and Stephen was therefore permitted the free use of his arms, in order to carry the poor little fellow. Thirteen years made a considerable load for seventeen, though Stephen's arms were exercised in the smithy, and it was a sore pull from the Guildhall. Jasper presently recovered enough to walk with a good deal of support. When he was laid on the bed he fell into an exhausted sleep, while Stephen kneeling, as the strokes of the knell smote on his ear, prayed—as he had never prayed before—for his comrade, for his enemy, and for all the unhappy boys who were being led to their death wherever the outrages had been committed.

Once indeed there was a strange sound coming across that of the knell. It almost sounded like an acclamation of joy. Could people be so cruel, thought Stephen, as to mock poor Giles's agonies? There were the knells still sounding. How long he did not know, for a beneficent drowsiness stole over him as he knelt, and he was only awakened, at the same time as Jasper, by the opening of his door.

He looked up to see three figures—his brother, his uncle, his master. Were they come to take leave of him? But the one conviction that their faces beamed with joy was all that he could gather, for little Jasper sprang up with a scream of terror, "Stephen, Stephen, save me! They will cut out my heart," and clung trembling to his breast, with arms round his neck.

"Poor child! poor child!" sighed Master Headley. "Would that I brought him the same tidings as to thee!"

"Is it so?" asked Stephen, reading confirmation as he looked from the one to the other. Though he was unable to rise under the weight of the boy, life and light were coming to his eye, while Ambrose clasped his hand tightly, choked by the swelling of his heart in almost an agony of joy and thankfulness.

"Yea, my good lad," said the alderman. "Thy good kinsman took my little wench to bear to the King the token he gave thee."

"And Giles?" Stephen asked, "and the rest?"

"Giles is safe. For the rest—may God have mercy on their souls."

These words passed while Stephen rocked Jasper backwards and forwards, his face hidden on his neck.

"Come home," added Master Headley. "My little Dennet and Giles cannot yet rejoice till thou art with them. Giles would have come himself, but he is sorely shaken, and could scarce stand."

Jasper caught the words, and loosing his friend's neck, looked up. "Oh! are we going home? Come, Stephen. Where's brother Simon? I want my good sister! I want nurse! Oh! take me home!" For as he tried to sit up, he fell back sick and dizzy on the bed.

"Alack! alack!" mourned Master Headley; and the jester, muttering that it was not the little wench's fault, turned to the window, and burst into tears. Stephen understood it all, and though he felt a passionate longing for freedom, he considered in one moment whether there were any one of his fellow prisoners to whom Jasper could be left, or who would be of the least comfort to him, but could find no one, and resolved to cling to him as once to old Spring.

"Sir," he said, as he rose to his master, "I fear me he is very sick. Will they—will your worship give me licence to bide with him till this ends?"

"Thou art a good-hearted lad," said the alderman with a hand on his shoulder. "There is no further danger of life to the prentice lads. The King hath sent to forbid all further dealing with them, and hath bidden my little maid to set it about that if their mothers beg them grace from good Queen Katherine, they shall have it. But this poor child! He can scarce be left. His brother will take it well of thee if thou wilt stay with him till some tendance can be had. We can see to that. Thanks be to Saint George and our good King, this good City is our own again!"

The alderman turned away, and Ambrose and Stephen exchanged a passionate embrace, feeling what it was to be still left to one another. The jester too shook his nephew's hand, saying, "Boy, boy, the blessing of such as I is scarce worth the having, but I would thy mother could see thee this day."

Stephen was left with these words and his brother's look to bear him through a trying time.

For the "Captain of Newgate" was an autocrat, who looked on his captives as compulsory lodgers, out of whom he was entitled to wring as much as possible—as indeed he had no other salary, nor means of maintaining his underlings, a state of things which lasted for two hundred years longer, until the days of James Oglethorpe and John Howard. Even in the rare cases of acquittals, the prisoner could not be released till he had paid his fees, and that Giles Headley should have been borne off from the scaffold itself in debt to him was an invasion of his privileges, which did not dispose him to be favourable to any one connected with that affair; and he liked to show his power and dignity even to an alderman.

He was found sitting in a comfortable tapestried chamber, handsomely dressed in orange and brown, and with a smooth sleek countenance and the appearance of a good-natured substantial citizen.

He only half rose from his big carved chair, and touched without removing his cap, to greet the alderman, as he observed, without the accustomed prefix of your worship—"So, you are come about your prentice's fees and dues. By Saint Peter of the Fetters, 'tis an irksome matter to have such a troop of idle, mischievous, dainty striplings thrust on one, giving more trouble, and making more call and outcry than twice as many honest thieves and pickpurses."

"Be assured, sir, they will scarce trouble you longer than they can help," said Master Headley.

"Yea, the Duke and my Lord Edmund are making brief work of them," quoth the jailer. "Ha!" with an oath, "what's that? Nought will daunt those lads till the hangman is at their throats."

For it was a real hurrah that reached his ears. The jester had got all the boys round him in the court, and was bidding them keep up a good heart, for their lives were safe, and their mothers would beg them off. Their shouts did not tend to increase the captain's good humour, and though he certainly would not have let out Alderman Headley's remaining apprentice without his fee, he made as great a favour of permission, and charged as exorbitantly, for a pardoned man to remain within his domains as if they had been the most costly and delightful hostel in the kingdom.

Master Hope, who presently arrived, had to pay a high fee for leave to bring Master Todd, the barber-surgeon, with him to see his brother; but though he offered a mark a day, (a huge amount at that time), the captain was obdurate in refusing to allow the patient to be attended by his own old nurse, declaring that it was contrary to discipline, and, (what probably affected him much more), one such woman could cause more trouble than a dozen felons. No doubt it was true, for she would have insisted on moderate cleanliness and comfort. No other attendant whom Mr. Hope could find would endure the disgrace, the discomfort, and alarm of a residence in Newgate for Jasper's sake; so that the draper's gratitude to Stephen Birkenholt, for voluntarily sharing the little fellow's captivity, was great, and he gave payment to one or two of the officials to secure the two lads being civilly treated, and that the provisions sent in reached them duly.

Jasper did not in general seem very ill by day, only heavy, listless and dull, unable to eat, too giddy to sit up, and unable to help crying like a babe, if Stephen left him for a moment; but he never fell asleep without all the horror and dread of the sentence coming over him. Like all the boys in London, he had gazed at executions with the sort of curiosity that leads rustic lads to run to see pigs killed, and now the details came over him in semi-delirium, as acted out on himself, and he shrieked and struggled in an anguish which was only mitigated by Stephen's reassurances, caresses, even scoldings. The other youths, relieved from the apprehension of death, agreed to regard their detention as a holiday, and not being squeamish, turned the yard into a playground, and there they certainly made uproar, and played pranks, enough to justify the preference of the captain for full grown criminals. But Stephen could not join them, for Jasper would not spare him for an instant, and he himself, though at first sorely missing employment and exercise, was growing drowsy and heavy limbed in his cramped life and the evil atmosphere, even the sick longings for liberty were gradually passing away from him, so that sometimes he felt as if he had lived here for ages and known no other life, though no sooner did he lie down to rest, and shut his eyes, than the trees and green glades of the New Forest rose before him, with all the hollies shining in the summer light, or the gorse making a sheet of gold.

The time was not in reality so very long. On the 7th of May, John Lincoln, the broker, who had incited Canon Beale to preach against the foreigners, was led forth with several others of the real promoters of the riot to the centre of Cheapside, where Lincoln was put to death, but orders were brought to respite the rest; and, at the same time, all the armed men were withdrawn, the City began to breathe, and the women who had been kept within doors to go abroad again.

The Recorder of London and several aldermen were to meet the King at his manor at Greenwich. This was the mothers' opportunity. The civic dignitaries rode in mourning robes, but the wives and mothers, sweethearts and sisters, every woman who had a youth's life at stake, came together, took boat, and went down the river, a strange fleet of barges, all containing white caps, and black gowns and hoods, for all were clad in the most correct and humble citizen's costume.

"Never was such a sight," said Jester Randall, who had taken care to secure a view, and who had come with his report to the Dragon court. "It might have been Ash Wednesday for the look of them, when they landed and got into order. One would think every prentice lad had got at least three mothers, and four or five aunts and sisters! I trow, verily, that half of them came to look on at the other half, and get a sight of Greenwich and the three queens. However, be that as it might, not one of them but knew how to open the sluices. Queen Katharine noted well what was coming, and she and the Queens of Scotland and France sat in the great chamber with the doors open. And immediately there's a knock at the door, and so soon as the usher opens it, in they come, three and three, every good wife of them with her napkin to her eyes, and working away with her sobs. Then Mistress Todd, the barber-surgeon's wife, she spoke for all, being thought to have the more courtly tongue, having been tirewoman to Queen Mary ere she went to France. Verily her husband must have penned the speech for her—for it began right scholarly, and flowery, with a likening of themselves to the mothers of Bethlehem, (lusty innocents theirs, I trow!) but ere long the good woman faltered and forgot her part, and broke out 'Oh! madam, you that are a mother yourself for the sake of your own sweet babe, give us back our sons.' And therewith they all fell on their knees, weeping and wringing their hands, and crying out, 'Mercy, mercy! For our Blessed Lady's sake, have pity on our children!' till the good Queen, with the tears running down her cheeks for very ruth, told them that the power was not in her hands, but the will was for them and their poor sons, and that she would strive so to plead for them with the King as to win their freedom. Meantime, there were the aldermen watching for the King in his chamber of presence, till forth he came, when all fell on their knees, and the Recorder spake for them, casting all the blame on the vain and light persons who had made that enormity. Thereupon what does our Hal but make himself as stern as though he meant to string them all up in a line. 'Ye ought to wail and be sorry,' said he, 'whereas ye say that substantial persons were not concerned, it appeareth to the contrary. You did wink at the matter,' quoth he, 'and at this time we will grant you neither favour nor goodwill.' However, none who knew Hal's eye but could tell that 'twas all very excellent fooling, when he bade them get to the Cardinal. Therewith, in came the three queens, hand in hand, with tears in their eyes, so as they might have been the three queens that bore away King Arthur, and down they went on their knees, and cried aloud 'Dear sir, we who are mothers ourselves, beseech you to set the hearts at ease of all the poor mothers who are mourning for their sons.' Whereupon, the door being opened, came in so piteous a sound of wailing and lamentation as our Harry's name must have been Herod to withstand! 'Stand up, Kate,' said he, 'stand up, sisters, and hark in your ear. Not a hair of the silly lads shall be touched, but they must bide lock and key long enough to teach them and their masters to keep better ward.' And then when the queens came back with the good tidings, such a storm of blessings was never heard, laughings and cryings, and the like, for verily some of the women seemed as distraught for joy as ever they had been for grief and fear. Moreover, Mistress Todd, being instructed of her husband, led up Mistress Hope to Queen Mary, and told her the tale of how her husband's little brother, a mere babe, lay sick in prison—a mere babe, a suckling as it were—and was like to die there, unless the sooner delivered, and how our Steve was fool enough to tarry with the poor child, pardoned though he be. Then the good lady wept again, and 'Good woman,' saith she to Mistress Hope, 'the King will set thy brother free anon. His wrath is not with babes, nor with lads like this other of whom thou speakest.'

"So off was she to the King again, and though he and his master pished and pshawed, and said if one and another were to be set free privily in this sort, there would be none to come and beg for mercy as a warning to all malapert youngsters to keep within bounds, 'Nay, verily,' quoth I, seeing the moment for shooting a fool's bolt among them, 'methinks Master Death will have been a pick-lock before you are ready for them, and then who will stand to cry mercy?'"

The narrative was broken off short by a cry of jubilee in the court. Workmen, boys, and all were thronging together, Kit Smallbones' head towering in the midst. Vehement welcomes seemed in progress. "Stephen! Stephen!" shouted Dennet, and flew out of the hall and down the steps.

"The lad himself!" exclaimed the jester, leaping down after her.

"Stephen, the good boy!" said Master Headley, descending more slowly, but not less joyfully.

Yes, Stephen himself it was, who had quietly walked into the court. Master Hope and Master Todd had brought the order for Jasper's release, had paid the captain's exorbitant fees for both, and, while the sick boy was carried home in a litter, Stephen had entered the Dragon court through the gates, as if he were coming home from an errand; though the moment he was recognised by the little four-year old Smallbones, there had been a general rush and shout of ecstatic welcome, led by Giles Headley, who fairly threw himself on Stephen's neck, as they met like comrades after a desperate battle. Not one was there who did not claim a grasp of the boy's hand, and who did not pour out welcomes and greetings; while in the midst, the released captive looked, to say the truth, very spiritless, faded, dusty, nay dirty. The court seemed spinning round with him, and the loud welcomes roared in his ears. He was glad that

Dennet took one hand, and Giles the other, declaring that he must be led to the grandmother instantly.

He muttered something about being in too foul trim to go near her, but Dennet held him fast, and he was too dizzy to make much resistance. Old Mrs. Headley was better again, though not able to do much but sit by the fire kept burning to drive away the plague which was always smouldering in London.

She held out her hands to Stephen, as he knelt down by her. "Take an old woman's blessing, my good youth," she said. "Right glad am I to see thee once more. Thou wilt not be the worse for the pains thou hast spent on the little lad, though they have tried thee sorely."

Stephen, becoming somewhat less dazed, tried to fulfil his long-cherished intention of thanking Dennet for her intercession, but the instant he tried to speak, to his dismay and indignation, tears choked his voice, and he could do nothing but weep, as if, thought he, his manhood had been left behind in the jail.

"Vex not thyself," said the old dame, as she saw him struggling with his sobs. "Thou art worn-out—Giles here was not half his own man when he came out, nor is he yet. Nay, beset him not, children. He should go to his chamber, change these garments, and rest ere supper-time."

Stephen was fain to obey, only murmuring an inquiry for his brother, to which his uncle responded that if Ambrose were at home, the tidings would send him to the Dragon instantly; but he was much with his old master, who was preparing to leave England, his work here being ruined.

The jester then took leave, accepting conditionally an invitation to supper. Master Headley, Smallbones, and Tibble now knew who he was, but the secret was kept from all the rest of the household, lest Stephen should be twitted with the connection.

Cold water was not much affected by the citizens of London, but smiths' and armourers' work entailed a freer use of it than less grimy trades; and a bath and Sunday garments made Stephen more like himself, though still he felt so weary and depressed that he missed the buoyant joy of release to which he had been looking forward.

He was sitting on the steps, leaning against the rail, so much tired that he hoped none of his comrades would notice that he had come out, when Ambrose hurried into the court, having just heard tidings of his freedom, and was at his side at once. The two brothers sat together, leaning against one another as if they had all that they could wish or long for. They had not met for more than a week, for Ambrose's finances had not availed to fee the turn-keys to give him entrance.

"And what art thou doing, Ambrose?" asked Stephen, rousing a little from his lethargy. "Methought I heard mine uncle say thine occupation was gone?"

"Even so," replied Ambrose. "Master Lucas will sail in a week's time to join his brother at Rotterdam, bearing with him what he hath been able to save out of the havoc. I wot not if I shall ever see the good man more."

"I am glad thou dost not go with him," said Stephen, with a hand on his brother's leather-covered knee.

"I would not put seas between us," returned Ambrose. "Moreover, though I grieve to lose my good master, who hath been so scurvily entreated here, yet, Stephen, this trouble and turmoil hath brought me that which I longed for above all, even to have speech with the Dean of Saint Paul's."

He then told Stephen how he had brought Dean Colet to administer the last rites to Abenali, and how that good man had bidden Lucas to take shelter at the Deanery, in the desolation of his own abode. This had led to conversation between the Dean and the printer; Lucas, who distrusted all ecclesiastics, would accept no patronage. He had a little hoard, buried in the corner of his stall, which would suffice to carry him to his native home and he wanted no more; but he had spoken of Ambrose, and the Dean was quite ready to be interested in the youth who had led him to Abenali.

"He had me to his privy chamber," said Ambrose, "and spake to me as no man hath yet spoken—no, not even Tibble. He let me utter all my mind, nay, I never wist before even what mine own thoughts were till he set them before me—as it were in a mirror."

"Thou wast ever in a harl," said Stephen, drowsily, using the Hampshire word for whirl or entanglement.

"Yea. On the one side stood all that I had ever believed or learnt before I came hither of the one true and glorious Mother-Church to whom the Blessed Lord had committed the keys of His kingdom, through His holy martyrs and priests to give us the blessed host and lead us in the way of salvation. And on the other side, I cannot but see the lewd and sinful and worldly lives of the most part, and hear the lies whereby they amass wealth and turn men from the spirit of truth and holiness to delude them into believing that wilful sin can be committed without harm, and that purchase of a parchment is as good as repentance. That do I see and hear. And therewith my master Lucas and Dan Tindall, and those of the new light, declare that all has been false even from the very outset, and that all the pomp and beauty is but Satan's bait, and that to believe in Christ alone is all that needs to justify us, casting all the rest aside. All seemed a mist, and I was swayed hither and thither till the more I read and thought, the greater was the fog. And this—I know not whether I told it to yonder good and holy doctor, or whether he knew it, for his eyes seemed to see into me, and he told me that he had felt and thought much the same. But on that one great truth, that faith in the Passion is salvation, is the Church built, though sinful men have hidden it by their errors and lies as befell before among the Israelites, whose law, like ours, was divine. Whatever is entrusted to man, he said, will become stained, soiled, and twisted, though the power of the Holy Spirit will strive to renew it. And such an outpouring of cleansing and renewing power is, he saith, abroad in our day. When he was a young man, this good father, so he said, hoped great things, and did his best to set forth the truth, both at Oxford and here, as indeed he hath ever done, he and the good Doctor Erasmus, striving to turn men's eyes back to the simplicity of God's

Word rather than to the arguments and deductions of the schoolmen. And for the abuses of evil priests that have sprung up, my Lord Cardinal sought the Legatine Commission from our holy father at Rome to deal with them. But Dr. Colet saith that there are other forces at work, and he doubteth greatly whether this same cleansing can be done without some great and terrible rending and upheaving, that may even split the Church as it were asunder—since judgment surely awaiteth such as will not be reformed. But, quoth he, 'our Mother-Church is God's own Church and I will abide by her to the end, as the means of oneness with my Lord and Head, and do thou the same, my son, for thou art like to be more sorely tried than will a frail old elder like me, who would fain say his *Nunc Dimittis*, if such be the Lord's will, ere the foundations be cast down.'"

Ambrose had gone on rehearsing all these words with the absorption of one to whom they were everything, till it occurred to him to wonder that Stephen had listened to so much with patience and assent, and then, looking at the position of head and hands, he perceived that his brother was asleep, and came to a sudden halt. This roused Stephen to say, "Eh? What? The Dean, will he do aught for thee?"

"Yea," said Ambrose, recollecting that there was little use in returning to the perplexities which Stephen could not enter into. "He deemed that in this mood of mine, yea, and as matters now be at the universities, I had best not as yet study there for the priesthood. But he said he would commend me to a friend whose life would better show me how the new gives life to the old than any man he wots of."

"One of thy old doctors in barnacles, I trow," said Stephen.

"Nay, verily. We saw him t'other night perilling his life to stop the poor crazy prentices, and save the foreigners. Dennet and our uncle saw him pleading for them with the King."

"What! Sir Thomas More?"

"Ay, no other. He needs a clerk for his law matters, and the Dean said he would speak of me to him. He is to sup at the Deanery tomorrow, and I am to be in waiting to see him. I shall go with a lighter heart now that thou art beyond the clutches of the captain of Newgate."

"Speak no more of that!" said Stephen, with a shudder. "Would that I could forget it!"

In truth Stephen's health had suffered enough to change the bold, high-spirited, active lad, so that he hardly knew himself. He was quite incapable of work all the next day, and Mistress Headley began to dread that he had brought home jail-fever, and insisted on his being inspected by the barber-surgeon, Todd, who proceeded to bleed the patient, in order, as he said, to carry off the humours contracted in the prison. He had done the same by Jasper Hope, and by Giles, but he followed the treatment up with better counsel, namely, that the lads should all be sent out of the City to some farm where they might eat curds and whey, until their strength should be restored. Thus they would be out of reach of the sweating sickness which was already in some of the purlieus of Saint Katharine's Docks, and must be specially dangerous in their lowered condition.

Master Hope came in just after this counsel had been given. He had a sister married to the host of a large prosperous inn near Windsor, and he proposed to send not only Jasper but Stephen thither, feeling how great a debt of gratitude he owed to the lad. Remembering well the good young Mistress Streatfield, and knowing that the Antelope was a large old house of excellent repute, where she often lodged persons of quality attending on the court or needing country air, Master Headley added Giles to the party at his own expense, and wished also to send Dennet for greater security, only neither her grandmother nor Mrs. Hope could leave home.

It ended, however, in Perronel Randall being asked to take charge of the whole party, including Aldonza. That little damsel had been in a manner confided to her both by the Dean of Saint Paul's and by Tibble Steelman—and indeed the motherly woman, after nursing and soothing her through her first despair at the loss of her father, was already loving her heartily, and was glad to give her a place in the home which Ambrose was leaving on being made an attendant on Sir Thomas More.

For the interview at the Deanery was satisfactory. The young man, after a good supper, enlivened by the sweet singing of some chosen pupils of Saint Paul's school, was called up to where the Dean sat, and with him, the man of the peculiarly sweet countenance, with the noble and deep expression, yet withal, something both tender and humorous in it.

They made him tell his whole life, and asked many questions about Abenali, specially about the fragment of Arabic scroll which had been clutched in his hand even as he lay dying. They much regretted never having known of his existence till too late. "Jewels lie before the unheeding!" said More. Then Ambrose was called on to show a specimen of his own penmanship, and to write from Sir Thomas's dictation in English and in Latin. The result was that he was engaged to act as one of the clerks Sir Thomas employed in his occupations alike as lawyer, statesman, and scholar.

"Methinks I have seen thy face before," said Sir Thomas, looking keenly at him. "I have beheld those black eyes, though with a different favour?"

Ambrose blushed deeply. "Sir, it is but honest to tell you that my mother's brother is jester to my Lord Cardinal."

"Quipsome Hal Merriman! Patch as the King calleth him!" exclaimed Sir Thomas. "A man I have ever thought wore the motley rather from excess, than infirmity, of wit."

"Nay, sir, so please you, it was his good heart that made him a jester," said Ambrose, explaining the story of Randall and his Perronel in a few words, which touched the friends a good deal, and the Dean remembered that she was in charge of the little Moresco girl. He lost nothing by dealing thus openly with his new master, who promised to keep his secret for him, then gave him handsel of his salary, and bade him collect his possessions, and come to take up his abode in the house of the More family at Chelsea.

He would still often see his brother in the intervals of attending Sir Thomas to the courts of law, but the chief present care was to get the boys into purer air, both to expedite their recovery and to ensure them against being dragged into the penitential company who were to ask for their lives on the 22nd of May, consisting of such of the prisoners who could still stand or go—for jail-fever was making havoc among them, and some of the better-conditioned had been released by private interest. The remainder, not more than half of the original two hundred and seventy-eight, were stripped to their shirts, had halters hung round their necks, and then, roped together as before, were driven through the streets to Westminster, where the King sat enthroned. There, looking utterly miserable, they fell on their knees before him, and received his pardon for their misdemeanours. They returned to their masters, and so ended that Ill May day, which was the longer remembered because one Churchill, a ballad-monger in Saint Paul's Churchyard, indited a poem on it, wherein he swelled the number of prentices to two thousand, and of the victims to two hundred. Will Wherry, who escaped from among the prisoners very forlorn, was recommended by Ambrose to the work of a carter at the Dragon, which he much preferred to printing.

CHAPTER XIX.

At The Antelope.

"Say, Father Thames, for thou hast seen
Full many a sprightly race,
Disporting on thy margent green,
The paths of pleasure trace."

Gray.

Master Hope took all the guests by boat to Windsor, and very soon the little party at the Antelope was in a state of such perfect felicity as became a proverb with them all their lives afterwards. It was an inn wherein to take one's ease, a large hostel full of accommodation for man and horse, with a big tapestried room of entertainment below, where meals were taken, with an oriel window with a view of the Round Tower, and above it a still more charming one, known as the Red Rose, because one of the Dukes of Somerset had been wont to lodge there. The walls were tapestried with the story of Saint Genoveva of Brabant, fresh and new on Mrs. Streatfield's marriage; there was a huge bed with green curtains of that dame's own work, where one might have said:—

"Above, below, the rose of snow,
Twined with her blushing foe we spread."

so as to avoid all offence. There was also a cupboard or sideboard of the choicer plate belonging to the establishment, and another awmry containing appliances for chess and backgammon, likewise two large chairs, several stools, and numerous chests.

This apartment was given up to Mistress Randall and the two girls, subject however to the chance of turning out for any very distinguished guests. The big bed held all three, and the chamber was likewise their sitting-room, though they took their meals down stairs, and joined the party in the common room in the evening whenever they were not out of doors, unless there were guests whom Perronel did not think desirable company for her charges. Stephen and Giles were quartered in a small room known as the Feathers, smelling so sweet of lavender and woodruff that Stephen declared it carried him back to the Forest. Mrs. Streatfield would have taken Jasper to tend among her children, but the boy could not bear to be without Stephen, and his brother advised her to let it be so, and not try to make a babe of him again.

The guest-chamber below stairs opened at one end into the innyard, a quadrangle surrounded with stables, outhouses, and offices, with a gallery running round to give access to the chambers above, where, when the Court was at Windsor, two or three great men's trains of retainers might be crowded together.

One door, however, in the side of the guest-chamber had steps down to an orchard, full of apple and pear trees in their glory of pink bud and white blossom, borders of roses, gillyflowers, and lilies of the valley running along under the grey walls. There was a broad space of grass near the houses, whence could be seen the Round Tower of the Castle looking down in protection, while the background of the view was filled up with a mass of the foliage of Windsor forest, in the spring tints.

Stephen never thought of its being beautiful, but he revelled in the refreshment of anything so like home, and he had nothing to wish for but his brother, and after all he was too contented and happy even to miss him much.

Master Streatfield was an elderly man, fat and easygoing, to whom talking seemed rather a trouble than otherwise, though he was very good-natured. His wife was a merry, lively, active woman, who had been handed over to him by her father like a piece of Flanders cambric, but who never seemed to regret her position, managed men and maids, farm and guests, kept perfect order without seeming to do so, and made great friends with Perronel, never guessing that she had been one of the strolling company, who, nine or ten years before, had been refused admission to the Antelope, then crowded with my Lord of Oxford's followers.

At first, it was enough for the prentices to spend most of their time in lying about on the grass under the trees. Giles, who was in the best condition, exerted himself so far as to try to learn chess from Aldonza, who seemed to be a proficient in the game, and even defeated the good-natured burly parson who came every evening to the Antelope, to imbibe slowly a tankard of ale, and hear any news there stirring.

She and Giles were content to spend hours over her instructions in chess on that pleasant balcony in the shade of the house. Though really only a year older than Dennet Headley, she looked much more, and was so in all her ways. It never occurred to her to run childishly wild with delight in the garden and orchard as did Dennet, who, with little five-years-old Will Streatfield for her guide and playfellow, rushed about hither and thither, making acquaintance with hens and chickens, geese and goslings, seeing cows and goats milked, watching butter churned, bringing all manner of animal and vegetable curiosities to Stephen to be named and explained, and enjoying his delight in them, a delight which after the first few days became more and more vigorous.

By and by there was punting and fishing on the river, strawberry gathering in the park, explorations of the forest, expeditions of all sorts and kinds, Jasper being soon likewise well enough to share in them. The boys and girls were in a kind of fairy land under Perronel's kind wing, the wandering habits of whose girlhood made the freedom of the country far more congenial to her than it would have been to any regular Londoner.

Stephen was the great oracle, of course, as to the deer respectfully peeped at in the park, or the squirrels, the hares and rabbits, in the forest, and the inhabitants of the stream above or below. It was he who secured and tamed the memorials of their visit—two starlings for Dennet and Aldonza. The birds were to be taught to speak, and to do wonders of all kinds, but Aldonza's bird was found one morning dead, and Giles consoled her by the promise of something much bigger, and that would talk much better. Two days after he brought her a young jackdaw. Aldonza clasped her hands and admired its glossy back and queer blue eye, and was in transports when it uttered something between "Jack" and "good lack." But Dennet looked in scorn at it, and said, "That's a bird tamed already. He didn't catch it. He only bought it! I would have none such! An ugsome great thieving bird!"

"Nay now, Mistress Dennet," argued Perronel. "Thou hast thy bird, and Alice has lost hers. It is not meet to grudge it to her."

"I! Grudge it to her!" said Dennet, with a toss of the head. "I grudge her nought from Giles Headley, so long as I have my Goldspot that Stephen climbed the wall for, his very self."

And Dennet turned majestically away with her bird—Goldspot only in the future—perched on her finger; while Perronel shook her head bodingly.

But they were all children still, and Aldonza was of a nature that was slow to take offence, while it was quite true that Dennet had been free from jealousy of the jackdaw, and only triumphant in Stephen's prowess and her own starling.

The great pleasure of all was a grand stag-hunt, got up for the diversion of the French ambassadors, who had come to treat for the espousals of the infant Princess Mary with the baby "Dolphyne." Probably these illustrious personages did not get half the pleasure out of it that the Antelope party had. Were they not, by special management of a yeoman pricker who had recognised in Stephen a kindred spirit, and had a strong admiration for Mistress Randall, placed where there was the best possible view of hunters, horses, and hounds, lords and ladies, King and ambassadors, in their gorgeous hunting trim? Did not Stephen, as a true verdurer's son, interpret every note on the horn, and predict just what was going to happen, to the edification of all his hearers? And when the final rush took place, did not the prentices, with their gowns rolled up, dart off headlong in pursuit? Dennet entertained some hope that Stephen would again catch some runaway steed, or come to the King's rescue in some way or other, but such chances did not happen every day. Nay, Stephen did not even follow up the chase to the death, but left Giles to do that, turning back forsooth because that little Jasper thought fit to get tired and out of breath, and could not find his way back alone. Dennet was quite angry with Stephen and turned her back on him, when Giles came in all glorious, at having followed up staunchly all day, having seen the fate of the poor stag, and having even beheld the King politely hand the knife to Monsieur de Montmorency to give the first stroke to the quarry!

That was the last exploit. There was to be a great tilting-match in honour of the betrothal, and Master Alderman Headley wanted his apprentices back again, and having been satisfied by a laborious letter from Dennet, sent per carrier, that they were in good health, despatched orders by the same means, that they were to hire horses at the Antelope and return—Jasper coming back at the same time, though his aunt would fain have kept him longer.

Women on a journey almost always rode double, and the arrangement came under debate. Perronel, well accustomed to horse, ass, or foot, undertook to ride behind the child, as she called Jasper, who—as a born Londoner—knew nothing of horses, though both the other prentices did. Giles, who, in right of his name, kindred, and expectations, always held himself a sort of master, declared that, "it was more fitting that Stephen should ride before Mistress Dennet." And to this none of the party made any objection, except that Perronel privately observed to him that she should have thought he would have preferred the company of his betrothed.

"I shall have quite enough of her by and by," returned Giles; then adding, "She is a good little wench, but it is more for her honour that her father's servant should ride before her."

Perronel held her tongue, and they rode merrily back to London, and astonished their several homes by the growth and healthful looks of the young people. Even Giles was grown, though he did not like to be told so, and was cherishing the down on his chin. But the most rapid development had been in Aldonza, or Alice, as Perronel insisted on calling her to suit the ears of her neighbours. The girl was just reaching the borderland of maidenhood, which came all the sooner to one of southern birth and extraction, when the great change took her from being her father's childish darling to be Perronel's companion and assistant. She had lain down on that fatal May Eve a child, she rose in the little house by the Temple Gardens, a maiden, and a very lovely one, with delicate, refined, beautifully cut features of a slightly aquiline cast, a bloom on her soft brunette cheek, splendid dark liquid eyes shaded by long black lashes, under brows as regular and well arched as her Eastern cousins could have made them artificially, magnificent black hair, that could hardly be contained in the close white cap, and a lithe beautiful figure on which the plainest dress sat with an Eastern grace. Perronel's neighbours did not admire her. They were not sure whether she were most Saracen, gipsy, or Jew. In fact, she was as like Rachel at the well as her father had been to a patriarch, and her descent was of the purest Saracen lineage, but a Christian Saracen was an anomaly the London mind could not comprehend, and her presence in the family tended to cast suspicion that Master Randall himself, with his gipsy eyes, and mysterious comings and goings, must have some strange connections. For this, however, Perronel cared little. She had made her own way for many years past, and had won respect and affection by many good offices to her neighbours, one of whom had taken her laundry work in her absence.

Aldonza was by no means indocile or incapable. She shared in Perronel's work without reluctance, making good use of her slender, dainty brown fingers, whether in cooking, household work, washing, ironing, plaiting, making or mending the stiff lawn collars and cuffs in which her hostess's business lay. There was nothing that she would not do when asked, or when she saw that it would save trouble to good mother Perronel, of whom she was very fond, and she seemed serene and contented, never wanting to go abroad; but she was very silent, and Perronel declared herself never to have seen any living woman so perfectly satisfied to do nothing. The good dame herself was industrious, not only from thrift but from taste, and if not busy in her vocation or in household business, was either using her distaff or her needle, or chatting with her neighbours—often doing both at once; but though Aldonza could spin, sew, and embroider admirably, and would do so at the least request from her hostess, it was always a sort of task, and she never seemed so happy as when seated on the floor, with her dark eyes dreamily fixed on the narrow window, where hung her jackdaw's cage, and the beads of her rosary passing through her fingers. At first Mistress Randall thought she was praying, but by and by came to the conviction that most of the time, "the wench was bemused." There was nothing to complain of in one so perfectly gentle and obedient, and withal, modest and devout; but the good woman, after having for some time given her the benefit of the supposition that she was grieving for her father, began to wonder at such want of activity and animation, and to think that on the whole Jack was the more talkative companion.

Aldonza had certainly not taught him the phrases he was so fond of repeating. Giles Headley had undertaken his education, and made it a reason for stealing down to the Temple many an evening after work was done, declaring that birds never learnt so well as after dark. Moreover, he had possessed himself of a chess board, and insisted that Aldonza should carry on her instructions in the game; he brought her all his Holy Cross Day gain of nuts, and he used all his blandishments to persuade Mrs. Randall to come and see the shooting at the popinjay, at Mile End.

All this made the good woman uneasy. Her husband was away, for the dread of sweating sickness had driven the Court from London, and she could only take counsel with Tibble Steelman. It was Hallowmas Eve, and Giles had been the bearer of an urgent invitation from Dennet to her friend Aldonza to come and join the diversions of the evening. There was a large number of young folk in the hall—Jasper Hope among them—mostly contemporaries of Dennet, and almost children, all keen upon the sports of the evening, namely, a sort of indoor quintain, where the revolving beam was decorated with a lighted candle at one end, and at the other an apple to be caught at by the players with their mouths, their hands being tied behind them.

Under all the uproarious merriment that each attempt occasioned, Tibble was about to steal off to his own chamber and his beloved books, when, as he backed out of the group of spectators, he was arrested by Mistress Randall, who had made her way into the rear of the party at the same time.

"Can I have a word with you, privily, Master Steelman?" she asked.

Unwillingly he muttered, "Yea, so please you;" and they retreated to a window at the dark end of the hall, where Perronel began—

"The alderman's daughter is contracted to young Giles, her kinsman, is she not?"

"Not as yet in form, but by the will of the parents," returned Tibble, impatiently, as he thought of the half-hour's reading which he was sacrificing to woman's gossip.

"An it be so," returned Perronel, "I would fain—were I Master Headley—that he spent not so many nights in gazing at mine Alice."

"Forbid him the house, good dame."

"Easier spoken than done," returned Perronel. "Moreover, 'tis better to let the matter, such as it is, be open in my sight than to teach them to run after one another stealthily, whereby worse might ensue."

"Have they spoken then to one another?" asked Tibble, beginning to take alarm.

"I trow not. I deem they know not yet what draweth them together."

"Pish, they are mere babes!" quoth Tib, hoping he might cast it off his mind.

"Look!" said Perronel; and as they stood on the somewhat elevated floor of the bay window, they could look over the heads of the other spectators to the seats where the young girls sat.

Aldonza's beautiful and peculiar contour of head and face rose among the round chubby English faces like a jessamine among daisies, and at that moment she was undertaking, with an exquisite smile, the care of the gown that Giles laid at her feet, ere making his venture.

"There!" said Perronel. "Mark that look on her face! I never see it save for that same youngster. The children are simple and guileless thus far, it may be. I dare be sworn that she is, but they wot not where they will be led on."

"You are right, dame; you know best, no doubt," said Tib, in helpless perplexity. "I wot nothing of such gear. What would you do?"

"Have the maid wedded at once, ere any harm come of it," returned Perronel promptly. "She will make a good wife—there will be no complaining of her tongue, and she is well instructed in all good housewifery."

"To whom then would you give her?" asked Tibble.

"Ay, that's the question. Comely and good she is, but she is outlandish, and I fear me 'twould take a handsome portion to get her dark skin and Moorish blood o'erlooked. Nor hath she aught, poor maid, save yonder gold and pearl earrings, and a cross of gold that she says her father bade her never part with."

"I pledged my word to her father," said Tibble, "that I would have a care of her. I have not cared to hoard, having none to come after me, but if a matter of twenty or five-and-twenty marks would avail—"

"Wherefore not take her yourself?" said Perronel, as he stood aghast. "She is a maid of sweet obedient conditions, trained by a scholar even like yourself. She would make your chamber fair and comfortable, and tend you dutifully."

"Whisht, good woman. 'Tis too dark to see, or you could not speak of wedlock to such as I. Think of the poor maid!"

"That is all folly! She would soon know you for a better husband than one of those young feather-pates, who have no care but of themselves."

"Nay, mistress," said Tibble, gravely, "your advice will not serve here. To bring that fair young wench hither, to this very court, mind you, with a mate loathly to behold as I be, and with the lad there ever before her, would be verily to give place to the devil."

"But you are the best sword-cutler in London. You could make a living without service."

"I am bound by too many years of faithful kindness to quit my master or my home at the Dragon," said Tibble. "Nay, that will not serve, good friend."

"Then what can be done?" asked Perronel, somewhat in despair. "There are the young sparks at the Temple. One or two of them are already beginning to cast eyes at her, so that I dare not let her help me carry home my basket, far less go alone. 'Tis not the wench's fault. She shrinks from men's eyes more than any maid I ever saw, but if she bide long with me, I wot not what may come of it. There be rufflers there who would not stick to carry her off!"

Tibble stood considering, and presently said, "Mayhap the Dean might aid thee in this matter. He is free of hand and kind of heart, and belike he would dower the maid, and find an honest man to wed her."

Perronel thought well of the suggestion, and decided that after the mass on All Soul's Day, and the general visiting of the graves of kindred, she would send Aldonza home with Dennet, whom they were sure to meet in the Pardon Churchyard, since her mother, as well as Abenali and Martin Fulford lay there; and herself endeavour to see Dean Colet, who was sure to be at home, as he was hardly recovered from an attack of the prevalent disorder.

Then Tibble escaped, and Perronel drew near to the party round the fire, where the divination of the burning of nuts was going on, but not successfully, since no pair hitherto put in would keep together. However, the next contribution was a snail, which had been captured on the wall, and was solemnly set to crawl on the hearth by Dennet, "to see whether it would trace a G or an H."

However, the creature proved sullen or sleepy, and no jogging of hands, no enticing, would induce it to crawl an inch, and the alderman, taking his daughter on his knee, declared that it was a wise beast, who knew her hap was fixed. Moreover, it was time for the rere supper, for the serving-men with the lanterns would be coming for the young folk.

London entertainments for women or young people had to finish very early unless they had a strong escort to go home with, for the streets were far from safe after dark. Giles's great desire to convoy her home, added to Perronel's determination, and on All Souls' Day, while knells were ringing from every church in London, she roused Aldonza from her weeping devotions at her father's grave, and led her to Dennet, who had just finished her round of prayers at the grave of the mother she had never known, under the protection of her nurse, and two or three of the servants. The child, who had thought little of her mother, while her grandmother was alert, and supplied the tenderness and care she needed, was beginning to yearn after counsel and sympathy, and to wonder, as she told her beads, what might have been, had that mother lived. She took Aldonza's hand, and the two girls threaded their way out of the crowded churchyard together, while Perronel betook herself to the Deanery of Saint Paul's.

Good Colet was always accessible to the meanest, but he had been very ill, and the porter had some doubts about troubling him respecting the substantial young matron whose trim cap and bodice, and full petticoats, showed no tokens of distress. However, when she begged him to take in her message, that she prayed the Dean to listen to her touching the child of the old man who was slain on May Eve, he consented; and she was at once admitted to an inner chamber, where Colet, wrapped in a gown lined with lambskin, sat by the fire, looking so wan and feeble that it went to the good woman's heart, and she began by an apology for troubling him.

"Heed not that, good dame," said the Dean, courteously, "but sit thee down and let me hear of the poor child."

"Ah, reverend sir, would that she were still a child—" and Perronel proceeded to tell her difficulties, adding, that if the Dean could of his goodness promise one of the dowries which were yearly given to poor maidens of good character, she would inquire among her gossips for some one to marry the girl. She secretly hoped he would take the hint and immediately portion Aldonza himself perhaps likewise find the husband. And she was disappointed that he only promised to consider the matter and let her hear from him. She went back and told Tibble that his device was nought, an old scholar with one foot in the grave knew less of women than even he did!

However it was only four days later, that, as Mrs. Randall was hanging out her collars to dry, there came up to her from the Temple stairs a figure whom for a moment she hardly knew, so different was the long, black garb, and short gown of the lawyer's clerk from the shabby old green suit that all her endeavours had not been able to save from many a stain of printer's ink. It was only as he exclaimed, "Good aunt, I am fain to see thee here!" that she answered, "What, thou, Ambrose! What a fine fellow thou art! Truly I knew not thou wast of such good mien! Thou thrivest at Chelsea!"

"Who would not thrive there?" said Ambrose. "Nay, aunt, tarry a little, I have a message for thee that I would fain give before we go in to Aldonza."

"From his reverence the Dean? Hath he bethought himself of her?"

"Ay, that hath he done," said Ambrose. "He is not the man to halt when good may be done. What doth he do, since it seems thou hadst speech of him, but send for Sir Thomas More, then sitting at Westminster, to come and see him as soon as the Court brake up, and I attended my master. They held council together, and by and by they sent for me to ask me of what conditions and breeding the maid was, and what I knew of her father?"

"Will they wed her to thee? That were rarely good, so they gave thee some good office!" cried his aunt.

"Nay, nay," said Ambrose. "I have much to learn and understand ere I think of a wife—if ever. Nay! But when they had heard all I could tell them, they looked at one another, and the Dean said, 'The maid is no doubt of high blood in her own land—scarce a mate for a London butcher or currier.'"

"'It were matching an Arab mare with a costard monger's colt,' said my master, 'or Angelica with Ralph Roister-Doister.'"

"I'd like to know what were better for the poor outlandish maid than to give her to some honest man," put in Perronel.

"The end of it was," said Ambrose, "that Sir Thomas said he was to be at the palace the next day, and he would strive to move the Queen to take her countrywoman into her service. Yea, and so he did, but though Queen Katharine was moved by hearing of a fatherless maid of Spain, and at first spake of taking her to wait on herself, yet when she heard the maid's name, and that she was of Moorish blood, she would none of her. She said that heresy lurked in them all, and though Sir Thomas offered that the Dean or the Queen's own chaplain should question her on the faith, it was all lost labour. I heard him tell the Dean as much, and thus it is that they bade me come for thee, and for the maid, take boat, and bring you down to Chelsea, where Sir Thomas will let her be bred up to wait on his little daughters till he can see what best may be done for her. I trow his spirit was moved by the Queen's hardness! I heard the Dean mutter, '*Et venient ab Oriente et Occidente.*'"

Perronel looked alarmed. "The Queen deemed her heretic in grain! Ah! She is a good wench, and of kind conditions. I would have no ill befall her, but I am glad to be rid of her. Sir Thomas—he is a wise man, ay, and a married man, with maidens of his own, and he may have more wit in the business than the rest of his kind. Be the matter instant?"

"Methinks Sir Thomas would have it so, since this being a holy day, the courts be not sitting, and he is himself at home, so that he can present the maid to his lady. And that makes no small odds."

"Yea, but what the lady is makes the greater odds to the maid, I trow," said Perronel anxiously.

"Fear not on that score. Dame Alice More is of kindly conditions, and will be good to any whom her lord commends to her; and as to the young ladies, never saw I any so sweet or so wise as the two elder ones, specially Mistress Margaret."

"Well-a-day! What must be must!" philosophically observed Perronel. "Now I have my wish, I could mourn over it. I am loth to part with the wench; and my man, when he comes home, will make an outcry for his pretty Ally; but 'tis best so. Come, Alice, girl, bestir thyself. Here's preferment for thee."

Aldonza raised her great soft eyes in slow wonder, and when she had heard what was to befall her, declared that she wanted no advancement, and wished only to remain with mother Perronel. Nay, she clung to the kind woman, beseeching that she might not be sent away from the only motherly tenderness she had ever known, and declaring that she would work all day and all night rather than leave her; but the more reluctance she showed, the more determined was Perronel, and she could not but submit to her fate, only adding one more entreaty that she might take her jackdaw, which was now a spruce grey-headed bird. Perronel said it would be presumption in a waiting-woman, but Ambrose declared that at Chelsea there were all manner of beasts and birds, beloved by the children and by their father himself, and that he believed the daw would be welcome. At any rate, if the lady of the house objected to it, it could return with Mistress Randall.

Perronel hurried the few preparations, being afraid that Giles might take advantage of the holiday to appear on the scene, and presently Aldonza was seated in the boat, making no more lamentations after she found that her fate was inevitable, but sitting silent, with downcast head, now and then brushing away a stray tear as it stole down under her long eyelashes.

Meantime Ambrose, hoping to raise her spirits, talked to his aunt of the friendly ease and kindliness of the new home, where he was evidently as thoroughly happy as it was in his nature to be. He was much, in the position of a barrister's clerk, superior to that of the mere servants, but inferior to the young gentlemen of larger means, though not perhaps of better birth, who had studied law regularly, and aspired to offices or to legal practice.

But though Ambrose was ranked with the three or four other clerks, his functions had more relation to Sir Thomas's literary and diplomatic avocations than his legal ones. From Lucas Hansen he had learnt Dutch and French, and he was thus available for copying and translating foreign correspondence. His knowledge of Latin and smattering of Greek enabled him to be employed in copying into a book some of the inestimable letters of Erasmus which arrived from time to time, and Sir Thomas promoted his desire to improve himself, and had requested Mr. Clements, the tutor of the children of the house, to give him weekly lessons in Latin and Greek.

Sir Thomas had himself pointed out to him books calculated to settle his mind on the truth and catholicity of the Church, and had warned him against meddling with the fiery controversial tracts which, smuggled in often through Lucas's means, had set his mind in commotion. And for the present at least beneath the shadow of the great man's intelligent devotion, Ambrose's restless spirit was tranquil.

Of course, he did not explain his state of mind to his aunt, but she gathered enough to be well content, and tried to encourage Aldonza, when at length they landed near Chelsea Church, and Ambrose led the way to an extensive pleasaunce or park, full of elms and oaks, whose yellow leaves were floating like golden rain in the sunshine.

Presently children's voices guided them to a large chestnut tree. "Lo you now, I hear Mistress Meg's voice, and where she is, his honour will ever be," said Ambrose.

And sure enough, among a group of five girls and one boy, all between fourteen and nine years old, was the great lawyer, knocking down the chestnuts with a long pole, while the young ones flew about picking up the burrs from the grass, exclaiming joyously when they found a full one.

Ambrose explained that of the young ladies, one was Mistress Middleton, Lady More's daughter by a former marriage, another a kinswoman. Perronel was for passing by unnoticed; but Ambrose knew better; and Sir Thomas, leaning on the pole, called out, "Ha, my Birkenholt, a forester born, knowst thou any mode of bringing down yonder chestnuts, which being the least within reach, seem in course the meetest of all."

"I would I were my brother, your honour," said Ambrose, "then would I climb the tree."

"Thou shouldst bring him one of these days," said Sir Thomas. "But thou hast instead brought us a fair maid. See, Meg, yonder is the poor young girl who lost her father on Ill May day. Lead her on and make her good cheer, while I speak to this good dame."

Margaret More, a slender, dark-eyed girl of thirteen, went forward with a peculiar gentle grace to the stranger, saying, "Welcome, sweet maid! I hope we shall make thee happy," and seeing the mournful countenance, she not only took Aldonza's hand, but kissed her cheek.

Sir Thomas had exchanged a word or two with Perronel, when there was a cry from the younger children, who had detected the wicker cage which Perronel was trying to keep in the background.

"A daw! a daw!" was the cry. "Is't for us?"

"Oh, mistress," faltered Aldonza, "'tis mine—there was one who tamed it for me, and I promised ever to keep it, but if the good knight and lady forbid it, we will send it back."

"Nay now, John, Cicely," was Margaret saying, "'tis her own bird! Wot ye not our father will let us take nought of them that come to him? Yea, Aldonza—is not that thy name?—I am sure my father will have thee keep it."

She led up Aldonza, making the request for her. Sir Thomas smiled.

"Keep thy bird? Nay, that thou shalt. Look at him, Meg, is he not in fit livery for a lawyer's house? Mark his trim legs, sable doublet and hose, and grey hood.—and see, he hath the very eye of a councillor seeking for suits, as he looketh at the chestnuts John holdeth to him. I warrant he hath a tongue likewise. Canst plead for thy dinner, bird?"

"I love Giles!" uttered the black beak, to the confusion and indignation of Perronel.

The perverse bird had heard Giles often dictate this avowal, but had entirely refused to repeat it, till, stimulated by the new surroundings, it had for the first time uttered it.

"Ah! thou foolish daw! Crow that thou art! Had I known thou hadst such a word in thy beak, I'd have wrung thy neck sooner than have brought thee," muttered Perronel. "I had best take thee home without more ado."

It was too late, however, the children were delighted, and perfectly willing that Aldonza should own the bird, so they might hear it speak, and thus the introduction was over. Aldonza and her daw were conveyed to Dame Alice More, a stout, good-tempered woman, who had too many dependents about her house to concern herself greatly about the introduction of another.

And thus Aldonza was installed in the long, low, two-storied red house which was to be her place of homelike service.

CHAPTER XX.

Cloth of Gold on the Seamy Side.

> "Then you lost
> The view of earthly glory men might say
> Till this time pomp was single; but now married
> To one above itself."

> Shakespeare.

If Giles Headley murmured at Aldonza's removal, it was only to Perronel, and that discreet woman kept it to herself.

In the summer of 1519 he was out of his apprenticeship, and though Dennet was only fifteen, it was not uncommon for brides to be even younger. However, the autumn of that year was signalised by a fresh outbreak of the sweating sickness, apparently a sort of influenza, and no festivities could be thought of. The King and Queen kept at a safe distance from London, and escaped, so did the inmates of the pleasant house at Chelsea; but the Cardinal, who, as Lord Chancellor, could not entirely absent himself from Westminster, was four times attacked by it, and Dean Colet, a far less robust man, had it three times, and sank at last under it. Sir Thomas More went to see his beloved old friend, and knowing Ambrose's devotion, let the young man be his attendant. Nor could those who saw the good man ever forget his peaceful farewells, grieving only for the old mother who had lived with him in the Deanery, and in the ninetieth year of her age, thus was bereaved of the last of her twenty-one children. For himself, he was thankful to be taken away from the evil times he already beheld threatening his beloved Saint Paul's, as well as the entire Church both in England and abroad; looking back with a sad, sweet smile to the happy Oxford days, when he, with More and Erasmus:

> "Strained the watchful eye
> If chance the golden hours were nigh
> By youthful hope seen gleaming round her walls."

"But," said he, as he laid his hand in blessing for the last time on Ambrose's head, "let men say what they will, do thou cling fast to the Church, nor let thyself be swept away. There are sure promises to her, and grace is with her to purify herself, even though it be obscured for a time. Be not of little faith, but believe that Christ is with us in the ship, though He seem to be asleep."

He spoke as much to his friend as to the youth, and there can be no doubt that this consideration was the restraining force with many who have been stigmatised as half hearted Reformers, because though they loved truth, they feared to lose unity.

He was a great loss at that especial time, as a restraining power, trusted by the innovators, and a personal friend both of King and Cardinal, and his preaching and catechising were sorely missed at Saint Paul's.

Tibble Steelman, though thinking he did not go far enough, deplored him deeply; but Tibble himself was laid by for many days. The epidemic went through the Dragon court, though some had it lightly, and only two young children actually died of it. It laid a heavy hand on Tibble, and as his distaste for women rendered his den almost inaccessible to Bet Smallbones, who looked after most of the patients, Stephen Birkenholt, whose nursing capacities had been developed in Newgate, spent his spare hours in attending him, sat with him in the evenings, slept on a pallet by his side, carried him his meals and often administered them, and finally pulled him through the illness and its effects, which left him much broken and never likely to be the same man again.

Old Mistress Headley, who was already failing, did not have the actual disease severely, but she never again left her bed, and died just after Christmas, sinking slowly away with little pain, and her memory having failed from the first.

Household affairs had thus slipped so gradually into Dennet's hands that no change of government was perceptible, except that the keys hung at the maiden's girdle. She had grown out of the child during this winter of trouble, and was here, there, and everywhere, the busy nurse and housewife, seldom pausing to laugh or play except with her father, and now and then to chat with her old friend and playfellow, Kit Smallbones. Her childish freedom of manner had given way to grave discretion, not to say primness, in her behaviour to her father's guests, and even the apprentices. It was, of course, the unconscious reaction of the maidenly spirit, aware that she had nothing but her own modesty to protect her. She was on a small scale, with no pretensions to beauty, but with a fresh, honest, sensible young face, a clear skin, and dark eyes that could be very merry when she would let them, and her whole air and dress were trimness itself, with an inclination to the choicest materials permitted to an alderman's daughter.

Things were going on so smoothly that the alderman was taken by surprise when all the good wives around began to press on him that it was incumbent on him to lose no time in marrying his daughter to her cousin, if not before Lent, yet certainly in the Easter holidays.

Dennet looked very grave thereon. Was it not over soon after the loss of the good grandmother? And when her father said, as the gossips had told him, that she and Giles need only walk quietly down some morning to Saint Faith's and plight their troth, she broke out into her girlish wilful manner, "Would she be married at all without a merry wedding? No, indeed! She would not have the thing done in a corner! What was the use of her being wedded, and having to consort with the tedious old wives instead of the merry wenches? Could she not guide the house, and rule the maids, and get in the stores, and hinder waste, and make the pasties, and brew the possets? Had her father found the crust hard, or missed his roasted crab, or had any one blamed her for want of discretion? Nay, as to that, she was like to be more discreet as she was, with only her good old father to please, than with a husband to plague her."

On the other hand, Giles's demeanour was rather that of one prepared for the inevitable than that of an eager bridegroom; and when orders began to pour in for accoutrements of unrivalled magnificence for the King and the gentlemen who were to accompany him to Ardres, there to meet the young King of France just after Whitsuntide, Dennet was the first to assure her father that there would be no time to think of weddings till all this was over, especially as some of the establishment would have to be in attendance to repair casualties at the jousts.

At this juncture there arrived on business Master Tiptoff, husband to Giles's sister, bringing greetings from Mrs. Headley at Salisbury, and inquiries whether the wedding was to take place at Whitsuntide, in which case she would hasten to be present, and to take charge of the household, for which her dear daughter was far too young. Master Tiptoff showed a suspicious alacrity in undertaking the forwarding of his mother-in-law and her stuff.

The faces of Master Headley and Tib Steelman were a sight, both having seen only too much of what the house wifery at Salisbury had been. The alderman decided on the spot that there could be no marriage till after the journey to France, since Giles was certainly to go upon it; and lest Mrs. Headley should be starting on her journey, he said he should despatch a special messenger to stay her. Giles, who had of course been longing for the splendid pageant, cheered up into great amiability, and volunteered to write to his mother, that she had best not think of coming, till he sent word to her that matters were forward. Even thus, Master Headley was somewhat insecure. He thought the dame quite capable of coming and taking possession of his house in his absence, and therefore resolved upon staying at home to garrison it; but there was then the further difficulty that Tibble was in no condition to take his place on the journey. If the rheumatism seized his right arm, as it had done in the winter, he would be unable to drive a rivet, and there would be every danger of it, high summer though it were; for though the party would carry their own tent and bedding, the knights and gentlemen would be certain to take all the best places, and they might be driven into a damp corner. Indeed it was not impossible that their tent itself might be seized, for many a noble or his attendants might think that beggarly artisans had no right to comforts which he had been too improvident to afford, especially if the alderman himself were absent.

Not only did Master Headley really love his trusty foreman too well to expose him to such chances, but Tibble knew too well that there were brutal young men to whom his contorted visage would be an incitement to contempt and outrage, and that if racked with rheumatism, he would only be an incumbrance. There was nothing for it but to put Kit Smallbones at the head of the party. His imposing presence would keep off wanton insults, but on the other hand, he had not the moral weight of authority possessed by Tibble, and though far from being a drunkard, he was not proof against a carouse, especially when out of reach of his Bet and of his master, and he was not by any means Tib's equal in fine and delicate workmanship. But on the other hand, Tib pronounced that Stephen Birkenholt was already well skilled in chasing metal and the difficult art of restoring inlaid work, and he showed some black and silver armour, that was in hand for the King, which fully bore out his words.

"And thou thinkst Kit can rule the lads!" said the alderman, scarce willingly.

"One of them at least can rule himself," said Tibble. "They have both been far more discreet since the fright they got on Ill May day; and, as for Stephen, he hath seemed to me to have no eyes nor thought save for his work of late."

"I have marked him," said the master, "and have marvelled what ailed the lad. His merry temper hath left him. I never hear him singing to keep time with his hammer, nor keeping the court in a roar with his gibes. I trust he is not running after the new doctrine of the hawkers and pedlars. His brother was inclined that way."

"There be worse folk than they, your worship," protested Tib, but he did not pursue their defence, only adding, "but 'tis not that which ails young Stephen. I would it were!" he sighed to himself, inaudibly.

"Well," said the good-natured alderman, "it may be he misseth his brother. The boys will care for this raree-show more than thou or I, Tib! We've seen enough of them in our day, though verily they say this is to surpass all that ever were beheld!"

The question of who was to go had not been hitherto decided, and Giles and Stephen were both so excited at being chosen that all low spirits and moodiness were dispelled, and the work which went on almost all night was merrily got through. The Dragon court was in a perpetual commotion with knights, squires, and grooms, coming in with orders for new armour, or for old to be furbished, and the tent-makers, lorimers, mercers, and tailors had their hands equally full. These lengthening mornings heard the hammer ringing at sunrise, and in the final rush, Smallbones never went to bed at all. He said he should make it up in the wagon on the way to Dover. Some hinted that he preferred the clang of his hammer to the good advice his Bet lavished on him at every leisure moment to forewarn him against French wine-pots.

The alderman might be content with the party he sent forth, for Kit had hardly his equal in size, strength, and good humour. Giles had developed into a tall, comely young man, who had got rid of his country slouch, and whose tall figure, light locks, and ruddy cheeks looked well in the new suit which gratified his love of finery, sober-hued as it needs must be. Stephen was still bound to the old prentice garb, though it could not conceal his good mien, the bright sparkling dark eyes, crisp black hair, healthy brown skin, and lithe active figure. Giles had a stout roadster to ride on, the others were to travel in their own wagon, furnished with four powerful horses, which, it possible, they were to take to Calais, so as to be independent of hiring. Their needments, clothes, and tools, were packed in the wagon, with store of lances, and other appliances of the tourney. A carter and Will Wherry, who was selected as being supposed to be conversant with foreign tongues, were to attend on them; Smallbones, as senior journeyman, had the control of the party, and Giles had sufficiently learnt subordination not to be likely to give himself dangerous airs of mastership.

Dennet was astir early to see them off, and she had a little gift for each. She began with her oldest friend, "See here, Kit," she said, "here's a wallet to hold thy nails and rivets. What wilt thou say to me for such a piece of stitchery?"

"Say, pretty mistress? Why this!" quoth the giant, and he picked her up by the slim waist in his great hands, and kissed her on the forehead. He had done the like many a time nine or ten years ago, and though Master Headley laughed, Dennet was not one bit embarrassed, and turned to the next traveller. "Thou art no more a prentice, Giles, and canst wear this in thy bonnet," she said, holding out to him a short silver chain and medal of Saint George and the Dragon.

"Thanks, gentle maid," said Giles, taking the handsome gift a little sheepishly. "My bonnet will make a fair show," and he bent down as she stood on the step, and saluted her lips, then began eagerly fastening the chain round his cap, as one delighted with the ornament.

Stephen was some distance off. He had turned aside when she spoke to Giles, and was asking of Tibble last instructions about the restoration of enamel, when he felt a touch on his arm, and saw Dennet standing by him. She looked up in his face, and held up a crimson silken purse, with S B embroidered on it within a wreath of oak and holly leaves.

With the air that ever showed his gentle blood, Stephen put a knee to the ground, and kissed the fingers that held it to him, whereupon Dennet, a sudden burning blush overspreading her face under her little pointed hood, turned suddenly round and ran into the house. She was out again on the steps when the wagon finally got under weigh, and as her eyes met Stephen's, he doffed his flat cap with one hand, and laid the other on his heart, so that she knew where her purse had taken up its abode.

Of the Field of the Cloth of Gold not much need be said. To the end of the lives of the spectators, it was a tale of wonder. Indeed without that, the very sight of the pavilions was a marvel in itself, the blue dome of Francis spangled in imitation of the sky, with sun, moon, and stars; and the feudal castle of Henry, a three months' work, each surrounded with tents of every colour and pattern which fancy could devise, with the owners banners or pennons floating from the summits, and every creature, man, and horse, within the enchanted precincts, equally gorgeous. It was the brightest and the last full display of magnificent pseudo chivalry, and to Stephen's dazzled eye, seeing it beneath the slant rays of the setting sun of June, it was a fairy tale come to life.

Hal Randall, who was in attendance on the Cardinal, declared that it was a mere surfeit of jewels and gold and silver, and that a frieze jerkin or leathern coat was an absolute refreshment to the sight. He therefore spent all the time he was off duty in the forge far in the rear, where Smallbones and his party had very little but hard work, mending, whetting, furbishing, and even changing devices. Those six days of tilting when "every man that stood, showed like a mine," kept the armourers in full occupation night and day, and only now and then could the youths try to make their way to some spot whence they could see the tournament.

Smallbones was more excited by the report of fountains of good red and white wines of all sorts, flowing perpetually in the court of King Henry's splendid mock castle; but fortunately one gulp was enough for an English palate nurtured on ale and mead, and he was disgusted at the heaps of country folk, men-at-arms, beggars and vagabonds of all kinds, who swilled the liquor continually, and, in loathsome contrast to the external splendours, lay wallowing on the ground so thickly that it was sometimes hardly possible to move without treading on them.

"I stumbled over a dozen," said the jester, as he strolled into the little staked inclosure that the Dragon party had arranged round their tent for the prosecution of their labours, which were too important to all the champions not to be respected. "Lance and sword have not laid so many low in the lists as have the doughty Baron Burgundy and the heady knight Messire Sherris Sack."

"Villain Verjuice and Varlet Vinegar is what Kit there calls them," said Stephen, looking up from the work he was carrying on over a pan of glowing charcoal.

"Yea," said Smallbones, intermitting his noisy operations, "and the more of swine be they that gorge themselves on it. I told Jack and Hob that 'twould be shame for English folk to drown themselves like French frogs or Flemish hogs."

"Hogs!" returned Randall. "A decent Hampshire hog would scorn to be lodged as many a knight and squire and lady too is now, pigging it in styes and hovels and haylofts by night, and pranking it by day with the best!"

"Sooth enough," said Smallbones. "Yea, we have had two knights and their squires beseeching us for leave to sleep under our wagon! Not an angel had they got among the four of them either, having all their year's income on their backs, and more too. I trow they and their heirs will have good cause to remember this same Field of Gold."

"And what be'st thou doing, nevvy?" asked the jester. "Thy trade seems as brisk as though red blood were flowing instead of red wine."

"I am doing my part towards making the King into Hercules," said Stephen, "though verily the tailor hath more part therein than we have; but he must needs have a breastplate of scales of gold, and that by tomorrow's morn. As Ambrose would say, 'if he will be a pagan god, he should have what's-his-name, the smith of the gods, to work for him.'"

"I heard of that freak," said the jester. "There be a dozen tailors and all the Queen's tirewomen frizzling up a good piece of cloth of gold for the lion's mane, covering a club with green damask with pricks, cutting out green velvet and gummed silk for his garland! In sooth, these graces have left me so far behind in foolery that I have not a jest left in my pouch! So here I be, while my Lord Cardinal is shut up with Madame d'Angoulême in the castle—the real old castle, mind you—doing the work, leaving the kings and queens to do their own fooling."

"Have you spoken with the French King, Hal?" asked Smallbones, who had become a great crony of his, since the anxieties of May Eve.

"So far as I may when I have no French, and he no English! He is a comely fellow, with a blithe tongue and a merry eye, I warrant you a chanticleer who will lose nought for lack of crowing. He'll crow louder than ever now he hath given our Harry a fall."

"No! hath he?" and Giles, Stephen, and Smallbones, all suspended their work to listen in concern.

"Ay marry, hath he! The two took it into their royal noddles to try a fall, and wrestled together on the grass, when by some ill hap, this same Francis tripped up our Harry, so that he was on the sward for a moment. He was up again forthwith, and in full heart for another round, when all the Frenchmen burst in gabbling; and, though their King was willing to play the match out fairly, they wouldn't let him, and my Lord Cardinal said something about making ill blood, whereat our King laughed and was content to leave it. As I told him, we have given the French falls enough to let them make much of this one."

"I hope he will yet give the mounseer a good shaking," muttered Smallbones.

"How now, Will! Who's that at the door? We are on his grace's work and can touch none other man's were it the King of France himself, or his Constable, who is finer still."

By way of expressing, "No admittance except on business," Smallbones kept Will Wherry in charge of the door of his little territory, which having a mud wall on two sides, and a broad brook with quaking banks on a third, had been easily fenced on the fourth, so as to protect tent, wagon, horses, and work from the incursions of idlers. Will however answered, "The gentleman saith he hath kindred here."

"Ay!" and there pushed in, past the lad a tall, lean form, with a gay but soiled short cloak over one shoulder, a suit of worn buff, a cap garnished with a dilapidated black and yellow feather, and a pair of gilt spurs. "If this be as they told me, where Armourer Headley's folk lodge—I have here a sort of a cousin. Yea, yonder's the brave lad who had no qualms at the flash of a good Toledo in a knight's fist. How now, my nevvy! Is not my daughter's nevvy—mine?"

"Save your knighthood!" said Smallbones. "Who would have looked to see you here, Sir John? Methought you were in the Emperor's service!"

"A stout man-at-arms is of all services," returned Fulford. "I'm here with half Flanders to see this mighty show, and pick up a few more lusty Badgers at this encounter of old comrades. Is old Headley here?"

"Nay, he is safe at home, where I would I were," sighed Kit.

"And you are my young master his nephew, who knew where to purvey me of good steel," added Fulford, shaking Giles's hand. "You are fain, doubtless, you youngsters, to be forth without the old man. Ha! and you've no lack of merry company."

Harry Randall's first impulse had been to look to the right and left for the means of avoiding this encounter, but there was no escape; and he was moreover in most fantastic motley, arrayed in one of the many suits provided for the occasion. It was in imitation of a parrot, brilliant grass-green velvet, touched here and there with scarlet, yellow, or blue. He had been only half disguised on the occasion of Fulford's visit to his wife, and he perceived the start of recognition in the eyes of the Condottiere, so that he knew it would be vain to try to conceal his identity.

"You sought Stephen Birkenholt," he said. "And you've lit on something nearer, if so be you'll acknowledge the paraquito that your Perronel hath mated with."

The Condottiere burst into a roar of laughter so violent that he had to lean against the mud wall, and hold his sides. "Ha, ha! that I should be father-in-law to a fool!" and then he set off again. "That the sober, dainty little wench should have wedded a fool! Ha! ha! ha!"

"Sir," cried Stephen hotly, "I would have you to know that mine uncle here, Master Harry Randall, is a yeoman of good birth, and that he undertook his present part to support your own father and child! Methinks you are the last who should jeer at and insult him!"

"Stephen is right," said Giles. "This is my kinsman's tent, and no man shall say a word against Master Harry Randall therein."

"Well crowed, my young London gamebirds," returned Fulford, coolly. "I meant no disrespect to the gentleman in green. Nay, I am mightily beholden to him for acting his part out and taking on himself that would scarce befit a gentleman of a company—*impedimenta*, as we used to say in the grammar school. How does the old man?—I must find some token to send him."

"He is beyond the reach of all tokens from you save prayers and masses," returned Randall, gravely.

"Ay? You say not so? Old gaffer dead?" And when the soldier was told how the feeble thread of life had been snapped by the shock of joy on his coming, a fit of compunction and sorrow seized him. He covered his face with his hands and wept with a loudness of grief that surprised and touched his hearers; and presently began to bemoan himself that he had hardly a mark in his purse to pay for a mass; but therewith he proceeded to erect before him the cross hilt of poor Abenali's sword, and to vow thereupon that the first spoil and the first ransom, that it should please the saints to send him, should be entirely spent in masses for the soul of Martin Fulford. This tribute apparently stilled both grief and remorse, for looking up at the grotesque figure of Randall, he said, "Methought they told me, master son, that you were in the right quarters for beads and masses and all that gear—a varlet of Master Butcher-Cardinal's, or the like—but mayhap 'twas part of your fooling."

"Not so," replied Randall. "'Tis to the Cardinal that I belong," holding out his sleeve, where the scarlet hat was neatly worked, "and I'll brook no word against his honour."

"Ho! ho! Maybe you looked to have the hat on your own head," quoth Fulford, waxing familiar, "if your master comes to be Pope after his own reckoning. Why, I've known a Cardinal get the scarlet because an ape had danced on the roof with him in his arms!"

"You forget! I'm a wedded man," said Randall, who certainly, in private life, had much less of the buffoon about him than his father-in-law.

"*Impedimentum* again," whistled the knight. "Put a halter round her neck, and sell her for a pot of beer."

"I'd rather put a halter round my own neck for good and all," said Hal, his face reddening; but among other accomplishments of his position, he had learnt to keep his temper, however indignant he felt.

"Well—she's a knight's daughter, and preferments will be plenty. Thou'lt make me captain of the Pope's guard, fair son—there's no post I should like better. Or I might put up with an Italian earldom or the like. Honour would befit me quite as well as that old fellow, Prosper Colonna; and the Badgers would well become the Pope's scarlet and yellow liveries."

The Badgers, it appeared, were in camp not far from Gravelines, whence the Emperor was watching the conference between his uncle-in-law and his chief enemy; and thence Fulford, who had a good many French acquaintance, having once served under Francis the First, had come over to see the sport. Moreover, he contrived to attach himself to the armourer's party, in a manner that either Alderman Headley himself, or Tibble Steelman, would effectually have prevented; but which Kit Smallbones had not sufficient moral weight to hinder, even if he had had a greater dislike to being treated as a boon companion by a knight who had seen the world, could appreciate good ale, and tell all manner of tales of his experiences.

So the odd sort of kindred that the captain chose to claim with Stephen Birkenholt was allowed, and in right of it, he was permitted to sleep in the wagon; and thereupon his big raw-boned charger was found sharing the fodder of the plump broad-backed cart horses, while he himself, whenever sport was not going forward for him, or work for the armourers, sat discussing with Kit the merits or demerits of the liquors of all nations, either in their own yard or in some of the numerous drinking booths that had sprung up around.

To no one was this arrangement so distasteful as to Quipsome Hal, who felt himself in some sort the occasion of the intrusion, and yet was quite unable to prevent it, while everything he said was treated as a joke by his unwelcome father-in-law. It was a coarse time, and Wolsey's was not a refined or spiritual establishment, but it was decorous, and Randall had such an affection and respect for the innocence of his sister's young son, that he could not bear to have him exposed to the company of one habituated to the licentiousness of the mercenary soldier. At first the jester hoped to remove the lads from the danger, for the brief remainder of their stay, by making double exertion to obtain places for them at any diversion which might be going on when their day's work was ended, and of these, of course, there was a wide choice, subordinate to the magnificent masquing of kings and queens. On the last midsummer evening, while their majesties were taking leave of one another, a company of strolling players were exhibiting in an extemporary theatre, and here Hal incited both the youths to obtain seats. The drama was on one of the ordinary and frequent topics of that, as of all other times, and the dumb show and gestures were far more effective than the words, so that even those who did not understand the language of the comedians, who seemed to be Italians, could enter into it, especially as it was interspersed with very expressive songs.

An old baron insists on betrothing his daughter and heiress to her kinsman freshly knighted. She is reluctant, weeps, and is threatened, singing afterwards her despair, (of course she really was a black-eyed boy). That song was followed by a still more despairing one from the baron's squire, and a tender interview between them followed.

Then came discovery, the baron descending as a thunderbolt, the banishment of the squire, the lady driven at last to wed the young knight, her weeping and bewailing herself under his ill-treatment, which extended to pulling her about by the hair, the return of the lover, notified by a song behind the scenes, a dangerously affectionate meeting, interrupted by the husband, a fierce clashing of swords, mutual slaughter by the two gentlemen, and the lady dying of grief on the top of her lover.

Such was the argument of this tragedy, which Giles Headley pronounced to be very dreary pastime, indeed he was amusing himself with an exchange of comfits with a youth who sat next him all the time—for he had found Stephen utterly deaf to aught but the tragedy, following every gesture with eager eyes, lips quivering, and eyes filling at the strains of the love songs, though they were in their native Italian, of which he understood not a word. He rose up with a heavy groan when all was over, as if not yet disenchanted, and hardly answered when his uncle spoke to him afterwards. It was to ask whether the Dragon party were to return at once to London, or to accompany the Court to Gravelines, where, it had just been announced, the King intended to pay a visit to his nephew, the Emperor.

Neither Stephen nor Giles knew, but when they reached their own quarters they found that Smallbones had received an intimation that there might be jousts, and that the offices of the armourers would be required. He was very busy packing up his tools, but loudly hilarious, and Sir John Fulford, with a flask of wine beside him, was swaggering and shouting orders to the men as though he were the head of the expedition.

Revelations come in strange ways. Perhaps that Italian play might be called Galeotto to Stephen Birkenholt. It affected him all the more because he was not distracted by the dialogue, but was only powerfully touched by the music, and, in the gestures of the lovers, felt all the force of sympathy. It was to him like a kind of prophetic mirror, revealing to him the true meaning of all he had ever felt for Dennet Headley, and of his vexation and impatience at seeing her bestowed upon a dull and indifferent lout like her kinsman, who not only was not good enough for her, but did not even love her, or accept her as anything but his title to the Dragon court. He now thrilled and tingled from head to foot with the perception that all this meant love—love to Dennet; and in every act of the drama he beheld only himself, Giles, and Dennet. Watching at first with a sweet fascination, his feelings changed, now to strong yearning, now to hot wrath, and then to horror and dismay. In his troubled sleep after the spectacle, he identified himself with the lover, sang, wooed, and struggled in his person, woke with a start of relief, to find Giles snoring safely beside him, and the watchdog on his chest instead of an expiring lady. He had not made unholy love to sweet Dennet, nor imperilled her good name, nor slain his comrade. Nor was she yet wedded to that oaf Giles! But she would be in a few weeks, and then! How was he to brook the sight, chained as he was to the Dragon court—see Giles lord it over her, and all of them, see her missing the love that was burning for her elsewhere. Stephen lost his boyhood on that evening, and, though force of habit kept him like himself outwardly, he never was alone, without feeling dazed, and torn in every direction at once.

CHAPTER XXI.

Sword or Smithy.

"Darest thou be so valiant as to play the coward with thy indenture, and to show it a fair pair of heels and run from it!"

Shakespeare.

Tidings came forth on the parting from the French King that the English Court was about to move to Gravelines to pay a visit to the Emperor and his aunt, the Duchess of Savoy. As it was hoped that jousts might make part of the entertainment, the attendance of the Dragon party was required. Giles was unfeignedly delighted at this extension of holiday, Stephen felt that it deferred the day—would it be of strange joy or pain?—of standing face to face with Dennet; and even Kit had come to tolerate foreign parts more with Sir John Fulford to show him the way to the best Flemish ale!

The knight took upon himself the conduct of the Dragons. He understood how to lead them by routes where all provisions and ale had not been consumed; and he knew how to swagger and threaten so as to obtain the best of liquor and provisions at each *kermesse*—at least so he said, though it might be doubted whether the Flemings might not have been more willing to yield up their stores to Kit's open, honest face and free hand.

However, Fulford seemed to consider himself one with the party; and he beguiled the way by tales of the doings of the Badgers in Italy and Savoy, which were listened to with avidity by the lads, distracting Stephen from the pain at his heart, and filling both with excitement. They were to have the honour of seeing the Badgers at Gravelines, where they were encamped outside the city to serve as a guard to the great inclosure that was being made of canvas stretched on the masts of ships to mark out the space for a great banquet and dance.

The weather broke however just as Henry, his wife and his sister, entered Gravelines; it rained pertinaciously, a tempestuous wind blew down the erection, and as there was no time to set it up again, the sports necessarily took place in the castle and town hall. There was no occasion for the exercise of the armourer's craft, and as Charles had forbidden the concourse of all save invited guests, everything was comparatively quiet and dull, though the entertainment was on the most liberal scale. Lodgings were provided in the city at the Emperor's expense, and wherever an Englishman was quartered each night, the imperial officers brought a cast of fine manchet bread, two great silver pots with wine, a pound of sugar, white and yellow candles, and a torch. As Randall said, "Charles gave solid pudding where Francis gave empty praise!"

Smallbones and the two youths had very little to do, save to consume these provisions and accept the hospitality freely offered to them at the camp of the Badgers, where Smallbones and the Ancient of the troop sat fraternising over big flagons of Flemish ale, which did not visibly intoxicate the honest smith, but kept him in the dull and drowsy state, which was his idea of the *dolce far niente* of a holiday. Meanwhile the two youths were made much of by the warriors, Stephen's dexterity with the bow and back-sword were shown off and lauded, Giles's strength was praised, and all manner of new feats were taught them, all manner of stories told them; and the shrinking of well-trained young citizens from these lawless men, "full of strange oaths and bearded like the pard," and some very truculent-looking, had given way to judicious flattery, and to the attractions of adventure and of a free life, where wealth and honour awaited the bold.

Stephen was told that the gentleman in him was visible, that he ought to disdain the flat cap and blue gown, that here was his opportunity, and that among the Badgers he would soon be so rich, as to wonder that he had ever tolerated the greasy mechanical life of a base burgher. Respect to his oaths to his master—Sir John laughed the scruple to scorn; nay, if he were so tender, he could buy his absolution the first time he had his pouch full of gold.

"What shall I do?" was the cry of Stephen's heart. "My honour and my oath. They bind me. *She* would weep. My master would deem me ungrateful, Ambrose break his heart. And yet who knows but I should do worse if I stayed, I shall break my own heart if I do. I shall not see—I may forget. No, no, never I but at least I shall never know the moment when the lubber takes the jewel he knows not how to prize! Marches—sieges—there shall I quell this wild beating! I may die there. At least they will allay this present frenzy of my blood."

And he listened when Fulford and Will Marden, a young English man-at-arms with whom he had made friends, concerted how he should meet them at an inn—the sion of the Seven Stars—in Gravelines, and there exchange his prentice's garb for the buff coat and corslet of a Badger, with the Austrian black and yellow scarf. He listened, but he had not promised. The sense of duty to his master, the honour to his word, always recurred like "first thoughts," though the longing to escape, the restlessness of hopeless love, the youthful eagerness for adventure and freedom, swept it aside again and again.

He had not seen his uncle since the evening of the comedy, for Hal had travelled in the Cardinal's suite, and the amusements being all within doors, jesters were much in request, as indeed Charles the Fifth was curious in fools, and generally had at least three in attendance. Stephen, moreover, always shrank from his uncle when acting professionally. He had learnt to love and esteem the *man* during his troubles, but this only rendered the sight of his buffoonery more distressing, and as Randall had not provided himself with his home suit, they were the more cut off from one another. Thus there was all the less to counteract or show the fallacy of Fulford's recruiting blandishments.

The day had come on the evening of which Stephen was to meet Fulford and Marden at the Seven Stars and give them his final answer, in time to allow of their smuggling him out of the city, and sending him away into the country, since Smallbones would certainly suspect him to be in the camp, and as he was still an apprentice, it was possible, though not probable, that the town magistrates might be incited to make search on inquiry, as they were very jealous of the luring away of their apprentices by the Free Companies, and moreover his uncle might move the Cardinal and the King to cause measures to be taken for his recovery.

Ill at ease, Stephen wandered away from the hostel where Smallbones was entertaining his friend, the Ancient. He had not gone far down the street when a familiar figure met his eye, no other than that of Lucas Hansen, his brother's old master, walking along with a pack on his back. Grown as Stephen was, the old man's recognition was as rapid as his own, and there was a clasp of the hand, an exchange of greeting, while Lucas eagerly asked after his dear pupil, Ambrose.

"Come in hither, and we can speak more at ease," said Lucas, leading the way up the common staircase of a tall house, whose upper stories overhung the street. Up and up, Lucas led the way to a room in the high peaked roof, looking out at the back. Here Stephen recognised a press, but it was not at work, only a young friar was sitting there engaged in sewing up sheets so as to form a pamphlet. Lucas spoke to him in Flemish to explain his own return with the English prentice.

"Dost thou dwell here, sir?" asked Stephen. "I thought Rotterdam was thine home."

"Yea," said Lucas, "so it be, but I am sojourning here to aid in bearing about the seed of the Gospel, for which I walk through these lands of ours. But tell me of thy brother, and of the little Moorish maiden?"

Stephen replied with an account of both Ambrose and Aldonza, and likewise of Tibble Steelman, explaining how ill the last had been in the winter, and that therefore he could not be with the party.

"I would I had a token to send him," said Lucas; "but I have nought here that is not either in the Dutch or the French, and neither of those tongues doth he understand. But thy brother, the good Ambrose, can read the Dutch. Wilt thou carry him from me this fresh tractate, showing how many there be that make light of the Apostle Paul's words not to do evil that good may come?"

Stephen had been hearing rather listlessly, thinking how little the good man suspected how doubtful it was that he should bear messages to Ambrose. Now, on that sore spot in his conscience, that sentence darted like an arrow, the shaft finding "mark the archer little meant," and with a start, not lost on Lucas, he exclaimed, "Saith the holy Saint Paul that?"

"Assuredly, my son. Brother Cornelis, who is one whose eyes have been opened, can show you the very words, if thou hast any Latin."

Perhaps to gain time, Stephen assented, and the young friar, with a somewhat inquisitive look, presently brought him the sentence, "*Et non faciamus mala ut veniant bona.*"

Stephen's Latin was not very fresh, and he hardly comprehended the words, but he stood gazing with a frown of distress on his brow, which made Lucas say, "My son, thou art sorely bestead. Is there aught in which a plain old man can help thee, for thy brother's sake? Speak freely. Brother Cornelis knows not a word of English. Dost thou owe aught to any man?"

"Nay, nay—not that," said Stephen, drawn in his trouble and perplexity to open his heart to this incongruous confidant, "but, sir, sir, which be the worst to break my pledge to my master, or to run into a trial which—which will last from day to day, and may be too much for me—yea, and for another—at last?"

The colour, the trembling of limb, the passion of voice, revealed enough to Lucas to make him say, in the voice of one who, dried up as he was, had once proved the trial, "'Tis love, thou wouldst say?"

"Ay, sir," said Stephen, turning away, but in another moment bursting forth, "I love my master's daughter, and she is to wed her cousin, who takes her as her father's chattel! I wist not why the world had grown dark to me till I saw a comedy at Ardres, where, as in a mirror, 'twas all set forth—yea, and how love was too strong for him and for her, and how shame and death came thereof."

"Those players are good for nought but to wake the passions!" muttered Lucas.

"Nay, methought they warned me," said Stephen. "For, sir,"—he hid his burning face in his hands as he leant on the back of a chair—"I wot that she has ever liked me better, far better than him. And scarce a night have I closed an eye without dreaming it all, and finding myself bringing evil on her, till I deemed 'twere better I never saw her more, and left her to think of me as a forsworn runagate rather than see her wedded only to be flouted—and maybe—do worse."

"Poor lad!" said Lucas; "and what wouldst thou do?"

"I have not pledged myself—but I said I would consider of—service among Fulford's troop," faltered Stephen.

"Among those ruffians—godless, lawless men!" exclaimed Lucas.

"Yea, I know what you would say," returned Stephen, "but they are brave men, better than you deem, sir."

"Were they angels or saints," said Lucas, rallying his forces, "thou hast no right to join, them. Thine oath fetters thee. Thou hast no right to break it and do a sure and certain evil to avoid one that may never befall! How knowst thou how it may be? Nay, if the trial seem to thee over great, thine apprenticeship will soon be at an end."

"Not for two years."

"Or thy master, if thou spakest the whole truth, would transfer thine indentures. He is a good man, and if it be as thou sayest, would not see his child tried too sorely. God will make a way for the tempted to escape. They need not take the devil's way."

"Sir," said Stephen, lifting up his head, "I thank you. This was what I needed. I will tell Sir John Fulford that I ought never to have heeded him."

"Must thou see him again?"

"I must. I am to give him his answer at the Seven Stars. But fear not me, Master Lucas, he shall not lead me away." And Stephen took a grateful leave of the little Dutchman, and charged himself with more messages for Ambrose and Tibble than his overburdened spirit was likely to retain.

Lucas went down the stairs with him, and as a sudden thought said at the foot of them, "'Tis at the Seven Stars thou meetest this knight. Take an old man's counsel. Taste no liquor there."

"I am no ale bibber," said Stephen.

"Nay, I deemed thee none—but heed my words—captains of landsknechts in *kermesses* are scarce to be trusted. Taste not."

Stephen gave a sort of laugh at the precaution, and shook himself loose. It was still an hour to the time of meeting, and the Ave-bell was ringing. A church door stood open, and for the first time since he had been at Gravelines he felt that there would be the calm he needed to adjust the conflict of his spirits, and comprehend the new situation, or rather the recurrence to the old one. He seemed to have recovered his former self, and to be able to perceive that things might go on as before, and his heart really leapt at finding he might return to the sight of Dennet and Ambrose and all he loved.

His wishes were really that way; and Fulford's allurements had become very shadowy when he made his way to the Seven Stars, whose vine-covered window allowed many loud voices and fumes of beer and wine to escape into the summer evening air.

The room was perhaps cleaner than an English one would have been, but it was reeking with heat and odours, and the forest-bred youth was unwilling to enter, but Fulford and two or three Badgers greeted him noisily and called on him to partake of the supper they had ready prepared.

"No, sir knight, I thank you," said Stephen. "I am bound for my quarters, I came but to thank you for your goodness to me, and to bid you farewell."

"And how as to thy pledge to join us, young man?" demanded Fulford sternly.

"I gave no pledge," said Stephen. "I said I would consider of it."

"Faint-hearted! ha! ha!" and the English Badgers translated the word to the Germans, and set them shouting with derision.

"I am not faint-hearted," said Stephen; "but I will not break mine oath to my master."

"And thine oath to me? Ha!" said Fulford.

"I sware you no oath, I gave you no word," said Stephen.

"Ha! Thou darest give me the lie, base prentice. Take that!"

And therewith he struck Stephen a crushing blow on the head, which felled him to the ground. The host and all the company, used to pot-house quarrels, and perhaps playing into his hands, took little heed; Stephen was dragged insensible into another room, and there the Badgers began hastily to divest him of his prentice's gown, and draw his arms into a buff coat.

Fulford had really been struck with his bravery, and knew besides that his skill in the armourer's craft would be valuable, so that it had been determined beforehand that he should—by fair means or foul—leave the Seven Stars a Badger.

"By all the powers of hell, you have struck too hard, sir. He is sped," said Marden anxiously.

"Ass! tut!" said Fulford. "Only enough to daze him till he be safe in our quarters—and for that the sooner the better. Here, call Anton to take his heels. We'll get him forth now as a fellow of our own."

"Hark! What's that?"

"Gentlemen," said the host hurrying in, "here be some of the gentlemen of the English Cardinal, calling for a nephew of one of them, who they say is in this house."

With an imprecation, Fulford denied all connection with gentlemen of the Cardinal; but there was evidently an invasion, and in another moment, several powerful-looking men in the crimson and black velvet of Wolsey's train had forced their way into the chamber, and the foremost, seeing Stephen's condition at a glance, exclaimed loudly, "Thou villain! traitor! kidnapper! This is thy work."

"Ha! ha!" shouted Fulford, "whom have we here? The Cardinal's fool a masquing! Treat us to a caper, quipsome sir?"

"I'm more like to treat you to the gyves," returned Randall. "Away with you! The watch are at hand. Were it not for my wife's sake, they should bear you off to the city jail; the Emperor should know how you fill your ranks."

It was quite true. The city-guard were entering at the street door, and the host hurried Fulford and his men, swearing and raging, out at a back door provided for such emergencies. Stephen was beginning to recover by this time. His uncle knelt down, took his head on his shoulder, and Lucas washed off the blood and administered a drop of wine. His first words were:

"Was it Giles? Where is she?"

"Still going over the play!" thought Lucas. "Nay, nay, lad. 'Twas one of the soldiers who played thee this scurvy trick! All's well now. Thou wilt soon be able to quit this place."

"I remember now," said Stephen, "Sir John said I gave him the lie when I said I had given no pledge. But I had not!"

"Thou hast been a brave fellow, and better broken head than broken troth," said his uncle.

"But how came you here," asked Stephen. "in the nick of time?"

It was explained that Lucas, not doubting Stephen's resolution, but quite aware of the tricks of landsknecht captains with promising recruits in view, had gone first in search of Smallbones, but had found him and the Ancient so deeply engaged in potations from the liberal supply of the Emperor to all English guests, that there was no getting him apart, and he was too much muddled to comprehend if he could have been spoken with.

Lucas then, in desperation, betook himself to the convent where Wolsey was magnificently lodged. Ill May Day had made him, as well as others, well acquainted with the relationship between Stephen and Randall, though he was not aware of the further connection with Fulford. He hoped, even if unable to see Randall, to obtain help on behalf of an English lad in danger, and happily he arrived at a moment when State affairs were going on, and Randall was refreshing himself by a stroll in the cloister. When Lucas had made him understand the situation, his dismay was only equalled by his promptitude. He easily obtained the loan of one of the splendid suits of scarlet and crimson, guarded with black velvet a hand broad, which were worn by the Cardinal's secular attendants—for he was well known by this time in the household to be very far from an absolute fool, and indeed had done many a good turn to his comrades. Several of the gentlemen, indignant at the threatened outrage on a young Englishman, and esteeming the craftsmen of the Dragon, volunteered to accompany him, and others warned the watch.

There was some difficulty still, for the burgher guards, coming up puffing and blowing, wanted to carry off the victim and keep him in ward to give evidence against the mercenaries, whom they regarded as a sort of wolves, so that even the Emperor never durst quarter them within one of the cities. The drawn swords of Randall's friends however settled that matter, and Stephen, though still dizzy, was able to walk. Thus leaning on his uncle, he was escorted back to the hostel.

"The villain!" the jester said on the way, "I mistrusted him, but I never thought he would have abused our kindred in this fashion. I would fain have come down to look after thee, nevvy, but these kings and queens are troublesome folk. The Emperor—he is a pale, shame-faced, solemn lad. Maybe he museth, but he had scarce a word to say for himself. Our Hal tried clapping on the shoulder, calling him fair coz, and the like, in his hearty fashion. Behold, what doth he but turn round with such a look about the long lip of him as my Lord of Buckingham might have if his scullion made free with him. His aunt, the Duchess of Savoy, is a merry dame, and a wise! She and our King can talk by the ell, but as for the Emperor, he speaketh to none willingly save Queen Katharine, who is of his own stiff Spanish humour, and he hath eyes for none save Queen Mary, who would have been his empress had high folk held to their word. And with so tongue—tied a host, and the rain without, what had the poor things to do by way of disporting themselves with but a show of fools. I've had to go through every trick and quip I learnt when I was with old Nat Fire-eater. And I'm stiffer in the joints and weightier in the heft than I was in those days when I slept in the fields, and fasted more than ever Holy Church meant; But, heigh ho! I ought to be supple enough after the practice of these three days. Moreover, if it could loose a fool's tongue to have a king and queen for interpreters, I had them—for there were our Harry and Moll catching at every gibe as fast as my brain could hatch it, and rendering it into French as best they might, carping and quibbling the while underhand at one another's renderings, and the Emperor sitting by in his black velvet, smiling about as much as a felon at the hangman's jests. All his poor fools moreover, and the King's own, ready to gnaw their baubles for envy! That was the only sport I had! I'm wearier than if I'd been plying Smallbones' biggest hammer. The worst of it is that my Lord Cardinal is to stay behind and go on to Bruges as ambassador, and I with him, so thou must bear my greetings to thy naunt, and tell her I'm keeping from picking up a word of French or Flemish lest this same Charles should take a fancy to me and ask me of my master, who would give away his own head to get the Pope's fool's cap."

"*Wer da? Qui va là?*" asked a voice, and the summer twilight revealed two figures with cloaks held high and drooping Spanish hats; one of whom, a slender, youthful figure, so far as could be seen under his cloak, made inquiries, first in Flemish, then in French, as to what ailed the youth. Lucas replied in the former tongue, and one of the Englishmen could speak French. The gentleman seemed much concerned, asked if the watch had been at hand, and desired Lucas to assure the young Englishman that the Emperor would be much distressed at the tidings, asked where he was lodged, and passed on.

"Ah ha!" muttered the jester, "if my ears deceive me now, I'll never trust them again! Mynheer Charles knows a few more tricks than he is fain to show off in royal company. Come on, Stevie! I'll see thee to thy bed. Old Kit is too far gone to ask after thee. In sooth, I trow that my sweet father-in-law set his Ancient to nail him to the wine pot. And Master Giles I saw last with some of the grooms. I said nought to him, for I trow thou wouldst not have him know thy plight! I'll be with thee in the morning ere thou partest, if kings, queens, and cardinals roar themselves hoarse for the Quipsome."

With this promise Hal Randall bestowed his still dulled and half stunned nephew carefully on the pallet provided by the care of the purveyors. Stephen slept dreamily at first, then soundly, and woke at the sound of the bells of Gravelines to the sense that a great crisis in his life was over, a strange wild dream of evil dispelled, and that he was to go home to see, hear, and act as he could, with a heartache indeed, but with the resolve to do his best as a true and honest man.

Smallbones was already afoot—for the start for Calais was to be made on that very day. The smith was fully himself again, and was bawling for his subordinates, who had followed his example in indulging in the good cheer, and did not carry it off so easily. Giles, rather silent and surly, was out of bed, shouting answers to Smallbones, and calling on Stephen to truss his points. He was in a mood not easy to understand, he would hardly speak, and never noticed the marks of the fray on Stephen's temple—only half hidden by the dark curly hair. This was of course a relief, but Stephen could not help suspecting that he had been last night engaged in some revel about which he desired no inquiries.

Randall came just as the operation was completed. He was in a good deal of haste, having to restore the groom's dress he wore by the time the owner had finished the morning toilet of the Lord Cardinal's palfreys. He could not wait to inquire how Stephen had contrived to fall into the hands of Fulford, his chief business being to put under safe charge a bag of coins, the largesse from the various princes and nobles whom he had diverted—ducats, crowns, dollars, and angels all jingling together—to be bestowed wherever Perronel kept her store, a matter which Hal was content not to know, though the pair cherished a hope some day to retire on it from fooling.

"Thou art a good lad, Steve," said Hal. "I'm right glad thou leavest this father of mine behind thee. I would not see thee such as he—no, not for all the gold we saw on the Frenchmen's backs."

This was the jester's farewell, but it was some time before the wagon was under way, for the carter and one of the smiths were missing, and were only at noon found in an alehouse, both very far gone in liquor, and one with a black eye. Kit discoursed on sobriety in the most edifying manner, as at last he drove heavily along the street, almost the last in the baggage train of the king and queens—but still in time to be so included in it so as to save all difficulty at the gates. It was, however, very late in the evening when they reached Calais, so that darkness was coming on as they waited their turn at the drawbridge, with a cart full of scullions and pots and pans before them, and a wagonload of tents behind. The warders in charge of the gateway had orders to count over all whom they admitted, so that no unauthorised person might enter that much-valued fortress. When at length the wagon rolled forward into the shadow of the great towered gateway on the outer side of the moat, the demand was made, who was there? Giles had always insisted, as leader of the party, on making reply to such questions, and Smallbones waited for his answer, but none was forthcoming. Therefore Kit shouted in reply, "Alderman Headley's wain and armourers. Two Journeymen, one prentice, two smiths, two wagoners."

"Seven!" rejoined the warder. "One—two—three—four—five. Ha! your company seems to be lacking."

"Giles must have ridden on," suggested Stephen, while Kit, growling angrily, called on the lazy fellow, Will Wherry, to wake and show himself. But the officials were greatly hurried, and as long as no dangerous person got into Calais, it mattered little to them who might be left outside, so they hurried on the wagon into the narrow street.

It was well that it was a summer night, for lodgings there were none. Every hostel was full and all the houses besides. The earlier comers assured Kit that it was of no use to try to go on. The streets up to the wharf were choked, and he might think himself lucky to have his wagon to sleep in. But the horses! And food? However, there was one comfort—English tongues answered, if it was only with denials.

Kit's store of travelling money was at a low ebb, and it was nearly exhausted by the time, at an exorbitant price, he had managed to get a little hay and water for the horses, and a couple of loaves and a haunch of bacon among the five hungry men. They were quite content to believe that Master Giles had ridden on before and secured better quarters and viands, nor could they much regret the absence of Will Wherry's wide mouth.

Kit called Stephen to council in the morning. His funds would not permit waiting for the missing ones, if he were to bring home any reasonable proportion of gain to his master. He believed that Master Headley would by no means risk the whole party loitering at Calais, when it was highly probable that Giles might have joined some of the other travellers, and embarked by himself.

After all, Kit's store had to be well-nigh expended before the horses, wagon, and all, could find means to encounter the miseries of the transit to Dover. Then, glad as he was to be on his native soil, his spirits sank lower and lower as the wagon creaked on under the hot sun towards London. He had actually brought home only four marks to make over to his master; and although he could show a considerable score against the King and various nobles, these debts were not apt to be promptly discharged, and what was worse, two members of his party and one horse were missing. He little knew how narrow an escape he had had of losing a third!

CHAPTER XXII.

An Invasion.

"What shall be the maiden's fate?
Who shall be the maiden's mate?"

Scott.

No Giles Headley appeared to greet the travellers, though Kit Smallbones had halted at Canterbury, to pour out entreaties to Saint Thomas, and the vow of a steel and gilt reliquary of his best workmanship to contain the old shoe, which a few years previously had so much disgusted Erasmus and his companion.

Poor old fellow, he was too much crest-fallen thoroughly to enjoy even the gladness of his little children; and his wife made no secret of her previous conviction that he was too dunderheaded not to run into some coil, when she was not there to look after him. The alderman was more merciful. Since there had been no invasion from Salisbury, he had regretted the not having gone himself to Ardres, and he knew pretty well that Kit's power lay more in his arms than in his brain. He did not wonder at the small gain, nor at the having lost sight of the young man, and confidently expected the lost ones soon to appear.

As to Dennet, her eyes shone quietly, and she took upon herself to send down to let Mistress Randall know of her nephew's return, and invite her to supper to hear the story of his doings. The girl did not look at all like a maiden uneasy about her lost lover, but much more like one enjoying for the moment the immunity from a kind of burthen; and, as she smiled, called for Stephen's help in her little arrangements, and treated him in the friendly manner of old times, he could not but wonder at the panic that had overpowered him for a time like a fever of the mind.

There was plenty to speak of in the glories of the Field of the Cloth of Gold, and the transactions with the knights and nobles; and Stephen held his peace as to his adventure, but Dennet's eyes were sharper than Kit's. She spied the remains of the bruise under his black curly hair; and while her father and Tib were unravelling the accounts from Kit's brain and tally-sticks, she got the youth out into the gallery, and observed, "So thou hast a broken head. See here are grandmother's lily-leaves in strong waters. Let me lay one on for thee. There, sit down on the step, then I can reach."

"'Tis well-nigh whole now, sweet mistress," said Stephen, complying however, for it was too sweet to have those little fingers busy about him, for the offer to be declined.

"How gatst thou the blow?" asked Dennet. "Was it at single-stick? Come, thou mayst tell me. 'Twas in standing up for some one."

"Nay, mistress, I would it had been."

"Thou hast been in trouble," she said, leaning on the baluster above him. "Or did ill men set on thee?"

"That's the nearest guess," said Stephen. "'Twas that tall father of mine aunt's, the fellow that came here for armour, and bought poor Master Michael's sword."

"And sliced the apple on thine hand. Ay?"

"He would have me for one of his Badgers."

"Thee! Stephen!" It was a cry of pain as well as horror.

"Yea, mistress; and when I refused, the fellow dealt me a blow, and laid me down senseless, to bear me off willy nilly, but that good old Lucas Hansen brought mine uncle to mine aid—"

Dennet clasped her hands. "O Stephen, Stephen! Now I know how good the Lord is. Wot ye, I asked of Tibble to take me daily to Saint Faith's to crave of good Saint Julian to have you all in his keeping, and saith he on the way, 'Methinks, mistress, our dear Lord would hear you if you spake to Him direct, with no go-between.' I did as he bade me, Stephen, I went to the high Altar, and prayed there, and Tibble went with me, and lo, now, He hath brought you back safe. We will have a mass of thanksgiving on the very morn."

Stephen's heart could not but bound, for it was plain enough for whom the chief force of these prayers had been offered.

"Sweet mistress," he said, "they have availed me indeed. Certes, they warded me in the time of sore trial and temptation."

"Nay," said Dennet, "thou *couldst* not have longed to go away from hence with those ill men who live by slaying and plundering?"

The present temptation was to say that he had doubted whether this course would not have been for the best both for himself and for her; but he recollected that Giles might be at the gate, and if so, he should feel as if he had rather have bitten out his tongue than have let Dennet know the state of the case, so he only answered—

"There be sorer temptations in the world for us poor rogues than little home-biding house crickets like thee wot of, mistress. Well that ye can pray for us without knowing all!"

Stephen had never consciously come so near lovemaking, and his honest face was all one burning glow with the suppressed feeling, while Dennet lingered till the curfew warned them of the lateness of the hour, both with a strange sense of undefined pleasure in the being together in the summer twilight.

Day after day passed on with no news of Giles or Will Wherry. The alderman grew uneasy, and sent Stephen to ask his brother to write to Randall, or to some one else in Wolsey's suite, to make inquiries at Bruges. But Ambrose was found to have gone abroad in the train of Sir Thomas More, and nothing was heard till their return six weeks later, when Ambrose brought home a small packet which had been conveyed to him through one of the Emperor's suite. It was tied up with a long tough pale wisp of hair, evidently from the mane or tail of some Flemish horse, and was addressed, "To Master

Ambrose Birkenholt, menial clerk to the most worshipful Sir Thomas More, Knight, Under Sheriff of the City of London. These greeting—"

Within, when Ambrose could open the missive, was another small parcel, and a piece of brown coarse paper, on which was scrawled—

"Good Ambrose Birkenholt,—I pray thee to stand, my friend, and let all know whom it may concern, that when this same billet comes to hand, I shall be far on the march to High Germany, with a company of lusty fellows in the Emperor's service. They be commanded by the good knight, Sir John Fulford.

"If thou canst send tidings to my mother, bid her keep her heart up, for I shall come back a captain, full of wealth and honour, and that will be better than hammering for life—or being wedded against mine own will. There never was troth plight between my master's daughter and me, and my time is over, so I be quit with them, and I thank my master for his goodness. They shall all hear of me some of these days. Will Wherry is my groom, and commends him to his mother. And so, commending thee and all the rest to Our Lady and the saints,

"Thine to command,

"Giles Headley,

"*Man-at-Arms in the Honourable Company of Sir John Fulford, Knight.*"

On a separate strip was written—

"Give this packet to the little Moorish maid, and tell her that I will bring her better by and by, and mayhap make her a knight's lady; but on thy life, say nought to any other."

It was out now! Ambrose's head was more in Sir Thomas's books than in real life at all times, or he would long ago have inferred something—from the jackdaw's favourite phrase—from Giles's modes of haunting his steps, and making him the bearer of small tokens—an orange, a simnel cake, a bag of walnuts or almonds to Mistress Aldonza, and of the smiles, blushes, and thanks with which she greeted them. Nay, had she not burst into tears and entreated to be spared when Lady More wanted to make a match between her and the big porter, and had not her distress led Mistress Margaret to appeal to her father, who had said he should as soon think of wedding the silver-footed Thetis to Polyphemus. "Tilley valley! Master More," the lady had answered, "will all your fine pagan gods hinder the wench from starving on earth, and leading apes in hell."

Margaret had answered that Aldonza should never do the first, and Sir Thomas had gravely said that he thought those black eyes would lead many a man on earth before they came to the latter fate.

Ambrose hid the parcel for her deep in his bosom before he asked permission of his master to go to the Dragon court with the rest of the tidings.

"He always was an unmannerly cub," said Master Headley, as he read the letter. "Well, I've done my best to make a silk purse of a sow's ear! I've done my duty by poor Robert's son, and if he will be such a fool as to run after blood and wounds, I have no more to say! Though 'tis pity of the old name! Ha! what's this? 'Wedded against my will—no troth plight.' Forsooth, I thought my young master was mighty slack. He hath some other matter in his mind, hath he? Run into some coil mayhap with a beggar wench! Well, we need not be beholden to him. Ha, Dennet, my maid!"

Dennet screwed up her little mouth, and looked very demure, but she twinkled her bright eyes, and said, "My heart will not break, sir; I am in no haste to be wed."

Her father pinched her cheek and said she was a silly wench; but perhaps he marked the dancing step with which the young mistress went about her household cares, and how she was singing to herself songs that certainly were not "Willow! willow!"

Ambrose had no scruple in delivering to Aldonza the message and token, when he overtook her on the stairs of the house at Chelsea, carrying up a lapful of roses to the still-room, where Dame Alice More was rejoicing in setting her step-daughters to housewifely tasks.

There came a wonderful illumination and agitation over the girl's usually impassive features, giving all that they needed to make them surpassingly beautiful.

"Woe is me!" was, however, her first exclamation. "That he should have given up all for me! Oh! if I had thought it!" But while she spoke as if she were shocked and appalled, her eyes belied her words. They shone with the first absolute certainty of love, and there was no realising as yet the years of silent waiting and anxiety that must go by, nay, perhaps an entire lifetime of uncertainty of her lover's truth or untruth, life or death.

Dame Alice called her, and in a rambling, maundering way, charged her with loitering and gadding with the young men; and Margaret saw by her colour and by her eyes that some strange thing had happened to her. Margaret had, perhaps, some intuition; for was not her heart very tender towards a certain young barrister by name Roper whom her father doubted as yet, because of his Lutheran inclinations. By and by she discovered that she needed Aldonza to comb out her long dark hair, and ere long, she had heard all the tale of the youth cured by the girl's father, and all his gifts, and how Aldonza deemed him too great and too good for her, (poor Giles!) though she knew she should never do more than look up to him with love and gratitude from afar. And she never so much as dreamt that he would cast an eye on her save in kindness. Oh yes, she knew what he had taught the daw to say, but then she was a child, she durst not deem it more. And Margaret More was more kind and eager than worldly wise, and she encouraged Aldonza to watch and wait, promised protection from all enforced suits and suitors, and gave assurances of shelter as her own attendant as long as the girl should need it.

Master Headley, with some sighing and groaning, applied himself to write to the mother at Salisbury what had become of her son; but he had only spent one evening over the trying task, when just as the supper bell was ringing, with Master Hope and his wife as guests, there were horses' feet in the court, and Master Tiptoff appeared, with a servant on another horse, which carried besides a figure in camlet, on a pillion. No sooner was this same figure lifted from her steed and set down on the steps, while the master of the house and his daughter came out to greet her, than she began, "Master Alderman Headley, I am here to know what you have done with my poor son!"

"Alack, good cousin!"

"Alack me no alacks," she interrupted, holding up her riding rod. "I'll have no dissembling, there hath been enough of that, Giles Headley. Thou hast sold him, soul and body, to one of yon cruel, bloodthirsty plundering, burning captains, that the poor child may be slain and murthered! Is this the fair promises you made to his father—wiling him away from his poor mother, a widow, with talking of teaching him the craft, and giving him your daughter! My son, Tiptoff here, told me the spousal was delayed and delayed, and he doubted whether it would ever come off, but I thought not of this sending him beyond seas, to make merchandise of him. And you call yourself an alderman! The gown should be stript off the back of you, and shall be, if there be any justice in London for a widow woman."

"Nay, cousin, you have heard some strange tale," said Master Headley, who, much as he would have dreaded the attack beforehand, faced it the more calmly and manfully because the accusation was so outrageous.

"Ay, so I told her," began her son-in-law, "but she hath been neither to have nor to hold since the—"

"And how should I be to have or to hold by a nincompoop like thee," she said, turning round on him, "that would have me sit down and be content forsooth, when mine only son is kidnapped to be sold to the Turks or to work in the galleys, for aught I know."

"Mistress!" here Master Hope's voice came in, "I would counsel you to speak less loud, and hear before you accuse. We of the City of London know Master Alderman Headley too well to hear him railed against."

"Ah! you're all of a piece," she began; but by this time Master Tiptoff had managed at least to get her into the hall, and had exchanged words enough with the alderman to assure himself that there was an explanation, nay, that there was a letter from Giles himself. This the indignant mother presently was made to understand—and as the alderman had borrowed the letter in order to copy it for her, it was given to her. She could not read, and would trust no one but her son-in-law to read it to her. "Yea, you have it very pat," she said, "but how am I to be assured 'tis not all writ here to hoodwink a poor woman like me."

"'Tis Giles's hand," averred Tiptoff.

"And if you will," added the alderman, with wonderful patience, "tomorrow you may speak with the youth who received it. Come, sit down and sup with us, and then you shall learn from Smallbones how this mischance befel, all from my sending two young heads together, and one who, though a good fellow, could not hold all in rule."

"Ay—you've your reasons for anything," she muttered, but being both weary and hungry, she consented to eat and drink, while Tiptoff, who was evidently ashamed of her violence, and anxious to excuse it, managed to explain that a report had been picked up at Romsey, by a bare-footed friar from Salisbury, that young Giles Headley had been seen at Ghent by one of the servants of a wool merchant, riding with a troop of Free Companions in the Emperor's service. All the rest was deduced from this intelligence by the dame's own imagination.

After supper she was invited to interrogate Kit and Stephen, and her grief and anxiety found vent in fierce scolding at the misrule which had permitted such a villain as Fulford to be haunting and tempting poor fatherless lads. Master Headley had reproached poor Kit for the same thing, but he could only represent that Giles, being a freeman, was no longer under his authority. However, she stormed on, being absolutely convinced that her son's evasion was every one's fault but his own. Now it was the alderman for misusing him, overtasking the poor child, and deferring the marriage, now it was that little pert poppet, Dennet, who had flouted him, now it was the bad company he had been led into—the poor babe who had been bred to godly ways.

The alderman was really sorry for her, and felt himself to blame so far as that he had shifted the guidance of the expedition to such an insufficient head as poor Smallbones, so he let her rail on as much as she would, till the storm exhausted itself, and she settled into the trust that Giles would soon grow weary and return. The good man felt bound to show her all hospitality, and the civilities to country cousins were in proportion to the rarity of their visits. So Mrs. Headley stayed on after Tiptoff's return to Salisbury, and had the best view feasible of all the pageants and diversions of autumn. She saw some magnificent processions of clergy, she was welcomed at a civic banquet and drank of the loving cup, and she beheld the Lord Mayor's Show in all its picturesque glory of emblazoned barges on the river. In fact, she found the position of denizen of an alderman's household so very agreeable that she did her best to make it a permanency. Nay, Dennet soon found that she considered herself to be waiting there and keeping guard till her son's return should establish her there, and that she viewed the girl already as a daughter—for which Dennet was by no means obliged to her! She lavished counsel on her hostess, found fault with the maidens, criticised the cookery, walked into the kitchen and still-room with assistance and directions, and even made a strong effort to possess herself of the keys.

It must be confessed that Dennet was saucy! It was her weapon of self-defence, and she considered herself insulted in her own house.

There she stood, exalted on a tall pair of pattens before the stout oaken table in the kitchen where a glowing fire burned; pewter, red and yellow earthenware, and clean scrubbed trenchers made a goodly show, a couple of men-cooks and twice as many scullions obeyed her behests—only the superior of the two first ever daring to argue a point with her. There she stood, in her white apron, with sleeves turned up, daintily compounding her mince-meat for Christmas, when in stalked Mrs. Headley to offer her counsel and aid—but this was lost in a volley of barking from the long-backed, bandy-legged, turnspit dog, which was awaiting its turn at the wheel, and which ran forward, yapping with malign intentions towards the dame's scarlet-hosed ankles.

She shook her petticoats at him, but Dennet tittered even while declaring that Tray hurt nobody. Mrs. Headley reviled the dog, and then proceeded to advise Dennet that she should chop her citron finer. Dennet made answer "that father liked a good stout piece of it." Mistress Headley offered to take the chopper and instruct her how to compound all in the true Sarum style.

"Grammercy, mistress, but we follow my grand-dame's recipe!" said Dennet, grasping her implement firmly.

"Come, child, be not above taking a lesson from thine elders! Where's the goose? What?" as the girl looked amazed, "where hast thou lived not to know that a live goose should be bled into the mincemeat?"

"I have never lived with barbarous, savage folk," said Dennet—and therewith she burst into an irrepressible fit of laughter, trying in vain to check it, for a small and mischievous elf, freshly promoted to the office of scullion, had crept up and pinned a dishcloth to the substantial petticoats, and as Mistress Headley whisked round to see what was the matter, like a kitten after its tail, it followed her like a train, while she rushed to box the ears of the offender, crying:

"You set him on, you little saucy vixen! I saw it in your eyes. Let the rascal be scourged."

"Not so," said Dennet, with prim mouth and laughing eyes. "Far be it from me! But 'tis ever the wont of the kitchen, when those come there who have no call thither."

Mistress Headley flounced away, dishcloth and all, to go whimpering to the alderman with her tale of insults. She trusted that her cousin would give the pert wench a good beating. She was not a whit too old for it.

"How oft did you beat Giles, good kinswoman?" said Dennet demurely, as she stood by her father.

"Whisht, whisht, child," said her father, "this may not be! I cannot have my guest flouted."

"If she act as our guest, I will treat her with all honour and courtesy," said the maiden; "but when she comes where we look not for guests, there is no saying what the black guard may take it on them to do."

Master Headley was mischievously tickled at the retort, and not without hope that it might offend his kinswoman into departing; but she contented herself with denouncing all imaginable evils from Dennet's ungoverned condition, with which she was prevented in her beneficence from interfering by the father's foolish fondness. He would rue the day!

Meantime if the alderman's peace on one side was disturbed by his visitor, on the other, suitors for Dennet's hand gave him little rest. She was known to be a considerable heiress, and though Mistress Headley gave every one to understand that there was a contract with Giles, and that she was awaiting his return, this did not deter more wooers than Dennet ever knew of, from making proposals to her father. Jasper Hope was offered, but he was too young, and besides, was a mercer—and Dennet and her father were agreed that her husband must go on with the trade. Then there was a master-armourer, but he was a widower with sons and daughters as old as Dennet, and she shook her head and laughed at the bare notion. There also came a young knight who would have turned the Dragon court into a tilt-yard, and spent all the gold that long years of prudent toil had amassed.

If Mistress Headley deemed each denial the result of her vigilance for her son's interests, she was the more impelled to expatiate on the folly of leaving a maid of sixteen to herself, to let the household go to rack and ruin; while as to the wench, she might prank herself in her own conceit, but no honest man would soon look at her for a wife, if her father left her to herself, without giving her a good stepmother, or at least putting a kinswoman in authority over her.

The alderman was stung. He certainly had warmed a snake on his hearth, and how was he to be rid of it? He secretly winked at the resumption of a forge fire that had been abandoned, because the noise and smoke incommoded the dwelling-house, and Kit Smallbones hammered his loudest there, when the guest might be taking her morning nap; but this had no effect in driving her away, though it may have told upon her temper; and good-humoured Master Headley was harassed more than he had ever been in his life.

"It puts me past my patience," said he, turning into Tibble's special work-shop one afternoon. "Here hath Mistress Hillyer of the Eagle been with me full of proposals that I would give my poor wench to that scapegrace lad of hers, who hath been twice called to account before the guild, but who now, for-sooth, is to turn over a new leaf."

"So I wis would the Dragon under him," quoth Tibble.

"I told her 'twas not to be thought of, and then what does the dame but sniff the air and protest that I had better take heed, for there may not be so many who would choose a spoilt, misruled maid like mine. There's the work of yonder Sarum woman. I tell thee, Tib, never was bull in the ring more baited than am I."

"Yea, sir," returned Tib, "there'll be no help for it till our young mistress be wed."

"Ay! that's the rub! But I've not seen one whom I could mate with her—let alone one who would keep up the old house. Giles would have done that pass-ably, though he were scarce worthy of the wench, even without—" An expres-sive shake of the head denoted the rest. "And now if he ever come home at all, 'twill be as a foul-mouthed, plundering scarecrow, like the kites of men-at-arms, who, if they lose not their lives, lose all that makes an honest life in the Italian wars. I would have writ to Edmund Burgess, but I hear his elder brother is dead, and he is driving a good traffic at York. Belike too he is wedded."

"Nay," said Tibble, "I could tell of one who would be true and faithful to your worship, and a loving husband to Mistress Dennet, ay, and would be a master that all of us would gladly cleave to. For he is godly after his lights, and sound-hearted, and wots what good work be, and can do it."

"That were a son-in-law, Tib! Of who speakest thou? Is he of good birth?"

"Yea, of gentle birth and breeding."

"And willing? But that they all are. Wherefore then hath he never made suit?"

"He hath not yet his freedom."

"Who be it then?"

"He that made this elbow-piece for the suit that Queen Margaret ordered for the little King of Scots," returned Tibble, producing an exquisite miniature bit of workmanship.

"Stephen Birkenholt! The fool's nephew! Mine own prentice!"

"Yea, and the best worker in steel we have yet turned out. Since the sickness of last winter hath stiffened my joints and dimmed mine eyes, I had rather trust dainty work such as this to him than to myself."

"Stephen! Tibble, hath he set thee on to this?"

"No, sir. We both know too well what becometh us; but when you were casting about for a mate for my young mistress, I could not but think how men seek far, and overlook the jewel at their feet."

"He hath nought! That brother of his will give him nought."

"He hath what will be better for the old Dragon and for your worship's self, than many a bag of gold, sir."

"Thou sayst truly there, Tib. I know him so far that he would not be the ingrate Jack to turn his back on the old master or the old man. He is a good lad. But—but—I've ever set my face against the prentice wedding the master's daughter, save when he is of her own house, like Giles. Tell me, Tibble, deemst thou that the varlet bath dared to lift his eyes to the lass?"

"I wot nothing of love!" said Tibble, somewhat grimly. "I have seen nought. I only told your worship where a good son and a good master might be had. Is it your pleasure, sir, that we take in a freight of sea-coal from Simon Collier for the new furnace? His is purest, if a mark more the chaldron."

He spoke as if he put the recommendation of the son and master on the same line as that of the coal. Mr. Headley answered the business matters absently, and ended by saying he would think on the council.

In Tibble's workroom, with the clatter of a forge close to them, they had not heard a commotion in the court outside. Dennet had been standing on the steps cleaning her tame starling's cage, when Mistress Headley had suddenly come out on the gallery behind her, hotly scolding her laundress, and waving her cap to show how ill-starched it was.

The bird had taken fright and flown to the tree in the court; Dennet hastened in pursuit, but all the boys and children in the court rushing out after her, her blandishments had no chance, and "Goldspot" had fluttered on to the gateway. Stephen had by this time come out, and hastened to the gate, hoping to turn the truant back from escaping into Cheapside; but all in vain, it flew out while the market was in full career, and he could only call back to her that he would not lose sight of it.

Out he hurried, Dennet waiting in a sort of despair by the tree for a time that seemed to her endless, until Stephen reappeared under the gate, with a signal that all was well. She darted to meet him. "Yea, mistress, here he is, the little caitiff. He was just knocked down by this country lad's cap—happily not hurt. I told him you would give him a tester for your bird."

"With all my heart!" and Dennet produced the coin. "Oh! Stephen, are you sure he is safe? Thou bad Goldspot, to fly away from me! Wink with thine eye—thou saucy rogue! Wottest thou not but for Stephen they might be blinding thy sweet blue eyes with hot needles?"

"His wing is grown since the moulting," said Stephen. "It should be cut to hinder such mischances."

"Will you do it? I will hold him," said Dennet.

"Ah! 'tis pity, the beauteous green gold-bedropped wing—that no armour of thine can equal, Stephen, not even that for the little King of Scots. But shouldst not be so silly a bird, Goldie, even though thou hast thine excuse. There! Peck not, ill birdling. Know thy friends, Master Stare."

And with such pretty nonsense the two stood together, Dennet in her white cap, short crimson kirtle, little stiff collar, and white bib and apron, holding her bird upside down in one hand, and with the other trying to keep his angry beak from pecking Stephen, who, in his leathern coat and apron, grimed, as well as his crisp black hair, with soot, stood towering above her, stooping to hold out the lustrous wing with one hand while he used his smallest pair of shears with the other to clip the pen-feathers.

"See there, Master Alderman," cried Mistress Headley, bursting on him from the gallery stairs. "Be that what you call fitting for your daughter and your prentice, a beggar lad from the heath? I ever told you she would bring you to shame, thus left to herself. And now you see it."

Their heads had been near together over the starling, but at this objurgation they started apart, both crimson in the cheeks, and Dennet flew up to her father, bird in hand, crying, "O father, father! suffer her not. He did no wrong. He was cutting my bird's wing."

"I suffer no one to insult my child in her own house," said the alderman, so much provoked as to be determined to put an end to it all at once. "Stephen Birkenholt, come here."

Stephen came, cap in hand, red in the face, with a strange tumult in his heart, ready to plead guilty, though he had done nothing, but imagining at the moment that his feelings had been actions.

"Stephen," said the alderman, "thou art a true and worthy lad! Canst thou love my daughter?"

"I—I crave your pardon, sir, there was no helping it," stammered Stephen, not catching the tone of the strange interrogation, and expecting any amount of terrible consequences for his presumption.

"Then thou wilt be a faithful spouse to her, and son to me? And Dennet, my daughter, hast thou any distaste to this youth—though he bring nought but skill and honesty!"

"O, father, father! I—I had rather have him than any other!"

"Then, Stephen Birkenholt and Dennet Headley, ye shall be man and wife, so soon as the young man's term be over, and he be a freeman—so he continue to be that which he seems at present. Thereto I give my word, I, Giles Headley, Alderman of the Chepe Ward, and thereof ye are witnesses, all of you. And God's blessing on it."

A tremendous hurrah arose, led by Kit Smallbones, from every workman in the court, and the while Stephen and Dennet, unaware of anything else, flew into one another's arms, while Goldspot, on whom the operation had been fortunately completed, took refuge upon Stephen's head.

"O, Mistress Dennet, I have made you black all over!" was Stephen's first word.

"Heed not, I ever loved the black!" she cried, as her eyes sparkled.

"So I have done what was to thy mind, my lass?" said Master Headley, who, without ever having thought of consulting his daughter, was delighted to see that her heart was with him.

"Sir, I did not know fully—but indeed I should never have been so happy as I am now.

"Sir," added Stephen, putting his knee to the ground, "it nearly wrung my heart to think of her as belonging to another, though I never durst utter aught,"—and while Dennet embraced her father, Stephen sobbed for very joy, and with difficulty said in broken words something about a "son's duty and devotion."

They were broken in upon by Mistress Headley, who, after standing in mute consternation, fell on them in a fury. She understood the device now! All had been a scheme laid amongst them for defrauding her poor fatherless child, driving him away, and taking up this beggarly brat. She had seen through the little baggage from the first, and she pitied Master Headley. Rage was utterly ungovernable in those days, and she actually was flying to attack Dennet with her nails when the alderman caught her by the wrists; and she would have been almost too much for him, had not Kit Smallbones come to his assistance, and carried her, kicking and screaming like a naughty child, into the house. There was small restraint of temper in those days even in high life, and below it, there was some reason for the employment of the padlock and the ducking stool.

Floods of tears restored the dame to some sort of composure; but she declared she could stay no longer in a house where her son had been ill-used and deceived, and she had been insulted. The alderman thought the insult had been the other way, but he was too glad to be rid of her on any terms to gainsay her, and at his own charge, undertook to procure horse and escort to convey her safely to Salisbury the next morning. He advised Stephen to keep out of her sight for the rest of the day, giving leave of absence, so that the youth, as one treading on air, set forth to carry to his brother, his aunt, and if possible, his uncle, the intelligence that he could as yet hardly believe was more than a happy dream.

CHAPTER XXIII.

Unwelcome Preferment.

"I am a poor fallen man, unworthy now
To be thy lord and master. Seek the king!
That sun I pray may never set."

Shakespeare.

Matters flowed on peaceably with Stephen and Dennet. The alderman saw no reason to repent his decision, hastily as it had been made. Stephen gave himself no unseemly airs of presumption, but worked on as one whose heart was in the business, and Dennet rewarded her father's trust by her discretion.

They were happily married in the summer of 1522, as soon as Stephen's apprenticeship was over; and from that time, he was in the position of the master's son, with more and more devolving on him as Tibble became increasingly rheumatic every winter, and the alderman himself grew in flesh and in distaste to exertion.

Ambrose meanwhile prospered with his master, and could easily have obtained some office in the law courts that would have enabled him to make a home of his own; but if he had the least inclination to the love of women, it was all merged in a silent distant worship of "sweet pale Margaret, rare pale Margaret," the like-minded daughter of Sir Thomas More—an affection which was so entirely devotion at a shrine, that it suffered no shock when Sir Thomas at length consented to his daughter's marriage with William Roper.

Ambrose was the only person who ever received any communication from Giles Headley. They were few and far between, but when Stephen Gardiner returned from his embassy to Pope Clement the Seventh, who was then at Orvieto, one of the suite reported to Ambrose how astonished he had been by being accosted in good English by one of the imperial men-at-arms, who were guarding his Holiness in actual though unconfessed captivity. This person had sent his commendations to Ambrose, and likewise a laborious bit of writing, which looked as if he were fast forgetting the art. It bade Ambrose inform his mother and all his friends and kin that he was well and coming to preferment, and inclosed for Aldonza a small mother-of-pearl cross blessed by the Pope. Giles added that he should bring her finer gifts by and by.

Seven years' constancy! It gave quite a respectability to Giles's love, and Aldonza was still ready and patient while waiting in attendance on her beloved mistress.

Ambrose lived on in the colony at Chelsea, sometimes attending his master, especially on diplomatic missions, and generally acting as librarian and foreign secretary, and obtaining some notice from Erasmus on the great scholar's visit to Chelsea. Under such guidance, Ambrose's opinions had settled down a good deal; and he was a disappointment to Tibble, whose views advanced proportionably as he worked less, and read and thought more. He so bitterly resented and deplored the burning of Tindal's Bible that there was constant fear that he might bring on himself the same fate, especially as he treasured his own copy and studied it constantly. The reform that Wolsey had intended to effect when he obtained the legatine authority seemed to fall into the background among political interests, and his efforts had as yet no result save the suppression of some useless and ill-managed small religious houses to endow his magnificent project of York College at Oxford, with a feeder at Ipswich, his native town.

He was waiting to obtain the papacy, when he would deal better with the abuses. Randall once asked him if he were not waiting to be King of Heaven, when he could make root and branch work at once. Hal had never so nearly incurred a flogging!

And in the meantime another influence was at work, an influence only heard of at first in whispered jests, which made loyal-hearted Dennet blush and look indignant, but which soon grew to sad earnest, as she could not but avow, when she beheld the stately pomp of the two Cardinals, Wolsey and Campeggio, sweep up to the Blackfriars Convent to sit in judgment on the marriage of poor Queen Katharine.

"Out on them!" she said. "So many learned men to set their wits against one poor woman!" And she heartily rejoiced when they came to no decision, and the Pope was appealed to. As to understanding all the explanations that Ambrose brought from time to time, she called them quirks and quiddities, and left them to her father and Tibble to discuss in their chimney corners.

They had seen nothing of the jester for a good while, for he was with Wolsey, who was attending the King on a progress through the midland shires. When the Cardinal returned to open the law courts as Chancellor at the beginning of the autumn term, still Randall kept away from home, perhaps because he had forebodings that he could not bear to mention.

On the evening of that very day, London rang with the tidings that the Great Seal had been taken from the Cardinal, and that he was under orders to yield up his noble mansion of York House and to retire to Esher; nay, it was reported that he was to be imprisoned in the Tower, and the next day the Thames was crowded with more than a thousand boats filled with people, expecting to see him landed at the Traitors' Gate, and much disappointed when his barge turned towards Putney.

In the afternoon, Ambrose came to the Dragon court.

Even as Stephen figured now as a handsome prosperous young freeman of the City, Ambrose looked well in the sober black apparel and neat ruff of a lawyer's clerk—clerk indeed to the first lawyer in the kingdom, for the news had spread before him that Sir Thomas More had become Lord Chancellor.

"Thou art come to bear us word of thy promotion—for thy master's is thine own," said the alderman heartily as he entered, shaking hands with him. "Never was the Great Seal in better hands."

"'Tis true indeed, your worship," said Ambrose, "though it will lay a heavy charge on him, and divert him from much that he loveth better still. I came to ask of my sister Dennet a supper and a bed for the night, as I have been on business for him, and can scarce get back to Chelsea."

"And welcome," said Dennet. "Little Giles and Bess have been wearying for their uncle."

"I must not toy with them yet," said Ambrose, "I have a message for my aunt. Brother, wilt thou walk down to the Temple with me before supper?"

"Yea, and how is it with Master Randall?" asked Dennet. "Be he gone with my Lord Cardinal?"

"He is made over to the King," said Ambrose briefly. "'Tis that which I must tell his wife."

"Have with thee, then," said Stephen, linking his arm into that of his brother, for to be together was still as great an enjoyment to them as in Forest days. And on the way, Ambrose told what he had not been willing to utter in full assembly in the hall. He had been sent by his master with a letter of condolence to the fallen Cardinal, and likewise of inquiry into some necessary business connected with the chancellorship. Wolsey had not time to answer before embarking, but as Sir Thomas had vouched for the messenger's ability and trustiness, he had bidden Ambrose come into his barge, and receive his instructions. Thus Ambrose had landed with him, just as a messenger came riding in haste from the King, with a kind greeting, assuring his old friend that his seeming disgrace was only for a time, and for political reasons, and sending him a ring in token thereof. The Cardinal had fallen on his knees to receive the message, had snatched a gold chain and precious relic from his own neck to reward the messenger, and then, casting about for some gift for the King, "by ill-luck," said Ambrose, "his eye lit upon our uncle, and he instantly declared that he would bestow Patch, as the Court chooses to call him, on the King. Well, as thou canst guess, Hal is hotly wroth at the treatment of his lord, whom he truly loveth; and he flung himself before the Cardinal, and besought that he might not be sent from his good lord. But the Cardinal was only chafed at aught that gainsaid him; and all he did was to say he would have no more ado, he had made his gift. 'Get thee gone,' he said, as if he had been ordering off a horse or dog. Well-a-day! it was hard to brook the sight, and Hal's blood was up. He flatly refused to go, saying he was the Cardinal's servant, but no villain nor serf to be thus made over without his own will."

"He was in the right there," returned Stephen, hotly.

"Yea, save that by playing the fool, poor fellow, he hath yielded up the rights of a wise man. Any way, all he gat by it was that the Cardinal bade two of the yeomen lay hands on him and bear him off. Then there came on him that reckless mood, which, I trow, banished him long ago from the Forest, and brought him to the motley. He fought with them with all his force, and broke away once—as if that were of any use for a man in motley!—but he was bound at last and borne off by six of them to Windsor!"

"And thou stoodst by, and beheld it!" cried Stephen.

"Nay, what could I have done, save to make his plight worse, and forfeit all chance of yet speaking to him?"

"Thou wert ever cool! I wot that I could not have borne it," said Stephen.

They told the story to Perronel, who was on the whole elated by her husband's promotion, declaring that the King loved him well, and that he would soon come to his senses, though for a wise man, he certainly had too much of the fool, even as he had too much of the wise man for the fool.

She became anxious, however, as the weeks passed by without hearing of or from him, and at length Ambrose confessed his uneasiness to his kind master, and obtained leave to attend him on the next summons to Windsor.

Ambrose could not find his uncle at first. Randall, who used to pervade York House, and turn up everywhere when least expected, did not appear among the superior serving-men and secretaries with whom his nephew ranked, and of course there was no access to the state apartments. Sir Thomas, however, told Ambrose that he had seen Quipsome Hal among the other jesters, but that he seemed dull and dejected. Then Ambrose beheld from a window a cruel sight, for the other fools, three in number, were surrounding Hal, baiting and teasing him, triumphing over him in fact, for having formerly outshone them, while he stood among them like a big dog worried by little curs, against whom he disdained to use his strength. Ambrose, unable to bear this, ran down stairs to endeavour to interfere; but before he could find his way to the spot, an arrival at the gate had attracted the tormentors, and Ambrose found his uncle leaning against the wall alone. He looked thin and wan, the light was gone out of his black eyes, and his countenance was in sad contrast to his gay and absurd attire. He scarcely cheered up when his nephew spoke to him, though he was glad to hear of Perronel. He said he knew not when he should see her again, for he had been unable to secure his suit of ordinary garments, so that even if the King came to London, or if he could elude the other fools, he could not get out to visit her. He was no better than a prisoner here, he only marvelled that the King retained so wretched a jester, with so heavy a heart.

"Once thou wast in favour," said Ambrose. "Methought thou couldst have availed thyself of it to speak for the Lord Cardinal."

"What? A senseless cur whom he kicked from him," said Randall. "'Twas that took all spirit from me, boy. I, who thought he loved me, as I love him to this day. To send me to be sport for his foes! I think of it day and night, and I've not a gibe left under my belt!"

"Nay," said Ambrose, "it may have been that the Cardinal hoped to secure a true friend at the King's ear, as well as to provide for thee."

"Had he but said so—"

"Nay, perchance he trusted to thy sharp wit."

A gleam came into Hal's eyes. "It might be so. Thou always wast a toward lad, Ambrose, and if so, I was cur and fool indeed to baulk him."

Therewith one of the other fools danced back exhibiting a silver crown that had just been flung to him, mopping and mowing, and demanding when Patch would have wit to gain the like. Whereto Hal replied by pointing to

Ambrose and declaring that that gentleman had given him better than fifty crowns. And that night, Sir Thomas told Ambrose that the Quipsome one had recovered himself, had been more brilliant than ever and had quite eclipsed the other fools.

On the next opportunity, Ambrose contrived to pack in his cloak-bag, the cap and loose garment in which his uncle was wont to cover his motley. The Court was still at Windsor; but nearly the whole of Sir Thomas's stay elapsed without Ambrose being able to find his uncle. Wolsey had been very ill, and the King had relented enough to send his own physician to attend him. Ambrose began to wonder if Hal could have found any plea for rejoining his old master; but in the last hour of his stay, he found Hal curled up listlessly on a window seat of a gallery, his head resting on his hand.

"Uncle, good uncle! At last! Thou art sick?"

"Sick at heart, lad," said Hal, looking up. "Yea, I took thy counsel. I plucked up a spirit, I made Harry laugh as of old, though my heart smote me, as I thought how he was wont to be answered by my master. I even brooked to jest with the night-crow, as my own poor lord called this Nan Boleyn. And lo you now, when his Grace was touched at my lord's sickness, I durst say there was one sure elixir for such as he, to wit a gold Harry; and that a King's touch was a sovereign cure for other disorders than the King's evil. Harry smiled, and in ten minutes more would have taken horse for Esher, had not Madam Nan claimed his word to ride out hawking with her. And next, she sendeth me a warning by one of her pert maids, that I should be whipped, if I spoke to his Grace of unfitting matters. My flesh could brook no more, and like a born nat-ural, I made answer that Nan Boleyn was no mistress of mine to bid me hold a tongue that had spoken sooth to her betters. Thereupon, what think you, boy? The grooms came and soundly flogged me for uncomely speech of my Lady Anne! I that was eighteen years with my Lord Cardinal, and none laid hand on me! Yea, I was beaten; and then shut up in a dog-hole for three days on bread and water, with none to speak to, but the other fools jeering at me like a rogue in a pillory."

Ambrose could hardly speak for hot grief and indignation, but he wrung his uncle's hand, and whispered that he had hid the loose gown behind the arras of his chamber, but he could do no more, for he was summoned to attend his master, and a servant further thrust in to say, "Concern yourself not for that rogue, sir, he hath been saucy, and must mend his manners, or he will have worse."

"Away, kind sir," said Hal, "you can do the poor fool no further good! but only bring the pack about the ears of the mangy hound." And he sang a stave appropriated by a greater man than he—

> "Then let the stricken deer go weep,
> The hart ungalled play."

The only hope that Ambrose or his good master could devise for poor

Randall was that Sir Thomas should watch his opportunity and beg the fool from the King, who might part with him as a child gives away the once coveted toy that has failed in its hands; but the request would need circumspection, for all had already felt the change that had taken place in the temper of the King since Henry had resolutely undertaken that the wrong should be the right; and Ambrose could not but dread the effect of desperation on a man whose nature had in it a vein of impatient recklessness.

It was after dinner, and Dennet, with her little boy and girl, was on the steps dispensing the salt fish, broken bread, and pottage of the Lenten meal to the daily troop who came for her alms, when, among them, she saw, somewhat to her alarm, a gipsy man, who was talking to little Giles. The boy, a stout fellow of six, was astride on the balustrade, looking up eagerly into the face of the man, who began imitating the note of a blackbird. Dennet, remembering the evil propensities of the gipsy race, called hastily to her little son to come down and return to her side; but little Giles was unwilling to move, and called to her, "O mother, come! He hath a bird-call!" In some perturbation lest the man might be calling her bird away, Dennet descended the steps. She was about to utter a sharp rebuke, but Giles held out his hand imploringly, and she paused a moment to hear the sweet full note of the "ouzel cock, with orange tawny bill," closely imitated on a tiny bone whistle. "He will sell it to me for two farthings," cried the boy, "and teach me to sing on it like all the birds—"

"Yea, good mistress," said the gipsy, "I can whistle a tune that the little master, ay, and others, might be fain to hear."

Therewith, spite of the wild dress, Dennet knew the eyes and the voice. And perhaps the blackbird's note had awakened echoes in another mind, for she saw Stephen, in his working dress, come out to the door of the shop where he continued to do all the finer work which had formerly fallen to Tibble's share.

She lifted her boy from his perch, and bade him take the stranger to his father, who would no doubt give him the whistle. And thus, having without exciting attention, separated the fugitive from the rest of her pensioners, she made haste to dismiss them.

She was not surprised that little Giles came running back to her, producing unearthly notes on the instrument, and telling her that father had taken the gipsy into his workshop, and said they would teach him bird's songs by and by.

"Steve, Steve," had been the first words uttered when the boy was out of hearing, "hast thou a smith's apron and plenty of smut to bestow on me? None can tell what Harry's mood may be, when he finds I've given him the slip. That is the reason I durst not go to my poor dame."

"We will send to let her know. I thought I guessed what black ouzel 'twas! I mind how thou didst make the like notes for us when we were no bigger than my Giles!"

"Thou hast a kind heart Stephen. Here! Is thy furnace hot enough to make a speedy end of this same greasy gipsy doublet? I trust not the varlet with whom I bartered it for my motley. And a fine bargain he had of what I trust never to wear again to the end of my days. Make me a smith complete, Stephen, and then will I tell thee my story."

"We must call Kit into counsel, ere we can do that fully," said Stephen.

In a few minutes Hal Randall was, to all appearance, a very shabby and grimy smith, and then he took breath to explain his anxiety and alarm. Once again, hearing that the Cardinal was to be exiled to York, he had ventured on a sorry jest about old friends and old wine being better than new; but the King, who had once been open to plain speaking, was now incensed, threatened and swore at him! Moreover, one of the other fools had told him, in the way of boasting that he had heard Master Cromwell, formerly the Cardinal's secretary, informing the King that this rogue was no true "natural" at all, but was blessed, (or cursed), with as good an understanding as other folks, as was well known in the Cardinal's household, and that he had no doubt been sent to serve as a spy, so that he was to be esteemed a dangerous person, and had best be put under ward.

Hal had not been able to discover whether Cromwell had communicated his name, but he suspected that it might be known to that acute person, and he could not tell whether his compeer spoke out of a sort of good-natured desire to warn him, or simply to triumph in his disgrace, and leer at him for being an impostor. At any rate, being now desperate, he covered his parti-coloured raiment with the gown Ambrose had brought, made a perilous descent from a window in the twilight, scaled a wall with the agility that seemed to have returned to him, and reached Windsor Forest.

There, falling on a camp of gipsies, he had availed himself of old experiences in his wild Shirley days, and had obtained an exchange of garb, his handsome motley being really a prize to the wanderers. Thus he had been able to reach London; but he did not feel any confidence that if he were pursued to the gipsy tent he would not be betrayed.

In this, his sagacity was not at fault, for he had scarcely made his explanation, when there was a knocking at the outer gate, and a demand to enter in the name of the King, and to see Alderman Sir Giles Headley. Several of the stout figures of the yeomen of the King's guard were seen crossing the court, and Stephen, committing the charge of his uncle to Kit, threw off his apron, washed his face and went up to the hall, not very rapidly, for he suspected that since his father-in-law knew nothing of the arrival, he would best baffle the inquiries by sincere denials.

And Dennet, with her sharp woman's wit, scenting danger, had whisked herself and her children out of the hall at the first moment, and taken them down to the kitchen, where modelling with a batch of dough occupied both of them.

Meantime the alderman flatly denied the presence of the jester, or the harbouring of the gipsy. He allowed that the jester was of kin to his son-in-law, but the good man averred in all honesty that he knew nought of any escape, and was absolutely certain that no such person was in the court. Then, as Stephen entered, doffing his cap to the King's officer, the alderman continued, "There, fair son, this is what these gentlemen have come about. Thy kinsman, it seemeth, hath fled from Windsor, and his Grace is mightily incensed. They say he changed clothes with a gipsy, and was traced hither this morn, but I have told them the thing is impossible."

"Will the gentlemen search?" asked Stephen.

The gentlemen did search, but they only saw the smiths in full work; and in Smallbones' forge, there was a roaring glowing furnace, with a bare-armed fellow feeding it with coals, so that it fairly scorched them, and gave them double relish for the good wine and beer that was put out on the table to do honour to them.

Stephen had just with all civility seen them off the premises when Perronel came sobbing into the court. They had visited her first, for Cromwell had evidently known of Randall's haunts; they had turned her little house upside down, and had threatened her hotly in case she harboured a disloyal spy, who deserved hanging. She came to consult Stephen, for the notion of her husband wandering about, as a sort of outlaw, was almost as terrible as the threat of his being hanged.

Stephen beckoned her to a storeroom full of gaunt figures of armour upon blocks, and there brought up to her his extremely grimy new hand!

There was much gladness between them, but the future had to be considered. Perronel had a little hoard, the amount of which she was too shrewd to name to any one, even her husband, but she considered it sufficient to enable him to fulfil the cherished scheme of his life, of retiring to some small farm near his old home, and she was for setting off at once. But Harry Randall declared that he could not go without having offered his services to his old master. He had heard of his "good lord" as sick, sad, and deserted by those whom he had cherished, and the faithful heart was so true in its loyalty that no persuasion could prevail in making it turn south.

"Nay," said the wife, "did he not cast thee off himself, and serve thee like one of his dogs! How canst thou be bound to him?"

"There's the rub!" sighed Hal. "He sent me to the King deeming that he should have one full of faithful love to speak a word on his behalf, and I, brutish oaf as I was, must needs take it amiss, and sulk and mope till the occasion was past, and that viper Cromwell was there to back up the woman Boleyn and poison his Grace's ear."

"As if a man must not have a spirit to be angered by such treatment."

"Thou forgettest, good wife. No man, but a fool, and to be entreated as such! Be that as it may, to York I must. I have eaten of my lord's bread too many years, and had too much kindness from him in the days of his glory, to seek mine own ease now in his adversity. Thou wouldst have a poor bargain of me when my heart is away."

Perronel saw that thus it would be, and that this was one of the points on which, to her mind, her husband was more than half a veritable fool after all.

There had long been a promise that Stephen should, in some time of slack employment make a visit to his old comrade, Edmund Burgess, at York; and as some new tools and patterns had to be conveyed thither, a sudden resolution was come to, in family conclave, that Stephen himself should convey them, taking his uncle with him as a serving-man, to attend to the horses. The alderman gave full consent, he had always wished Stephen to see York, while he himself with Tibble Steelman, was able to attend to the business; and while he pronounced Randall to have a heart of gold, well worth guarding, he still was glad when the risk was over of the King's hearing that the runaway jester was harboured at the Dragon. Dennet did not like the journey for her husband, for to her mind it was perilous, but she had had a warm affection for his uncle ever since their expedition to Richmond together, and she did her best to reconcile the murmuring and wounded Perronel by praises of Randall, a true and noble heart; and that as to setting her aside for the Cardinal, who bad heeded him so little, such faithfulness only made her more secure of his true-heartedness towards her. Perronel was moreover to break up her business, dispose of her house, and await her husband's return at the Dragon.

Stephen came back after a happy month with his friend, stored with wondrous tales and descriptions which would last the children for a month. He had seen his uncle present himself to the Cardinal at Cawood Castle. It had been a touching meeting. Hal could hardly restrain his tears when he saw how Wolsey's sturdy form had wasted, and his round ruddy cheeks had fallen away, while the attitude in which he sat in his chair was listless and weary, though he fitfully exerted himself with his old vigour.

Hal on his side, in the dark plain dress of a citizen, was hardly recognisable, for not only had he likewise grown thinner, and his brown cheeks more hollow, but his hair had become almost white during his miserable weeks at Windsor, though he was not much over forty years old.

He came up the last of a number who presented themselves for the Archiepiscopal blessing, as Wolsey sat under a large tree in Cawood Park. Wolsey gave it with his raised fingers, without special heed, but therewith Hal threw himself on the ground, kissed his feet, and cried, "My lord, my dear lord, your pardon."

"What hast done, fellow? Speak!" said the Cardinal. "Grovel not thus. We will be merciful."

"Ah! my lord," said Randall, lifting himself up, but with clasped hands and tearful eyes, "I did not serve you as I ought with the King, but if you will forgive me and take me back—"

"How now? How couldst thou serve me? What!"—as Hal made a familiar gesture—"thou art not the poor fool, Quipsome Patch? How comest thou here? Methought I had provided well for thee in making thee over to the King."

"Ah! my lord, I was fool, fool indeed, but all my jests failed me. How could I make sport for your enemies?"

"And thou hast come, thou hast left the King to follow my fallen fortunes?" said Wolsey. "My poor boy, he who is sitting in sackcloth and ashes needs no jester."

"Nay, my lord, nor can I find one jest to break! Would you but let me be your meanest horse-boy, your scullion!" Hal's voice was cut short by tears as the Cardinal abandoned to him one hand. The other was drying eyes that seldom wept.

"My faithful Hal!" he said, "this is love indeed!"

And Stephen ere he came away had seen his uncle fully established, as a rational creature, and by his true name, as one of the personal attendants on the Cardinal's bed-chamber, and treated with the affection he well deserved. Wolsey had really seemed cheered by his affection, and was devoting himself to the care of his hitherto neglected and even unvisited diocese, in a way that delighted the hearts of the Yorkshiremen.

The first idea was that Perronel should join her husband at York, but safe modes of travelling were not easy to be found, and before any satisfactory escort offered, there were rumours that made it prudent to delay. As autumn advanced, it was known that the Earl of Northumberland had been sent to attach the Cardinal of High Treason. Then ensued other reports that the great Cardinal had sunk and died on his way to London for trial; and at last, one dark winter evening, a sorrowful man stumbled up the steps of the Dragon, and as he came into the bright light of the fire, and Perronel sprang to meet him, he sank into a chair and wept aloud.

He had been one of those who had lifted the brokenhearted Wolsey from his mule in the cloister of Leicester Abbey, he had carried him to his bed, watched over him, and supported him, as the Abbot of Leicester gave him the last Sacraments. He had heard and treasured up those mournful words which are Wolsey's chief legacy to the world, "Had I but served my God, as I have served my king, He would not have forsaken me in my old age." For himself, he had the dying man's blessing, and assurance that nothing had so much availed to cheer in these sad hours as his faithful love.

Now, Perronel might do what she would with him—he cared not.

And what she did was to set forth with him for Hampshire, on a pair of stout mules with a strong serving-man behind them.

CHAPTER XXIV.

The Soldier.

"Of a worthy London prentice
My purpose is to speak,
And tell his brave adventures
Done for his country's sake.
Seek all the world about
And you shall hardly find
A man in valour to exceed
A prentice' gallant mind."

The Homes of a London Prentice.

Six more years had passed over the Dragon court, when, one fine summer evening, as the old walls rang with the merriment of the young boys at play, there entered through the gateway a tall, well-equipped, soldierly figure, which caught the eyes of the little armourer world in a moment. "Oh, that's a real Milan helmet!" exclaimed the one lad.

"And oh, what a belt and buff coat!" cried another.

The subject of their admiration advanced muttering, "As if I'd not been away a week," adding, "I pray you, pretty lads, doth Master Alderman Headley still dwell here?"

"Yea, sir, he is our grandfather," said the elder boy, holding a lesser one by the shoulder as he spoke.

"Verily! And what may be your names?"

"I am Giles Birkenholt, and this is my little brother, Dick."

"Even as I thought. Wilt thou run in to your grandsire, and tell him?"

The bigger boy interrupted, "Grandfather is going to bed. He is old and weary, and cannot see strangers so late. 'Tis our father who heareth all the orders."

"And," added the little one, with wide-open grave eyes, "Mother bade us run out and play and not trouble father, because uncle Ambrose is so downcast because they have cut off the head of good Sir Thomas More."

"Yet," said the visitor, "methinks your father would hear of an old comrade. Or stay, where be Tibble Steelman and Kit Smallbones?"

"Tibble is in the hall, well-nigh as sad as uncle Ambrose," began Dick; but Giles, better able to draw conclusions, exclaimed, "Tibble! Kit! You know them, sir! Oh! are you the Giles Headley that ran away to be a soldier ere I was born? Kit! Kit! see here—" as the giant, broader and perhaps a little more bent, but with little loss of strength, came forward out of his hut, and taking up the matter just where it had been left fourteen years before, demanded as they shook hands, "Ah, Master Giles, how couldst thou play me such a scurvy trick?"

"Nay, Kit, was it not best for all that I turned my back to make way for honest Stephen?"

By this time young Giles had rushed up the stair to the hall, where, as he said truly, Stephen was giving his brother such poor comfort as could be had from sympathy, when listening to the story of the cheerful, brave resignation of the noblest of all the victims of Henry the Eighth. Ambrose had been with Sir Thomas well-nigh to the last, had carried messages between him and his friends during his imprisonment, had handed his papers to him at his trial, had been with Mrs. Roper when she broke through the crowd and fell on his neck as he walked from Westminster Hall with the axe-edge turned towards him; had received his last kind farewell, counsel, and blessing, and had only not been with him on the scaffold because Sir Thomas had forbidden it, saying, in the old strain of mirth, which never forsook him, "Nay, come not, my good friend. Thou art of a queasy nature, and I would fain not haunt thee against thy will."

All was over now, the wise and faithful head had fallen, because it would not own the wrong for the right; and Ambrose had been brought home by his brother, a being confounded, dazed, seeming hardly able to think or understand aught save that the man whom he had above all loved and looked up to was taken from him, judicially murdered, and by the King. The whole world seemed utterly changed to him, and as to thinking or planning for himself, he was incapable of it; indeed, he looked fearfully ill. His little nephew came up to his father's knee, pausing, though open-mouthed, and at the first token of permission, bursting out, "Oh! father! Here's a soldier in the court! Kit is talking to him. And he is Giles Headley that ran away. He has a beauteous Spanish leathern coat, and a belt with silver bosses—and a morion that Phil Smallbones saith to be of Milan, but I say it is French."

Stephen had no sooner gathered the import of this intelligence than he sprang down almost as rapidly as his little boy, with his welcome. Nor did Giles Headley return at all in the dilapidated condition that had been predicted. He was stout, comely, and well fleshed, and very handsomely clad and equipped in a foreign style, with nothing of the lean wolfish appearance of Sir John Fulford. The two old comrades heartily shook one another by the hand in real gladness at the meeting. Stephen's welcome was crossed by the greeting and inquiry whether all was well.

"Yea. The alderman is hale and hearty, but aged. Your mother is tabled at a religious house at Salisbury."

"I know. I landed at Southampton and have seen her."

"And Dennet," Stephen added with a short laugh, "she could not wait for you."

"No, verily. Did I not wot well that she cared not a fico for me? I hoped when I made off that thou wouldst be the winner, Steve, and I am right glad thou art, man."

"I can but thank thee, Giles," said Stephen, changing to the familiar singular pronoun. "I have oft since thought what a foolish figure I should have cut had I met thee among the Badgers, after having given leg bail because I might not brook seeing thee wedded to her. For I was sore tempted—only thou wast free, and mine indenture held me fast."

"Then it was so! And I did thee a good turn! For I tell thee, Steve, I never knew how well I liked thee till I was wounded and sick among those who heeded neither God nor man! But one word more, Stephen, ere we go in. The Moor's little maiden, is she still unwedded?"

"Yea," was Stephen's answer. "She is still waiting-maid to Mistress Roper, daughter to good Sir Thomas More; but alack, Giles, they are in sore trouble, as it may be thou hast heard—and my poor brother is like one distraught."

Ambrose did indeed meet Giles like one in a dream. He probably would have made the same mechanical greeting, if the Emperor or the Pope had been at that moment presented to him; but Dennet, who had been attending to her father, made up all that was wanting in cordiality. She had always had a certain sense of shame for having flouted her cousin, and, as his mother told her, driven him to death and destruction, and it was highly satisfactory to see him safe and sound, and apparently respectable and prosperous.

Moreover, grieved as all the family were for the fate of the admirable and excellent More, it was a relief to those less closely connected with him to attend to something beyond poor Ambrose's sorrow and his talk, the which moreover might be perilous if any outsider listened and reported it to the authorities as disaffection to the King. So Giles told his story, sitting on the gallery in the cool of the summer evening, and marvelling over and over again how entirely unchanged all was since his first view of the Dragon court as a proud, sullen, raw lad twenty summers ago. Since that time he had seen so much that the time appeared far longer to him than to those who had stayed at home.

It seemed that Fulford had from the first fascinated him more than any of the party guessed, and that each day of the free life of the expedition, and of contact with the soldiery, made a return to the monotony of the forge, the decorous life of a London citizen, and the bridal with a child, to whom he was indifferent, seem more intolerable to him. Fulford imagining rightly that the knowledge of his intentions might deter young Birkenholt from escaping, enjoined strict secrecy on either lad, not intending them to meet till it should be too late to return, and therefore had arranged that Giles should quit the party on the way to Calais, bringing with him Will Wherry, and the horse he rode.

Giles had then, been enrolled among the Badgers. He had little to tell about his life among them till the battle of Pavia, where he had had the good fortune to take three French prisoners; but a stray shot from a fugitive had broken his leg during the pursuit, and he had been laid up in a merchant's house at Pavia for several months. He evidently looked back to the time with gratitude, as having wakened his better associations, which had been well-nigh stifled during the previous years of the wild life of a soldier of fortune. His host's young daughter had eyes like Aldonza, and the almost forgotten possibility of returning to his love a brave and distinguished man awoke once more. His burgher thrift began to assert itself again, and he deposited a nest-egg from the ransoms of his prisoners in the hands of his host, who gave him bonds by which he could recover the sum from Lombard correspondents in London.

He was bound by his engagements to join the Badgers again, or he would have gone home on his recovery; and he had shared in the terrible taking of Rome, of which he declared that he could not speak—with a significant look at Dennet and her children, who were devouring his words. He had, however, stood guard over a lady and her young children whom some savage Spaniards were about to murder, and the whole family had overpowered him with gratitude, lodged him sumptuously in their house, and shown themselves as grateful to him as if he had given them all the treasure which he had abstained from seizing.

The sickness brought on by their savage excesses together with the Roman summer had laid low many of the Badgers. When the Prince of Orange drew off the army from the miserable city, scarce seven score of that once gallant troop were in marching order, and Sir John Fulford himself was dying. He sent for Giles, as less of a demon than most of the troop, and sent a gold medal, the only fragment of spoil remaining to him, to his daughter Perronel. To Giles himself Fulford bequeathed Abenali's well-tested sword, and he died in the comfortable belief—so far as he troubled himself about the matter at all—that there were special exemptions for soldiers.

The Badgers now incorporated themselves with another broken body of Landsknechts, and fell under the command of a better and more conscientious captain. Giles, who had been horrified rather than hardened by the experiences of Rome, was found trustworthy and rose in command. The troop was sent to take charge of the Pope at Orvieto, and thus it was that he had fallen in with the Englishmen of Gardiner's suite, and had been able to send his letter to Ambrose. Since he had found the means of rising out of the slough, he had made up his mind to continue to serve till he had won some honour, and had obtained enough to prevent his return as a hungry beggar.

His corps became known for discipline and valour. It was trusted often, was in attendance on the Emperor, and was fairly well paid. Giles was their "ancient" and had charge of the banner, nor could it be doubted that be had flourished. His last adventure had been the expedition to Tunis, when 20,000 Christian captives had been set free from the dungeons and galleys, and so grand a treasure had been shared among the soldiery that Giles, having completed the term of service for which he was engaged, decided on returning to England, before, as he said, he grew any older, to see how matters were going.

"For the future," he said, "it depended on how he found things." If Aldonza would none of him, he should return to the Emperor's service. If she would go with him, he held such a position that he could provide for her honourably. Or he could settle in England. For he had a good sum in the hands of Lombard merchants; having made over to them spoils of war, ransoms, and arrears when he obtained them; and having at times earned something by exercising his craft, which he said had been most valuable to him. Indeed he thought he could show Stephen and Tibble a few fresh arts he had picked up at Milan.

Meantime his first desire was to see Aldonza. She was still at Chelsea with her mistress, and Ambrose, to his brother's regret, went thither every day, partly because he could not keep away, and partly to try to be of use to the family. Giles might accompany him, though he still looked so absorbed in his trouble that it was doubtful whether he had really understood what was passing, or that he was wanted to bring about an interview between his companion and Aldonza.

The beautiful grounds at Chelsea, in their summer beauty, looked inexpressibly mournful, deprived of him who had planted and cherished the trees and roses. As they passed along in the barge, one spot after another recalled More's bright jests or wise words; above all, the very place where he had told his son-in-law Roper that he was merry, not because he was safe, but because the fight was won, and his conscience had triumphed against the King he loved and feared.

Giles told of the report that the Emperor had said he would have given a hundred of his nobles for one such councillor as More, and the prospect of telling this to the daughters had somewhat cheered Ambrose. They found a guard in the royal livery at the stairs to the river, and at the door of the house, but these had been there ever since Sir Thomas's apprehension. They knew Ambrose Birkenholt, and made no objection to his passing in and leaving his companion to walk about among the borders and paths, once so trim, but already missing their master's hand and eye.

Very long it seemed to Giles, who was nearly despairing, when a female figure in black came out of one of the side doors, which were not guarded, and seemed to be timidly looking for him. Instantly he was at her side.

"Not here," she said, and in silence led the way to a pleached alley out of sight of the windows. There they stood still. It was a strange meeting of two who had not seen each other for fourteen years, when the one was a tall, ungainly youth, the other well-nigh a child. And now Giles was a fine, soldierly man in the prime of life, with a short, curled beard, and powerful, alert bearing, and Aldonza, though the first flower of her youth had gone by, yet, having lived a sheltered and far from toilsome life, was a really beautiful woman, gracefully proportioned, and with the delicate features and clear olive, skin of the Andalusian Moor. Her eyes, always her finest feature, were sunken with weeping, but their soft beauty could still be seen. Giles threw himself on his knee and grasped at her hand.

"My love!—my only love!" he cried.

"Oh! how can I think of such matters now—now, when it is thus with my dear mistress," said Aldonza, in a mournful voice, as though her tears were all spent—yet not withholding her hand.

"You knew me before you knew her," said Giles. "See, Aldonza, what I have brought back to you."

And he half drew the sword her father had made. She gave a gasp of delight, for well she knew every device in the gold inlaying of the blade, and she looked at Giles with eyes full of gratitude.

"I knew thou wouldst own me," said Giles. "I have fought and gone far from thee, Aldonza. Canst not spare one word for thine old Giles?"

"Ah, Giles—there is one thing which if you will do for my mistress, I would be yours from—from my heart of hearts."

"Say it, sweetheart, and it is done."

"You know not. It is perilous, and may be many would quail. Yet it may be less perilous for you than for one who is better known."

"Peril and I are well acquainted, my heart."

She lowered her voice as her eyes dilated, and she laid her hand on his arm. "Thou wottest what is on London Bridge gates?"

"I saw it, a sorry sight."

"My mistress will not rest till that dear and sacred head, holy as any blessed relic, be taken down so as not to be the sport of sun and wind, and cruel men gaping beneath. She cannot sleep, she cannot sit or stand still, she cannot even kiss her child for thinking of it. Her mind is set on taking it down, yet she will not peril her husband. Nor verily know I how any here could do the deed."

"Ha! I have scaled a wall ere now. I bare our banner at Goletta, with the battlements full of angry Moors, not far behind the Emperor's."

"You would? And be secret? Then indeed nought would be overmuch for you. And this very night—"

"The sooner the better."

She not only clasped his hand in thanks, but let him raise her face to his, and take the reward he felt his due. Then she said she must return, but Ambrose would bring him all particulars. Ambrose was as anxious as herself and her mistress that the thing should be done, but was unfit by all his habits, and his dainty, scholarly niceness, to render such effectual assistance as the soldier could do. Giles offered to scale the gate by night himself carry off the head, and take it to any place Mrs. Roper might appoint, with no assistance save such as Ambrose could afford. Aldonza shuddered a little at this, proving that her heart had gone out to him already, but with this he had to be contented, for she went back into the house, and he saw her no more. Ambrose came back to him, and, with something more like cheerfulness than he had yet seen, said, "Thou art happy, Giles."

"More happy than I durst hope—to find her—"

"Tush! I meant not that. But to be able to do the work of the holy ones of old who gathered the remnants of the martyrs, while I have indeed the will, but am but a poor craven! It is gone nearer to comfort that sad-hearted lady than aught else."

It appeared that Mrs. Roper would not be satisfied unless she herself were present at the undertaking, and this was contrary to the views of Giles, who thought the further off women were in such a matter the better. There was a watch at the outer entrance of London Bridge, the trainbands taking turns to supply it, but it was known by experience that they did not think it necessary to keep awake after belated travellers had ceased to come in; and Sir Thomas More's head was set over the opposite gateway, looking inwards at the City. The most suitable hour would be between one and two o'clock, when no one would be stirring, and the summer night would be at the shortest. Mrs. Roper was exceedingly anxious to implicate no one, and to prevent her husband and brother from having any knowledge of an act that William Roper might have prohibited, as if she could not absolutely exculpate him, it might be fatal to him. She would therefore allow no one to assist save Ambrose, and a few more devoted old servants, of condition too low for anger to be likely to light upon them. She was to be rowed with muffled oars to the spot, to lie hid in the shadow of the bridge till a signal like the cry of the pee-wit was exchanged from the bridge, then approach the stairs at the inner angle of the bridge where Giles and Ambrose would meet her.

Giles's experience as a man-at-arms stood him in good stead. He purchased a rope as he went home, also some iron ramps. He took a survey of the arched gateway in the course of the afternoon, and shutting himself into one of the worksheds with Ambrose, he constructed such a rope ladder as was used in scaling fortresses, especially when seized at night by surprise. He beguiled the work by a long series of anecdotes of adventures of the kind, of all of which Ambrose heard not one word. The whole court, and especially Giles number three, were very curious as to their occupation, but nothing was said even to Stephen, for it was better, if Ambrose should be suspected, that he should be wholly ignorant, but he had—they knew not how—gathered somewhat. Only Ambrose was, at parting for the night, obliged to ask him for the key of the gate.

"Brother," then he said, "what is this work I see? Dost think I can let thee go into a danger I do not partake? I will share in this pious act towards the man I have ever reverenced."

So at dead of night the three men stole out together, all in the plainest leathern suits. The deed was done in the perfect stillness of the sleeping City, and without mishap or mischance. Stephen's strong hand held the ladder securely and aided to fix it to the ramps, and just as the early dawn was touching the summit of Saint Paul's spire with a promise of light, Giles stepped into the boat, and reverently placed his burden within the opening of a velvet cushion that had been ripped up and deprived of part of the stuffing, so as to conceal it effectually. The brave Margaret Roper, the English Antigone, well knowing that all depended on her self-control, refrained from aught that might shake it. She only raised her face to Giles and murmured from dry lips, "Sir, God must reward you!" And Aldonza, who sat beside her, held out her hand.

Ambrose was to go with them to the priest's house, where Mrs. Roper was forced to leave her treasure, since she durst not take it to Chelsea, as the royal officers were already in possession, and the whole family were to depart on the ensuing day. Stephen and Giles returned safely to Cheapside.

CHAPTER XXV.

Old Haunts.

"O the oak, and the birch, and the bonny holly tree,
They flourish best at home in my own countree."

When the absence of the barbarous token of the execution was discovered, suspicion instantly fell on the More family, and Margaret, her husband, and her brother, were all imprisoned. The brave lady took all upon herself, and gave no names of her associates in the deed, and as Henry the Eighth still sometimes had better moods, all were soon released.

But that night had given Ambrose a terrible cough, so that Dennet kept him in bed two days. Indeed he hardly cared to rise from it. His whole nature, health, spirits, and mind, had been so cruelly strained, and he was so listless, so weak, so incapable of rousing himself, or turning to any fresh scheme of life, that Stephen decided on fulfilling a long-cherished plan of visiting their native home and seeing their uncle, who had, as he had contrived to send them word, settled down on a farm which he had bought with Perronel's savings, near Romsey. Headley, who was lingering till Aldonza could leave her mistress and decide on any plan, undertook to attend to the business, and little Giles, to his great delight, was to accompany them.

So the brothers went over the old ground. They slept in the hostel at Dogmersfield where the Dragon mark and the badge of the Armourers' Company had first appeared before them. They found the very tree where the alderman had been tied, and beneath which Spring lay buried, while little Giles gazed with ecstatic, almost religious veneration, and Ambrose seemed to draw in new life with the fresh air of the heath, now becoming rich with crimson bells. They visited Hyde Abbey, and the well-clothed, well-mounted travellers received a better welcome than had fallen to the lot of the hungry lads. They were shown the grave of old Richard Birkenholt in the cloister, and Stephen left a sum to be expended in masses for his behoof. They looked into Saint Elizabeth's College, but the kind warden was dead, and a trembling old man who looked at them through the wicket hoped they were not sent from the Commissioners. For the visitation of the lesser religious houses was going on, and Saint Elizabeth's was already doomed. Stephen inquired at the White Hart for Father Shoveller, and heard that he had grown too old to perform the office of a bailiff, and had retired to the parent abbey. The brothers therefore renounced their first scheme of taking Silkstede in their way, and made for Romsey. There, under the shadow of the magnificent nunnery, they dined pleasantly by the waterside at the sign of Bishop Blaise, patron of the woolcombers of the town, and halted long enough to refresh Ambrose, who was equal to very little fatigue. It amused Stephen to recollect how mighty a place he had once thought the little town.

Did mine host know Master Randall? What Master Randall of Bad-desley? He should think so! Was not the good man or his good wife here every market-day, with a pleasant word for every one! Men said he had had some good office about the Court, as steward or the like—for he was plainly conversant with great men, though he made no boast. If these guests were kin of his, they were welcome for his sake.

So the brothers rode on amid the gorse and heather till they came to a broad-spreading oak tree, sheltering a farmhouse built in frames of heavy timber, filled up with bricks set in zigzag patterns, with a high-pitched roof and tall chimneys. Barns and stacks were near it, and fields reclaimed from the heath were waving with corn just tinged with the gold of harvest. Three or four cows, of the tawny hue that looked so homelike to the brothers, were being released from the stack-yard after being milked, and conducted to their field by a tall, white-haired man in a farmer's smock with a little child perched on his shoulder, who gave a loud jubilant cry at the sight of the riders. Stephen, pushing on, began the question whether Master Randall dwelt there, but it broke off half way into a cry of recognition on either side, Harry's an absolute shout. "The lads, the lads! Wife, wife! 'tis our own lads!"

And as Perronel, more buxom and rosy than London had ever made her, came forth from her dairy, and there was a *mêlée* of greetings, and Stephen would have asked what homeless little one the pair had adopted, he was cut short by an exulting laugh. "No more adopted than thy Giles there, Stephen. 'Tis our own boy, Thomas Randall! Yea, and if he have come late, he is the better loved, though I trow Perronel there will ever look on Ambrose as her eldest son."

"And by my troth, he needs good country diet and air!" cried Perronel. "Thou hast had none to take care of thee, Ambrose. They have let thee pine and dwine over thy books. I must take thee in hand."

"'Tis what I brought him to thee for, good aunt," said Stephen, smiling.

Great was the interchange of news over the homely hearty meal. It was plain that no one could be happier, or more prosperous in a humble way, than the ex-jester and his wife; and if anything could restore Ambrose it would surely be the homely plenty and motherly care he found there.

Stephen heard another tale of his half-brother. His wife had soon been disgusted by the loneliness of the verdurer's lodge, and was always finding excuses for going to Southampton, where she and her daughter had both caught the plague, imported in some Eastern merchandise, and had died. The only son had turned out wild and wicked, and had been killed in a broil which he had provoked: and John, a broken-down man, with no one to enjoy the wealth he had accumulated, had given up his office as verdurer, and retired to an estate which he had purchased on the skirts of the Forest.

Stephen rode thither to see him, and found him a dying man, tyrannised over and neglected by his servants, and having often bitterly regretted his hardness towards his young brothers. All that Stephen did for him he received as tokens of pardon, and it was not possible to leave him until, after a fortnight's watching, he died in his brother's arms. He had made no will, and Ambrose thus inherited a property which made his future maintenance no longer an anxiety to his brother.

He himself seemed to care very little for the matter. To be allowed to rest under Perronel's care, to read his Erasmus' Testament, and attend mass on Sundays at the little Norman church, seemed all that he wished. Stephen tried to persuade him that he was young enough at thirty-five to marry and begin life again on the fair woodland river-bordered estate that was his portion, but he shook his head. "No, Stephen, my work is over. I could only help my dear master, and that is at an end. Dean Colet is gone, Sir Thomas is gone, what more have I to do here? Old ties are broken, old bonds severed. Crime and corruption were protested against in vain; and, now that judgment is beginning at the house of God, I am thankful that I am not like to live to see it."

Perronel scolded and exhorted him, and told him he would be stronger when the hot weather was over, but Ambrose only smiled, and Stephen saw a change in him, even in this fortnight, which justified his forebodings.

Stephen and his uncle found a trustworthy bailiff to manage the estate, and Ambrose remained in the house where he could now be no burthen. Stephen was obliged to leave him and take home young Giles, who had, he found, become so completely a country lad, enjoying everything to the utmost, that he already declared that he would much rather be a yeoman and forester than an armourer, and that he did not want to be apprenticed to that black forge.

This again made Ambrose smile with pleasure as he thought of the boy as keeping up the name of Birkenholt in the Forest. The one wish he expressed was that Stephen would send down Tibble Steelman to be with him. For in truth they both felt that in London Tib might at any time be laid hands on, and suffer at Smithfield for his opinions. The hope of being a comfort to Ambrose was perhaps the only idea that could have counterbalanced the sense that he ought not to fly from martyrdom; and as it proved, the invitation came only just in time. Three days after Tibble had been despatched by the Southampton carrier in charge of all the comforts Dennet could put together, Bishop Stokesley's grim "soumpnour" came to summon him to the Bishop's court, and there could be little question that he would have courted the faggot and stake. But as he was gone out of reach, no further inquiries were made after him.

Dennet had told her husband that she had been amazed to find how, in spite of a very warm affection for her, her husband, and children, her father hankered after the old name, and grieved that he could not fulfil his old engagement to his cousin Robert. Giles Headley had managed the business excellently during Stephen's absence, had shown himself very capable, and gained good opinions from all. Rubbing about in the world had been very good for him; and she verily believed that nothing would make her father so happy as for them to offer to share the business with Giles. She would on her part make Aldonza welcome, and had no fears of not agreeing with her. Besides—if little Giles were indeed to be heir to Testside was not the way made clear?

So thus it was. The alderman was very happy in the arrangement, and Giles Headley had not forfeited his rights to be a freeman of London or a member of the Armourers' Guild. He married Aldonza at Michaelmas, and all went well and peacefully in the household. Dennet never quitted her father while he lived; but Stephen struggled through winter roads and floods, and reached Baddesley in time to watch his brother depart in peace, his sorrow and indignation for his master healed by the sense of his martyrdom, and his trust firm and joyful. "If this be, as it is, dying of grief," said Hal Randall, "surely it is a blessed way to die!"

A few winters later Stephen and Dennet left Giles Headley in sole possession of the Dragon, with their second son as an apprentice, while they themselves took up the old forest life as Master and Mistress Birkenholt of Testside, where they lived and died honoured and loved.

THE END

www.ingramcontent.com/pod-product-compliance
Lightning Source LLC
Chambersburg PA
CBHW031959240626
47153CB00003B/1036